Praise for LOVE STUCK

'Get ready for the most original book of the year with one girl, two blokes and three endings!' – *B Magazine*

'A quirky romantic comedy with a choose-your-own-ending' – *Mirror*

'You, the reader, get the chance to choose which man she ends up with. So good you'll want to read all the endings' – *New Woman*

'Refreshingly unpredictable' – *Company*

'A *Sliding Doors* situation . . . Jess's chaotic life provides plenty of laughs, while leaving the reader to choose her destiny is a really clever idea' – *Shine*

Also by Susie Gilmour

Love Stuck

About the author

Holding Out or Giving In is the follow-up to Susie Gilmour's highly-acclaimed first novel *Love Stuck*. She has recently returned from a teaching-trip to Africa.

HOLDING OUT
or GIVING IN

SUSIE GILMOUR

FLAME
Hodder & Stoughton

Grateful acknowledgement is made to the Estate of
James MacGibbon for permission to reprint 'To the Tune
of the Coventry Carol' by Stevie Smith.

First published in Great Britain in 2002 by Hodder and Stoughton
A division of Hodder Headline

The right of Susie Gilmour to be identified as the Author of the Work
has been asserted by her in accordance with the Copyright,
Designs and Patents Act 1988.

A Flame Paperback

1 3 5 7 9 10 8 6 4 2

A CIP catalogue record is available from the British Library

ISBN 0340 79358 9

Typeset in Monotype Plantin
by Palimpsest Book Production Limited,
Polmont, Stirlingshire
Printed and bound in Great Britain by
Mackays of Chatham plc, Chatham, Kent

Hodder and Stoughton
A division of Hodder Headline
338 Euston Road
London NW1 3BH

For my mum, for always believing in me.

Acknowledgements

With grateful thanks to the following for preventing this book being called 'Holding Off and Giving Up':

My agent, Simon Trewin and Sarah Ballard, for looking after me so professionally and keeping me sane and smiling through the long, dark hours of writing.

My editor, Philippa Pride and everyone at Hodder for their patience, enthusiasm and wise judgement.

Alan Bateman and all at Pembroke House, Kenya for giving me the opportunity to live and write in such a beautiful place, and for being so accommodating, helpful and friendly. Also for introducing me to many generous and hospitable Kenyans, who showed me much more of their country than I would otherwise have seen.

Fi, a true friend, for always being there; my flatmates for so graciously putting up with *me* always being there; Lucy, my sister, for being such a great listener; Linz for her help in the beginning; Layla for her celebrity knowledge; and Sonja for her speedy, efficient and invaluable research.

Life is, of course, made immeasurably better by the companionship of all my friends, and would be horribly empty without the love and support of my family.

PS A special thank you to family friends and relatives for not collapsing from shock after ignoring all warnings and reading *Love Stuck* anyway. Please have a stiff drink on standby if you plan to be equally disobedient with this one!

To the Tune of the Coventry Carol

The nearly right
And yet not quite
In love is wholly evil
And every heart
That loves in part
Is mortgaged to the devil.

I loved or thought
I loved in sort
Was this to love akin
To take the best
And leave the rest
And let the devil in?

O lovers true
And others too
Whose best is only better
Take my advice
Shun compromise
Forget him and forget her.

Stevie Smith

PROLOGUE

Hiding in my bedroom after an unsuccessful attempt to convince Mum and Dad that any smell of cigarettes was coming from the dog. Tummy going mad due to mistaking a lump of blue candlewax for a delicious icing globule. Making myself feel popular by re-reading any birthday card not from a relative.

Dear Jess,

Happy 27th birthday – although I must say it feels very strange to be wishing someone else a happy birthday on my birthday – like a weird kind of Christmas. Since mine has been as near to happy as sitting in a dentist's waiting room is to being relaxing, I've cheered myself up by imagining yours . . .

	My Birthday	*Your Birthday*
7.30 a.m.	*Mum wakes me up with birthday cards: one mysterious tantalising one alluding to an exciting sender (Miles Willoughby?), one squashy one suggesting enclosed stash of juicy twenty-pound notes, one pink one with bubbles on the envelope and one intriguing one from Glasgow. Utter disappointment: mysterious one is from the A1 Driving School, squashy one is a revolting padded kitten-sitting-in-basket-playing-with-yarn-ball number, bubble one is from the goldfish, and intriguing Glasgow one is not a birthday card at all but a leaflet about interest rate changes to my Post Office Savings Account.*	*Your husband wakes you up with birthday cards: one from Miles Willoughby who still regrets snogging Kerry outside the Dragon and Egg, several from all the fantastic friends you made at university, one from a couple you met when you went travelling around the world, a joint one from all the office with witty comments about how much you are loved and valued, and one your husband has hand-painted himself (because he is creative as well as rich, good-looking, funny, popular, kind, generous, sensitive, caring, intelligent, thoughtful, and absolutely nothing whatsoever like Miles Willoughby).*
10.00 a.m.	*Double geography.*	*Important executive strategy meeting to discuss your successful job as presenter of* The Holiday Programme.

1.30 p.m.	Horrible canteen sausage lunch. Stanners finds out it's my birthday, stands on his chair and tells everybody I want Miles Willoughby's sausage. I am lunchtime laughing stock.	Delicious lunch in a sunny pavement café with your work colleagues who have all clubbed together to buy you a beautiful sophisticated objet d'art for your newly renovated home.
4.00 p.m.	Maths.	Bouquet to fill Britain arrives from your husband. Everyone is jealous. Inside one of the rosebuds is a set of keys to an idyllic French château he has just bought you.
7.30 p.m.	Wander seedy Inverness back lanes stepping on dog turds and downing warm Diamond White in order to pluck up enough courage to enter the Dragon and Egg. Get chucked out of the Dragon and Egg. Look for Kerry in the hope she will know where Miles Willoughby is. Find Kerry with her tongue rammed down someone's throat. It is Miles Willoughby's throat. Hate Kerry. Hate Miles Willoughby. Hate LIFE!	Sophisticated dinner party with lovely couples you met on safari in Africa. Everyone is drinking wine and laughing, in awe of how you can hold down a successful television career and still provide a sumptuous Delia banquet. You catch your husband looking at you lovingly as he reaches over, strokes your tiny bump and tells the guests you are expecting a baby in September. Everyone cries tears of joy.

And I'm picturing you now, curled up with your husband and possibly a little fluffy Andrex puppy, laughing over mortgages and Babygros. What is a mortgage? And did you meet your husband when you were travelling? And what's it like to be in love – to have found 'the one'? Kerry says it's as though all the love songs on the radio have been written especially for you, but Kerry thinks it's perfectly all right to go round snogging the one boy your best friend, ex-best friend has fancied all year. Did you ever forgive her for snogging Miles Willoughby? Did you ever snog Miles Willoughby?

There are so many questions I want to ask you but I know that by the time you can reply I will be totally uninterested in the answers – like doing exams and immediately wanting to know how you've done, convinced you'll never be able to stand the suspense of waiting, then getting the envelope three months later and being so far removed from the event that you don't give the slightest flying fig what it says.

Anyway, I hope this letter finds you happy. I've been trying to imagine where you might be when you read it and keep getting this alarmingly recurring image of the Dragon and Egg. Will start praying now that this is not the case. Enjoy the next ten years.

Lots of love,
Jess, 17 today
xxx

PS If the baby is a boy, promise me you won't, whatever you do, call him Miles.

Jess folded up the letter and did not so much feel as though she'd failed to make the grade as not even made it to the exam hall. The idea of her as a widely travelled expectant mum with devoted husband, fabulous job and boisterous Labrador smacked more of an advertising campaign for Norwich Union than anything resembling her own life. It seemed a cruel irony indeed that the only thing she'd predicted accurately was that she would still be sitting in the Dragon and Egg.

But even this, she realised, as she stared out into what was now a trendy restaurant, had managed to mature into something a whole lot more sophisticated. If only she'd had the foresight to predict that such a notorious underage drinking hovel associated with Diamond White, teenage snogging and non-inhaling smokers could attract the richest and most élite of Inverness's population simply by converting it into an aircraft hangar and erecting some stainless steel furniture. She wondered what the natural extension of minimalism might be, and imagined herself returning in another ten years to find lots of naked people sitting in a vast open space drinking nothing out of thin air.

'Here's to the birthday girl!' Alex announced, returning to the table with a pint of beer and something that looked as though it had just been dredged up from the bottom of Loch Ness.

Jess watched as he placed the two glasses meticulously on the shiny surface and arranged himself on an oblong piece of metal claiming to be a chair. Maybe this was the husband from the letter. Maybe this was the person she was meant to be with.

'This is supposed to be a treat, is it?' she said, gesturing to the algae.

Alex nodded. 'To be downed in one. And none of those nose-pinching girly sips.'

Jess smiled. He knew her through and through. Knew every little foible, every phobia, every shortcoming. And loved her because of them.

'Long-lost friend or secret admirer?'

She looked up at him blankly.

'That,' he said, pointing to the letter. 'It's either from someone I don't know, or someone you don't want me to know.'

'Oh, you know them all right,' she said, attempting to sip the sludge. 'Very well, in fact.'

'And do I like them?'

Jess pretended to think about this. 'Last count you said you loved them.'

Alex pretended to look confused. 'So that whittles it down to Manchester United or . . . you,' he said, grinning.

'Glad to know I'm up there with the best of them,' Jess replied, smirking.

'And as far as I know Man U aren't recruiting at the moment,' he continued, still grinning, 'so that means it must be from you.' He took her hand. 'Jess, if I'd known you were that desperate for friends I would have lent you some of mine.'

She laughed despite herself. 'I'm perfectly happy with my own friends, thank you.'

'So, why the letter to yourself?' he asked, then looked concerned. 'Oh, no. It's not some weird analytical thing, is it?' Alex lived in fear of being subjected to one of Jess's psychological testing games, which she was adamant unearthed vital clues to their compatibility. The very fact she believed this said everything he needed to know about their compatibility.

'I wrote it ten years ago on my seventeenth birthday,' she announced, picking up the letter and staring fondly at a bonneted Holly Hobbie motif in the corner, 'to see if what I hoped my life would be was what it became.'

'So it *is* some weird analytical thing.'

Sometimes, Jess thought, she and Alex could feel so right, so bonded, so in tune with one another. This was not one of those moments. 'Weird only to those who put Manchester United before their girlfriend,' she retorted.

'So what hopes came true – apart from me?' Alex asked, grinning.

'None,' Jess said, then felt the weight of the word. 'I've let her down.'

Alex tried not to look offended. 'Let who down?'

'Me. I was supposed to have gone travelling, got married, presented *The Holiday Programme*, owned a puppy and now be smiling smugly at my bump as I wander, deliriously happy, round the Babygro department of Mothercare.'

Alex laughed. 'Well, I think Mothercare's still open if you fancied—'

'Alex, it's not funny,' she whined. 'I'm twenty-seven and a failure. I've achieved nothing.' She watched his expression crumple.

'What about a successful three-year relationship with someone who loves you?'

He was right, she mused, as they looked at each other across the minimalist olive bowl, and yet if this was something she truly valued, why did it have to take him to point it out?

'I was meaning job, life things,' she added, relieved to see a waitress scurrying towards them.

But the food ordering, rather than providing a welcome distraction, turned out to be an intensive French tutorial where the menu required the kind of translation only those carrying a sizeable Collins would attempt. For a restaurant that sold itself on simplicity and lack of fuss, Jess thought, it seemed incongruous to present its food as an A-level interpretation paper.

'So, what d'you mean "job, life things"?' Alex continued, once the ordeal was over. 'You've got a fantastic job.'

'Scouting for commitment-phobic dogs and teenage mums with suicidal tendencies is hardly presenting *The Holiday Programme*.'

'At least it's television. When I was seventeen I wanted to be an Australian bush-walker.'

Jess entertained images of Alex skipping down mountain tracks with a knapsack and Stetson singing 'Waltzing Matilda' at passing kookaburras. 'Well, a lawyer's not a million miles away,' she said. 'Anyway, you don't understand. It's less tangible than just a job, it's a whole lifestyle thing. It's about living the life you meant to lead, doing what you set out to do, what you hoped to do, before you got lost along the way.'

'It's called idealism,' Alex said, with such an irritating laugh that she felt like belting him over the head with the chrome salt cellar. 'The pursuit of unattainable goals.'

'But that's the whole point,' Jess said, exasperated. 'How are you ever going to know they're unattainable if you don't at least try?' She dipped her ciabatta into what looked suspiciously like a bowl of urine. 'I need to find out if my ideals can be real, Alex,' she said, then paused and added, as if it were the penultimate scene in an American feel-good movie and she was about to disappear indefinitely over a horizon, 'I owe it to the person I used to be.'

Just then the waitress arrived with two plates each containing, contrary to everything the tutorial had previously promised, one asparagus spear. It seemed, Jess decided as she bit off the tip, that every part of her life was destined to fall short of her expectations.

'So where are you going to begin on this "quest for perfection"?' Alex said, swallowing his starter in a mouthful. 'I could get the puppy if that would help.'

Jess stared him straight in the eye. 'I'm going to go travelling.'

There was a stunned silence. Alex looked as though the asparagus had just whacked him across the face. 'Oh. Why?'

'I've told you why, Alex,' she said, then paused. 'Don't you see?'

He tried to look as if he did by nodding, then staring pensively into the distance.

'I need to know that this is all I can hope for. That this is it.' She glanced up but he was still doing his Rodin's *Thinker* bit and refused to catch her eye. 'Not with us,' she added, with more conviction than she felt, 'just with everything.'

'How long for?'

'Six months, a year. I don't know.'

Alex moved to study a hole in his ciabatta. 'Where?'

'Africa, I think.'

She watched, feeling like eight different kinds of murderer, as he absorbed the news.

'So. Where do we fit into all of this?' he said, finally looking up at her.

Jess gave a meek smile. It was like turning over an exam paper, she thought as she played snooker with a crumb: there were several questions she'd prepared for, and it was just Sod's Law that this wasn't one of them. 'I'm not sure,' she replied, choosing to become mesmerised by the crumb.

Alex reached over and took her hand. 'It sounds like this is something you need to do on your own.'

Jess froze. He was supposed to dissolve into tears, collapse in a begging bundle at her feet and swear on his life that he would do everything within his power to make her stay. He was not supposed to smile and suggest they split up.

'So you want us to finish, then?' she said, in retaliation.

'I want us to do whatever will make you happiest,' he replied, with such compassion she did not feel so much reassured of *his* feelings as horribly ashamed of her own. He loved her unconditionally. She loved him on the condition that he loved *her*. And that, she conceded, probably wasn't love.

'Even if it means us splitting up?' she persisted.

'If that's what will make you happy,' he said, removing his hand. 'Yes.'

Suddenly Jess wasn't at all sure that this would make her happy. She felt like a child who'd pestered to be let out to play, not because she necessarily wanted to go but because she thought she wouldn't be allowed to. Now she'd been led out into the playground and wasn't convinced that that was where she wanted to be.

'I don't *know* what will make me happy, Alex,' she said, as the waitress returned and started stacking plates up her arms. 'That's the whole problem.'

Alex reached down into the heavy-duty Sainsbury's bag he'd been carrying all night and brought out something whose wrapping had clearly been inspired by *Blue Peter*. 'Maybe your present might change things, then,' he said, handing over the tin-foil gift. 'Happy birthday.'

Jess picked it up and ripped it open excitedly. In the midst of all her self-wallowing she'd forgotten it was her birthday. 'Oh, Alex, it's lovely,' she squawked, in the pre-programmed fake voice she reserved for opening presents she wasn't sure she would like. She was holding up a three-quarter-length leather jacket with a weird detachable hood. Like everything in their relationship, it was almost right.

'It suits you,' he said, as she put it on and tried subtly to get rid of the hood.

'Naturally,' she replied, thrusting her hands into the pockets and doing a little twirl. Suddenly her fingers touched something metal and she pulled out a set of keys, studying them with the measured curiosity of a toddler. 'What are these?'

'At a guess, I'd say they were house keys,' Alex said, grinning.

'Ye-es,' she said, as though speaking to a three-year-old, 'but whose?'

'Well,' he said, slowly, looking like the three-year-old's naughtier brother, 'I think you'll find they might be . . . well, maybe, sort of . . . ours.'

Jess blinked as the restaurant started going fuzzy. 'Ours?'

'Sixty-eight C Ranley Gardens,' he announced. 'I take ownership as of next week. Fully fitted kitchen, leaking shower, nice swirly granny carpet in the hall.' He paused. 'Oh, and a spare bedroom for when I get sick of you.'

Jess gawped in a mixture of bewilderment and the more practical need to work out what he was talking about. 'You're . . . sick of me?' she managed.

'Not yet, no. I've bought a flat and I thought – before this evening, that is – that we might,' he looked up at her coyly, 'move in together.'

Jess collapsed into her seat, speechless.

'But if you're going off to search for perfection in Africa,' he said, picking up the keys and putting them in his pocket, 'I guess we won't.'

Suddenly Jess saw exactly what she would be giving up. It was one thing contemplating being the brave and independent traveller when things at home were drab and stagnant. It was quite another to know she was leaving behind someone who would make her life so comfortable, so contented and so full of love that she would never need to be brave or independent again.

'Alex, I don't—'

'Sssh,' he whispered, taking both her hands in his. 'Don't say anything now. I've sprung this on you and you need time to think. If it's Africa, I'll understand. If it's me . . . well . . .' he said, with a look of love so intense, so unfaltering she felt like screeching, 'I am not worthy,' and scuttling under the tablecloth.

Luckily, she was saved from such a confession by the arrival of the waitress, who was smiling and carrying plates the size of small paddling pools. 'The mussels?'

'That's me,' Alex volunteered. 'Can't you tell?' Then he pulled up his sleeve and flexed his right arm.

The waitress giggled politely. 'And the chicken?'

'Here,' Jess mumbled, feeling that if anyone was more suited to their choice of meal, it was her.

'The kitchen's closing in ten minutes,' the waitress said, pulling out a pad from her apron, 'so if you'd like dessert I'll take your order now.'

After the minimalist asparagus, Alex was taking no risks. 'I'll have the chocolate fudge gateau with extra ice-cream, please.'

'I can't decide,' Jess drawled, scrutinising the menu as if it were an instruction manual – which, given the translation torment of earlier, would clearly have been a preferable alternative. 'It's between two.'

'Close your eyes,' the waitress advised, 'and think of one. Then go for the other.'

Jess did as she was told, but rather than images of profiteroles versus lemon sorbet, she found her mind drifting to an altogether bigger dilemma. Camping safaris or couply Sundays? Sunny days or cosy nights? Wildlife or shared life? Africa or Alex?

She waited, eyes closed, thinking. By the time she opened them again, her decision had been made . . .

Should Jess hold out?

Turn to page 147

Should Jess give in?

Turn over to the next page

LONDON

GIVING IN

Twice upon a time . . .

To: Claire. Voyant@hotmail.com
Date: Sunday 16 April
Subject: Twice upon a time . . .

*Crouched in a room resembling an Argos delivery
van. Wondering why it is I can find a soufflé
dish and even small ceramic hippo, but no
chair. Hoping Alex does not intend to display
small ceramic hippo.*

Dear Claire,
  *Moving in with your boyfriend is not, as adverts for savings
accounts would lead us to believe, all about balancing half-way up
step-ladders in matching painting smocks and back-to-front baseball caps, heads tossed back in hilarious laughter as a Dulux dog
walks white-paint pawprints over the floorboards. It is one long
interminable hunt for the tin-opener. Had I known that five days
into being here we would still be using the television aerial as a
coat-hanger, I would have enrolled myself on an army survival
course right away. As it is, I am slumped in an inactive heap
against the ironing-board wondering whether I want to survive at
all.*
  *It is entirely predictable that the minute you leave the country
I am faced with a dilemma only you can help me with. I don't
know whether to feel ashamed or acutely pissed off, but either way
I am going totally bonkers not being able to tell someone. One of
the main drawbacks of living with your boyfriend is that there's
no one around to moan to about him.*
  *The whole thing kicked off on Tuesday when I was searching
for the box the mugs had been packed in. I'd just got to the point*

of giving up and drinking my coffee out of a champagne flute when I happened to glance – because in the process of moving, things can get terribly mixed up – into a box marked 'Alex's personal stuff'. The trouble, however, with looking for mugs in a box full of intriguing bits of paper is that you tend to become less mug-focused and more inclined to do a spot of reading. Thus, without intending to, I found myself leafing through Alex's old diaries.

After several minutes of scanning the weekend entries for girls' names and finding, instead, tedious and laboriously detailed accounts of football passes, I decided to move on to some appealing-looking airmail letters, until I noticed a smaller box peeking tantalisingly from beneath them. On hauling it out, I was perturbed to find it labelled 'K', which, being a woman and therefore instinctively alert to the slightest whiff of an ex-girlfriend, I realised stood for Kate. This girl is like some horrible extra from Ghost Busters, *flitting around unseen for weeks, then popping up just when you think she's been exorcised to cause more chaos and devastation.*

Against my better judgement, I took off the lid and started raking through the contents, which seemed to be a collection of dog-eared letters and a photo of K wearing a bikini made from three postage stamps, looking as though her first name should be 'Special'. After scrutinising her body for cellulite, I took meagre consolation in the fact she couldn't spell 'beach', before moving on to find fault with her sense of humour.

Then, among some nauseating snaps of the two of them looking blissfully happy in some French café, I spotted an envelope with Alex's writing on it. I picked it up and deduced from its unsealed nature that it had never been sent. Intrigued, I removed the note inside and read the following:

> *Kate,*
> *I know that whatever happens, wherever I go, whoever I meet, there will always be a place in my heart, an empty seat in my soul, which only you can fill.*
> *A.*

Now I know that (a) he was nineteen when he wrote this (b) the relationship ended eight years ago and (c) he had a crush on Keats, but however much I rationalise with myself – and I have been doing so non-stop since Tuesday – I can't help feeling furiously jealous. The thought of him writing such things to someone other than me is ego-denting enough. The discovery that he has preserved them in a shrine makes me want to throw myself head first off the London Eye.

But therein lies the problem: I can't. I have to behave as if all is fine because while everyone knows that keeping an old-girlfriend file is wrong, treacherous and the kind of thing you expect from a fourteen-year-old boy-band groupie, everyone also knows that snooping in someone else's private stuff is, unfortunately, the greater crime. So, instead of confronting him, making him swear he feels nothing but genuine indifference towards her (because hate, for all its negative connotations, still suggests an unnatural strength of feeling), then enjoying a celebratory bonfire, I must smile insipidly whenever he looks lost in thought, and obsess internally over which fond memory of his and Kate's happy life together he has chosen to reminisce about this time.

I hate the pair of them. I thought moving in with your boyfriend was meant to put a seal on your relationship, not bring bikini-clad skeletons out of the shoebox. What would you do? I admit this is a pointless question given that you and John have been going out so long that any relationship he might've had previously would have to have happened before the invention of photography.

Oh, God. Maybe I should just forget about it all and come and join you in your ecologically (and booze?) friendly Spanish commune. How's it all going? I read an article on a self-sustaining community in Peru where, in order to wash, they have to perform an energetic two-hour rain-dance to the water god. While I'm sure the hills of southern Spain have a slightly more reliable irrigation system, I can't help imagining the two of you in little cowhide thongs jigging and whooping and offering yourselves up as human fish.

Do you think you'll be able to last a year of pooing down holes and growing your own Weetabix? Or will the prospect of a Chinese takeaway in front of Friends *become – just perhaps – the more appealing option?*

You're certainly not missing anything at work. It's been hideous since you left, with Michael deciding, half an hour before we go on air, to drop the 'Guess the Granny' slot in favour of a late news item on obesity, thus leaving me in a room full of half-eaten cheese-spread sandwiches to entertain sixteen OAPs from Basingstoke. Sometimes I feel as though I'm not so much a researcher for daytime telly as an overworked performing seal.

To make matters worse they have replaced you with an annoying girl called Chyani – pronounced 'Shan-yah' – who thinks, just because she used to work on Kilroy, *she is entitled to treat me like a two-year-old. The other day I overheard her on the phone saying she would get her assistant to fax through the details, causing me to embark on a furious internal dilemma as to why I hadn't been given an assistant, until she hailed me from across the room, thrust a wodge of paper at my chest and cautioned me not to try to send it all through the fax machine at once.*

I have no idea where people like her get such arrogance but I would very much like to borrow some. If that were me nine days into a new job, I would be behaving like some kind of deferential mouse, which probably explains why, aged twenty-seven, I am still a lowly researcher – or, as would now appear to be the case, assistant researcher – while 'Shan-yah', aged twenty-two and barely out of college, is two light-entertainment programmes away from directorship of Carlton Television.

It is hardly surprising, therefore, that by the weekend I was so drained by my seal and slave duties that the thought of devoting my only two free days to moving furniture nearly tipped me over the edge. I kept myself buoyant, however, with delicious images of the two of us celebrating our first night of cohabitation, panting and sweating our way through the house, christening every room in a mind-blowing sexual extravaganza. Two hours in, however, it became miserably apparent that the only panting and sweating we'd be doing was up three flights of stairs carrying a wardrobe.

I had forgotten how hellish the moving-house process is, imagining it instead as some vast social gathering where I and all my wonderfully helpful friends would sit around on boxes chatting, laughing and gorging ourselves on junk food. This proved to be wrong on every count, particularly the one relating to the helpful friends who did not so much turn out to be helpful as not turn out at all.

I hate it when this happens because rather than telling them in a nonchalant manner that I have no use for fair-weather friends, I immediately start thinking that the only reason they do not want to come and lug bookcases around all day is not because it is arduous, boring, unpaid and there are myriad other things they would rather be doing with their Saturday, but because they don't like me. Had I been the popular person of the junk-food fantasy, the mere mention of blocked sewage pipes would have had them piling round to help me in droves.

As it was, we had Alex's friend Dave – a lawyer who seems to have missed his vocation as a packer at Sainsbury's – and a very hung-over Lou. The idea had been to meet at the van-hire place, move my stuff first, then whiz up to Maida Vale to get Alex's. Unfortunately, however, when we got to the van-hire place it was an Indian takeaway.

This set the tone for the rest of the day. Alex went into the foulest mood imaginable but kept insisting, annoyingly, that he was fine. Dave spent half an hour studying the street sign then tried to convince us all there was a misprint in both A–Zs. Lou threw up at the sight of a poppadom, and I, after explaining we had not come to get a Bengali curry at eleven thirty in the morning, discovered I had managed to hire a van from a company that didn't exist.

After wandering into the kind of fenced wastelands inhabited only by pierced skateboarders, we ended up squashed into a vehicle from an outfit calling itself 'Miracle Van Hire' for reasons that did not become obvious until we tried to drive it, when we discovered

23

that with only one windscreen wiper, no right indicator and a gear-stick that came off in your hand when you changed up to third, it was not so much a miracle as a supernatural phenomenon it functioned at all.

By the time we'd rocked up – literally – at mine, I had almost forgotten that the point of the day wasn't to sit in traffic jams chewing the heads off jelly babies, gossiping with Lou and listening to the same song eight times on Capital FM. It therefore came as a rude awakening to discover that my bedroom resembled the after-math of a long-standing strike by the bin men. Alex thought the debris was rubbish and started hauling several black bin-liners towards the stairwell until I pointed out that he was just about to dispose of half my winter wardrobe, at which point he cast a terri-fied, furious eye over the other thirty-eight bulging monstrosities and said he needed a gin and tonic.

I don't know what it is about blokes and doing a tedious job like carting furniture or loading vans but they seem to turn from being fun, light-hearted, wise-cracking guys into nothing-is-a-laughing-matter weirdos. Thus, while Lou and I pissed ourselves over the fact that the large bag containing all my toiletries had just burst and spilt all the way down the stairs, Alex and Dave were standing as if they were at a state funeral, glowering at an armchair. They seemed to think they were taking part in an episode of Changing Rooms, *casting anxious glances at their watches every time they couldn't fit something into the van. Then, when Lou and I said we wanted to stop for a coffee, they looked at us as if we'd just abandoned stencilling the bathroom in favour of a leisurely three-course dinner.*

I ended up having to phone Miracle Van Hire and beg to hold on to the van till six, but the bloke couldn't speak English and kept telling us he only had five vans, not six. I tried to make a joke about actually needing *five vans – it took one trip for my photo albums and old letters alone – but the humourless ones just gave me a filthy look and continued discussing how best to stack the hi-fi speakers.*

When finally we got round to moving Alex's stuff it was like going from a car boot sale to a library. He had everything organised in packing cases, all clearly labelled with things like 'CDs (A–M)' and 'Books – light fiction'. He had even thought to put the bulkier stuff nearer the door to make loading easier. Had he been any more sensible he would have combusted with tedium!

Fortunately – or maybe unfortunately – this library effect has not been in evidence since we moved in. Instead of filing the towels and arranging the mantelpiece ornaments in alphabetical order, he has made a half-hearted stab at unpacking a soup ladle and spent the rest of the time fiddling with a cable behind the telly. I had no idea our priorities for sorting out a house would be quite so diametrically opposed:

My Priorities	*Alex's Priorities*
(1) Inspect the hygiene levels of loo, bath, kitchen cupboards and fridge.	(1) Inspect the best location for optimal television reception.
(2) Go to corner shop and buy Flash Excel, bleach, rubber gloves, scouring pads and unnecessary-yet-cleverly-marketed-so-as-to-appear-vital alpine-fresh Toilet Duck.	(2) Go to Tottenham Court Road and buy a television connector socket.
(3) Spend following two hours with head in loo or fridge trying to elicit praise, sympathy and/or guilt from Alex.	(3) Spend following two hours with head in television instruction manual.
(4) Decide which cupboard to put the saucepans in.	(4) Decide which socket to put the television connector socket in.

(5) Figure out why the immersion heater isn't working.	(5) Figure out why, even with new connector socket, television still isn't working.
(6) Ring up for pizza to be enjoyed in front of juicy Channel Four film.	(6) Blame dodgy bloke on Tottenham Court Road for fact that juicy Channel Four film is pitch black and silent.

The only good thing about it is that he has been so consumed with AC adapters that I have had free rein to put things exactly where I want them. It is by far the best bit of moving into a new house and is, I suppose, the human equivalent to peeing on lampposts.

The trouble is, I'm so indecisive about what kind of 'feel' I want a room to have: I spend ages trying to create, say, an ethnic one, with some African salad servers, a wooden picture frame and an elephant-patterned throw painstakingly draped over the sofa to give the impression it has just been casually flung there, then I wake up the next day, resolve to be sophisticated and trendy, and display instead a thick glass dish with three expensive pebbles from Heal's.

Yesterday morning, however, I had less a change of heart than a full-blown heart-attack. I was just wondering whether the candlesticks on the dining-room cabinet didn't look a bit too symmetrically placed when I caught sight of a figure looming by the stereo in the sitting room. It was too tall to be Alex and, anyway, he'd already left for work, so unless we had an over-friendly postman, I deduced that we were being burgled.

With no escape route and still wearing my dressing-gown, I grabbed one of the candlesticks and crept stealthily, pulse racing, towards the intruder. As I approached the connecting doors between the two rooms wishing I'd thought to choose a more vicious-looking weapon I heard the toot of a car horn directly beneath the window. Presuming this was his accomplice and that, consequently, he would be forced to go to the window to signal progress, I seized my opportunity, threw open the doors then let out a high-pitched scream. There, standing not three feet away from me, was David Beckham.

It turns out that Alex's one contribution to the interior design of our new home is not a beautifully crafted vase, stylish oil-painting or even functional neutral-coloured rug but a life-sized cardboard cut-out of a footballer. The idea that he considered this an attractive object to display was mind-boggling. The idea that it should take pride of place in our sitting room was simply not on. So I picked it up, fleetingly relished the prospect of being so close to the real-life version, then flat-packed it away behind the freezer never to see it again.

Or so I thought. I got back from work to find that not only had it come back to life, it is watching the end credits of – ironically – They Think It's All Over. I put it calmly to Alex that I'd understood I was here to live with my boyfriend rather than a Manchester United centre-forward. He gave me an exasperated look, accused me of being impossible to please and announced haughtily that Beckham was a midfielder, not a centre-forward.

It transpires that my complaints about him taking no part in the décor of the house have somewhat backfired on me – even though the notion of 'décor' and a cardboard David Beckham is not exactly a pairing that leaps instantly to mind. He said I was in no position to ban him from displaying one photo when I had littered the room with so many girly ones I could start up my own wallpaper company. He then tried to claim he hadn't been given a fair chance to put up his photos until I pointed out that this was because he is a typical bloke and doesn't have any photos. So, after much bickering, we have compromised with keeping David in the downstairs loo. Although this is a definite improvement on the sitting room, it makes doing a wee feel as if you're performing in a peep show.

Oh, God – peeping. I'd forgotten momentarily about my crime. What if Alex finds out I've been snuffling around his personal stuff? I'm terrified I put a letter back in the wrong place and his *library-brain notices. I will not just be in trouble for prying, but doubly so for not owning up. Right. That's it. I'm going to get this out in the open and be done with it. We are supposed to be in a functioning relationship, not a fraudulent one. And, anyway, honesty is always much the best policy.*

Hope John's surviving the solar-baked chickpea burgers.

Lots of love,

Jess

xxx

PS Might just say the box fell open, rather than give him the I-went-snooping-intentionally line.

Benefit of the Doubt

'So you're saying this letter was lying on top of the toaster?'
Alex was pacing the bedroom with his arms behind his back
in a manner that would have been authoritative had he not
been wearing boxer shorts with googly-eyed reindeers.

'Yes,' Jess said, nodding assertively.

'And you thought it was a bill.'

She nodded again, less assertively, wishing she'd thought
up a more convincing lie.

'And despite it not having a reference number, not demanding payment, not being addressed to you, and, when we think
about it, not really looking like a bill at all, you read it.'

'No, well, I didn't. It wasn't so much that it was—'

'Did you or did you not read it?'

'Well . . . sort of, but the thing is the toaster was—'

'Yes or no?'

Jess busied herself with a duvet popper. One of the drawbacks of going out with a lawyer, she decided, apart from
perpetually picturing his clients as bustier versions of Ally
McBeal, was that trying to hold your own in an argument
was like playing Monopoly with a merchant banker. 'Yes,' she
squeaked, and hid under a pillow.

Alex moved silently to his section of the wardrobe –
originally a rail and three cupboards until Jess unpacked her
jumpers and left him with half a shelf and some wire coat-
hangers. Without saying a word, he pulled on a sweatshirt and
jeans and made for the bathroom.

'I don't know why I'm being made to feel the criminal,'
Jess shouted defensively, throwing the pillow across the room,
'when it was you who wrote the stupid thing.'

Alex turned to face her. He looked so calm she wanted to

hit him. 'I was nineteen, Jess.' He picked up the pillow and put it back on the bed. 'And everyone has a past.'

This, Jess realised, was the problem: he was not supposed to have a past. He was supposed to have spent any life prior to her as an amorphous abstract blob floating around in the ether, without direction, motive, thought, emotion or, most crucially, girlfriend.

'Anyway, you would have done the same,' she retorted, yanking the duvet around her shoulders, 'if you found a box with—' She paused. 'If a letter from James was sitting on the toaster.'

Alex looked at her as if she'd just accused him of having a crush on Westlife. 'Of course I wouldn't.'

Even though she knew this was the honest answer, the right answer and, when she thought about him reading her emails to Claire, the safest answer, she couldn't help feeling that the reason he wouldn't snoop into her personal belongings was not one of deference or moral decency but simply because he wasn't interested. And this prospect opened up a new can of paranoid worms. 'So, my life's not interesting to you, is that it?'

He let out an exasperated sigh. 'No, Jess. I just respect your privacy.' Then he strode into the bathroom, pulled down his trousers, sat on the toilet and pointedly shut the door.

Jess lay there as she always did on the rare occasions she and Alex argued; she felt, humiliatingly, that she was the nastier human being. No matter how often his love for her was confirmed, she couldn't help doubting it, suspecting it, needing to push and challenge it. And then an uncomfortable thought struck her: maybe the reason she felt this way was not because Alex's feelings were in dispute but because hers were.

In an attempt to make amends, she scurried downstairs and embarked on trying to cook a fry-up without oil. When Alex eventually appeared, she'd managed to burn some sausages, make an egg resemble a sunburnt nipple and coat everything else with the bottom layer of the frying pan, all in time for the opening sequence of *Grandstand,* which was, she conceded, the only bit of the five-hour tedium worth watching. They proceeded to sit in silence – enthralled, in Alex's case – in front of a football match whose outcome was not only already established but emblazoned across half the screen for anyone still in doubt.

'What's that white thing on the pitch?' Jess asked, in a rare moment of interest.

'Think you'll find it's the ball, Jess,' Alex said, fracturing his jaw on a sausage. 'Right, watch this goal.'

'No, I'm talking about that stuff there,' she continued, pointing at the foreground.

'Way-hey!' he roared, shooting his arms in the air and knocking over his mug. 'Tell me that wasn't skill.'

'I think it could be loo paper.'

Alex shifted excitedly to the edge of the sofa. 'This next one's a beauty,' he enthused, as Jess started to crawl towards the telly obstructing his view. 'Move, Jess!'

'I think it *is* loo paper.'

'Get out of the way!'

'It's loo paper!' she squealed, turning round in disbelief. 'Why do they put loo paper on the pitch?'

Alex thumped the armrest. 'Oh, for arse's sake, Jess.' He sighed as the goalpost was swallowed up into a large football icon and whizzed off into the corner of the screen to reveal Gary Lineker and a man wearing a silver shirt launching into a tedious discussion about a pass. 'I missed it.'

'I wouldn't worry,' Jess breezed, reaching for the phone and dragging it towards the door. 'I'm sure they'll show it twenty-four more times in slow motion.'

But this, she discovered, after a fifty-minute analysis of a potentially flirty email Lou had been sent, was by no means an exaggeration. Football's tragic downfall was that it couldn't just *be*: it had to be subjected to the kind of post-mortem so dull that the video-instruction manual seemed an enticing alternative. Perhaps, she conceded, it had only been invented so that sportsmen past their prime could still feel valued and sit in comfy studios in disgusting shirts.

'I thought the idea was to spend today in Ikea,' she said, returning to the sofa and looking ostentatiously at her watch, 'not slumped—'

'On the phone for an hour to someone you saw twelve hours ago.' Alex was looking at her with raised eyebrows.

'It was important,' she protested. 'Paul sent her a really ambiguous email.'

'Oh, God, why didn't you tell me?' he said, in alarm. 'I'd have arranged a conference call with the White House.'

Jess picked up a cushion and threw it at him. 'You were too busy analysing a penalty kick with Gary,' she retorted, before the cushion hit her in the face.

Whether it had been the excitement of too many goal replays or the exertions of his morning's trip to the bathroom, Alex spent the car trip to Ikea in a peculiar mood. Instead of chatting and laughing like a normal human being, he drifted off into silent contemplation as if the single act of driving the car rendered him exempt from any obligation to be social.

Jess hated it when he did this. It made her worry that he was thinking about their relationship – or, more specifically, its flaws. As much as she tried to tell herself he was just having a moment or two of quiet reflection, it never worked and before long she was gibbering increasingly dire rubbish to fill the airwaves, while simultaneously whipping herself up into a state of paranoia over what she had said or done to piss him off. Which was exactly what was happening now.

'. . . so then Lou and I went into the viewing gallery and Jake was watching some footage about this bloke who's been doing all this weird experimental stuff with cell mutation and so I said to Jake, "Ooh, that looks a bit intellectual," and Jake said, "Yes, it is, where have you two been?" so I said, "We've been at the pub," and then Lou said, "I don't think we can talk to you any more, Jake," and so Jake said, "Why not?" and then Lou said, "Because you're too cerebral for us," and then Jake said, "Too what?"' Jess paused for dramatic effect. 'D'you get it?'

Alex looked at her blankly.

'We were accusing him of being intelligent – right? – but he didn't know what cerebral—'

'Oh, yeah. Yeah, I see.'

Silence.

'So. Who's Jake, then?'

'Alex,' Jess whined, 'he's my old flatmate.'

Paranoia suspected. Round 1.

'You OK?'

'Hmm?'

'I said, are you OK?'

'Fine, why?'

'I don't know, you're being all weird and silent.'

Silence.

'You sure you're OK?'

'Yes.'

'Why are you being silent, then?'

'I'm just thinking, that's all.'

Paranoia substantiated. Round 2.

'What about?'

'Hmm?'

'What about?'

'What?'

'You said you were thinking. What are you thinking about?'

Silence.

Paranormal paranoia. Round 3.

Jess sat, tense with anticipation as all sorts of possibilities whizzed through her brain: he was thinking about them, about her, about how she found loo paper more interesting than

Gary Lineker, about how incompatible they were, how they shouldn't be living together, how he missed his flat with his friends, Nintendo PlayStation and empty pizza boxes, how he would rather be living with someone else, how he would rather be living with someone pretty who didn't make sunburnt-nipple eggs, who liked cardboard cut-out David Beckhams, who *was* David Beckham, who didn't wander around the flat in BhS knickers or use the telly aerial as a clothes horse or snoop in his . . . Jess froze in horror. He was thinking about Kate.

'I was just thinking,' Alex said, turning down the stereo, looking around at her and smiling, 'about the time me and my brother went body-surfing in Cornwall.'

Game over.

By the time they'd sat in a two-hour traffic jam, gone six times round the same roundabout and entered the car park via the exit-only lane, they did not need a knife with which to cut the atmosphere, but a two-foot-long machete. Having spent all week in dreamy fantasies of the two of them wandering hand in hand through aisles of Scandinavian pine furniture, stopping occasionally to admire a hanging linen sock cupboard, Jess was miserably disappointed to discover seven hundred others with the same idea.

'I'm getting agoraphobia,' she moaned, as Alex produced a tape measure from his pocket, pulled it out to a length of two and a half metres and stood squinting at it with one eye.

'Might just be a couple of centimetres out,' he concluded, 'but at twenty-eight fifty that's fourteen twenty-five each.' He reached up and hauled down something the size of a Rice Krispies box that purported to be a bookcase.

Jess stared morosely into the trolley, wondering whether she was ready to share half a bookcase with someone who carried a tape measure in his jacket and split shared costs to the penny. It seemed an irony indeed that while the rest of her friends devoted their lives to getting their boyfriends to commit, she'd found one eager to be part of the furniture – only she wasn't sure whether she wanted his feet under the table.

'Dinner plates are next to the ceramic salt cellars,' he said, whipping out a list and circling 'lightbulbs'. 'And then we need to make a decision on roller blinds.'

'Alternatively we could just shag on the bed,' Jess suggested, collapsing next to a 'Please do not sit here' sign.

A bearded assistant looked hopeful. Alex was ticking his list.

'That sounds good,' a voice announced behind her.

She turned to discover a grinning Mark, hand in hand with a grinning Jo. Jo was her old flatmate, a fellow believer in finding 'the one', until eight years of searching and a fairly dogged show of persistence from Mark had culminated in the compromised relationship she was now in. But Jo would never admit it was a compromise. And there was something about her own relationship with Alex that prevented Jess pushing her to do so.

'What are you guys doing here?' Jess squealed.

'Obviously not what you two are, babes,' Jo said, gesticulating suggestively at the bed.

Jess didn't think it was the moment to point out that the only thing currently making Alex tick was an Ikea shopping list.

'We've just spent two hours looking at candles,' Mark said, rolling his eyes at Alex as if this held some deeper significance.

'Know what you mean, mate,' Alex replied, in the tone he reserved for when he decided to be a lad. 'If you thought this morning's hangover was bad, try shopping in Ikea with your girlfriend.' They guffawed.

It was a source of much fascination to Jess how quickly Alex could effect a sex change that turned him from being essentially a girl into something found mooning into the camera on *Ibiza Uncovered.*

'What is it they say again, babes?' Jo retaliated, joining Jess on the bed. 'Big hangover, small—'

Just then the bearded assistant arrived and told them, in rather limited English, that they weren't allowed to shit on the bed. Their meeting disrupted, they said their goodbyes, Jo sealing hers with several rounds of demonstrative air-kisses. 'See you tonight at Sophie's,' she chirped, and guided a bored-looking Mark towards Soft Furnishings.

Three hours later, however, they saw rather more of Jo than they had expected. She seemed to have translated the invitation to a dress-down dinner literally and was wearing something more usually at home in the slinkier range of Marks & Spencer's underwear department. Sophie, in contrast, was swaddled in a knitted polo-necked black dress.

'This looks familiar,' she said, as Jess proffered a bottle of upmarket Australian Chardonnay and realised, too late, that she'd just handed back Sophie's flat-warming gift.

'Well, you know . . .' Jess giggled nervously. 'Alex and I decided we couldn't possibly drink it without you guys.' Alex looked bemused and helped himself to a passing carrot stick.

Jess scanned the hall, which was bedecked with silver-framed photos of the married couple: Sophie with a bridesmaid up her dress and a balding Richard gazing at her adoringly; the two of them suntanned and laughing astride a camel with flowers in its ears; months later in matching bobble hats balanced precariously on a nursery slope. Photos, she realised, represented the window through which she viewed everyone else's relationships: happy, problem-free, and better than her own.

'Avocado canapé?' Sophie offered, waving a plate of immaculately prepared doll's house food. She was always inviting people for what she termed a 'spot of supper', to give the impression of a relaxed affair, when in fact she spent all morning with her head in the oven, all afternoon in a Little Mermaid apron and all evening elbow deep in washing-up water.

'It's the new cohabitees,' Richard announced, approaching with two glasses of wine as Jess and Alex made self-conscious small-talk about a light fitting. 'Come through! We're all just chilling out,' he said, leading them into a room full of couples standing awkwardly in a circle sipping drinks and making conversation about the Northern Line. The idea that Richard conceived this as 'chilling out' made Jess feel genuinely concerned for his more stressful moments.

'It's all very well to say, "Take a bus", but do they have any idea how gridlocked the roads are at seven in the morning?' someone called Digby implored.

'Or indeed at eight in the morning?' his girlfriend added usefully.

'And, of course, there's no direct route to the City,' piped up a girl in a navy suit, 'so we would have to take . . . How many is it, Michael?'

'Well, at least three and that only gets us to Westminster,' Michael replied, looking round in anticipation for shocked faces.

Jess suspected that a more entertaining evening could be had from studying Richard's accountancy textbooks and sidled over to the bookcase. The world of dating would be made a great deal simpler, she decided, by a quick recce of someone's book collection: a manual on computer programming, for example, or an Alan Titchmarsh novel was all one needed to know that a relationship wasn't going to be a winner.

'Allure,' a soft, throaty voice announced in her right ear.

Jess lifted her head from *Accountancy Can Be Fun!* and turned to meet its owner. He was tall with dark, floppy hair and the kind of grin that managed to be innocently seductive. Immediately she wanted to show him how unattractive she found him – always a sign, she had learned, of the reverse.

'Allure,' he said again, still grinning. 'Am I right?'

Despite herself, she grinned back. 'About what?'

'Your perfume.'

This was the conversational equivalent of foreplay. She wanted to find it invasive. Instead she found it intimate. 'Wrong.'

'Damn,' he said, clicking his fingers. 'It should be, though.'

'Should be what?'

'Called Allure. It smells, you know . . .' He trailed off and ran a hand through his hair. 'You smell nice.'

Jess didn't know how to respond. Acknowledging it felt a bit like saying 'Thank you' to 'I love you'.

'So,' he continued, gesturing to the book, 'you're an accountant.'

Jess was horrified. 'Oh, good God, no.' She closed it and returned it to the shelf. 'I'm not *that* boring.'

'Really?' he said. 'So what would you call reading a text-book at a dinner party?'

She laughed, then bent forward and said in a confiding stage-whisper, 'Escaping the boring sods who *are* accountants.'

He moved to whisper in her ear. She felt a surge of excitement at his proximity. 'I'd watch out,' he said. She could feel his breath tickling her neck. It felt thrillingly as though he might kiss her – there, in front of the whole room. A forbidden brush of his lips on the nape of her— 'My girlfriend's one of those "boring accountants".'

Jess froze; she hadn't just been led up the garden path but through the front door and straight to the bedroom. Before she had time to reassemble her expression into one of indifference, Sophie arrived clutching a seating plan and started guiding people to the table with the ease of a lollipop lady.

'Geoffrey,' announced a ruddy-cheeked bloke in a pinstriped shirt.

'Jess,' she replied, wondering why Sophie had deemed them compatible dinner-party companions. Geoffrey scratched at his dandruff.

'Andy.' Jess took the confidently stretched-out hand and looked up into a familiar face. 'Not an accountant.'

She shook his hand. 'Jess. Not that I would think any less of you if you were.'

As they all delved into some home-made pâté and waited for Jo to return from pinning her 'dress', which, not content with being transparent, had now decided to unravel itself from her cleavage, Jess surveyed the rest of the party. It wasn't, she decided, helping herself to a fifth glass of wine, that any of Sophie's friends were horrible. Quite the opposite, they were perfectly pleasant. It was just that all of them, Sophie at times included, would clearly have benefited from a personality lobotomy at birth.

'Mmm, this is lovely, Soph,' said a girl who was wearing the kind of blouse one would only contemplate in the event of a severe laundry crisis.

'Dee-lish,' her boyfriend agreed eagerly.

'You'll have to bring the recipe next time you're round at ours.'

'Or, better still, come round to ours and cook it for us,' he chortled.

They had that couples' disease, Jess noticed, of classifying their lives like the word sheep: nothing had a singular.

'Anna and I once tried to make pâté,' Geoffrey volunteered, mid-munch.

'Tell them about that time we made it for your parents,' Anna said, pulling at his shirt as if he were a puppet.

'Oh, yeah, *that*,' he replied. They looked at each other and laughed.

As Geoffrey launched into the story, prompted at every turn by Anna who seemed happier to ruin it by butting in than tell it uninterrupted herself, Jess felt a strange sense of jealousy. Although she had no desire to hurtle up the corporate climbing frame, save up for a semi-detached in Clapham, and settle for someone called Geoffrey with no charisma and visible dandruff, she couldn't help wishing she felt as smug and contented with *her* life as they plainly did with theirs. As she gazed round the table, the couples seemed to become an army: tightly flanked, totally impenetrable and about to attack.

'So, Jess, how's cohabitation?'

'I wouldn't know,' she said, slurping at more wine. 'It's trihabitation at the moment.'

Everyone looked perplexed. Geoffrey looked aroused. 'You crafty devil,' he said, smirking at Alex. Alex reverted to lad mode and grunted.

'The third occupant is a bloke, Geoffrey,' Jess said, wondering why the prospect of potential bisexuality was a bigger male turn-on than short skirts or lacy underwear. 'A cardboard David Beckham.'

Rather than damaging Alex's reputation, this seemed to confirm his status as chief lad, and by the time the pudding arrived, he was hosting his own pissed, even more tedious version of *Grandstand*.

'So. You and Alex are lovers, then?' Andy had pulled up a chair beside her. He was holding on to the back rest and straddling the seat in a way that suggested furniture wasn't the only thing he had a talent for mounting.

'Um . . . well . . .' Jess stuttered, as if she'd just been catapulted back to primary three and asked whether she wanted to kiss Paddy Delaney on the roundabout. It seemed odd to refer to Alex as her 'lover' – like calling Burger King a restaurant.

'But you're in a serious relationship,' he said, pulling out a packet of cigarettes from his back pocket and sticking one in the corner of his mouth.

It was a statement that required an answer. Jess discovered, to her shame, that she wanted to respond in the negative. 'Only marriage is serious,' she replied, evasively.

He lit the cigarette, inhaled slowly and began to blow a

series of wispy haloes into the air above them. For such a revolting habit, Jess decided, smoking was uncannily sexy on the right person.

'Tell me about it,' he said.

Jess flinched. He'd done it again, intoxicated her with flirtation then whacked her back into consciousness with the inference that he wasn't just unavailable he was married. She pretended to be fascinated by a lump of candlewax. A girl-friend was salvageable. A girlfriend was running to the boarding gate just as the flight was closing. Marriage was getting there to watch the plane take off.

'So you and her,' Jess nodded in the direction of a mousy-blonde talking earnestly to the girl of the laundry crisis, 'are married?'

'Oh, good God, no,' he protested, smiling, 'we're not *that* boring.'

Jess laughed with relief. She was back at the boarding gate, unsure where the plane was heading but alarmingly certain she wanted to find out. 'Lovers?'

Andy ran a finger round the rim of his glass. 'Maybe. Once.'

'And now?' she said, unable to look at him.

He bent forward and tapped some ash into the pâté dish. 'Now is something I'm not very good at confronting.'

Jess tried to look as though she was unaffected by this news. It was easy when Andy was the flirt, the one-dimensional wanker who swanked in with his good looks and perfume chat-up lines. She could enjoy it, ignore it and trot home superior with her lovely, deep, multi-dimensional Alex. But when he started showing signs of having something more – a brain, a sense of self, and, more specifically, reservations about his girlfriend – it wasn't easy at all. It was exciting.

'What is there to confront?' she asked, hoping the direct-ness of her question wouldn't send him scuttling back to co-host *Grandstand*.

'Have you ever loved someone so much you feel consumed

by them, as if your emotions, your senses, your entire being only exist in relation to them?'

Jess stared crestfallen. He was not partially in love with his girlfriend. He was *too* in love with her. 'I guess,' she replied, limply.

'And then have you experienced what it's like to have someone feel that way for you?'

She tried to remember whether she had.

'Only not to feel it back. To love them,' he added, insistently, 'to want to protect them, care for them, help them. But to know that you are capable of feeling an uncontrollability, an intensity beyond those measured sentiments.' He looked up from the strawberry cheesecake he'd been addressing. 'To know that they are feeling something for you that you will never feel for them.'

Jess sat, frozen to the spot, wondering if he hadn't just stuck a tape player inside her head, recorded every thought she'd had about her relationship with Alex, subjected it to an editor, a relationship counsellor and a dictionary, then played it back to check whether she was happy with it. The answer was a resounding yes – but not for what it said about her and Alex.

'Surely if it's not right you should walk away. Find someone with whom it *is* right,' she said, then felt uncomfortable – as though he'd been loitering on the edge of the disco and she'd offered herself as his partner for the slow dance.

'What about you and Alex?' he said, stubbing out his cigarette. 'Do you ever have doubts?'

She paused. 'Everyone has doubts,' she replied, swiping her finger round the remains of the cheesecake.

'I don't think Alex does.'

Jess looked down the table where, right on cue, Alex turned towards her and winked.

'But I think you do.'

She swung round and, for the first time since she'd met

him, looked Andy directly in the eye. He grinned. She wanted to throw him on to the table and do forbidden things with the cheesecake. He was unbelievably attractive. He understood her. And he was unavailable.

'Can I interrupt to sort out taxis?' Geoffrey had just appeared with the timing of a broken clock. 'Anna's a bit sleepy,' he said, nodding in the direction of his comatose girlfriend, slumped at the table with her hair in the cream jug. With Geoffrey as a boyfriend, it was a wonder she hadn't done it sooner, Jess thought.

'Alex and I are south,' she said, as Andy's girlfriend sidled up and placed a proprietary arm around his shoulders.

'And Andy and I are north,' the girlfriend said pointedly.

'The south taxi's leaving now,' Geoffrey announced, causing a selection of couples to start shuffling towards the door, saying repeatedly, 'Lovely, thank you,' like well-trained cockatoos.

Jess got up and stood opposite Andy, hovering hopefully for a goodbye kiss.

'It was lovely to meet you,' he said, proffering his hand as if they had not just emerged from an intimate connecting of souls, but a successful business meeting.

'You too,' she said, then left reluctantly to join a taxi load of tweed jackets laboriously discussing the best route back.

In the darkness of the ride home, Jess mulled over the evening, replaying her time with Andy like a detective sifting through CCTV footage. Having talked to him of doubt, it seemed paradoxical that now she was never more sure of what she wanted.

Sects Education

To: Claire.Voyant@hotmail.com
Date: Monday 29 May
Subject: Sects Education

Confused – but not in the way bastards claim to
be when they want to dump you and can't be
arsed to explain it's because they've shagged
someone else. Wishing to shag someone else.
Wishing, now I think about it, just to shag.

Dear Claire,

It would appear that Alex and I are taking part in the sex equivalent of the Slimfast diet. We have forgone scrumptious, leisurely three-course dinners for an occasional quick, functional yet unexciting substitute, to such an extent that the before and after images are so frighteningly dissimilar you begin to wonder whether we are actually the same two people.

A sample evening before moving in together	A sample evening after moving in together
Greeted at Alex's warm, cosy flat with a glass of wine and sensuous kiss.	Alex incapable of acknowledging me due to being at level four of Tomb Raider.
Sit in a snuzzly bundle on the sofa munching a delicious meal Alex has spent two hours toiling over.	Pick at the remains of Alex's Burger King.

Retire to Alex's bedroom ostensibly to watch telly but really to begin lengthy foreplay.	Watch telly.
Sex.	Change into oversized T-shirt and discuss which of us is going to come back from work to let the plumber in.
Drift into post-coital slumber holding each other in a loving embrace.	Pass out holding a book.

I knew that moving in together meant that you became more relaxed with each other and didn't try as hard, but I had no idea this was because you turned into your parents. I feel sure it isn't normal to waddle round in greying pants, squeeze some blackheads in the mirror, then slob into bed and stare at a book for fifteen minutes, but I have no means of finding out. When you are in a long-term relationship like ours it is not the done thing to go about divulging the intricacies of your sex life and, unfortunately, the only people who are willing to talk openly on the subject are single people who actually have sex. Thus, instead of empathising and laughing in shared acknowledgement of once-weekly efforts wearing scrotty PJs, you end up convinced you've become some sexless freak, torturing yourself with why you are the only ones not smearing each other with whipped cream and having oral sex in the airing cupboard.

I keep hoping it might just be an adjustment thing and that at any moment now I will come home from work to find Alex straddling the fridge starkers with a rose between his buttocks. But the nearest we have come was last Friday when, although he was naked, he was about as ready to make erotic love as a Nigella Lawson raspberry Pavlova. He was looking furious, clutching a plunger and a spanner and cursing the loo, which had blocked, refused to flush, then flooded all over the bathroom floor. As a result, we spent the rest of the evening mopping up wee and talking about rubber washers.

And this is the other thing. Where before our conversations were sparky, stimulating and, if not intellectual, at least good fun, they now have the interest-value of an afternoon cookery programme. For example, a typical pre-dinner chat:

Alex (unpacking the shopping):   'I popped into Habitat today and they do sell those metallic soap dishes but only ones that clip over the bath, not the wall-fixture ones.'

Me (rummaging in the fridge):   'I'm sure I saw some wall-fixture ones there before . . . d'you think these mushrooms need to be eaten up?'

Alex (stacking tins):   'Unless they were in Wall Hangings rather than Bathroom Accessories. We could put them in the salad.'

Me (sniffing inside a bowl):   'No, it was definitely Bathroom Accessories. Did you get anywhere with the gas bill?'

Alex (also sniffing bowl):   'Apparently, the second part relates to the previous owners but – I'd chuck that sauce – the price per unit figure is . . .'

Arghhhhh!! I am going slowly mad with – oh, Christ, hold on, the plumber wants me . . .

I was under the impression that coming back from work mid-afternoon to let a workman in was the slacker, more preferable option. That was before I discovered it meant turning into a coffee percolator and staring at excrement. I'm sure he knows I'm trying to write an email because every time I sit down and start typing, a "'Scuse me, love,' bellows up from inside the toilet bowl and I'm summoned to search the house for something called a pipe wrench or to sit on the edge of the bath and flush the loo repeatedly, while he slurps at his mug and says, 'Not a problem, Gary,' eight times into his phone.

This last excursion, however, seems to have borne fruit – or something a little less appealing. Having spent half an hour standing with a gigantic plunger and telling me in disappointed tones that it was 'just a blockage, love' he has taken great delight in escorting me to the manhole in the front garden and showing me, barely able to control his excitement, what the problem is. I have never seen anyone quite so thrilled with a festering mound of turds and used Tampax. He is now trailing a hose through the house and telling a twelve-year-old in a shell-suit to 'Blast it,' while the Le Creuset casserole dish collects orange drips from the U-bend.

The idea that I chose this plumbing outfit because it was called Running Free now seems lunatic. It is not, as the name tantalisingly suggests, about racing across the plains of Kenya, warm wind in your hair and the soundtrack to Out of Africa, but about spending all afternoon as Steve's overworked apprentice to have a loo that is neither running nor – at one hundred and twenty-three pounds sixty exclusive of VAT – free.

Oh, God, listen to me – I'm talking shit again, so to speak. I may as well have done with it and trade in my personality for a weekly subscription to Good Housekeeping. In fact, the only thing that's preventing me having twenty-four-hour conversations on desirable artefacts to brighten up your conservatory is a desirable artefact of a decidedly different variety. It is six feet tall, dark and attractive and, in the absence of a conservatory, has brightened up my life.

Its name is Andy and I think I am falling in love. I should probably stop writing now, particularly as this is Alex's computer and the sheer mention of another bloke feels tantamount to shagging them several times in his bed but, unfortunately, one of the most pressing desires about starting to fancy someone new is to share this news with someone else.

That's it, though. If it was just a fancying thing, everything would be dandy. I'd admire him as one would a conservatory artefact, occasionally fantasise about him as a bedroom artefact, then remind myself, in a restrained and sensible manner, that artefacts – bedroom, conservatory or otherwise – don't possess a personality. But herein lies the problem: this one does. Admittedly, I'm basing this on half an hour at one of Sophie's daughter-of-Delia dinner parties where anyone capable of holding a conversation on a subject other than tube journeys takes on an interest-factor of seismic proportions, but he read and understood me as easily as a large print Topsy and Tim. Given that I have yet to achieve this I take it as a very positive sign.

It is, of course, absolutely typical that the minute I decide to commit to Alex, a seemingly more attractive alternative pops up. I feel as though, after scouring every shop on the high street for the ideal dress, I've settled for something that's almost right – bought it, cut off the tag, put it on, and am just on the way to the ball – when, lo and behold, there in the window of the most unpromising-looking shop is the dress I have been searching for all along. But rather than strip naked, seize it and take the other back for a refund, I am stuck with the knowledge that while it both suits and fits me, it is regrettably on hold for someone else.

I have now become obsessed with the idea that if I can see him just once more my craving will be satiated, which is, of course, total bollocks – the equivalent of going out on a Friday night and saying you're only going to stay for one drink. I keep trying to figure out how I could see him, concocting all sorts of ridiculous scenarios involving him driving half-way across London to get a sandwich from the Putney Waitrose. The only glimmer of hope is a dinner party Alex is mumbling about hosting, to pay back all the people who've had us. But I fear it might be difficult to justify a place on the invite list for Andy plus girlfriend, whom we don't owe, know or, in her case, like.

Anyway, I should not be plotting like this. Any investigative skills I possess should be channelled into my job, which demands them, rather than into a bloke who doesn't. Talking of work, I suppose I'd better go. It's three thirty-five – not quite late enough to warrant taking the rest of the afternoon off but late enough to ensure that by the time I actually get there it will be time to go home.

To be honest, they'd probably prefer I stayed at home anyway. 'Shan-yah', in her capacity to make me feel delinquent, has succeeded in turning me into one. Carol, the woman who writes the autocue and on-screen captions, was off ill the other day, but instead of hiring a temp or digging the runner out from inside the photocopier toner tray, she decided it would be easier to get the poor woman to dictate the script from what sounded suspiciously like the confines of the toilet bowl, send a courier to Enfield to collect the tape and get some overworked, over-qualified slave, i.e. me, to type up the wretched thing.

Ordinarily I would have told her where to stick it – or some feeble, less confrontational equivalent – but, given that the alternative was finding eight pregnant mothers willing to do a Victoria Beckham yoga class by lunchtime, it seemed by far the least challenging option. Then I tried to do it.

I don't know if you've ever worked a Dictaphone machine, but it's like being a cross between a seamstress and a pilot. You sit there wearing padded headphones, foot on pedal, hands on keyboard, awaiting your orders. The difference is that where a pilot receives word from Air Traffic Control, you receive word by the tapping of a toe – not as easy as Michael Flatley would have us believe. Tap the toe too much and Carol becomes Mickey Mouse on E, release the pressure and she's stuck inside the digestive system of a dinosaur. Consequently, I spent most of the time in search of the 'real' Carol, to little avail, and paying no attention whatsoever to what I was transcribing.

Later, when I was back at my desk persuading Mrs Forbes that she wanted to don Lycra and contort her pregnant body on national TV for free, I glanced up at one of the overhead screens and saw the presenter looking as though she'd sat on a cactus. Assuming this to be the result of an unscreened comment from a religious wacko – they were doing a phone-in on religious sects within the community – I didn't give it much thought until everyone around me burst out laughing. I looked up again to read the following captions being intermittently displayed across the screen:

'Do you think religion in the community encourages practising sex?'

'Do you welcome different sex in your church?'

'Have you felt drawn to any religious sex?'

'Do you think sex can be inclusive if approached with an open mind?'

There were more, but I suspect you get the gist. The rest of the day went by in one of those fuzzy-headed blurs normally associated with a hangover. Michael, fuelled by angry phone-calls from the Anne Robinson of the clergy and half of the Broadcasting Standards Commission, hauled me into a room where a vision mixer on the verge of a nervous breakdown was protesting his innocence. I tried tentatively to pin the blame on Chyani by pointing out that if she'd hired a professional who knew what they were doing, rather than me, none of this would have happened, but he just looked at me with a crazed glint in his eye and said, 'You were supposed to be the professional.' Unfortunately, I dissolved after that, proving, among other things, the apposite use of the past tense with the term 'professional'.

Alex has been lovely, getting angry and indignant on my behalf and trying to reassure me that if it came to suing – which I was alarmed to discover it might – they didn't have a leg to stand on because transcribing caption text was not within the remit of my job as researcher. I didn't have the heart to tell him that everything short of shagging the gay production controller comes within my remit.

Anyway, apparently Vivienne, whose skills as a presenter I am no longer going to slag off so vehemently, salvaged the situation by passing it off as a belated April Fool. She now wanders round the studio being hailed as some kind of returning war veteran. I am now called April.

Ergh. I so wish I was out there with you, tilling the fields and building adobe huts – whatever adobe might be. You sound so happy and calm, as if the transition from telly researcher to ecological earthchild is a natural one. I thought perhaps you might be suffering some kind of disturbing culture shock, but then I remembered that wouldn't be possible because you came from daytime telly, i.e. no culture. Still, I suspect the fried ants take a bit of getting used to.

Right, I'd better go and face the music – or, as is more likely, seventeen telephones ringing off the hook. I can't send this now because POP3 error keeps flashing up on the screen followed by instructions written by MI6. I'm going to have to find a complicated way of saving it so that I can still retrieve it but Alex cannot read it. Speak to you later . . .

Oh, God. I am pissed. I am also in the process of falling (a) in love (b) out with Alex (c) off this swivel chair and (d) for the strategically timed Dial-a-Pizza ad on ITV. I'm afraid, however, that try as I might, I am incapable of falling asleep and, if I don't talk to someone soon, am in danger of falling apart.

I have met Andy again. Almost as randomly as at the sandwich counter at Putney's Waitrose only not quite because it was a pub in Soho known to be frequented by media people (he works in advertising).

Lou and I had gone in for a post-work drink because we were both feeling miserable: Lou because she'd spent all day lining up six cat-owners from Folkestone for the 'Pet Your Pet' outside broadcast, only to be told after she'd arranged several shipments of Kit-E-Kat and an electric blanket (for a cat, not an owner) that the Martine McCutcheon interview had overrun and they were cutting straight to the news, and me because, well, they think I'm shit. Anyway, we were just sitting in the corner with a Diet Coke having a moan when, out of the corner of my eye, I spotted him. I knew immediately it was him because he was doing the sexy-straddling-of-a-bar-stool routine and because, as a result, my body was in the first stages of a seizure.

Initially the plan was to act as if I hadn't spotted him, then be all cool and confident when he spotted me, but after ten minutes of watching him talk earnestly to a bloke with a long chin, I realised that any spotting would have to come from me and used the excuse of going to the ladies' to do it. Unfortunately, though, by the time I got there I was so conscious of the need to act surprised that I ended up behaving as though I'd just stumbled across Tony Blair rifling through my underwear drawer.

He did look pleased to see me, though, and gave a much better performance of genuine surprise, but then rather irritatingly introduced me as 'Alex's girlfriend', thereby pigeonholing me from the start as 'that which is out of bounds'. I searched his friend's face vainly for some glint of recognition – 'Ah, that Alex's girlfriend, the one you haven't stopped talking about for weeks, the one you think you've fallen in love with, your one true soulmate' etc. – but he just looked annoyed that I'd interrupted them, downed his pint and said he had to go.

Andy came over to join us, whereupon I underwent a dramatic personality transition: why is it that you can be sipping limply at a Coke, wanting only to go home to bed, and generally behaving as though you're suffering from a premature form of ME, then someone you fancy turns up and suddenly you've got enough energy to power the National Grid?

Lou was great, obeying the unspoken female etiquette of staying long enough to suss him out, but not too long as to present potential competition, although when she decided to leave Andy insisted that she stayed. (I'm choosing to put this down to his affable character, rather than anything sinister.) And then the two of us sat and drank and talked and laughed and got on like a house not just on fire but blazing with raging flames of passion.

This is what I now know about him and am sending to you for further lab analysis:

(1)   He has been going out with Sarah for eight and a half
       years (bad).
       Sarah is an accountant (good).
(2)   He lives with Sarah (bad).
       He says if it wasn't for the dog they would have split
       up years ago (good).
(3)   Sarah is pressuring him to get married (bad).
       Sarah is pressuring him to get married (good).
(4)   Sarah called him four times on his mobile (bad).
       He ignored all four calls (good).
(5)   He says 'gotcha' (bad).
       He grabbed my waist when he said it (absolutely bloody
       fantastic)!

The whole thing is so confusing. Everything points to the fact
that we are soulmates and should be together, yet there are two
large obstacles in our way: (a) Sarah — maybe not large, but
certainly big-hipped, and (b) Alex.

But do I want to leave Alex? And would I really have a couple-
sipping-cocktails-lying-on-joke-inflatable-frog-in-Sandals-holiday-
brochure relationship with Andy? I remember reading about a
woman stuck in this dilemma. Cosmopolitan labelled it Twenty-
Four-Seven Fatigue and told her that her partner was an oak tree
and the bloke she thought she fancied was a flower. The flower
looks fresh and pretty in the shop, but bring it home and it wilts
in days; the oak tree is sturdy, rooted, dependable and always there
for her to lean on. When I think of Alex like this there is no way
I can abandon him for . . . Urgh, suddenly had a discomfiting
image of Andy as a carnation.

Unfortunately, however, by the time I'd made it home, I was so
caught up with the idea of Andy and me eloping in a camper-
van, making soul-binding love en route and setting up a life
together somewhere in the vicinity of cloud nine, that when I stumbled into the bedroom to find Alex sitting bolt upright in bed wearing
stripy PJs and staring earnestly at the law pages of The Times,

I nearly hurled myself straight through the skylight. I told him – because when I have something on my mind I am rarely able to leave it there – that we had the sex life of a slug and were in real danger of forgetting how to do it, so consumed were we with soap dishes and plumbing bills. He looked at me in bewilderment and said he'd been ready since ten, making it sound as though I'd arrived late for a client meeting.

Now we're not speaking to each other, which means bedtime will be a silent farce of the back-turning, toe-retracting, duvet-snatching variety. Why did I have to do this when everyone knows that starting an argument in the bedroom is tantamount to lighting a fag at an Esso garage? And now I seem to have broken his swivel chair. Oh, God. I'm going to have a pepperoni and mushroom Dial-a-Pizza and abscond with the delivery boy. Hope this gets to you this time.

Lots of love,
Jess
xxx

PS Forgot to say – am contemplating jacking job. Before they jack me.

Brief Encounters

'Can I have a word, Jess?' Michael had just strode up, placed his palms aggressively on the desk and was staring menacingly down at her in a manner that suggested the word might very likely be 'fired'.

'Which one would you like?' Jess said, realising the minute she'd opened her mouth that cheekiness to one's boss was the equivalent of walking across a field of landmines: one wrong foot and you're a goner. He nodded towards his glass partition. She'd clearly just blown herself up.

'So,' he began, reclining in his chair and placing his hands behind his head, 'how do you feel you're getting on?'

Jess tried to look calm. It was like being asked what your weaknesses were in an interview: the negative had to be couched in the positive. 'I'm learning from my mistakes.'

'That'll be a pretty steep learning curve, then, eh?'

Jess pretended to find this amusing.

'This is not amusing, Jess,' he said, catapulting forward and hitting the space bar on his computer, whereupon the dancing minimally clothed S Club 7 girls became an inbox file. 'You are here as a researcher, not a reformed drug addict on work experience.'

Just at that moment, the work-experience girl came in. She was wearing black leather trousers and a fake designer T-shirt that said 'Bed Taker'. 'The printed emails you were requesting,' she said, as though she were a Bond girl bringing Sean Connery a cocktail named after a piece of female anatomy. She flashed Jess a condescending smile and sashayed out in a way that suggested 'Job Taker' should have been emblazoned across her back.

Michael picked up one of the letters and perched a pair

of half-moon glasses on his nose. 'Dear Michael,' he read. 'It has come to my attention that the research team is not as cohesive as of old. I understand this is due to the distracting influence of Jess,' he paused, peering over his glasses as though she were a toddler who'd just peed on the sofa, 'who seems more interested in researching the avenues of her social life than that requested of her by her superior, Shan-*yah* Devesh.'

Jess flinched. The idea that her job appeared to be on the line faded into the realms of negligible importance next to hearing that twenty-two-year-old Chyani was her boss. 'Shan-yah isn't exactly—'

'*Dear* Michael,' he cut in, in a loud booming voice. 'As per our telephone conversation, I am writing to express how disappointed I am in Jess's continual inability to support the research ethos of our department. For someone who is obviously a natural on the phone . . .' He looked up and did the peering thing again. She smiled in modest acceptance of the praise. '. . . it would seem she is perhaps more suited to a job as receptionist.'

Jess felt a lump crawl up her throat and rest in a strangulating position.

He snatched at the next one. 'I find it increasingly hard to work with someone whose idea of research is staring at *Heat* and making inane comments about the size of Britney Spears's chest.'

'But it's obvious she's had—' Jess bleated, before catching sight of Michael's expression: however extensive her research into celebrity breast enlargements, it was not going to compensate for her lack of research into everything else.

'I like you, Jess,' Michael remarked – inexplicably.

She smiled. It was like spending all night preparing to be dumped, then being presented with a sparkly engagement ring.

'But I cannot ignore the comments of my workers,' he continued, as if they were in the midst of a nineteenth-century steel-factory revolt. 'I believe in keeping one's private life just that,' he said emphatically, placing the letters back on his desk alongside a copy of *Now* opened at a page headed, 'The Secrets of Madonna's Relationship with Guy Ritchie – REVEALED!'. 'Bringing it in to work is one sure-fire way of having *no* work.'

Suddenly the sparkly engagement ring had been yanked off her finger. 'But sometimes Shan-yah doesn't—'

'This is not about Shan-*yah*, Jess. Her letter only concurred with what every—'

'What?' she erupted, staring at the pile of complaints as though they'd metamorphosed into a ticking bomb. 'Did Shan-yah write one of those?'

'It is of no consequence who wrote what,' he replied, sternly. 'The point, which you seem to be spectacularly slow to get the hang of, is that you are sailing dangerously close to being sacked.'

Jess felt the lump clamp with the tenacity of a greedy tarantula around her tonsils. It was like having a crap boyfriend: she moaned about wanting rid of him, but when he turned round and suggested wanting rid of *her*, it was all she could do not to collapse on her knees pleading forgiveness and a second chance. 'But—' she squeaked, before the tarantula swallowed her voice box.

'I'm not interested in excuses,' he bellowed, like a scary headmaster about to march the whole school off to detention, 'I want guarantees. We are paying you to do a job, not organise a perpetual game of playground kiss-chase.'

Jess felt slightly cheered by this. If she was going to be chastised for putting her social life before her work, it might as well be because it was viewed as a hectic round of snogging, bed-swapping and eager, pursuant males.

'I am prepared to let you off with an official warning if you promise me that from now on your personal life will not enter this office.'

Just then there was a knock at the door and a figure clad head-to-toe in black was standing holding a large white oblong box with a bow on top, panting as though he'd just leaped off the set of the Milk Tray ad.

'Jessica?' he announced, looking uncertainly from one to the other as if it were possible that the besuited, overweight, prematurely balding specimen sitting legs apart behind the desk was female.

'That's me!' Jess exclaimed, springing to her feet and charging at the courier in a way, she suspected, he wasn't in the habit of being approached by women.

'This wouldn't be a personal delivery, would it?' Michael enquired.

'Er . . . great,' Jess enthused, snatching the box. 'Those giraffe X-rays Alan wanted.' Then she scuttled out of sight to the loos in the manner of a squirrel with a particularly large nut, before Michael had time to remember that Alan had left six months previously.

Once in the safety of a toilet cubicle, she tore at the box as if she hadn't eaten for a fortnight and it contained a pizza. Then she lifted off the lid and let out a high-pitched squeak. There, awash in a sea of soft cream tissue paper, were a pair of bright red lacy knickers and provocative matching bra.

She stared in a mixture of delight and puzzlement. Tentatively, she picked up the bra and dangled it in front of her chest. Whoever had sent it had obviously had a pleasingly inflated impression of her . . . Who the hell *had* sent it? There was no note. A horrible thought hit her. Maybe it wasn't meant for her. Maybe she had just intercepted the beginnings of an illicit office affair or the guilt-appeasing offering of a cheating partner. A cheating partner! Could Andy have . . . No! She was not going to allow herself to wander down that particular fantasy avenue. She'd learned on many occasions in the past that it led to shattered illusions, unfulfilled hope and a dead-end state of delirium.

And then she spotted it: a small white card protruding from the crotch of the knickers.

Saw this and thought of me.
A.
xxx

She studied it, barely daring to breathe, as if she'd just dug up the remains of a Roman jug that might disintegrate if it came into contact with modern air. Enraptured, she tried hard not to leap around the cubicle shouting, 'Andy, Andy,' like a crazed, over-energised children's TV presenter, but instead to search maturely and calmly for further proof. It was like Valentine's Day, she decided, only more cryptic because nothing could be gleaned from analysing the sausagy handwriting that, unless Andy was in fact a woman, clearly belonged to the lingerie assistant.

She picked up the bra and checked the size. Then, joyously, it all became clear. There on the label, just above a picture of a bowl of water with a dismembered hand floating in it, was its trademark name: Allure. It was confirmed. He'd left his calling card. Andy, her sexy, sensitive and now by all accounts not-quite-so-unavailable soulmate had made the first move in the game of love-chess. There was no going back. She was going for checkmate.

'Hi, it's Jess,' she shouted half-an-hour later into her mobile, as the traffic did its best to imitate the climaxing of a thunderstorm. It was typical, she thought, as her phone cut out for the second time, that the one day something important and exciting happened that required the detailed analytical perspective of at least five friends, she was banned from discussing her personal life in the office. It felt unsettling to be calling him cold – like entering an exam hall without having revised.

'Hi, sorry, it's me again,' she said, instantly regretting her over-familiar tone.

'I can't hear,' crackled the reply. 'Who is this?'

Hoping Sophie hadn't given her the wrong number, she

59

scurried into the welcoming peace-haven of Carlton Cards whereupon a rendition of 'I Want Your Sex' started belting out from the overhead speakers. 'It's Jess,' she repeated, crouching beside an inflatable penguin with a fist in her ear. 'I'm fine.'

After a prolonged silence at the other end it dawned on her that she'd just answered the question she'd intended to ask. 'Alas, not a 34C, though,' she added, by way of salvation.

'Jess, have you been drinking?' Andy sounded bemused.

'Oh, goodness me, *no*,' she protested, grinning. 'But funny you should say that, because, well, I thought maybe we could—'

'Look, Jess, I'm about to go into a meeting, can I call you—'

'The love of your life?' She gave a tinkly laugh. 'The sexiest woman ever to have crossed your path? Your one true—'

'Back,' he said, rather sharply.

'Yes, I mean, no, I mean, what I mean is . . .' she swallowed hard '. . . meet me for a drink, Andy. Tonight.' She'd read in *Marie Claire* that the direct, almost commanding approach worked well. Research showed that it suggested danger and urgency, and presented an erotic mix of dominant woman versus sexually compliant one. Unfortunately, as she was to discover, they hadn't included Andy in this study.

'But, well, didn't we go for a drink the other night?' he asked.

'Oh, I'm sorry,' she chirped. 'I wasn't aware the drinks police issued quotas.'

He softened at this. 'One a month, apparently.'

She laughed, then panicked that this might be his polite way of declining. 'More for good behaviour, I gather,' she said. This was the kind of banter she missed so much with Alex.

'Oh . . . hold on,' he said, distractedly. 'Yup, yup, I'll pick her up.'

Jess waited patiently, hoping whoever she was, he was just

picking her up metaphorically. 'So. We on then?' she continued, feeling that the dominant woman had turned a bit desperate.

'On for what?' he said, disappointingly with no sexual innuendo.

'The drink.'

'Oh, yes, that,' he said, as if she'd just reminded him to put the rubbish out. 'I think you can probably lure me.'

Jess felt a ripple of thrill race up her spine. He was using a derivative of 'allure'. It was another calling card. 'Seven thirty at our usual place?' she said, a bit too excitedly.

'Our usual place being . . . ?'

'The Sun Inn?'

There was an ominous pause. 'Gotcha!' he replied, then put the phone down.

By the time Jess had squirmed out of work and into the sexy red lingerie, it was nearly eight. Apart from two gigantic builders in green gnome hats and LOVE tattooed across their knuckles, the pub was empty. As she sidled up to the bar trying to give the impression that she was comfortable with the idea of drinking alone and being gawped at, an unsettling thought struck her. Of all the myriad meanings 'gotcha' might have, as an answer to a request to meet for a drink, could it have stood for 'no'?

'Gotcha!' a familiar voice erupted from behind her. He grabbed her waist, causing the bottle of tonic water she was holding to projectile-vomit into the air.

'Hi,' she gushed, turning and hoping that their new-found intimacy called for a kiss on the lips.

'You've met Ben?' he said, eschewing any further physical contact in favour of gesturing to a bloke with a long chin hovering uncertainly behind him.

Crestfallen, Jess stared at this unwelcome intrusion as if Andy had just offered her a stool sample. 'Nice to see you again,' she lied, hoping he was there as a cling-on from work and not as an uglier version of Kevin Costner's bodyguard.

As they drank their way into the evening, it became clear that while he was certainly amenable to the odd, stolen flirtatious exchange, any fantasy she'd entertained of Andy flinging her to the ground and ravaging her red-laced body would have to take second place to Ben's marital problems. As a conversational contraceptive, he was a genius.

'She says I lack dynamism,' he drawled, in an I-bore-for-Britain voice. 'And that I think foreplay is a football-pitch formation.'

'Have you tried spicing things up a bit?' Andy enquired, as though he were a celebrity chef and Ben had just phoned in for advice on gravy. 'Sexy underwear always goes down a treat,' he said, flashing a smile at Jess.

'I tried a G-string once,' he droned, 'but she just said I looked like John Prescott in a bikini.'

Jess tried not to let this image put her off her gin.

'I was thinking more for . . . her,' Andy said. 'Something a bit, you know . . .'

'Like this?' Jess suggested, seductively pulling her top off her shoulder and sliding her thumb up and down behind the red bra strap.

'Indeed,' Andy cooed, and followed it up with the kind of appreciative noise that implied she had not only raised his eyebrows.

Ben, overawed, scuttled off to the loo in a way that, Jess couldn't help noticing, did not seem entirely bladder-related.

'That's very sexy, you know,' Andy said, the minute they were alone.

Jess smiled winsomely. 'I guess you're hoping to see the rest,' she purred, enjoying the way the evening was headed.

Andy looked a little taken aback. 'Well, um, I don't quite . . . I think Sarah might have different ideas.'

'I wasn't planning,' Jess said, smirking provocatively and moving closer, 'on showing Sarah.'

He smirked back. 'So. What about Alex? Doesn't he get a look in?'

It struck Jess as odd to buy one's lover secret sexy underwear then propose it be shared with another man. 'I think we'll just keep it between you and me, if that's OK with you,' she said, at which he seemed surprised, then gave her a look to suggest it was very OK.

'I've decided,' announced boring Ben, returning to the table and, to Jess's joy, reaching for his jacket. 'I'm going to tell Diane straight that it's not what's on the outside it's what's inside that counts.'

'Without wishing to state the obvious, mate,' Andy said, 'isn't that precisely the problem?' The two then dissolved into a lively display of mateyness, which seemed to involve making derogatory comments about the size of each other's penis.

'Right. I'm off,' Andy announced suddenly, getting up and pulling on his coat.

'But . . . What . . . Now?' Jess stammered, failing to hide her disappointment.

'Can't keep the missus waiting,' Ben cautioned, conjuring up images of a fearsome Sarah prowling the empty house with a food trolley before taking a mallet to Andy's ankles.

'Have a good night,' Andy said, nodding suggestively in the direction of her chest.

Jess pulled a fraction of the knicker lace into view. 'Just a "brief" glimpse of what you're missing,' she teased, and felt sure she saw a flicker of regret flit across his face.

When she got home, the house was silent and dark. It was Alex's football night so he would still be in a pub analysing a forward pass. She climbed the stairs, entered the pitch black of the bedroom, collapsed on to the bed and let out a high-pitched scream of terror.

'Where have you been?' an accusatory voice demanded, as she catapulted towards the door and lunged at the light switch.

Alex was lying fully clothed on the bed, hands behind his head, staring at the ceiling.

'You scared the living—' Jess panted, breathlessly. 'Why aren't you at football?'

'It was cancelled. And you?'

'They said my goal-defence skills weren't up to scratch,' she said, regaining her composure and joining him on the bed. 'Can you believe it? After all that training I'd done.'

Alex refused to smile. 'Where were you?' he repeated, stony-faced.

Jess paused. 'With Lou,' she said, getting up and developing an unnatural urge to ensure that all the coat-hangers faced the same direction.

'Really,' he said, still staring at the ceiling. 'And how was Lou?'

'Oh, you know,' Jess breezed, rushing manically around the room, picking things up and putting them down again.

'No. Tell me.'

She was unsure whether he was acting suspicious because he *was* suspicious or because she felt guilty and therefore *imagined* him to be suspicious. 'You know Lou,' she said, throwing herself back on to the bed and sidling up to him, 'moaning about being single, wishing she had a nice, wonderful, lovely boyfriend who was all shnuggly-wuggly-woojlee.' She buried her face in his neck.

To her relief, Alex seemed to warm to this blatant act of overcompensatory love and kissed her forehead. It was a while since they had been so affectionate with each other. Jess couldn't help feeling it a rather bizarre state of affairs that in order to recapture their lost passion she had had to embark on an affair with someone else.

'Now,' he whispered, licking her ear as he began seductively to lift her top, 'I wonder what we have up here?'

Jess smiled into the darkness, rejoicing in her powers as a warm, golden, sexual goddess. Then she froze. The underwear!

'Shall I do us a hottie?' she squealed, springing out of his arms and pulling down her top. 'A hottie would be nice, wouldn't it? All shnuggly.'

Alex looked at her in stunned disbelief. If there was one thing the moment required, it was not a hot-water bottle. 'And to think *I* was being accused of taking the life out of our sex,' he shouted at her retreating back.

Once downstairs, Jess pulled off her clothes as if she'd discovered she had fleas. Of all the scenarios she'd envisaged for the evening, stripping off alone in a dark kitchen wasn't one of them. Shivering and naked, she grabbed the lingerie and scanned the room for a suitable hiding place where she could be certain Alex wouldn't look. The cleaning-products cupboard seemed an obvious one, as did any that contained a more sophisticated cooking utensil than a saucepan. Eventually, however, she plumped for the miscellaneous kitchen drawer in which was stuffed a bewildering array of threadbare dishcloths, tubes of Uhu, French francs, dried up felt-tips, plastic farmyard animals, aftersun and a sprig of fake holly – the addition of some underwear was unlikely to raise alarm. Then she filled the hot-water bottle, gathered up her clothes and scampered back upstairs.

'Come and get me,' she purred, standing naked in the doorway, clothes in one hand, hottie in the other, like a deranged escapee from an old folks' home.

A strange pig-like snuffling was coming from the pillow. Alex had fallen asleep.

The Sarah Doorstep Challenge

To: *Claire.Voyant@hotmail.com*
Date: *Sunday 18 June*
Subject: *The Sarah Doorstep Challenge*

Desiring for Alex never to wake up. Watching
   EastEnders *omnibus in the hope of finding*
   someone – possibly Pauline Fowler? – whose
   existence is bleaker than mine. Discovering, in
   the process, I've developed an alarming crush
   on half-my-age Jamie.

Dear Claire,
   I want to be you. Your life sounds so idyllic and fun – though
I do realise the whole point of sending communal emails when
abroad is to convey this very impression. Did John really lay a
trail of bougainvillea and light candles round the bathing-pool? If
so, please tell me there was a reason for doing so, e.g. post argu-
ment/weird Spanish tradition/subtle way of getting you to wash. I
will explode with envy if it was another one of his just-becauses.
   Rest assured, you're missing out on bugger all here. Life is crap
and, on top of everything else that's conspiring against me, I've
just discovered, miserably, that Pauline Fowler isn't real but merely
a construct dreamed up by a group of shaven-headed scriptwriters
in Soho. All this time I've been consoling myself with the notion
that I could be a lot worse, i.e. yellow hair, dead husband, pinnacle
of career = washing-machine supervisor, when in fact the object of
my pity is happy and well and wearing expensive Chanel suits
doing book signings in Ottakar's.
   I can't help feeling cheated by this. It reminds me of being back
at school when an important exam was looming and everyone went

around claiming they were cool and hadn't done any revision and I believed them and – coolly – didn't do any either. But then the exam came and, flukily, out of nowhere, they could do it. I, of course, couldn't and had to spend the rest of term admiring their congratulatory new leather jackets with a D+ and the prospect of a polytechnic in Slough.

Right now, however, imprisonment in Slough would be appealing. The only possible explanation for the last twelve hours is that God works on a system similar to that of the Sainsbury's Reward Card. You clock up points every time you buy something/a shit thing happens to you, then when you've got enough points/ enough shit has happened to you, you are rewarded with a £2.50 voucher/a flirtatious evening with Andy. I am now clearly back at the stage of accruing points, the only consolation being that last night's unparalleled horror must have earned me the equivalent of buying up the entirety of the fresh-produce aisle.

We had a party. This notion in itself should have been enough to warn me that the evening was going to be dismal, since when, in the history of party-hosting, does one think that apart from . . . (1) the beginning, when you're convinced no one's going to turn up, (2) the middle, when they have turned up but you're worried they're having a crap time so you turn into a bumblebee trying to pollinate each of them in turn, resulting in three-second chit-chats about nothing and the avoidance of any topic that might actually be interesting, and, (3) the end, when they leave at eleven saying they've had a nice time when you know that if they'd really had a nice time they wouldn't be leaving at eleven, . . . yes, indeed, apart from these minor little hitches, I've had a really fantastic party.

I guess I've only myself to blame since it was me who suggested having the stupid thing in the first place. I declared it an open house-warming, not, I have to confess, out of any desire to welcome my friends into the bosom of my hearth, but simply so that I could invite Andy without raising any undue suspicion. Unfortunately, it was raised before Andy even arrived.

*I was just arranging all the chairs against the wall in antici-
pation of turning the dining room into a trendy basement club
dance-floor, imagining lots of Craig David-type guests gyrating to
something trendy (Lou was bringing her CDs), while illegal
substances were being sniffed off the loo seat, when Alex appeared
holding a bowl of Twiglets. He looked at me oddly and asked me
to 'account for an item in the kitchen' (even on Saturdays he
speaks as if he's in the midst of compiling a law document). I
wandered through and was directed to peer into the kitchen drawer.*

*I have to admit, I did think perhaps he'd bought me a lovely
pre-party present in the form of a Tiffany necklace or a joke blow-
up bottle of Veuve Clicquot, so was careful to make a conscious
effort of pretending I didn't know what I was supposed to be looking
for. Then he pointed to a bit of red lace twisted round a tube of
Uhu. I squeaked in a mouse-like manner. It was the sexy underwear and card Andy had sent me. The sexy underwear and card
I had hidden in there precisely so that Alex wouldn't find it.*

*I truly didn't know what to say or do, so opted for standing in
the gormless pose adopted by a teenager caught with fags in their
blazer. He looked at me with raised eyebrows, waiting for an explanation. My mind whizzed round like a roulette wheel with the ball
boinging uncontrollably between black (own up) and red (lie). It
soon became obvious the safe bet was red: I'd bought them for
myself in an M&S sale. I felt quite proud of this spur-of-the-
moment variation on the truth and was just working out why I
would choose to keep them in the kitchen drawer beside the toaster
rather than, say, in the bedroom, when he pulled out the bra and
said, 'Hmm, now, where is that M&S label, again?' in an infuriating you-have-just-told-a-whopping-lie-and-I-know-it voice. I
hadn't counted on an anal lawyer also being a lingerie specialist.*

*In the end, I had to confess that, yes, I had lied, but only to
protect him from the truth, which was a lie: that I had been given
them as a gift by a bloke at work who's in love with me, but in
whom I have absolutely no interest, him having warts, halitosis
and nostril hair. Alex looked personally insulted by this, then started*

firing questions at me with Jeremy Paxman-like intensity as I gibbered a spectacular array of lies and counter-lies about Paulo, Paulo's resemblance to the Elephant Man and my near-vomiting reaction to anything Paulo-related. I actually started to feel a bit sorry for Paulo.

Then he hit me with the big one: why did Paulo sign the card 'A'? It was like being in a tense high-court drama where everything is going marvellously until an attractive young hotshot discovers tiny evidence at the last minute, e.g. the caretaker doesn't eat doughnuts, and the whole defence is blown out of the water. I stood there, opening and closing my mouth like a goldfish.

'Could it be, in fact,' he continued, biting off a knobbly bit of Twiglet, 'that you did not receive this gift from Paulo at all?' He paused for courtroom suspense. 'Could it be, in fact, that you received this gift from someone whose name begins with A?' It was turning into a hideous version of I-Spy only instead of the spied object being a grazing cow or electricity pylon, it was Andy.

'Maybe A stands for Agripaulos?' I said, weakly.

He looked vaguely amused and replied, 'Or maybe A stands for Alex.'

Horror beyond all known measure of horror. I had not for one moment considered that the underwear donor might be my boyfriend. I felt as though I'd sat through a thriller only to discover in the final scene that the murderer wasn't who I'd believed it to be all along.

Crippled with disappointment, I started to leap around over-compensatorily, punching the air and flinging my arms around his neck like a contestant from Big Brother who's just been told they've been chucked out of the house and, despite the point of the game being to stay in the house, is pretending it's the best thing that's ever happened to them. Alex stood motionless, staring at a fork.

Then the second missile was fired: who had I been with on the night of the underwear delivery? Attempted a joke of Lou-with-the-lead-piping-in-the-bedroom variety, hoping deftly to manoeuvre *the conversation away from me as a criminal lie-infused adulterer to the possibility of lesbian sex, but he was having none of it.*

'If you were "out with Lou",' he barked, in full scary-lawyer mode, 'how come Lou wasn't out with you?' Turns out Lou had called the flat asking to speak to me shortly before I'd returned home.

Luckily I was saved from disentangling this horrible mass of mangled deceit by the bell, which actually transpired to be anything but lucky. I opened the door to reveal a shiny, happy couple standing hand in hand on the doorstep grinning like extras from the show-room forecourt of a Carpet World commercial. Andy and Sarah.

In all the turmoil, I'd overlooked the Andy angle, i.e. that the last time I'd been with him I was flashing bits of knicker elastic and insinuating he wanted to sleep with me. It's quite remarkable how one minute you don't think you're going to be capable of surviving unless you see your 'love' every day and the next you're positively praying you'll never have to face them again.

It was hideous. He took one look at me and said, 'It's the Lady in Red,' then continued to smirk knowingly as I conformed to this description by turning puce and offering round the Twiglets.

The rest of the evening was shit. Alex gave me death stares and did loud raucous laughing whenever he talked to anyone female. Lou arrived late – flouting the rule of party-friendship, which everyone knows is to support one's friend by turning up early and going through the no-one-will-come dilemma, then making them look popular and fun when someone does come. She spent the rest of the night reassuring me she was 'spying' on Andy, which seemed to involve supplying him with drinks and tossing her hair around provocatively. Jo didn't come at all, Sophie and Richard were talking about a baby – I cannot cope with the thought of it being their own – and I was left with a whole lot of people I'd only invited so I could smuggle in Andy, like distracting the airport check-in girl with inane questions about departure gates so that she won't notice your hand luggage is the size of Terminal Three.

The only saving grace, although I don't suspect I was particularly graceful about saving it, was that I got utterly wasted on sambuca and by ten o'clock was floating round the room feeling like a happy little harp-playing cherub. Come morning, however, the harp had turned into someone learning to play the cymbals inside my head and my cherub garb had to be discarded because I was sick on it.

I don't think Alex . . . oh, fuck. Shit. A little boy dressed as Oliver Twist has just appeared on ITV to remind me it's Father's Day. Bugger. Although it's obviously just one big marketing ploy dreamed up by Carlton Cards and is manipulative, indulgent (wrong to be spending money on 'Luv Ya Dad' inflatable silver hearts, surely, when millions need rice in Africa?) and inconsistent – after all, where is Daughter's Day? – Dad went into the most ridiculous huff last year because he only got a card from Mum (warped Electra-complex situation). So I must just drag the amateur cymbal-player and myself down to the corner shop before it closes and I'm reduced to covering a loo roll in tin foil and claiming it's a Father's Day pen holder. Back in a tick . . .

Oh, thank goodness. Everything is much, much better. Nurofen has killed the cymbals, I've got a card with a father and son fly-fishing and 'World's Best Dad' written at the top (no wonder kids say 'bestest' when the world has so many best dads) and Alex has forgiven me. Lou told him the reason I lied about having a drink with her was because I was actually having a drink with the be-warted Paulo, by way of a thank-you for his underwear, but didn't want to own up in case Alex assumed Paulo to be a six-foot hunk of throbbing muscle.

Now the only thing I have to worry about – apart from job, money, life, etc. – is Andy. The trouble is that when someone you fancy does something nice, like sends you underwear – or you think sends you underwear – you automatically fancy them twenty times more. The underwear becomes a symbol, confirming that all your fantasies relating to romantic meals in expensive restaurants and all-night shagging in front of roaring fires are reciprocated and about to come true. So all I have to do is reverse my thought processes, like when you think you've got lots of money in your bank account and go round buying up whatever takes your fancy and planning fun, expensive things with your friends, then a horrible letter arrives telling you that you have exceeded your overdraft limit, and suddenly you're a pauper who has to bring in sandwiches from home and stand in freezing cold night-bus queues with weirdos.

Anyway, I have decided. If this whole débâcle of deceit has taught me anything it is that I should be more careful next time. Alex is paid *to detect inconsistencies and loopholes: lying to him is the equivalent of trying to short-change an accountant. Not that I want to lie to Alex. He is lovely and kind and the giver of a truly wonderful set . . . Then why do I still feel forbidden things for Andy? Why? I love Alex, honestly, I do. He makes me feel loved and secure and cosy, and he's my best friend, yet whenever I think of Andy it's as though my stomach turns into one of those fireworks that whoosh up into the air exploding in a kaleidoscopic cascade of twinkly sparks.*

Obviously the solution is not to think of Andy and concentrate instead on – oh, my God, the doorbell! Someone's just rung the doorbell. This doesn't happen in London. Well, it does *happen, people* do *ring doorbells, but they tend just to be the postman or strange headscarfed people with clipboards wanting money for showing you horrifying pictures of mutilated limbs. Anyone you want to see makes an arrangement to meet, since trekking halfway across London on the off-chance someone might be in is like thinking all your money problems will be solved by spending your last tenner on lottery tickets.*

And now Alex has just emerged from the kitchen and we're looking at each other as if it is The Sound of Music *and we have to hide the children quickly because the Gestapo are outside. This is ridiculous. It's only the bloody doorbell. Hang on . . .*

Wild, abandoned, unleashed ECSTASY (not, obviously, of the pill variety)! It wasn't the postman or a headscarfed activist, but

Sarah, red-eyed and suicidal-looking. She just stood there not saying a word, doing something almost pneumatic-drill like with her shoulders. For a horrible, lurching moment I thought Andy had been shot or run over and a policeman was going to appear from behind her with a notebook and take us to identify the body. Then she managed to squeak out, 'He's had a th-th-thing with someone else,' and I realised, totally thrilled, though obviously unable to show it, that we were very much back in the realm of the living.

I hadn't a clue what to do. It felt as though someone had dumped a bawling baby on my doorstep then run away. I barely know Sarah and hugging her seemed the equivalent of greeting my doctor with a lip-kiss (not an altogether unappealing thought). I couldn't just do nothing, so I sort of patted her then invited her in.

The minute we were in the sitting room, though, I started panicking. Did Sarah know the 'thing' was me? Had she come round to kill me? Would Alex and his Stephen-Hawking mind put two and two together and want to kill me too? Should I just kill myself? Am I a 'thing'? It became clear, however, that any slaughtering would have to wait until Sarah could speak – she was doing whooping-crying, and breathing like a drowning person. The commotion encouraged Alex to pop a concerned face round the corner but I got rid of him by telling him it was a girlie thing, always a sure-fire way of ensuring a bloke loses interest straight away.

It turned out, once Sarah had stopped suffocating in snot, that Andy had taken her to the bandstand in Clapham Common and confessed to the 'thing' (I can't help thinking this is a strange place to admit adultery, more like a location for proposing, or having gay sex). He refused to tell her who the 'thing' was, claiming it was irrelevant, though why he thought it relevant to say anything escapes me – like getting away with parking on double yellows then owning up to a traffic warden.

Sarah is devastated and has translated 'thing' into all sorts of lurid semi-bestial orgies with cucumbers. I told her I was sure it wasn't as bad as she imagined – after all, we haven't even kissed yet – then felt like Judas Iscariot as I gave her another little pat. She is torturing herself with whom it might be, which is doubly torturing for me, especially when she started blubbering, 'I came to you because . . . becah – becah—' then left me in a frenzied state of limbo, trying to look patient with a head full of increasingly horrifying potential sentence endings.

Unbelievably, she has plumped for Lou as the perpetrator based, as far as I can gather, on absolutely no evidence. She says she can't explain, it's just a 'feeling'. While I'm a keen believer in women's intuition, I fear in this case that it has got rather muddled up with 'women's denial' and 'women's paranoia of anyone blonde, attractive and single'. I found myself stuck in a kind of peat bog of torn loyalties: clearly I didn't want to bad-mouth Lou but neither did I want to attract suspicion to myself by suggesting Sarah was headed off on a wild-goose chase. So I tried to change the subject by asking what Sophie had said. Sophie is, after all, one of her closest friends and therefore officially responsible for dealing with such man-crises. But it transpired that she hadn't told Sophie because Sophie never has man-crises, the implication being, I suppose, that I do.

If only she knew. I do not have a man-crisis but a man in love with me! Two, actually. Without wishing to sound over-modest, I had no idea Andy felt so strongly. Confessing our 'relationship' to Sarah is clearly his way of communicating this. I can feel myself falling more and more in love by the second.

Lots of love (of a slightly different variety)

Jess

xxx

The Star-cross-wired Lovers

'It's not love, Jess,' Jo said, holding a teaspoon to her lips and looking pensively into the distance. They were sitting in her kitchen drinking cappuccino from cups that appeared to have shrunk in the dishwasher.

'Then what?' Jess replied. 'It feels like love.'

Jo smiled sweetly. 'And what does "love" feel like?' she said, as if to suggest she had long outgrown such infantile emotions.

'You know,' Jess said, catching sight of a photo of Mark in yellow Speedos and realising that there was every good reason Jo wouldn't. 'Sparky, exciting, intimate.'

'Intimate.'

'Yeah, like knowing each other really well,' Jess said, eagerly.

'How many times have you *seen* Andy, babes?' Jo enquired, as if Jess had just confessed to being in touch with the spiritual underworld and Andy were a recurring ghost.

'Four, but that's—'

'Four,' she repeated, leaning back and lighting a cigarette. 'Four times. And which of these *four* times did you get to know Andy really well?'

Jess wasn't sure she liked where Jo was going with this. 'It's a qualitative thing,' she said, haughtily. 'You can spend years with someone without really knowing them. Time is irrelevant. It's about connecting. And we click.'

'A bit like a BT advert, then.'

Jess grimaced. Just because Jo had spent most of her early twenties campaigning for the 'spark' as if it were a moral right on a par with the minimum wage, then ended up in a relationship without enough flicker to light a gas hob, didn't mean she had *carte blanche* to disparage everyone else's endeavours to escape such a fate. 'How are you and Mark?' she snapped.

Jo started laughing. 'We're fine, babes,' she said, with the infuriating smugness of someone who'd just walked out of an exam hall declaring the paper a cinch. 'But it's you we're talking about.'

Jess softened.

'In what way do you and Andy click?'

'In what we feel we ought to have in life,' Jess said, after a thoughtful pause, 'but don't have.'

Jo was nodding slowly and seriously, like a thick person trying to look as though they understood. 'Like . . . what? Money?'

'This is a spiritual connection we're talking about, Jo, not an Internet one.'

Jo looked slightly put off. 'He's not some religious freakoid, is he?'

'He's not an anything freakoid. He's sensitive and deep and thinks in the same way as I do.'

'Poor bloke,' Jo said.

'He recognises the limitations of what he has,' Jess continued, dreamily, 'and aches for more.'

Jo stared at her blankly. Then her face lit up. 'Oh, I get it, babes,' she said, as Jess smiled encouragingly. 'But have you told him it's what he *does* with it that counts?'

Jess blinked in bafflement. Jo could reduce a lecture on traditional Viking basketry to sex. 'It's a mind-soul thing. Not a penis-hole thing,' she said indignantly, though privately hoping it would soon be both.

'Really,' Jo murmured, in thinly disguised disappointment.

'As he himself said,' Jess announced, grandly, ' "to know that you are capable of feeling an uncontrollability, an intensity beyond those measured sentiments".'

Jo was now looking bored. 'He sounds a bit of a twat, babes.'

Coming from someone whose boyfriend wore a medallion and yellow Speedos, Jess didn't feel inclined to bow to this judgement. 'Well, twat or no twat, he—'

'I think you'll find no twat,' Jo interjected, smirking.

'Jo!' Jess exploded. 'Please can we keep this conversation away from genitalia for half a second?'

There was an awkward silence. Jo had adopted the look of a betrayed schoolgirl whose friend had suddenly decided to stop exchanging rude notes about pencils and sharpeners and instead, settled to do some work. 'So what about Alex?'

'That's precisely it,' Jess said, excitedly, staring at Jo as if she'd just discovered quantum physics. 'Alex is part of it.'

'Ye-es,' Jo drawled. 'He's your boyfriend.'

'No. Part of me and Andy.'

Jo suddenly regained interest. 'Really? You mean you three are—'

'The reason Andy and I click is because we both have doubts about our relationship.'

'But you two don't have a relationship,' she said, confused. 'Apart from this soul, mind, penis—'

'Our *own* relationships,' Jess articulated slowly. 'Alex. Sarah. We both feel there's something missing.'

'Well . . . I did notice Alex was thinning a bit on top. Maybe that's it.' She gave a tinkly laugh.

If Alex's hair was thinning, Jess thought, then Mark's was in an eating-disorders clinic.

'So what is it, then? What's missing?' Jo continued, reaching for a fag.

'I don't know.' Jess paused, pensively. 'It's indefinable.'

'If it's indefinable, babes,' Jo said, blowing smoke-rings at the ceiling, 'then how do you know it's missing?'

'Because I feel it.'

Jo looked unconvinced. 'In the same way you *feel* in love with Andy?'

Jess sat bolt upright. 'Yes. Exactly!' she said, enlightened.

'But you say you love Alex.'

'Of course I love Alex,' Jess replied, in a dismissive what-has-that-got-to-do-with-anything way. 'He's lovely.' Then she hit herself on the forehead.

Jo stared, cigarette drooping from her mouth.

'That's it, though, isn't it? That's just fucking it. He's lovely. Wonderful, great, fantastic, marvellous, super-fucking-jim-dandy.'

Jo looked as if she wanted to phone for an ambulance. 'Jess, babes, are you—'

'I could get a dictionary,' Jess threatened, barely stopping for breath while Jo's eyes moved suspiciously from right to left as though 'dictionary' were a euphemism for 'AK-47 Kalashnikov assault rifle', 'and list every positive adjective I could find. And do you know what?'

'You'd die of boredom?'

'Every single one of them would be applicable to Alex. Every one. I hear myself all the time, "Yeah, isn't he great?", "Oh, I know, he's so kind and understanding", "Alex? Oh, he's super. Delightful. Surprised he isn't God, actually." ' She threw herself back dramatically in the chair. 'But that's all it is. Just a list. A list of nice words. And it's not that I don't mean them,' she protested to a dumbstruck Jo. 'I do. I mean them all. He is all of these nice words and more. But every time I talk about him, every time I use these words, there's no energy behind my voice. No enthusiasm. No spirit.' She thumped the table. 'I list them like I'm doing some fucking French-conjugation homework. I like Alex. You like Alex. They like Alex. The whole fucking world likes Alex. As if the more I say the words, the less conscious I will be of *having* to say them.' She looked beseechingly at Jo. 'But it's not about a list, is it?'

Jo shook her head obediently.

'A list is the sum of the parts. It's about the whole. And the whole is greater than the sum of the parts.' Jess collapsed at the table and made a noise like a goat.

Jo sat, motionless, staring. 'Blimey, babes,' she said, when it became clear that Jess had stopped for more than breath, 'so does Andy have these grammar-cum-algebra-lesson thoughts about Sarah?'

'*Yes!*' Jess exclaimed, like a teacher who had finally got through to her pupil. 'He does.'

Jo furrowed her brow. 'How long has he been going out with her?'

'Eight and a half years,' Jess replied, in a tone that suggested this in itself was evidence of how flawed the relationship was.

'And there's been no talk of marriage?'

'She's not right for him, Jo,' Jess said, unable to stop herself grinning at the prospect of who she considered *was* right. 'He's not going to marry someone who's not right for him.'

'Maybe he's not going to marry at all.'

Jess looked at Jo as if she'd suggested he'd eaten a baby. 'What's that supposed to mean?'

'I just think that if he doubts it as much as you say he does he wouldn't still be going out with her eight and a half years on. Equally, if he wanted to marry her he wouldn't still be going out with her eight and a half years on.'

'Your point being?' Jess said, irritated that Jo was ignoring her duty of friendship – to interpret everything in Jess's favour.

'He sounds like someone whose problem is not one of doubt, babes, but of dedication.' She pursed her lips.

'It is one of dedication,' Jess retorted, '*because* it is one of doubt.'

Jo looked blank.

'If he was with the right person,' Jess continued, 'he would be able to devote – because he wouldn't doubt.'

'And you believe that?'

'Of course I do. How often do you hear of blokes who spend years with one person unable to commit to them, then the relationship ends and before they've sawed the sofa in half he's married someone else?'

Jo stared searchingly at the kitchen tiling. 'You really think someone can change like that?'

'I think meeting the right person can effect a change, yes,' Jess replied, as if they were taking part in a studio discussion on foreign policy with David Frost. 'I know for a fact I could change Andy.'

Jo looked aghast. 'Uh-oh, babes,' she cautioned, shaking her head and wagging a finger, 'never think you can change a bloke. Never. As my granny used to say, changing a man is like changing a tyre: they're the only ones who can do it.'

Jess exploded. 'Bollocks. One, I am perfectly capable of changing a tyre,' she shouted, banishing memories of being stuck on the hard shoulder of the M25 fiddling with a jack and looking hopefully at any passing male driver. 'And two, it's obvious I would change him because he would discover in a cataclysmic blinding revelatory flash, what it's *really* like to be in love.' Then she laughed.

'I just think you need to be careful, babes,' Jo said gravely, not laughing.

Why was it, Jess wondered, that she could walk home alone at two in the morning, take dodgy powder at a party, or drive a car over black ice, yet the one occasion guaranteed to invoke genuine, heartfelt and serious concern for her well-being was the possibility that she might be a bit too keen on a bloke? 'I'll use a condom, if that's what you mean,' she said, smirking.

'I just don't think you should trust him,' Jo continued, in a doctors-are-doing-everything-they-can voice. 'He hasn't left her yet, and there's no certainty that he—'

Suddenly, Jess's bag started ringing. 'Ooh, that'll be Andy,' she announced, in mock-presumption. 'Yes, Andy, I would love to come round and shag you,' she chirped, fishing around for her mobile. 'And what? Oh, you've left Sarah and want to marry me instead? Yes, of course I do. Yes. OK. I'll just ask Jo if she wants to be my bridesmaid, hold on.'

Jo was licking the foam from around her cup and giggling. Jess located the phone, looked quizzically at the unknown number and pressed yes. 'Hello?'

Jo watched expectantly.

Jess's face erupted. 'Oh . . . um, hi, Andy.'

Jo burst out laughing. 'Don't marry Jess, Andy,' she shouted at the handset. 'She's got genital warts.'

'Who's that?' Andy asked, sounding irritable.

Jess wanted the entire Formica kitchen fittings to collapse on top of her. 'Oh, ha-ha,' she tittered. 'Just Jo being . . . pissed. So. How are you?'

'Desperately, uncontrollably in love with you,' Jo shouted, through more laughter.

'Sorry, Andy,' Jess squeaked, attempting a karate kick at Jo's face and scuttling out of the room. 'Jo really is paralytic.'

'Listen,' Andy said brusquely, as though they were in a meeting and Jess was fussing around with the biscuits, 'what are you doing now?'

'Nothing,' she said hastily and – given that she was supposed to be having dinner with Jo – deceitfully.

'Can you meet me for a drink in half an hour?'

Jess felt her whole body explode with joy. 'Of course I can, Andy,' she gushed.

'I really need to talk to you,' he said, softly. 'Seven at the Sun Inn?'

Delirious, she accepted. 'Gotcha!' she quipped, and felt the sparks of their compatibility igniting all the way down the line.

Seven at the Sun Inn

'We're in a mess,' Andy wailed, clawing his forehead with his hands as if in the midst of an oriental stress-relieving exercise that was obviously, from the way the rest of his body convulsed, not really working.

'We're not in a mess,' Jess said soothingly, stroking his back reassuringly. 'We're in . . .' she wondered if it was too early in their relationship to introduce the concept of love '. . . we're in a position all I—'

'We?' he said, startled, peering up at her through his fingers as if he were a five-year-old too scared to watch the bunny being boiled to death in *Fatal Attraction*.

Jess smiled. He had obviously been attributing the mess to him and Sarah, not him and her. *They* were in something a lot more positive. 'We collective, I mean,' she said, arms flailing wildly.

'I should never have told her,' he continued, addressing the ashtray, 'and then everything would have been fine.'

'Everything *will* be fine,' Jess said, glancing at him to see if this might be the moment for them to look searchingly into each other's eyes and whisper softly, yet urgently, 'I need you. I want you. I—'

'I love her,' he said, banging the table with his fist.

Jess tried not to look hurt by this insensitivity. 'Of course you love her,' she said, understandingly, fighting back the desire to shout, 'What about *me*? Do you love *me*?'

'And I want her back.'

Jess froze, pint glass hovering in mid-air, mouth unattractively ajar. 'Has she left you?' she said, unable to convert the excitement in her voice to sympathy.

He nodded and stared forlornly at the exit sign. 'That's why I wanted to see you.'

Jess felt her stomach nose-dive into her groin. 'Really?' she whispered.

He looked at her earnestly. 'You don't need to answer this if you feel your loyalty to—'

'Sssh,' she hushed, keen not to let the conversation stray into practicalities like Alex. 'My loyalty is to you.'

Andy smiled. She concentrated on not letting her face give away what she knew was coming next.

'I know, well . . .' he stuttered. She smiled encouragingly, feeling as though she might combust with pent-up anticipation. 'I know she came to see you on Sunday.'

Her face fell. 'Who?'

'Sarah.'

'Yes. And?'

'And, well, I need to know if she said anything that might suggest . . . well, that might suggest she—'

'She doesn't,' Jess cut in, reassuringly. 'In fact, she seems to think the "thing", as you so nicely referred—'

'Did she say it, though?' he pleaded. 'Did she say, "I no longer love him"?'

Jess blinked at him, confused. The idea was to talk about *their* love.

'She did, didn't she?' he said, looking as though he might walk out into the road and stand in front of a bus. 'I've fucked up.'

'You have not "fucked up",' Jess began, trying not to dwell on the notion of their relationship being described in a doomed Romeo-and-Julietesque way. 'You were just led by your emotions and did—'

'Emotions?' he yelled. 'Jess, I was led by my dick.'

Jess flinched. The idea that a bloke might actually confess to such a thing was as bizarre as a woman admitting to being irrational. It seemed even more bizarre when she considered how much further his dick still had to lead him.

'Everything's ruined,' he continued, hurling his head at his hands. 'Ruined.'

Jess waited until a respectful pause had passed. 'It's not all ruined,' she said, coyly. 'There's still a chance for . . .' She blushed.

He brought his head up and turned to look at her, a thrillingly determined glint in his eye. 'You're right, Jess,' he said, assertively. 'There's still a chance she'll come back to me.'

Jess tried not to look crestfallen. She'd jumped ahead of herself – like arranging the christening for a baby that was still an embryo. She smiled wanly and resolved to wait patiently for their mutual declaration of love.

Eight at the Sun Inn . . .
'It's a love of friendship, of respect, of compatibility, of . . .'
Andy gazed melancholically into his pint '. . . of love.' He
paused again. 'Sarah is a wonderful woman.'

Nine at the Sun Inn . . .
'It's a love of passion, of compassion, of . . . adoration, adula-
tion, desire, of . . .'

Ten at the Sun Inn . . .
'It's a love of—'
   'Christ!' Jess exploded.
   Andy looked up in alarm. 'What?'
   'Oh, I mean, Christ, is that the time?' she stuttered, pulling
up her sleeve and checking her watch ostentatiously. 'Told
Alex I'd be back hours ago,' she said, snatching her coat. 'So,
well . . . better be off then.'
   Andy grabbed her hand. It was typical of the evening, Jess
thought, that this urgent, passionate gesture coincided with
her leaving. 'Thank you, Jess,' he said, looking up at her and
smiling, as if she'd just walked into his office with the files
he'd spent all morning searching for. 'You're a star.'
   'Twinkle, twinkle,' she said, cocking her head from side to
side like a puppet. Then she made her way, as dignified as
possible, to the door, trying to extrapolate something non-
platonic from the word 'star'.
   As she rounded the corner to the tube, she felt, for the
first time in a long while, a genuine desire to return home to
her lovely, dependable, female-free Alex.

Has Alex Got News For You

To:	*Claire.Voyant@hotmail.com*
Date:	*Saturday 24 June*
Subject:	*Has Alex Got News For You*

Desiring never to see vile adulterous Alex again.
  Staying at Lou's feeling like an abandoned
  puppy she has taken in because its yelping was
  waking up the neighbours, not because she
  wants a dog. Watching, helpless, as my life goes
  to the dogs.

Dear Claire,

Alex has snogged someone. However skew-whiff my trajectory through life might be, I'd never suspected Alex would be unfaithful. He is supposed to be good and sensible and in love with me. He is not supposed to get pissed at a work do and stick his tongue down the throat of someone called Leonie.

It's as if he's a very expensive stereo that I'd bought from John Lewis, rather than from a man with a microphone standing on a podium in Oxford Street, shouting, 'Hurry, hurry, everything half-price just for today,' to a gathering of permed women in leggings and anoraks. While it's perfectly clear that Microphone Man is an escaped convict trying his luck with a Betamax video-player and some urine in a Coco Chanel bottle, you do not expect practical parent-place-for-purchasing John Lewis to sell things that go wrong. And even though Alex/expensive stereo is under guarantee, I have a horrible sinking feeling that if I try to take it back and get it fixed, I will be told that the fault is not with the product but with my careless and brutal treatment of the product, and if I want it to work again, I'll have to pay.

I'm certainly paying at the moment, that's for sure. One of the hideous things about hearing bad news is that in addition to throwing up, howling uncontrollably and feeling as if your intestines have been wrenched out and strung round your neck, you also seem to contract Alzheimer's. Thus after emotionally exhausting yourself for a good few hours, you will finally, peacefully and happily be absorbed in something else, e.g. putting on a coloureds wash, when suddenly, without any warning, the bad news comes flooding back again. Only it doesn't arrive in a gentle, lapping, muted, oh-that-little-problem ripple, but in a grotesque, tumultuous tidal wave, hitting you with the same ferocity as if it were the first time you'd heard it.

Oh, God – Alex has been unfaithful. Typically, of course, he's not couching it as such: he refers to it as a random drunken incident that meant nothing. Why, oh, why do blokes insist on thinking that what will reassure you are not descriptions of a lard-arsed gorilla with Hoover lips, or protestations of out-of-hand games of Truth or Dare, but simply that it 'didn't mean anything'? This is clearly bollocks on two fronts: (1) because if it was so devoid of any kind of meaning, why did it prompt him to jeopardise a trusting, happy, long-term relationship? And (2) because as far as the trusting, happy, long-term relationship is concerned, it holds more bloody meaning than the entire Oxford English Dictionary.

What makes the whole thing doubly depressing is that rather than tell me straight away, i.e. on Thursday night when he was so revoltingly pissed and kebab-coated that the thought of him snogging would elicit feelings not of jealousy, outrage or hurt, but of genuine sympathy for the poor woman, he decided to wait a couple of days and regale me instead with a number of unfunny jokes he'd remembered being told that evening.

I feel sure God must have skived off a few physics lessons when in heaven because however successfully the rest of His human-body-assembling task might have been, he certainly fucked up on the wiring of the male memory. How else does one account for the fact that a bloke can always remember word for word any joke he is told (without, as tends to be the case with me, forgetting the punch-line/remembering it but forgetting the joke/announcing it half-way through the joke and/or getting it mixed up with a different joke) yet if you tell them you're going to wear what you wore last night at Jane's they haven't got an inkling what that might have been?

He claimed, in a soft, tender tone, that the reason he took two days to tell me was because he was 'waiting for the right moment', at which I went mad and pointed out that that was like planning to have a car accident on a Monday night because A and E would be a bit less busy.

Oh, Jesus, I'm so miserable. It's Midsummer's Day and I should be at an open-air performance of A Midsummer Night's Dream with little fairy-lights in the trees and picnic hampers with warm wine, not contemplating sticking my head in the oven and leaving it there.

Looking back with hindsight, of course, it all makes perfect sense. He was doing that overcompensating thing of being extra nice, which everyone knows, when it comes to a bloke, means he has either done something wrong or is about to do something wrong. And then on Friday morning he initiated spontaneous sex when he was already rushing for a meeting, which is the equivalent of me suggesting doing it when I've had a shower, blow-dried my hair and got all dolled up.

The trouble was, in our haste – and, in my case, shock – we forgot that I'd stopped taking the pill. After all, what's the point of putting on weight and having madwoman mood swings just so that you can have the odd shag on a Sunday? It's as insane as paying forty quid a month for gym membership and going once. By eight twenty-five, we'd not only made ourselves late for work but also, potentially, a baby.

For someone who is a lawyer and therefore trained to insure him-self against the unlikely, Alex was surprisingly blasé. He claimed that the 'chances were slim', until I told him he might regret this when he came home to find me anything but slim. So it was agreed that we'd go to the Family Planning Clinic for the morning-after *pill – or, as Alex seemed to find it amusing to call it, the afternoon-after pill.*

Making a bloody appointment, though, was a nightmare. It is one thing trying to disguise the fact that you are on a personal call at work; it is quite another trying to make up lies about condoms splitting with scary producers walking past. And getting out of work to attend the appointment was akin to a Mission Impossible plot. Ended up telling everyone I had an emergency dental appointment, which was about as convincing as claiming that a purple lovebite on my neck was the result of an unfortunate encounter with a felt-tip pen.

It was a hideous experience. I expected to walk into an empty waiting room, smile feebly at a pregnant mum in the corner, then settle down in silence to read the knitting patterns in last Christmas's edition of Bella. *I was not expecting to enter what might have been mistaken for the community disco. Fatboy Slim was blasting 'You've Come A Long Way, Baby', rather inappropriately given that the reception area was crammed full of sulky teenage girls there to ensure their babies didn't come at all. Each of them was chewing gum, and was accompanied by a fellow sulky friend whose job as supportive companion seemed to involve issuing filthy looks to anyone bold enough to catch her eye.*

Of course, the minute Alex and I walked in they stared at us as if we were not a sprightly young twosome caught short by our unbridled sexual eagerness but a middle-aged couple coming to collect our Viagra prescription. Intimidated, I sat down in a corner and buried my head in Just Seventeen, *while Alex studied a leaflet, somewhat pointlessly, on baby care.*

Eventually I was summoned into the surgery where a stick-thin woman with frizzy hair and thick-lensed glasses was seated behind a desk, scribbling furiously. She glowered at me, then launched into an MI5 investigation of my sex life.

I don't know why, when the job entails dealing with matters of a sexual nature, they employ someone who has clearly never had sex. It felt wrong to be telling her things, especially as she kept pronouncing the word 'sex-u-al' as if it did not relate to passion and love, but to an industrial-strength antiseptic. Only when I'd convinced her that I would take more care in the future was I allowed to go, clutching the hard-fought-for pills and a brown paper bag of condoms – the equivalent of buying a cycle helmet after you've crashed.

I walked back into the waiting room and spotted Alex deep in conversation with an earnest-looking couple. Horror of all horrors, it was Sophie and Richard. Bizarre as the idea was, I assumed they, too, had been caught short and suggested we all buy shares in the morning-after pill. Everyone went silent and stared at the diamond design on the floor, then Alex explained, as if we'd all been transported to an American self-help class and had to tell the group what was wrong with the person sitting next to us, 'Sophie and Richard are having problems conceiving.' Two thoughts went whizzing through my head in rapid succession:

(1) I'd forgotten that the function of sex was to procreate: I'd always just seen it as a recreational exercise. And,

(2) That while I'd been laboriously analysing whether Alex was right for me, Sophie had got married, bought a house, and was now, albeit unsuccessfully, trying for a baby.

I must say, though, it's good to know that even the most perfect couples have their problems. Mind you, right now I can't help wishing mine were of the infertility rather than the infidelity variety.

In fact, I seem to be haunted by infidelity every which way I turn – like when you discover something you didn't know before, e.g. what chlamydia means, and suddenly chlamydia is in every bloody nook and cranny, though not, I hope, in mine.

Michael came storming into work yesterday and, 'inspired' in a seemingly Nabokov manner by some girl wearing a pink vest on the tube, announced he had a marvellous, topical and forward-thinking item for next Wednesday's 'Out'n'About' slot. Felt immediately inclined to encourage said idea, whatever it was because *they have put me in charge of this slot – I suspect mainly to get me to do my fuck-ups* out *of the office – and I'm always looking for ways to squirm out of it. After all, where is the enjoyment in standing outside Prêt à Manger saying, 'What influenced your choice of sandwich today?' while thrusting a microphone at the only person who isn't looking at you as though you're a talking turd? Then, before I know it, he's dragged three of us into his office and is scrawling 'Summer: The Salacious Season?' in gigantic letters on a whiteboard, licking his lips and grinning, well, salaciously.*

It turns out that the idea involved me and Jim, the cameraman, going to Golden Square at lunchtime and perving on lots of semi-naked sunbathing girls, then finding any bloke who was perving too and springing them. Aside from the fact that this was (a) derogatory to women, (b) derogatory to me, and (c) mind-bogglingly crap TV of American proportions, I agreed to go, mainly because I hoped to get in a bit of sunbathing too. When we got there, however, Golden Square had become Tenerife with pigeons. I do find it bizarre how one minute Londoners are sitting in a tube doing their utmost to ignore everyone and the next they're flaunting all sorts of fleshy white bits as if their aim is to secure a role as an extra in Baywatch.

Jim made a beeline for a girl who'd shaped herself in tribute to Pamela Anderson – or, at least, her surgeon had – and zoomed the camera lens in a way that Freud would have had little difficulty in interpreting. 'Pamela' pretended, ridiculously, that she hadn't noticed, while surreptitiously – and deftly – transforming her Whistles suit into a bikini.

I called a halt when we had enough footage to keep Eurotrash *in production for a decade, and pointed out that we were here to jump the blokes, not jump-start Jim's libido. The blokes, in a reversal-of-gender-convention way, were sitting in the shade preserving their skin, except for a couple of topless tattooed scaffolders who seemed to work on the principle – as is often the case with those of limited beauty – 'If you've got it, flaunt it; if you haven't, flaunt it even more.' Asking them if they felt guilty for 'admiring' the sunbathing girls (the euphemism I was told to use for 'perving') was a bit like asking an investment banker if he had qualms about spending the equivalent of the Third World debt on lunch at Coq d'Argent. They told me, with dazzling originality, that, 'Even though you drive a Mini, there's no harm in looking at a Merc.' Couldn't help suspecting that if what surrounded them in Golden Square were lots of Mercedes, their Minis were fit only for the scrap heap.*

Any hope of keeping to our brief – which, let's face it, was never going to be a winner (what bloke is going to admit that, yes, he has a girlfriend, but, yes, he is also perving at girls in the park?) – was annihilated by the supposition that we were the crew from Streetmate. *This meant that every time I caught a bloke ogling a girl, pounced on him and asked if he was single, he looked at me as though I'd offered him a night with Britney Spears and a rubber catsuit and was so quick to say yes that I began to wonder how Davina McCall can make the date-search span a whole episode.*

I soon remembered, however, that I was not there to turn Golden Square into a high-school prom but to expose men in a bad light. Returned to the office, hot and sweaty, to discover it was the women I had exposed, in every kind of light, and the men whose integrity remained firmly intact – which, I bitterly suspect, was the point of the exercise.

Michael was so excited* by the footage that now he wants to do a phone-in on where people draw the line on what constitutes infidelity and . . . Ergh! Tidal wave has just hit again. Horrible images of him slurping at Leonie's ear. Alex, not Michael. Feel as though I'm a celebrity and every time my brain thinks about it/I open a tabloid, a new and horrifying angle is exposed.

It's the details that get to you. The amorphous 'Alex snogged someone' doesn't necessarily make you suicidal. It's when you hear he spilled wine on her top or she told him he had cute stubble that the pain strikes.

---

*Turned on

Oh, God. I must stop this and calm myself. That river-mud massage you were talking about would be good – if the banks of the Thames could first be cleared of used condoms and sanitary towels. Did the massage guy insist you were naked or did his bronzed six-pack and 'melting azure' eyes (what have you been reading?) mean that you were the one doing the insisting? And since when did you start smoking?

Mmm . . . maybe a fag is the answer, or a drink. I could swallow the gin bottle – that would be quite calming. Or possibly just have a bath. That idea seems particularly appealing, but it always does until I get into it. Within five minutes I'm sweating and wheezing and panicking that I'm about to die of heat exhaustion and generally getting so not *calm that I have to clamber out and stand dripping, slimy and gasping for air in the hallway. Suspect the gin bottle might be more sensible. In fact . . .*

Oh, my God. On my way to Lou's drink cabinet, i.e. a bottle of duty-free vodka and some gloopy Austrian schnapps, I happened to notice she'd written something on the back of an envelope, and because it looked like important instructions to the washing machine, I read it. This is what it said:

Saturday

9.30 a.m.	*Run round Clapham Common with Cassie.*
11.00 a.m.	*Go shopping: strappy slingbacks and Karen Millen dress.*
1.00 p.m.	*Meet yoga class friends for lunch.*
2.30 p.m.	*Tate Modern.*
5.00 p.m.	*Hook up with Janet to discuss Greek Island holiday.*
7.30 p.m.	*Seb's dinner party.*
12.00 p.m.	*Clubbing with Matt, etc.?*

ARGHHHHHH . . . Feel as though I have missed the point of Saturday. I was under the impression it was all about coloureds washes, Sainsbury's shopping and slobbing in front of Blind Date *with a takeaway, not a triathlon organised with the intensity of a military exercise where it is vital to get the right balance of cardiovascular activity/stamina building/muscle toning or, if you are single, wild social life/cultural museum visits/credit-card flexing.*

Mind you, anything is preferable to spending the day fending off tidal waves. Wish Lou would come back from her single person's sensational Saturday and help me with my suicidal one. Does she not understand that my boyfriend has committed a vile and atrocious crime? Oh, God, misery. Need gin . . .

Miss you.

Lots of love,

Jess

xxx

High Infidelity

'Vile and atrocious, Jess?' Lou said, looking at her with brow furrowed as if she'd just announced she had a contagious fungal disease. 'He snogged someone, not shot them.'

'It's still a crime,' Jess replied, picking a shaving scab on her leg, 'when you're supposed to be going out with someone else.'

'And what is having secret drinks with someone you think you might be in love with,' she sniggered, 'when you're supposed to be going out with someone else?'

'That's different,' Jess snapped, as blood oozed from where the scab had been.

'In . . . what way?' Despite a bewildering choice of freshly washed outfits, Lou had decided to wear a crumpled sequined top from her dirty laundry basket and was sniffing at it hopefully.

'I haven't *done* anything with Andy.'

'So, if Alex had pursued this Leonie for several weeks, told all his friends he thought she was his soulmate, engineered a variety of situations to see her, but at the end of the day hadn't *done* anything with her, that would be OK?'

Jess felt like strangling Lou with her sequined top. Best friends were supposed to be the equivalent of defence lawyers: no matter how glaringly guilty the evidence proved one to be, it was their job to make out it didn't. 'Yes,' she lied, trying to dam the blood with her thumb.

'I'm not saying what Alex did was right,' Lou continued, spraying perfume at the top – the single woman's substitute for the dry-cleaners, 'but blaming him and walking out isn't going to solve the more intrinsic problem in your relation- ship.'

'Which is, Claire Rayner?'

Lou smiled. 'By your own admission, that Alex is not the right person for you.'

Jess flinched. The trouble with being honest about your relationship problems with your friends was that however much of an emotionally cleansing experience it was at the time, it always came back at you on the one occasion you would rather be *dis*honest. 'Alex *is* the right person for me,' she said, sulkily.

'You're only saying that, Jess, because for once he hasn't been Mr Nice Guy.'

Jess slumped back on the bed. She was with Lou to be looked after, felt sorry for and fed consoling junk food, not preached at by Woody Allen in a sparkly top. After all, she thought, as Lou slithered into a pair of leather trousers, why should she listen to someone whose high expectations of a boyfriend had left her without one for three years? She threw her head indignantly on to the pillow and contemplated whether Alex's role as adulterer had really made him more appealing. And then an uncomfortable thought washed over her: was she angry because Lou was single or because Lou was right?

'Hair-clip or no hair-clip?'

She was awoken from her self-analysis by Lou sporting a rosebud on her head.

'Depends. Will you be singing "Who Will Buy This Beautiful Morning?" in the local am-dram performance of *Oliver*?'

Lou laughed. 'Got the message,' she said and dismantled the church-hall costume-box look then applied a lipstick that looked as though it belonged to the church-hall crayon-box. 'Can I borrow your hair mousse?'

Jess rummaged in her bag and handed it to her. She'd forgotten the enjoyment to be had from getting ready for an evening with someone who didn't think all that was required was a change of T-shirt and the running of a wet hand through greasy hair. She picked up the lipstick. 'Uuu gaaaing oww?' she garbled, mid-application.

Lou looked at her blankly, the way dentists did when they asked their patient a question seconds before ramming several implements down their throat.

'Sorry,' Jess said, rolling her lips together. 'You going out?'

Lou squirted a golfball of mousse into her palm. 'Nah. Just wanted to look my best for slouching in front of the telly.'

'So. Where you going, then?' Jess said, pouting at herself in the mirror.

'Out.'

'Out where?'

'Outside.'

'Outside where?'

'You,' Lou said, dabbing a blob of mousse on Jess's nose, 'should learn to be less nosy.'

A comment like this was one sure-fire way to guarantee the opposite. 'You've got a date, haven't you?'

'Alex may have to account for his every movement, bowel or otherwise,' Lou replied, running her hands through her hair, 'but I am in no way obliged to account for mine.' She got up, swept some makeup into an open bag with the adeptness of a burglar and scampered towards the front door.

'But . . . when are you coming back?' Jess stammered, following her like a child being dragged through Asda.

'You've been married too long,' Lou said, turning to give Jess a hug. 'Who says I'm coming back at all?' She gave a wink. 'Feel free to help yourself to anything in the fridge that isn't sprouting green fuzz, and don't kill the goldfish.' Then she was gone.

Jess stood in the hallway fighting back tears. She'd forgotten that having a boyfriend meant you had someone who loved you, looked after you and – when they didn't choose to investigate Leonie's tonsils – was always there for you. Spending Saturday night outside that happy, hermetically sealed bubble felt a bit like being dropped out of the sky, landing on your head and finding yourself in the middle of nowhere without the slightest idea of how to get back. She wandered through to the television.

'. . . and a simple diamanté tiara gives the bride a look of . . .'

'. . . revolting smugness,' Jess shouted, grabbing the remote control and searching for people less successful in love. Unfortunately *Blind Date* was over, replaced by a monstrous woman from Basingstoke telling Matthew Kelly she was Kylie Minogue.

It was a cruel, evil thing about Saturday-night television, Jess decided, as she flicked mindlessly from one channel to the next, that there was never anything worth watching. It was clearly a conspiracy from somewhere up high in Television Centre to make those not out having fun and laughing feel like social rejects of the lowest order. It was their way of saying, 'We are transmitting utter crap because anyone worthy of good television is out doing something better.'

Just as she slumped further into the sofa, while Kylie Minogue's less than identical twin belted out, rather appropriately, 'I Should Be So Lucky', the phone rang. It had that promising, exciting feel to it that usually meant it was for someone else.

'Oh, um, hello,' a startled man's voice began. 'Um, gosh, I was expecting an answerphone. Didn't think anyone would be in.' He paused. 'Saturday night and all that.'

'I'm not in . . . actually,' Jess said. Then, suspecting that such a supernatural feat required clarification, she added, 'What I mean is, I won't be in for long. Rushing out . . . to a party, in fact. Hectic stuff.'

She flinched, appalled that the pressure to be doing something wild and young had become so intense that she needed to lie to a stranger. She'd be inventing imaginary friends next and having conversations with the sink.

'Can you tell Lou that Paul phoned?' he said. ''Anks, 'bye.'

Lou had not only left her alone and boyfriendless on a Saturday night, she had also left her to be social secretary to any potential boyfriends of *hers*. In disgust, Jess switched on the answermachine, slobbed over to the kitchen and peered into the fridge with the same sense of expectation she'd approached the other comfort box in her life – the telly. Unfortunately, with half a pint of milk and a lemon, even the fridge was shouting, 'Look at me, I'm so busy and popular all my contents have gone out to do much better things than sit around going off!' She slammed it shut, contemplated eating the goldfish and phoned for a pizza.

Forty-five minutes later the doorbell rang.

'Nine-inch Hawaiian,' announced a small leather-clad man who, with receding red hair and freckles, was neither Hawaiian nor, Jess suspected, if the shoe-size theory had any validity, nine inches.

'How much?'

'Seven ninety-five,' replied the self-professed well-endowed exotic-islander.

'Oh . . . um, gosh,' Jess said, fumbling in her wallet in the hope that some loose change and a stamp might metamorphose into something a little closer to the required sum. 'D'you take cheques?'

'That girlfriend of yours been spending all your dosh, then?'

'You know Lou?' Jess said, startled.

He grinned proudly. 'She's one of my regulars,' he said, then looked pensively into the hallway and added, lovingly, 'Lou and Margherita,' as if they were not a customer and a pizza but his two favourite call-girls.

'Here,' she said, handing him a cheque and taking her nine-inch packet before it tried to take her.

Once alone, she gobbled down its contents in the Neanderthal style she adopted whenever no one was around to witness it. Then, she chucked the empty pizza box on to the floor and belched. After watching the goldfish chase what appeared to be a giant flake of dandruff round and round its bowl, she realised that her Saturday night was no longer making her miserable, it was turning her mad. And then the phone rang:

'I'm not in,' Lou's voice announced to the room, 'but luckily my machine is. Leave him a message.'

'*Him?*' Jess was incredulous. Was this what you were driven to when you didn't have a boyfriend? she wondered. The masculine machine began emitting lots of beeps to show the unsuspecting caller that a queue of people wanted to speak to Lou and that if they wanted to join it they'd have to think up something headline-grabbing to attract her. Unfortunately, by the time the beeping had finished, the caller couldn't seem to think of *anything* to say – either that or, Jess deduced from the background rumble, they were going to *do* something headline-grabbing instead, like throw themselves in front of—

She sat bolt upright. Maybe it was Alex. She leaned forward and listened intently. Maybe right at that moment he was waiting on a track at Kings Cross for the 22.41 from Manchester to do the business, stabbing a voodoo doll of Leonie in the back, so replete with desolation and despair he could no longer . . .

'I don't recall saying you were sexy.' It was a girl.

Jess lurched in horror. The voodoo doll had come alive.

'A snog doesn't mean . . .' the voice sounded familiar '. . . you are so *cheeky.*' There was a high-pitched giggle, then more muffled conversation. If it was the voodoo she must have inadvertently pressed Lou's number and didn't know she was being listened to. '. . . and big-headed . . . Even my goldfish kisses better!'

Jess gave a squeak of delight. It was Lou flirting with a bloke. She smiled at her own stupidity then sat back excitedly to see what happened next.

'. . . only because you said . . . a thing . . .' More laughter, followed by the voice of a man, tantalisingly out of earshot.

'. . . no you can't,' Lou squealed. 'I only . . . married men
. . .' Then the voice got louder, things were being rustled
around. She'd obviously opened her bag. 'How much?'

Jess flinched as vile images of Lou and a goldfish-kissing
gigolo flashed up. It would make sense, she reflected, as rather
odd sucking noises squelched out of the machine, given how
weird she'd been about where she was going.

'Maybe you're a *bit* sexy, then,' Lou teased, in a splendidly
flirtatious manner.

'Mmm, you're a lot sexy,' the gigolo replied, before the
squelching noises returned. Jess felt as though she was no
longer eavesdropping on a conversation, but renting a porn
movie.

'. . . and my lips are sealed,' Lou said, which, Jess deemed,
given what she'd overheard seconds earlier, to be untrue,
'. . . call you.' Then everything was drowned out by traffic
noises.

Jess got up, disappointed not to have been party to anything
juicier, and wandered over to Lou's CD collection intent on
finding something a little more relaxing to listen to than buses
and diesel engines. Just as she was selecting a suitably maudlin
Smiths track, Lou's voice, loud and clear, cut through the
motoring mêlée: 'Night, Andy.'

Jess froze. The machine bleeped off. A car door slammed.
The horror hit.

'I'm home, darling.' Lou was bustling into the room, keys
jangling, hair tossing, grinning. Then she stopped in her tracks.
'Good God, Jess, you look as if you've seen a ghost.'

Jess stood, mouth agape, staring white-faced like a . . .
ghost.

'It's me. Lou,' Lou said, waving both hands in the air as
though she were a teenager doing self-conscious swaying on
Top of the Pops. 'Your best friend.'

'Best friend, my arse,' Jess blurted, the full nightmare

impacting on her. The room spun, as the world of her and Andy collapsed around her. He was her everything. Lou was his 'thing'. She was his nothing.

'Jess? Whatever's the—'

'"Night, Andy",' Jess mimicked, hurling the CD case at the floor as Lou's eyes moved suspiciously from left to right as if she was a cartoon character unsure which way to run.

There was a moment's silence while she chose her route. 'Is Andy *here*?' she said, peering forward. 'Is he? Where is he?' she continued, pretending to look for him beneath a cushion. 'Sleeping under the sofa?'

'No,' Jess replied, staring at her coldly. 'Sleeping with my "best friend".' Then, before Lou had time to say anything more, she pressed play.

'You have one message,' the pseudo-boyfriend declared. Jess stood with folded arms, glowering. '. . . I don't recall saying you were sexy . . . a snog doesn't mean . . . you are so *cheeky* . . .'

Jess watched as Lou's expression turned from one of mild amusement into something that would not have been out of place in an A and E waiting room. She pressed fast-forward. '. . . my lips are sealed . . . Night, Andy.'

Lou collapsed on to a chair and stared at the carpet.

'So?' Jess barked.

There was a strange strangled noise, then Lou looked up at her. 'So, OK, I snogged him, but I—'

'OK?' Jess screeched, kicking at the chair. 'OK? On what fucking planet, pray tell me, is it OK to snog the bloke your best friend – *ex*-best friend fancies?'

Lou stared at the carpet again. Although Jess was shocked, hurt, furious and jealous, she couldn't help relishing the rather heady sensation afforded by occupying the moral high ground.

'The planet where your best friend already *has* a fucking bloke.'

Jess lurched: the moral high ground had obviously been

erected on a fault line. She scrabbled around for *terra firma* and found it, moments later, on an island called Emotional Blackmail. 'You *knew*,' she whined, throwing herself melodramatically at the sofa, 'you knew I liked him. You knew how much I felt for him and yet you still did it. Why?'

'Because, Jess,' Lou said, getting to her feet to demonstrate just how sturdy *her* turf was, 'I could.'

'You *could* with half the population of London,' Jess shouted. 'Why did you have to choose my one?'

Lou looked as though she'd trodden on the goldfish. '*Your* one?'

'Yes,' Jess said, limply.

'And Alex is . . . ?'

'Alex is irrelevant,' Jess snapped, irritated that the austere-headmistress-scolding-naughty-pupil had become naughty-pupil-pointing-out-headmistress-has-made-a-mistake-on-the-blackboard.

'I'm sure he'd be delighted to know that,' Lou replied, walking through to the kitchen. 'But if he's that irrelevant how come you're round here moping about like damp bog roll.'

Jess concentrated hard on not bursting into tears. She'd never argued with Lou. Not properly. And arguing with a best friend was always the worst. You sort of *expected* to argue with a boyfriend. It came with the package, like moving into a house and discovering that the beautiful, spacious, south-facing dining room had dry rot and a cracked ceiling. But the whole point of friendship was compatibility: when that broke down it was much more serious than rot or cracks – the entire house collapsed.

'Fine,' Jess shouted, jumping to her feet. 'I'll go.'

'Suits me,' Lou shouted back.

'And God forbid we do anything that *doesn't* suit you,' Jess screamed, hurling a cushion at the telly.

'Meaning?' Lou was standing, hands on hips, looking as if

she might flick her wrists in the air, produce two loaded revolvers and shoot the living daylights out of the place.

'That I'm sick of having to tread on egg-shells listening to you moan about being single as if it's some kind of terminal cancer when the only fucking reason you don't have a boy-friend is because your expectations are as high as your over-bloated opinion of yourself.'

Lou stared at her very hard in the manner of an axe-murderer. 'At least I don't kid myself I'm feeling things I'm not,' she said, icily. 'And, for your information,' she added, moving towards the door, 'I'm not single.'

Jess stood, stunned, as she disappeared out of the room. The news that Lou had snogged Andy was enough to send her to an early grave. The news that this was because she was *going out* with him encouraged her to consider the carving knife as a means of getting there.

'But . . .' she stammered, following Lou as she stomped her way upstairs. 'You and Andy . . . what? When?'

Lou turned round and looked down at Jess as if she were a servant who'd stolen the bread rations from the pantry. 'I would tell you,' she said, still with the axe-murderer expres-sion, 'but I understand you're sick of listening to me.' Then she walked calmly into her bedroom, glanced fleetingly back at a begging Jess and added, 'Don't make too much noise on your way out. Goodbye,' then slammed the door behind her.

Jess slumped on the stairs feeling not so much as if the rug had been pulled from under her, as yanked out all her innards in the process. Why was it, she reflected tearfully, that she was the one feeling like a criminal when it was Lou who'd committed the crime?

Just as she was contemplating the effort required to hurl herself over the banisters, her mobile rang. She checked the time. It was late. Only one person called her when it was late. With the first ounce of enthusiasm she'd experienced all day, she sprang to her feet and charged downstairs to tell him all was forgiven, to tell him how much she missed him, to tell him that she hated being apart, cast out into a world where everyone was in a happy couple. Euphorically, she pressed yes.

'Guess what, babes?' It wasn't Alex. It was Jo. 'Mark and I are getting married!'

In the Doghouse

To: Claire.Voyant@hotmail.com
Date: Wednesday 19 July
Subject: In the Doghouse

*Alex and I are getting a puppy. Not to fill a gap
in the way unhappy couples have babies. Nor
as a quick-fix solution, e.g. surgeon putting
Band-Aid on head-gash of crash victim. But so
that we can play with it in the dunes wearing
tight white T-shirts and knickers, hair blowing
in the wind and laughing like happy Calvin
Klein people.*

Dear Claire,

Alex and I have kissed and made up. Well, to be frank, it was
more of a kiss and make out – several times around the house.
Given the nunnery the place had become, this was a marvellously
welcome change, except, unfortunately, for the bathroom towel rail
which is now dangling from a wall that looks as if it's made a
narrow escape from the Gaza Strip.

If I'd known that all we had to do to relight the spark was get
Alex to have a random snog, I would have been organising Spin-
the-Bottle parties months ago. It's like when the boiler doesn't work
and you don't have a clue what's wrong with it and are too scared
to fiddle with any of the dials in case you explode the house, so
you phone up an electrician who takes one look at it, reignites the
pilot light and charges you a £58 call-out charge. Should I be
paying Leonie? I wonder.

Thanks for your last email, and congratulations on becoming
an aunt. Does this mean you'll start wearing Crimplene dresses

and make fudge for coffee mornings? And has it brought John any nearer to changing his mind or is he still describing kids as 'life imprisonment'?

As an extension of our new-found passionate love, we're getting a puppy. The other day we went to the dog home to have a 'look', which was, I rapidly discovered, the equivalent of saying you're just window-shopping when passing Armani: impossible to walk away without wanting to take everything with you. The trouble was I was torn between waves of genuine heartfelt love for all the forlorn, abandoned creatures – working out, in my new role as heroic Mother Teresa of the canine world, how we could convert our bedroom into a refuge centre – and the jarring-with-saintly idea spawned by corruptive adverts for loo paper that what I really wanted was not a scrotty flea-ridden mongrel thing with one ear but a little honeycomb-coloured fluffy ball of joy that would bound out of a big box with a bow on top and skid around on shiny floors. After a barrage of plaintive yelping – our eardrums felt as though they were being cheese-grated – we told a rather fraught-looking woman that we needed to think about it, Alex repeating, as everyone blinked in the dazzling July sunlight, that a puppy wasn't just for Christmas.

It turns out that a puppy might not be for any other time of the year either, if next door's dog is anything to go by. They suggested we looked after it for a day to get a feel for what it would be like, then handed us a matted grey yappy nightmare and announced it was called Jess (which I'm choosing to be flattered about, rather than obsessing over which of its bewilderingly hideous deformities had prompted them to think of me).

'She' did nothing but sit in the corner and bark until I took her grudgingly to the park whereupon, knowing full well I was walking her out of duty not devotion, she set about depositing a runny brown number under the 'No Fouling' sign. I was all ready to disclaim it, like pretending it isn't you when the whole room goes, 'Yuk, who's farted?' but a patrolling do-gooder had clocked us, thus challenging me to fashion a pooper-scooper out of a Walker's *crisp packet and a twig in the manner of an ingenious* Blue Peter *Mother's Day gift. Just as I was in the process of catapulting a lumpy bit into the open goal, a sexy 'All right there?' made me jump and sent the lump pinging into my trouser leg, while the owner of the voice – an extremely attractive Levi-clad backside – sprinted off down the hill, black Labrador in hot pursuit.*

I dumped the crisp packet in a bin marked NO DOG DO, *wondering what Walker's would say were I to inform them how much more fitting their slogan 'New Taste, New Texture' had become, and went in search of a lost Jess, whom I found three minutes later mounting the black Lab in a way that, alarmingly, epitomised my lust for its owner. (Why do dogs do this? They lick you into thinking they're your cute and cuddly best friend and the minute they've got you shovelling shit – wham – they're off doing their humiliate-a-human routine. However, I think she learned the lesson that no matter how PC the New Millennium claims to be, a girl is still a slapper if she tries to shag a man.)*

And while I'm on the subject of slappers and, indeed, mutts that are supposed to be your best friend, have you heard from Lou? I'm still not talking to her because of Andy, which I realise may sound like the kind of thing you do aged fourteen after too much strawberry Hooch, but it is now no longer simply your best friend kissing cute Marty from double geography under the pool table, but your best friend poaching someone with whom you had planned three kids, twice-yearly holidays, and what kind of toothbrush-holder to have in the upstairs bathroom.

I say 'poached' and obviously there is something fishy going on between them, but I was experiencing such a gamut of knife-stabbingly painful sensations when I first found out that before I had time to twist the blade and discover all the vile details, we were slamming doors and gesticulating things that would not have earned us a Friends of the Deaf badge had we still been Brownies. And now, instead of being mature, calling a truce and wishing them every happiness for their future together, I am marooned in mute hell with only my imagination for company – always a hideous prospect where bad news is concerned – as I try to convince myself I never really wanted Andy anyway.

Certainly, it's going well so far. At the end of the day, what is the appeal of someone who's going to drop their trousers the minute they're in the vicinity of an attractive female, when you could have someone whose only trouser-dropping antics happen with the Sunday Times *and the toilet bowl? The minute I walked in and saw Alex's anxious little face break into a gigantic smile of the sort more commonly seen on Colgate adverts, I knew I'd done the right thing. It was just so nice and reassuring to be back with him in our safe little haven of familiarity – like when you're reading the accompanying manual to an electrical gadget and all you can find is gobbledegook instructions in Swahili and Russian then suddenly you spot the English version and it all becomes joyously clear – except, of course, if it's the video instructions where it is all just Chinese physics.*

I must say, though, a large reason I went back to Alex was because I'd fallen out with Lou, which, given that I'd gone to hers because I'd fallen out with him, makes me slightly anxious as to what the next permutation might be. Tent in the garden while Lou and Alex fall in love? Reconciliatory threesome in the goldfish bowl? Sod the lot of them and run off to Thailand with a puppy?

One thing's for sure: it will in no way involve Andy. I've come to realise, in a mature problem-page-solving way, that I was seeing him as if I was peering in through the sitting-room window of a mansion in Chelsea where everything is vases of lilies and trendy chrome lights. All seems *perfect but there is no guarantee that the rest of the house will be so too. There may be something dodgy going on with floral curtains in the bedroom – or, as would appear to be the case,* behind *dodgy floral curtains in the bedroom – only you're not going to find out unless you go in and look. Since Lou has flouted all the codes of friendship and gone in for me, I suspect I've been spared the horror of a lot more than just some unappealing furnishings.*

Anyway, I don't know why I'm boring on about Andy when what is important is lovely Alex. We've been having a wonderful time together: whenever I'm feeling even slightly in need of attention I just mention Leonie and immediately he becomes this apologetic sheep thing, bleating all sorts of protestations of love and wanting to rush out and buy up all the flowers in Covent Garden.

What is somewhat ironic about this admittedly blatant act of emotional blackmail on my part is that it seems the person I should really be jealous of is not Leonie but Alex's friend Dave. They appear to have spent the duration of his and my time apart having a hilarious time together, so much so that whenever Alex tells me a story about him – this is becoming frighteningly frequent and tedious – he does this infuriating chuckling thing, which not only prolongs the already unfunny anecdote but implies that he could have nowhere near as much fun with me.

It's got to the point where he's incapable of mentioning Dave's name without grinning and looking besottedly into the distance as if they were, well, lovers. While I'm happy that he's found such a good 'friend', I can't help feeling I'm some kind of poor substitute dragged on to the pitch because Beckham's injured his ankle. And although I endeavour to show interest in a tiresomely detailed account of a transfer, it's clear that I'm not making the right noises in the right places – like when a kid tries out the latest school joke on its younger sibling and the whole thing falls flat because they don't yet know what cunnilingus means.

A tiny part of me – and after the comfort eating I did at Lou's this part is no longer, alas, my bottom – thinks that if Alex and I were really right for each other I would find his every utterance fascinating and he would not find everything related to Dave fascinating.

I can't decide whether this is something I'm entitled to be pissed off about. It's like going into a restaurant with a bloke and both of you ordering the chicken. You start eating yours and notice it tastes a bit funny but don't know whether it's because you've

imagined it tastes funny/it's supposed *to taste funny/you're only
used to eating Chicken McNuggets and not posh Coq au Citron.
Then the bloke takes one mouthful, spits it out on the plate in
disgust and demands to see the manager. Suddenly you realise
that it's not unreasonable to complain about something that will
give you diarrhoea, salmonella and possibly a mutant version of
BSE.*

*Obviously, I don't always need others' confirmation to tell me
what's acceptable – for instance, I am perfectly capable (on most
mornings, at least) of choosing something to wear without having
to check with someone else whether it suits me. But when it comes
to relationships my brain is as much use as a goat's. For example:*

Abysmal relationship with ex-boyfriend, James

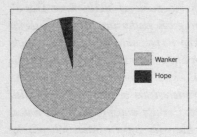

Brain blocks out 96 per cent of wanker activity and clings on to the hope that 4 per cent of ability to behave like a normal decent human being might grow over time.

Amazing relationship with current boyfriend, Alex

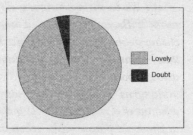

Brain takes for granted 96 per cent of lovely-person activity and obsesses that 4 per cent of doubt about the relationship might never go away.

*Of course, none of this is made any easier when I'm feeling
perpetually conscious of every chink in my relationship armour and
all other couples seem to be swanking about in shiny seamless suits*

looking as though they've never had to pick up a sword, let alone been in battle. As much as I tell myself that there's no knowing what kind of nasty sweaty stuff might be lurking under their shields, it doesn't stop me drawing unfavourable comparisons between how I feel behind my shield, i.e. vulnerable, unsure, insecure, and the rest of the 387 negative emotions in the dictionary, and how they appear on the outside of theirs, i.e. perfect. I know this is pointless, like putting the mangled entrails of a pig side by side with a cuddly toy Babe then asking everyone which is cuter, but when you find yourself in the midst of a circle of contented couples it's hard not to see Anne Robinson's bespectacled face scowling down at you, snapping, 'You are the weakest link. Goodbye.'

Fortunately, Anne had been replaced by Chris Tarrant for the night of Jo's engagement party, meaning that while the surroundings were still as intimidating, we had three lifelines: fifty-fifty gin to tonic, ask the hosts for Class A drugs and, if all else fails, phone a taxi. We were doing quite well for a while, with Alex winning all sorts of Brownie points – rather than, unfortunately, £250,000 cheques – being charming and knowledgeable and making people laugh. But then he got a question on women's lingerie and lost the whole bloody lot.

It turns out that on Monday night he'd been in the pub with some workmates and they'd got on to the subject of Ann Summers and whether anyone had bought anything there. Alex owned up to the red lacy underwear and everyone had thought him really cool until he also owned up to thinking a studded dog collar was a suspender belt, and spent the rest of the evening getting slagged off.

The minute he'd finished telling this story I went into a very black mood indeed. Not because of the underwear but because Alex hadn't told me he'd been out with work friends on Monday night. I realise this may sound a trifle petty, but I can't stand the idea that there is even a fraction of his life I do not know about. It's at times like this that I feel he is not my boyfriend but a Boeing 747 whose route I'm supposed to be navigating from a tall air-traffic-control building: not being able to track him on my radar screen at any moment of day or night immediately suggests he is cruising perilously close to other aircraft – like, for example, a Leonie 747.

I'd feel marginally less of a freakoid about this if he showed the same obsession with the intricacies of my day. But he seems quite content with getting the join-the-dot version and filling it in for himself, unable to see why I require the full-blown illustrated encyclopedia. He says that the only reason he doesn't tell me things is because I wouldn't find them interesting, but that is not the point. I want to know all information available to me, not have it preselected by someone else, like fruit and veg from Tesco's home-delivery service.

Anyway, he promised resolutely to go through every microscopic detail of his day (which I should imagine, judging from yesterday's head-eatingly tedious private client story, will shortly kill all inquisitive cells in my body) and assured me he keeps nothing from me. I know this is true and . . . hold on, just got to get the phone . . .

Bollocking, bollocking FUCK. Alex is a lying, deceitful wank – oh, God, I simply cannot cope. Why is it that just when you think life is coming together, and you're not going to end up alone and miserable eating Be Good To Yourself apricot yoghurts, it all falls apart like a home-made Christmas card whose glittery angel keeps coming unstuck from the green felt tree?

It was Alex's mum on the phone enquiring, despite it being the height of summer, whether I could locate Alex's salopettes. This was a request on a par with going into Waterstones and asking the sales assistant where the latest Harry Potter novel is. After promising to call her back with the size, make and – given that she is related to Alex – bar code, I went upstairs to wardrobe W2, right-hand shelving unit, third up, where, neatly filed under 'Sportswear', I located Alex's salopettes. Unfortunately, however, I also happened to locate something else which not only broke all filing regulations but most of my heart: a crumpled and much 'read' porn mag.

I couldn't believe it. I just stood there, stunned, caught between *feelings of sheer repulsion and an unsettling desire to have a look. Knowing that porn is staring down at you from a newsagent's top shelf is something you can choose to ignore; discovering it on your boyfriend's sportswear shelf is something you'd never choose and certainly cannot ignore. I brought it down and held it in the palm of my hand trying desperately to convince myself it might just be a particularly raunchy ski brochure, while all the time fighting off vile and disturbing images of what exactly Alex's hand had last been doing with it. Then, just as I'd plucked up courage to turn to the page that it seemed to want to turn automatically, I heard Alex's key in the door. Panicked, I ran through my options:*

(a) *Put it into his alphabetised 'Light Bedside Reading' pile and wait for him to discover it.*

(b) *Hide it somewhere then confront him with it later, e.g. at dinner with his parents.*

(c) *Tell him I bought it and watch his reaction.*

In the event I ended up doing (d) putting it back exactly where it was and staring at him as though I'd just discovered he was a girl. If only. Somehow the idea of him turning out to be female seems easier to cope with than the idea of him turned on *by lots of females – or whatever Debbie's freakily pubeless pubic area entitles her to be. (No wonder women feel inadequate when men choose to fantasise about a twelve-year-old with blow-up tits coated in yoghurt.)*

Oh, God, this is simply horrific. Finding porn in your boyfriend's wardrobe is vile: when your boyfriend is sensible pinstriped pyjama-wearing Alex it is the repulsive and traumatic equivalent of imagining your parents having sex. Alex reads the law pages of The Times *and the instruction manual to the storage heater. He does not 'read' Big'n'Busty. Oh, misery. What the hell am I going to do? I'm scared if I confront him he'll give me the all-men-have-porn line, which, as well as being a deeply revolting statistic in its own right, misses the point that one wants one's boyfriend to be different from 'all men' – except, of course, when the shower has* to be fixed. Or you need help with a heavy box. And if the car's making a funny noise.

I could try the Germaine Greer I-find-it-offensive-to-women line, which, although true, is a bit like saying you're outraged by the injustices of the budget increases when really what you mean is you're pissed off that you personally are going to have to pay more for booze. Maybe I could . . . oh, sod it – why should I be the one worrying when it is he who has the criminal, degrading material stashed guiltily in his salopettes? Yuk. He deserves to be shouted at. Bastard! I'm going to give him a bollocking.

Hope you're living in porn-free peace.

Jess

xxx

PS Germaine wouldn't give bollockings, though. And she is always very effective. I've decided – I'm to approach it like Germaine, in a subtle, mature and intelligent manner.

Indecent Proposal

'Do you use porn?'

Alex remained suspiciously silent at the other end of the phone.

'*Do* you use porn?' Jess shouted, uncaring that the rest of the office were pretending not to listen by typing with their heads in their chests.

'Oh, crikey,' Alex said, chuckling, 'don't tell me Michael's got you performing pornography on national telev—'

'Michael hasn't got me doing anything,' she snapped, prompting Chyani to look pointedly at Jess's bulging in-tray and raise her eyebrows very high. 'I want to know if you use porn.'

'And you can guarantee that I will not be hauled into the studio and made to answer this question while a naked lady does something unconventional with a champagne—'

'This is *nothing* to do with my work,' she snarled, immediately deducing from the fact that everyone else in the office was raising their eyebrows that this reply was tantamount to sitting under a bright neon light flashing, 'ALERT: Employee on a Personal Call'.

'Well,' Alex sighed, sounding slightly disappointed not to be making his television début as a porn king, 'in that case I suggest you go and do something that *is* to do with your work and let me get on with proofreading this case file.' He had the knack of making his job sound the fascinating and stimulating equal of standing on Oxford Street holding a large pole attached to a sign saying, 'Golf Sale'.

'It's a simple yes or no,' Jess persisted.

'Nothing is ever a simple yes or no, Jess,' Alex replied, in full pedantic lawyer mode.

'So that's a yes, then.'

'Yes, you are asking a totally inappropriate question at eleven thirty in the morning, and no, I am not going to talk about it now.'

Jess waited patiently, knowing that the best way to get him to talk about it now was not to say anything at all.

'All right,' he said, finally and begrudgingly. 'Yes, I sometimes look at pictures.'

Jess froze, mouth agape. The idea had been for him to deny it, her to confront him with the evidence, him to feel doubly guilty for being a liar as well as a pervert, and her to spend the next year and a half giving him a hard time – the different sort of hard time he'd got from *Big 'n' Busty*. He was not supposed to own up and use the word 'pictures' as if he'd merely enjoyed the occasional trip to the Tate Modern. 'What d'you mean *pictures?*' she spat.

'Oh, you know, just stuff,' Alex replied, evasively.

She knew exactly what stuff. 'No. What?'

'Just stuff, Jess.'

'What stuff?' And then, as if she'd just thought of it, 'Magazines?'

There was an ominous silence. She was intrigued to hear how he would describe his sordid hobby, wondering whether he would opt for the it's-just-tits-and-butts-and-doesn't-mean-anything route or try to make it sound a bit more classy by alluding . . .

'No.'

Jess flinched. 'No what?'

'No, not magazines.'

This was not just a sordid hobby: it was his vocation.

'Well? What, then?' she snapped, as Alex metamorphosed into something found lurking in a trenchcoat outside shops with black windows.

'What then, what? Jesus, Jess, what is this?'

'If you don't look at magazines, how come you sometimes look at pictures?'

'Oh, for God's sake, this is getting ridiculous. I'm at work. We'll talk about this later.'

Panicked that she wasn't going to unearth the truth – in all its deformity – she decided to try a different approach. 'Look, you don't need to worry,' she soothed. 'I'm not going to go all mad or anything. I'd just rather know, that's all. Now,' she continued, still calmly, 'what pictures?'

Alex gave a long sigh. 'Just stuff from the Internet.'

'Naked stuff?'

'Well,' he said, chortling in the horrid, gravelly manner of a pervert, 'obviously.'

Jess let out a furious yelp. 'Wanker!' she shrieked, stating the obvious, and threw down the phone.

'It's a sexual thing, babes,' Jo pointed out astutely several minutes later.

Having sent herself mad conjuring up lurid images of Alex slavering over computer-enhanced nipples, saliva dribbling down his chin, Jess was keen to hear a more positive take on the situation.

'You're pissed off because he can just as easily get off on two tits on a monitor as he can on you. More easily, probably,' she added, never one to stint on honesty.

'And d'you think it's the same with all blokes?' Jess asked, falteringly.

'Totally, babes, yeah.'

'Mark?'

Jo paused. 'No, well . . . Mark doesn't use porn.'

Jess paused. 'Mark doesn't use porn.'

'No.'

'But you've just said it's the same with all blokes.'

'Yeah, well, blokes generally. But Mark's different.'

For someone who rejoiced in dispensing hurtful home truths, Jo was in remarkable denial of her own.

'Is Mark a girl, then?'

'I just know he doesn't use porn. So,' she said, in a breezy subject-changer voice, 'what are you going to do?'

'I don't know,' Jess replied, inserting her finger in and out of the spirally phone cord in a way that left no interpretation problems for the pupil of psychoanalysis. 'It's not so much the fact that he does it I object to,' she lied, 'it's the secrecy – like he knows it's wrong.'

'Yeah, I get what you're saying, babes, but you've got to remember, he is a *bloke*. It's just simple formulas with them: a tit, a buttock – can you tell them I'll call back? – a strand of blonde hair. They're not like us, babes. We need sophistication, a personality, a sense of soul – the whole package.' Then she added, laughing, 'They just haven't evolved yet, that's all.'

Jess liked Jo's theory. It certainly explained why Alex was no less of a sleazoid than the rest of the male population. One thing troubled her, though: if women were looking for something more, something refined, something sensitive and deep, why, then, were the majority of them seeking it in men?

'What are you doing, Jess?' Echo-like, as if her *alter ego* could speak, a voice struck up behind her.

'What are we all doing?' she replied rhetorically, staring mesmerised at her computer as little windows whizzed through the darkness towards her like *Play School* on speed.

'*We* are all doing some work.'

She jolted back into consciousness, then let out a high-pitched squawk: her ego had altered – into Michael.

'What, Jess, are *you* doing?'

'Um . . . work,' she replied limply, then hit the mouse, at which point the flying windows were replaced with her email file and the subject header, 'Wank Off!'

'Really,' he said, glowering down at her, arms folded with the self-importance of a traffic warden who was not about to fall for the I-was-just-leaving line. 'What work?'

'Um . . . well, I'm . . . you see, what I'm . . . well, obviously, I'm researching.'

'Goodness me. A researcher who's researching. Fabulous news. What are you researching?'

She couldn't tell whether he was taking an interest or the piss. 'We-ell,' she began, frantically closing down the inbox file then finding herself with a blank screen and a blank mind, 'porn.'

His face broke into a frothy grin. 'Researching porn, eh? Must remember that one next time the wife catches me, hrumph,' he grunted, rearranging his trousers. 'Was this "porn research" for the Guess the Granny slot, or Tuesday's Food for Thought?'

'Actually,' Jess said, sensing she was not just sailing close to the wind but heading into a potential gale force nine, 'it was something Shan-yah asked me to do.'

Chyani, who'd been doing smug things with bits of paper, looked as though she'd swallowed the stapler. 'I . . . excuse me—'

'And?' Michael persisted.

'And . . . it's . . . it's an item on . . . on how women feel about doing porn.'

There was a prolonged silence as Michael did a series of slow blinks and Jess stared blankly, feeling as though she'd just tried to say something in German to a native and couldn't tell whether their lack of reply was because they hadn't understood her or because she'd just insulted their family.

'Fantastic,' he roared. 'Absolutely fan-bloody-tastic.'

Jess flashed a self-satisfied grin at a bemused Chyani.

'Jess's boss ain't just a pretty face, is she?' he said, guffawing over to Chyani and ruffling her hair as if she were a dog. Jess stared, incredulous. 'Come on, what are you waiting for? Chop-chop,' he ordered, plunging his hands into his pockets and fiddling frenetically with something Jess hoped was just his keys. 'We're going to lead with this tomorrow!' he shouted, then disappeared into his office.

Tomorrow

Jess hovered excitedly in the viewing gallery as the programme was counted down. Having complained for months that she was never given anything meaty to research, she felt a swelling sense of pride that her very own item, albeit somewhat hastily conceived and assembled, was about to lead the show. 'Women Pour Scorn on Porn' would become known as a seminal piece of television journalism, she would become known as the best friend of Germaine Greer, and Alex would become known as the boyfriend who was so overcome with guilt at his wanton enjoyment of something so degrading to women that he almost drowned himself in the Thames, then dedicated the rest of his life to the cause of feminism while still . . .

'Good morning and welcome to *Carpe Diem*, the show where we don't just seize the day but bring it right into your homes.'

Jess catapulted back to reality as the presenter beamed a panty-liner-commercial smile into Camera One.

'Acrobatic dogs, grow your own banana tree and a psychic policeman who claims he can predict a crime *before* it happens are just a few of the treats we've got in store for you this morning, but first,' she cooed calmly – as Michael flew around shouting, 'Where the fuck are you, Camera Three? Get yer fucking arse' – 'have you ever caught your partner with pornography and wondered what it might be like for the poor woman forced to relinquish all dignity to expose herself for the sheer *tit*-illation of men?'

Jess felt the corners of her mouth curl into an involuntary smile. They were *her* words being spoken on national television.

'Today we are lucky enough to have one of those women

here to tell us just how humiliating and derogatory her work as a porn model is – Chantelle.'

Jess's jaw dropped as camera three spun round to reveal not some orange mass of heaving silicone licking provocatively at a Mr Whippy, but something that bore an uncanny resemblance to Cherie Blair. She was wearing a navy suit and a neckerchief.

'Hiya,' Chantelle chirped, in incongruous Essex accent. It was remarkable, Jess thought, how easy it was to create a picture of a person from a voice at the end of a telephone and how tragically removed that image invariably was from the, in this case, deeply inappropriate reality.

'Tell us, Chantelle,' the presenter continued, 'how do you feel about being a porn model?'

Chantelle beamed into the wrong camera. 'I really, really like it, you know. It gives me, like, you know, lots of self-insurance.'

Jess felt the entire viewing gallery implode with horror. Michael, to *her* horror, exploded: 'Who the fuck booked this moron?'

Jess tried to scuttle out of sight behind a monitor. 'She *seemed* all right when I—'

'A researcher checks, then checks again,' Chyani butted in haughtily.

'Get 'er off, get 'er off!' Michael yelled, as the vision mixer frantically stabbed at buttons and dials and the presenter made lame attempts to emulate the tenacity of Jeremy Paxman.

'But you find the whole concept of pornography very demeaning.'

'No, no,' Chantelle continued, happily, 'I don't know about them other models and stuff but for me, like, porn has a lot of meaning.'

'Cutting straight to phone-in, straight to fucking phone-in,' Michael bellowed, as the presenter nodded in a distracted manner at an auto-gibbering Chantelle.

'. . . I'd envise more women to do it, cos, you know, men need to be, you know, stimulated and stuff and it's flatterin' to know, like, you know, you're giving them a stiffy—'

'*Aaand* that's all we've got time for just now,' the presenter swooped in, 'but if you'd like to share your views on women and the pornography industry, then join us after the break for our phone-in: "Scorn on Porn". Seize the day!'

While the rest of the nation sat back and watched mouthwash being poured on to a sanitary towel, the studios of *Carpe Diem* were not so much seizing the day as seizing.

'Mother of all . . . Bollocking blazes . . . Off, off, get her fucking off!'

Michael was yelling, rolls of film were whirring backwards, phones were ringing, screens were showing eight different shots of an empty chair, lights were flashing, smoke was puffing and men with beards were saying, 'Schedule,' a lot.

'Can I do anything?' Jess finally plucked up courage to squeak.

Michael threw her a look from Eminem's chainsaw-wielding repertoire. 'Evidently not.'

'I've got a chap on line three who says his wife's a porn model and loathes it,' Chyani cut in, cradling the phone to her ear as if it were her and Michael's first-born. 'Shall I—'

'Yes-*yes*-YES!' Michael crescendoed excitedly, jiggling up and down in a manner that suggested Chyani hadn't just relieved a flagging programme. 'My little beauty, line him up, line him up.' Chyani put her hand on her chest and looked around the gallery, eyelashes fluttering in mock astonishment, as if she'd just been awarded an Oscar and was about to deliver her acceptance speech.

'On air in sixty,' a voice boomed, as Jess watched a large clock count down her fate. She had not so much shot herself in the foot as blown off both her legs. Chyani – Myra Hindley disguised as Florence Nightingale – was now stitching them back on.

'Don't worry, Jenny,' Michael hollered into the presenter's earpiece. 'Shan-yah's saved the day. Got us some callers who'll actually talk some sense,' he said, looking pointedly at Jess.

'Thirty seconds, standing by . . .'

'Leading with Casper from Birmingham,' Chyani announced, as the presenter nodded her appreciation into a camera that seemed to have focused *its* appreciation on something nearer her hemline.

'And welcome back to *Carpe Diem*, the show where we don't just seize the day, but—'

'Fuck it up,' Michael muttered.

The plastic-smiling presenter battled on: '. . . Casper from Birmingham.'

'Hi,' a deep voice announced.

Chyani sat back, arms folded in self-congratulation, as if she'd just single-handedly solved the Middle East crisis.

'Now, Casper, you say your wife is a pornography model.'

'That's right.'

Jess froze in unparalleled horror. It wasn't Casper from Birmingham. It was Alex from London. And it was the last straw.

'And finds it degrading and demeaning,' the presenter told him rather than asked.

'Absolutely,' 'Casper' exclaimed, as Michael flashed a grin and a wink at Chyani, 'not!' He gave a little laugh. 'She loves it, finds it exceptionally fulfilling.'

Very slowly, with expressions of car-crash witnesses, everyone in the viewing gallery turned round and stared at Chyani. Chyani looked like she was going to cry, Michael looked like he was going to make her cry and Jess looked at them both and, unable to stop the beginnings of a revengeful smile, announced, haughtily, 'A researcher checks, then checks again.'

*

'. . . and the minute whatever-her-name-was – Chantelle? – opened her mouth I knew Michael would be shouting at you so I phoned up to check you were OK.'

Jess watched as Alex patiently gave way to a stream of cars trying to turn out of a side-road. You could tell a lot about a bloke by the way he drove, she decided. If cars were really a penis extension, Alex didn't shaft his fellow drivers, he made love to them.

'But I got Shan-yah instead. She sounded so smug and pleased with herself that I wanted to get back at her for you.' He reached over and gave her thigh a reassuring squeeze. 'Silly cow.'

Jess smiled across at him and thought, for the first time in a while, that she might really be in love with him. It was a relieving thought, as though she'd gone into the supermarket and actually wanted to buy the broccoli, not just because it was good for her and she felt she ought to. But then an unsettling suspicion struck: surely you *felt* love rather than thought it.

'Her, not you.'

Jess stared ahead blankly.

'Shan-yah,' Alex said, mistaking her distraction for confusion. 'She's the silly cow, you're just the slightly dozy one.'

Suddenly, Jess snapped back into consciousness. 'Wait a minute, I'm still pissed off with you over the porn,' she said, thumping him on the shoulder.

'Help,' Alex shouted out the window. 'Porn rage!'

'Don't think you can make it up to me by framing Shan-yah and collecting me from work,' she said, intent on getting maximum argumentative mileage out of his smut-fuelled tank.

'Damn,' he joked, hitting the steering-wheel. 'She's found me out.'

'More than you know,' she said, in the foreboding tones of a Bond girl about to put up an unfeasibly close fight with Sean Connery. This, she decided, was her moment to attack.

'If you're referring to that porn mag in the wardrobe,' Alex said, calmly, 'Dave bought it for me.'

Jess blinked in disbelief. Him owning up was something she hadn't expected. Him owning up to *not* owning it was something she'd done when she was ten. 'I suppose Dave told you to say that,' she said, sourly.

'Ask him yourself. It was just a gag.' He smiled, in fond recollection of the hilarity. 'He was trying to perk me up after you walked out.'

'And did Debbie's besiliconed thirty-eight double-D yoghurt-smeared photographically manipulated image "perk" you up?'

'Of course it didn't,' he soothed. 'If anything it made me feel more alone.'

'I thought that was the whole point of porn mags – you "feel" yourself alone.'

Alex chose not to rise to it. 'I just wanted you back. And no amount of double-D Debbies was going to achieve that.' He turned and smiled and Jess fell back into the love-thought groove again.

Half an hour later, she was no closer to understanding her fluctuating feelings than they were to getting home. 'I know I'm crap at directions but surely we should be going east not west.'

'You're right,' he said, as she smiled smugly. 'You are crap at directions.'

'But Putney's the other way.'

'Oh, bollocks, is it?' Alex said, throwing his palm to his forehead. 'Never mind, maybe we'll get to it this way.' He was grinning.

Jess glanced up at the signpost. 'Alex. The sign says Heathrow.'

'Thanks,' he replied, following it. 'Can't see shit without my glasses.'

'Alex!' she squealed, with mounting intrigue. 'Where are we going?'

'You told me Heathrow,' he said, still grinning, then signalled into the lane for Terminal Four.

Jess studied his face excitedly for clues, as little seeds of hope shot up in her with the speed of a time-release film into fully developed images of Caribbean beaches and palm-fringed hotel verandas. It was the kind of thing that happened in films – except that the heroine would only twig what was going on once she'd boarded the plane, and wouldn't have to spend the previous hour faking moronic naïvety while wondering whether the airport shops sold hairdryers and hoping Alex had packed the right bikini.

'You coming?' Alex had parked in the long-stay car park and was holding the car door open for her.

'Where?' she asked, giggling.

'I dunno. Told you, don't have my glasses.' He took her hand, pulled her up, then led her towards the terminal building.

As they approached the exit, Jess realised they'd forgotten the luggage. 'What about the . . .' she remembered she wasn't supposed to have guessed that they were going away yet '. . . the parking ticket?' she added, lamely.

Alex didn't seem to have heard her. He was striding purposefully towards Departures. She trotted behind him, scanning for possible places their bags might be hidden, like an eager dog being taken for a walk and casing out all the interesting wee smells on the way.

Then, without any warning, Alex disappeared through the Arrivals door.

'Gosh. What are we doing here?' Jess said, as if he'd just escorted her to the men's urinals. And then disappointment hit: they weren't going to the Caribbean, they weren't going on a plane, they weren't even going to the men's urinals. They were waiting for someone else.

This was typical of their relationship, she thought, as she followed Alex into the throng of arriving passengers: it was nice and fun but just never quite took off – in this case, literally.

'You ask too many questions,' Alex said, removing his jacket. He was still grinning. Maybe this was all part of his elaborate plan – make her *think* they were waiting for someone then, just when she'd given up all hope, whisking her next door and on to a plane to – 'Now it's my turn,' he said, as someone knocked his jacket to the floor. He bent down to pick it up. She used the chance to glance sneakily up at the departures board. A rather tantalising flight to Thailand was leaving in under an hour. Maybe he'd done something clever with a phone check-in. But didn't you need jabs for . . . ?

Suddenly she was aware of a fat woman pointing at her. Was this who they were waiting for? Had they come all the way out here to meet one of Alex's aged aunts? She felt her mouth tighten into a polite smile.

'Oww *Gaaad*,' the woman exclaimed. Oww *Gaaad* indeed, Jess thought – not only an aged aunt, an American one. 'Isn't that just adorable?' She was still pointing and grabbing the arm of something swamped by a sombrero.

Jess turned to Alex for an explanation.

'Jess,' he said, looking up from bended knee. 'Will you marry me?'

Otherwise Engaged

To: *Claire.Voyant@hotmail.com*
Date: *Thursday 24 August*
Subject: *Otherwise Engaged*

Engaged. Not in the manner of a telephone –
although we do both have the optional ring-
back feature. But in a way that means you
can't stop grinning at your left hand.

Dear Claire,
   I am in a state I can only describe as engagement euphoria. In
fact, I'm on such a high I'm beginning to wonder whether it
mightn't be substance-generated and I will find myself, believing I
am a pigeon, having to be talked down from the roof of a tall
building.
   I certainly have my head in the clouds at the moment. Lots of
fluffy number nine ones. It was just so incredible. He took me to
the Arrivals lounge at Heathrow to the exact spot we'd met when
he came back from China because that was where he said he first
knew he was in love with me. And then he just said it: 'Will you
marry me?' Like they do in films or you say as a joke – oh, Christ,
hideous clunk of paranoia: what if it was a joke? What if he was
just pissing about and I took it seriously and said yes and now he
feels he has to go through with it for fear of me boiling his head
and, right at this minute, is devising a complicated legal get-out
clause with Dave while I obsess over what font we should use for
the engagement party invites? No – relief – paranoia averted.
Suddenly remembered that Alex is stingy and would not fork out
three grand for a joke, even if the 'joke' did involve the oh-so-
hilarious comedic powers of Dave.

I really must calm down and stop thinking anything good that happens to me is only a precursor for myriad shit things. I have joined the élite of the engaged, where life glides serenely towards matching cut-glass champagne flutes from John Lewis and a genuine interest in ironing-board covers. Although not quite at the stage of prefixing all sentences with 'we', I have certainly stopped picking our relationship to bits as if it is a pluke not yet ripe for the squeeze. And I now know that the reason little doubts about Alex kept popping into my head before was not because there was anything wrong with the relationship but because it was a bit directionless – like when you're sitting on a Virgin train and it grinds to a halt and doesn't move for ages and no one tells you what's happening, so you get pissed off and assume there's something wrong with the train when actually the train itself is perfectly OK, it's just the signalling that's buggered. But now we've got the green light – or, strictly speaking, frighteningly expensive emerald from Tiffany's – and it's all systems go.

You'd be amazed how much there is to do once the question's been popped:

- *lengthy phone calls to friends detailing every word, thought, sentiment, and romantic value of the proposal*
- *lengthy phone calls to friends detailing every word, thought, sentiment, and financial value of the ring*
- *laborious moisturising and nail-painting so that left hand is in the most desirable state for 'ring-viewing' sessions*
- *remembering to do everything ostentatiously with left hand for those who have failed to notice/forgotten to notice/ strangers*
- *remembering to say fiancé a lot*
- *waking up in a paranoid frenzy that the ring has jumped down the plug-hole*
- *remembering to remove the ring when washing up (though not, obviously, leaving it near plug-hole)/having a shower/ tying a shoelace/walking in a dodgy area of*

*London/cooking/sleeping/working/eating/sweating, while
promising yourself that you won't just keep it for special
occasions in the manner of my grandad who spent all his
savings on an expensive suit, never felt an event quite
merited getting it out of the wardrobe and ended up
wearing it for the first time at his funeral.*

I can't help feeling slightly guilty about the whole thing, though.
It's not actually stated or anything, but it's obvious that getting
married is basically a race – like swimming across a river. It's all
very well for me, waving and shouting for joy, dry, happy and about
to crack open the champagne and smoked-salmon-filled picnic
hamper, but I can hardly expect the other swimmers to do the same
when they're still battling against all sorts of unpredictable currents
with no certainty that they're ever going to make it to the other
side.

I must say, however, they were all very magnanimous and
sounded genuinely happy for me – even my single friends who, let's
face it, have yet to put on their swimsuits. The only person whose
congratulation sounded as if it coincided with the raising of their
middle finger was Abbey from home who has now been going out
with Neil for six and a half years without even the merest glimmer
of the M-word. Telling her I'd got engaged felt a bit like being the
unsuspecting friend of a wannabe model who only accompanies
her to the casting session for moral support then ends up getting
selected instead. The idea that if you really want something in life,
you get it, appears to be total bollocks: it's if you're not particularly fussed either way that it seems to happen.

I was especially dreading phoning Lou because (1) we hadn't
spoken since the Andy thing, and (2) I'd only ever been negative
about Alex. But she was great and lovely and we exchanged a
string of escalating apologies: 'No, I was the one at fault.', 'No, I
shan't hear of it, it was me.', 'Curse me down, I am evil . . .', etc.,
which was nice and relieving and the equivalent of post-argument
sex with a boyfriend. She said that if I was happy, she was happy,

then listened patiently as I gushed about Alex and explained that the only reason I'd concentrated on the bad things about him in the past was because I had needed her advice – because, let's face it, you don't go to the doctor when you're well!

But when we eventually got round to talking about her I felt as if I'd not just done the jolly picnic-hamper-waving thing, but peed in the water on my way across. It turns out that she was not going out with Andy but merely thought she was, based on a heavily over-analysed snog and a phone call where he'd told her things with her felt 'different'. Naturally, she'd built the rest of their life on this, and waited in vain for his next call. Perplexed, but believing he was just playing 'the game', she'd refrained from phoning him, instead torturing herself with ever-unlikelier interpretations as to why he hadn't phoned her. Unfortunately, the whole trauma culminated in the frantic assumption that he'd been run over and a panicked late-night call during which he informed her that he was perfectly well and happy and car-accident free, and back together with Sarah.

Poor Lou. She sounds miserable. I'm going to try to set her up with someone nice at our engagement party as a way of – oh, gosh, without knowing it I've already turned into a smug couple-person whose romantic life is so complete they feel equipped to sort out those whose isn't. Which reminds me, I must check whether we're inviting single people and whether twenty-five helium-filled heart-shaped balloons will be enough. Also, do you think people will want a finger buffet or actuallllllllllllll I love Jess verry muck and she is going to be my wif – sorry, that was my fiancé. I think he's a bit pissed. Apparently I've got to stop writing to you and come and show his aunt my ring – do sincerely hope she means the one on my finger. Being engaged isn't all roses, you know – it's endless champagne celebrations, tra-la-la-la-la-la-la-la-la . . .

Oh, God. Apologies for that insane, unnaturally happy, over-confident version of me above. Think I thought I was Carol Smillie.

I'm sorry I haven't sent this yet – the ring-viewing turned into dinner, turned into frenzied phone-calls about goat's cheese canapés, turned into whether we had enough chairs, turned into my skirt looking weird, turned into arguments with Alex for not taking my skirt looking weird seriously, turned into sex, turned into engagement party (though not, obviously, gang-bang), turned into Sunday morning with a hideous hangover and desire to marry not Alex but the Nurofen packet.

Urgh. Can't get over how much this whole engagement thing is just like a funeral. You're so busy running around announcing the news, trying to get hold of ministers, having long chats with people you haven't spoken to for seven years, working out sandwich quantities, selecting the wine and scrabbling around attempting to turn Moulinex food mixers into vases as the house mutates into a florist's that the fact that there is a dead person at the centre of it all passes you by. Until, that is, the service is over and you're left with some rotting gerberas and depression.

Not that I'm depressed exactly. More just back in the horrible doubting den again. It's like the penultimate scene of a scary film where she's just killed the baddy and you're finally able to sit back in your seat and take your fist out of your mouth, then suddenly, even though he's been hit over the head with a ceramic vase, pushed down three flights of stairs, shot at and has a knife through his neck, he jolts back to life and grabs her round the throat. Only difference is that, with the film, you know she doesn't die because she was in last week's Heat *wearing a low-cut Versace dress, whereas with real life anything could happen – except, I suspect, the Versace dress.*

The particular throat-grabbing incident I'm referring to is our engagement party. Everything had been going swimmingly with me the centre of attention getting lots of presents, Alex saying 'very lucky' and 'beautiful' a lot, then Andy arrived. Alone. Felt my stomach turn into a huge magnet with one end furiously repelling any association with the bastard who had fucked up Lou, our friendship and very nearly my relationship, and the other end virtually wrenching itself out of my body to have contact with him. Before I'd decided which end I was going to obey, he came up to me, performed perfunctory air-kisses as though they were the prelude to a night of steamy love-making, took my hands in his and said, looking at me intently, 'Congratulations. I'm so happy for you.'

I realised then and there the horrific reality of my feelings. I did not want him to be happy for me. I did not want him to be pleased for me. I did not want him to be even mildly content for me. I wanted him to be torturously JEALOUS! And that, I figured, on the spectrum of emotions one should be feeling at one's engagement party was not normal. So I decided to block it out and ignore him, convincing myself that my feelings for him were based purely on the aesthetic. But then we ended up talking and getting on so well that by the time the evening was over I found myself about as confused as I did when I was faced with the Standard Grade Arithmetic paper and discovered I'd forgotten my calculator.

But this is not something that can be worked out simply with the pressing of a button – although, admittedly, Andy has the knack of pressing all the right ones – it is a deeper, more profound issue. We understand each other, we connect. And the fact that he chose to tell me at my engagement party that he has split up with Sarah because they don't understand each other and they don't connect was like ordering spag bol from the menu, then discovering – once the waiter has gone and the order been processed – I could have had fresh penne carbonara with oyster mushrooms, if I'd only checked the specials board.

And now I'm stuck in a horrible quagmire trying to talk myself out of feeling right things for Andy while simultaneously trying to talk myself into feeling right things for Alex – like having to do that unnatural co-ordination game where one hand is supposed to rub your stomach while the other pats your head.

Jo says I need to forget about Andy as he is bad news. She claims that the only reason I feel this 'clicking' thing is because he's like a mobile phone, i.e. he will work anywhere there is a signal. If he gets good reception from me there is every likelihood he gets good reception elsewhere – e.g. Lou, Sarah – but very shortly his battery will run down and the one time I need him most he won't work. She's probably right. After all, he does seem to go rather in and out of range with Sarah (and, from what he was insinuating, in and out in a more literal sense with Angie, his assistant). But it's hard not to see this as a fault with them, rather than a fault with him.

Lou swears categorically that he is a bastard and that the very function of a bastard is to make whichever female they happen to be talking to at the time feel as if there is some magical, unexplainable force at play, uniting them in a special bond. The trouble comes when the female fixates on this special bond, the bastard goes off and forges many more special bonds, and then they come together and all hell breaks loose because each has been under a different impression of what was going on.

I can't help feeling that, although Alex is a far cry from the bastard, similarly opposed thought processes are happening in our relationship. There's me, riddled with doubt and focused on all the negative, and then there's Alex, blissfully content and oblivious to the fact that anything's wrong. It seems bizarre indeed to think that the same relationship can be interpreted so differently – like those optical illusions where you either see the old haggard woman or the young girl. Oh, God. Have just had a vile bolt of vision. What if: Alex's interpretation of our relationship is to my interpretation of our relationship what my interpretation of Andy and me is to Andy's interpretation of Andy and me?

Ergh. It's turning into my arithmetic paper again, with the added possibility of my finals philosophy essay if we are to take on board the fact that we don't know what Andy thinks or, indeed, what anyone really – arghhhhh! Am going completely bonkers with this. Surely love is not supposed to be such analytical torture.

I need to calm down and start channelling my energies into something constructive for a change, like my job – or, more accurately, finding a job. In my absurd Carol Smillie persona of earlier I decided I was far too happy to work for the likes of drongo

Michael and merrily handed in my notice, which would have been fine if I was Carol and could swan around wrecking people's homes while winning Rear of the Year contests, but not quite so fine given I'm totally unemployable, two grand in debt on my Visa card and only likely to win Arrears of the Year contests.

So now I'm having to see out my contract, which means I'm reduced to going into an office where everyone hates me, pretending I'm not working on my CV or checking the Net for vacancies and claiming all interviews are recurring dental problems – because trying to get a job once you're unemployed is like trying to get a boyfriend when you're single: people only ever want you when you're in something else. In fact, it feels horribly as though I've decided to dump my boyfriend but still have to get into bed with him every night because the moment of dumping can only happen after his grandad's eightieth.

Oh, God. Just had horror thought of being at my own grandad's eightieth – particularly horrifying, obviously, as Grandad is dead – with neither boyfriend nor job. I suddenly realise that the only reason I'm negative about Alex is because I already have him, and that the minute I think about not having him, all the negatives become positive. The answer, then, is to imagine he is dead too: that way I will only think nice things, since it's especially wrong to think bad things about dead people. I might not keep up the dead theory at night, though – there's something a bit creepy about having sex with a corpse – but I'm glad I've found a solution.

Anyway, how are things with you and your man? Presumably not having to imagine one of you is dead. Do you think you might make it over for my wedding? Oh, Jesus, 'my wedding' – can't cope with enormity and surety and finality and . . . must think dead, dead, Alex is dead. This is fucking ridiculous. I should not be having to imagine my fiancé – gah! It's happened again. Oh, God. Oh, God. Please tell me this is normal. Pre-wedding jitters coming early, or New Millennium commitment bug selectively targeting women, as opposed to its more usual victim, i.e. all males.

I blame Andy, to be honest. If he hadn't swanked in and charmed my socks and, as I imagine was the general idea, knickers off, then I would not now be thinking, What if? But, then, maybe it was fate. Maybe he was supposed to be there to show me what I could have if I was just brave enough to let go of what I do have. The whole thing feels like one long drawn out game of Who Wants to be a Millionaire? *with Alex, a perfectly acceptable already-won thirty-two grand, and Andy, a potential six-figure cheque that Chris Tarrant is teasingly waving under my nose. Do I take the gamble on getting more and risk losing what I already have? Or do I just settle for what I've got?*

    Must go. Head about to explode.

    Jess

    xxx

Who Wants To Be a Married?

'Don't risk it,' Alex shouted, at a woman with an unfortunate nose. He was sitting in front of the telly with an open pizza box on his lap.

'Risk what?' Jess said, dumping her bag and keys, then collapsing next to him on the sofa and picking at a grey blob of slime that was masquerading as chicken. 'Food poisoning?'

'D, squirrel,' he yelled, as the woman gave a laborious run-down on why she was going for A, mole. 'Oh, God, I can't bear it, Jess. She's going to lose the lot.'

Jess took her head out of the pizza box and stared with interest at the screen. Her recurring commitment problem had made her particularly sensitive to the notion of 'losing the lot'.

'Sure?' Chris Tarrant said, in a way that suggested she shouldn't be. 'You've *got* sixteen thousand pounds. If you get this next question right you would have *thirty-two thousand pounds* – it's a lot of money, Tracey.'

Tracey beamed obediently.

'But if you answer this question incorrectly, I have to tell you, you *would* lose fifteen thousand pounds.'

'And might even fit into your dress, Tracey,' Alex said, chortling. Tracey was the size of a Range Rover.

'Sure? Positive?' Chris tortured on. Tracey nodded and looked about as positive as an electron. 'That your final answer?'

'Uh-oh, Trace,' Alex sirened. 'Big mistake. Should have stuck with what you had.'

'But she might be right,' Jess said, excitedly. 'And then she'll win.'

'Or wrong. And then she'll lose,' Alex replied, proving again his suitability to a career in law.

Just then dramatic music started up, as if someone had inadvertently sat on the remote control and switched to a horror film. From the tormenting way Chris was delivering the answer, Jess decided, it wasn't far off a horror film.

'You said A, mole. Tracey? You *had* sixteen thousand pounds . . .' prolonged horror silence '. . . you've just . . .' more horror silence as knife-wielding murderer goes for the kill '. . . lost fifteen thousand.'

Jess watched in sympathy as Tracey waved goodbye to her fortune. She'd had it, she'd gambled for more, she'd lost it. After all the lessons of Sunday school, Jess couldn't help feeling it somewhat of an irony that the one to impact most on her life would come from an ITV game-show.

'See what happens when you want too much?' Alex said, swigging at a pint of beer, burping, stuffing the remains of a half-chewed chunk of cold pizza into his mouth, then holding the box upside down over the sofa to demonstrate its emptiness. 'You end up with nothing.'

Jess stared despondently at a globule of mozzarella. Maybe Alex was right. Maybe giving him up for the hope of something more would not lead to happiness and a full life, but loneliness and empty pizza boxes.

'You OK, gorgeous?' He was studying her with the look of undiluted love. She wished she didn't need the diluting effect of three glasses of wine to return it. 'What's up?'

Jess tried to smile. 'Just thinking.'

'Oh dear,' he announced, grabbing a cushion and pretending to hide behind it. 'Beware, everyone! Jess is thinking.'

Jess suspected it wasn't the moment to point out that if anyone should beware it was Alex.

'If you need some food for thought,' he said, reaching over and whispering in her right ear, 'your favourite pizza's waiting in the kitchen.'

He mightn't always nourish her soul, but he was adept at caring for the rest of her. She leaned over and hugged him as a flicker of genuine love ignited inside her. But, like the optimistic spark of a cigarette lighter without enough lighter fuel, it died just as quickly as it came to life: a Quattro Formaggi with extra mushrooms was not enough to base a marriage on.

'Thanks,' she said, getting up and leaving Alex to watch television his way – four channels viewed consecutively in ten-second snippets, unless a nipple appeared on Channel Five.

She made her way to the kitchen and put the pizza in the microwave, then scanned the room for something to nibble while she waited. Undecided whether the mould on a hunk of cheese was supposed to be there, she opted for yesterday's potatoes, until a pile of half-opened mail on the table caught her eye. She ambled over and began to rifle through it. A circular from an insurance company, the electricity bill, something dull addressed to The Homeowner, and a letter from an Internet company Alex subscribed to, which began, seemingly without irony, 'Dear Big Member'.

Then, just as she was about to fetch another potato, she noticed an airmail sticker poking out from underneath the circular. Letters that had been stamped rather than franked were rare and exciting. Letters that came from abroad were gold-dust. Eagerly, she yanked it out. It was addressed to Alex and had a Kenyan stamp although, from the look of the envelope, it had done a few jungle safaris *en route*.

She picked it up and peered into the neatly serrated opening: Alex was the only person she knew who used a paper-knife. Only slightly guiltily, she removed the contents to reveal a handmade card with two elephants facing each other, their trunks knotted together under the words, 'Trying the Knot'. Whoever had made it had clearly been more of an artist than a linguist – either that, Jess decided, or they had a frighteningly spooky insight into her own feelings. She opened it up:

To Dearest A,
Congratulations, or, as they say here, vizuri sana!
She is very lucky.
  Wishing you a long and happy life together,
  J
  xxx

Jess stared at the words as a knot of a very different variety tightened around her gut. 'She is very lucky.' She read it again. 'She is very lucky.' She repeated it over and over: 'Lucky, lucky, lucky. She is very lucky,' until it lost all meaning and turned into a Kylie Minogue song. And then it hit her: she might *be* lucky, but she didn't *feel* lucky, and that, surely, wasn't the right sentiment for a bride-to-be.

Suddenly, as if she'd just worked out how to disentangle a necklace, the rest of her emotions unfurled. Like falling dominoes, they hurtled towards a conclusion she felt sure would not be a grand finale, but a horrible truth: she couldn't marry Alex. It wasn't love. It was lovely. And that wasn't enough.

She stood motionless, stunned that after so much internal analysis this realisation had been brought about by the words of a stranger. Then, as if she'd given the correct answer on a game-show, the microwave pinged to a standstill.

'You coming to join me?' Alex.

She jolted back to the living. It was one thing confronting the truth for herself. It was several things – possibly smashed crockery – confronting it with Alex. She took the pizza, felt sick and went next door.

'Decided to go to Italy for the real thing, did we?' Alex was slouched exactly where she'd left him, smiling playfully.

'No,' she said, feeling bereft of both sense and humour.

He studied her closely. 'Uh-oh, you've been thinking again, haven't you? I knew it! You've been standing too close to that microwave and all its little electromagnetic waves have gone,

"Yippee!" ' – He picked a mushroom from her pizza and waved it around in the air – ' "Jess's brain! We're going to fry all her little thought cells so that they whiz around – wheeeeeeee, ZAP! – and then we're going to—" '

'Alex!' she shouted, punching off the telly, as he gobbled the mushroom, sat on his hands and grinned. 'This is serious.'

He bowed his head, removed the pizza from her lap, placed it carefully on the floor, took both her hands in his and said, 'Tell Dr Alex all about it.'

Jess swallowed. 'I can't go through with it.' She searched his face, waiting in horror for the moment when he . . .

'With the pizza? It's OK, honestly. Just eat as much as you can and then—'

'With us, Alex.'

There was a long, painful silence. She felt as though she were telling a small child his mother had just been killed.

Alex sat, motionless, staring at her. If the eyes were really the windows of the soul, then his soul was currently in a crumpled heap on the floor. Slowly, he withdrew his hands from hers and ran them through his hair. 'What d'you mean "us"?'

'Us – as in us getting married.'

He looked instantly relieved. '*Okaay*,' he said, addressing the carpet and nodding. 'So you need more time. That's understandable, I mean, it *has* all been a bit rushed and—'

'It's not about time, Alex.'

He shot her a quizzical look.

'It's about feelings . . . and—'

'And thoughts,' he added, with a hint of a smile.

'And . . . well—' she stuttered.

'And you think and feel you can't go through with it.'

'Yes,' she said, taken aback by the ease with which he was accepting it.

'OK, well, let's talk about it, then,' he said, as if he'd metamorphosed into a character from *Dawson's Creek* and was about to deliver an unfeasibly articulate analysis of the meaning of love by alluding to emotions clearly beyond the scope of his own teenage experience and much nearer that of the middle-aged scriptwriter.

'I just . . . oh, Alex . . . I—' Suddenly, without any warning, she was crying.

'Come here,' he said, reaching over and enveloping her in a hug. This, though comforting, felt wrong – like the stabbed victim consoling his attacker. 'You're just overwhelmed, that's all.'

For a fraction of a second Jess wondered if he was right. After all, getting married wasn't something you did every day, unless, of course, you were Elizabeth Taylor in which case it would not be overwhelming, merely exhausting. But then she remembered it wasn't marriage that was the problem: it was Alex.

'I just don't think, well . . . I don't think I feel the right things,' she said, freeing herself from the hug and looking at him nervously, as if he were a firework that hadn't gone off properly.

He smiled. 'Jess, it's not an exam. There is no *right* way to feel.'

She had known that breaking the news was not going to be easy: she just hadn't anticipated breaking it to a deaf person. 'For you,' she said, fixing him intently. 'I don't think I feel the right things for *you*.'

She waited, feeling as though she hadn't so much driven the point home as crashed it into his living room.

'But you still love me, right?' He was looking down at the cushion, picking at a thread.

'I care so much for you,' she said, instantly realising the inadequacy of her words. 'I just don't think it's enough.'

Alex still picked at the thread. 'What would make it enough?'

Jess thought for a while. The obvious answer was Andy, but

she suspected that wasn't what he was after. And then a bitter sensation washed over her: what if Andy wasn't what *she* was after either? She'd fantasised that he was but maybe it was like holidays: you dreamed about the Bahamas when you were stuck in Putney, but only because you didn't live there.

'I don't know,' she said, finally.

He looked up. He was crying. She had only seen him cry once before, when England had been knocked out of the World Cup. It was reassuring and distressing to know she could elicit the same response.

'So what do you want?' he asked, in a small voice.

She knew what she wanted to want. She wanted to want Alex more than anything in the world. But no end of trying, denying or convincing was going to get her there. That was the problem with being with someone you weren't totally in love with – it was like taking the wrong route in a maze. You kept going, hitting dead ends and running around in circles, knowing you were lost, hoping that if you persevered you would eventually find a route out. But deep down you knew that what you really had to do was go back to the point at which you first got lost and start again. Which was where, with a sinking heart, Jess was headed.

'I want to call off the engagement.'

Alex stared in disbelief as a large lone tear rolled down his cheek and plopped into his lap. 'For now or for ever?'

Jess answered by not answering.

His face crumpled like a deflating blow-up toy: not content on removing his stop valve, she was now trampling the life out of him. 'I'm sorry, Alex. I'm so . . . so sorry,' she managed, before she too crumpled.

'Why?' he wailed, head in hands. 'I've done nothing but love you.'

'I know, Alex, I know. That's why I can't do this to you, to us. It wouldn't be fair.'

He looked up at her as if they were *Jerry Springer* guests

and she'd just announced she'd been sleeping with his sister. 'And this *is*?'

'It mightn't seem it now, but, yes, in the long run.' She felt like his mother trying to convince him into a pair of brown buckled Clark's shoes on the understanding that they might not be the height of fashion now but he'd thank her for it when he was bunion-free at fifty.

'Please, Jess, don't do this,' he begged, grabbing both her hands. 'Think about it.'

Of all the requests Alex could have made of her, she wouldn't instinctively have imagined he would be pleading for the thinking one. 'No, Alex, I—'

'We can work it out. Whatever it is. I know we can.'

She gave a meek smile of resignation. 'Love shouldn't have to be worked at.'

There was a long silence as the penny crashed to the ground with a thud. 'So what are you saying? That this is it? That it's over?'

She nodded slowly, taking in, for the first time, the full impact of her decision. The world had gone blurry – partly through tears, partly through terror. She studied him, trying to gauge his reaction, willing him to stop crying. Her own pain was acute but finite. She could only imagine his, and to know that she had been the cause of it made her feel like checking into prison.

'So what happens now?' he said, wiping his eyes.

She thought about it. In a film, she'd leave, it'd be pissing with rain, she'd go and stay at a friend's house, there'd be several shots of her wearing a baggy sweatshirt looking at old photos of them together, a couple of days would pass and then she'd just happen to be sitting in their favourite coffee bar – which would be empty except for a waiter wiping the counter – and he'd come in looking like shit, his dog would be peering mournfully in at the window, they'd sit side by side in silence, then he'd say something cute like, 'Bozo misses you,' the credits would roll, Gabrielle would burst into song and they'd kiss and laugh their way down the middle of a road, Bozo barking for joy behind them. But this was real life.

'Well. You'll hate me for a good two years, then—'

'Jess, I don't hate you. I just hate that you don't love me.'

'I do,' she pleaded.

'But not enough to repeat those two words in church.'

She hung her head. 'No.'

The room fell into a deathly silence disturbed only by their alternating sniffs, as if it were a funeral and the organist had forgotten to turn up. Wishing to be the dead person, Jess got up quietly and went upstairs. She reached under the bed, pulled out her suitcase, two pairs of twisted knickers and a cloud of dust, then, tears streaming, began grabbing at her belongings.

Alex stood watching her in the doorway. 'What are you doing?'

She looked up from where she was forcing a shampoo bottle into a makeup bag designed for a lipstick. The honest answer was that she didn't know. She didn't know what she was doing or where she was going, but even so, even then, hidden in the midst of all the sadness, all the confusion and all the heartache was the belief that finally she had done the right thing. It didn't feel so much like a weight off her mind as an enormous back-breaking rucksack lifted off her shoulders: the bruises and aches would take a long time to heal, but the constant digging-in had gone.

'I'm doing what is best for both of us,' she said, then gathered her baggage, both literally and metaphorically, and made for the door.

What would have happened if Jess had held out?

To find out turn to page 147 . . .

Otherwise turn to page 285 . . .

KENYA

HOLDING OUT

Twice Upon a Time . . .

To:	*Claire.Voyant@hotmail.com*
Date:	*Sunday 16 April*
Subject:	*Twice upon a time . . .*

Sitting in the middle of Kenya. Not in a little mud hut with tin roof and insects the size of small lorries. Nor by a dust-track boiling rice for ninety. But in front of a state-of-the-art computer with modem, printer, scanner, fax machine and hi-fi system so trendy and modern I can't find the on button.

Dear Claire,

Moving out to Africa is not, as VSO and gap-year students would lead us to believe, all about building schools from baboon dung, playing football with a coconut, and eating brown sludge out of a bowl with your fingers while dressed in brightly coloured pantaloons. It is one relaxing meander through the ethnic-artefacts department of Harrods. I had no idea that accepting the school's offer of a job as nanny to a Kenyan family would be identical to doing it in Chelsea, despite a little more sunshine and not quite so many designer-dress boutiques. For example:

Job Description	How I imagined it	How it really is
Take and collect children from school	Wandering along red dusty roads at sunrise holding hands with lots of little barefoot black children, possibly some on an elephant, wearing a sarong and baby in a sling.	Driving a four-wheel-drive Land Cruiser listening to Westlife downloaded from nine-year-old Noah's mini-disc player.
Shop for groceries	Buying exotic vegetables from a little shack by the roadside while walking around with a pot of grain on my head.	Driving a four-wheel-drive Land Cruiser to a super-market the size of Manchester and loading up with crisps, fizzy drinks and Nestlé KitKats.
Supervise homework	Lying in a hammock on the veranda at sunset with a small infant in my arms, telling them about a strange faraway place called Britain where they have magical things like moving pictures in a little box called a television.	Confiscating Noah's Gameboy until he switches off Sky Sports so that Bea can watch her geography video, while gently trying to coax him into writing a story that does not involve drugs or the Internet.

| Help, if required, with evening meal | Sitting on a little footstool under an acacia tree and singing 'Kum Ba Ya' with neighbouring large-breasted women while peeling indeterminate crops into a gigantic tin bucket. | Swigging champagne with Quentin, Marjorie and the entire polo club while consuming vast amounts of English food and shouting loud out-of-tune versions of 'Auld Lang Syne' in the manner of football hooligans. |
| Put children to bed | Scrubbing tiny infants in the same gigantic tin bucket then tucking them into the hammock on the veranda while humming poignant Swahili nursery rhymes as a local villager plays a flute made of bamboo. | Leaving them both to have piping hot electrically fuelled power-showers before chasing them under their Harry Potter duvet and 'reading' to them from their Pokémon album. |

In addition to me, they seem to have employed half of Kenya to do anything they can't be arsed to — which, they assure me, is perfectly normal, but then I'm sure the Queen assumes everyone has a butler. It's like Back to the Future where the 'future' is colonial Britain and we are travelling back there in a T-reg Land Cruiser, with Britney Spears, a dishwasher and the entire gadgetry of the Conran shop. To complete this distorted juxtaposition of worlds, the local Maasai wander around with nothing except a herd of emaciated cattle, a long stick and, in what I'm hoping is not a grotesquely unethical advertising stunt by the Edinburgh Woollen Mill, red tartan travel rugs.

The family, I must say, are lovely. I'm not quite sure what Quentin does – I never get an answer I entirely understand – but whatever it is keeps him in Nairobi and Marjorie in rather nice Prada footwear. He tends to stop by unannounced, drink most of the gin bottle, take us all out in a safari truck to look at elephant droppings, then vanish, leaving Marjorie to explain why Bea missed her Swahili lesson. Marjorie makes African animals – or, more accurately, oversees a task force of shoeless Africans who make African animals – then, as far as I can tell, sells them to other wives who also make African animals.

They have two kids: Noah, nine, whose similarities to his Biblical namesake extend as far as building a computer-animated ark on level five of 'Missiles Attack!', and Bea, seven, who's just discovered glittery eye-shadow. They both go to the local school, where Noah seems to be a whiz at maths and Bea, as her mum compensatorily puts it, 'has a lot of friends'.

I'm staying in what they term the 'outhouse', which is similar to something I saw in the window of Foxtons for £330,000. Admittedly, the rooms are quite small and basic, e.g. kitchen cooker is smaller than Bea's Sindy one, but I don't imagine the £330,000 cupboard in Clapham could boast views over the Rift Valley – or, indeed, views over anything.

I've yet to make it all a bit more homely, starting with a rug I'm planning to buy from someone called Joseph for the extortionate equivalent of 4p. I must remember, however, that the temptation to kit out the rest of the place with similarly tiny-priced purchases is only exciting until you try to take them all home, whereupon they become easily breakable, impossible to fit into your suitcase and, with a £285 excess baggage fine, ever so slightly uneconomically viable.

The only thing I miss is my stereo. As I didn't wish to sit in the departure lounge looking like a sixteen-year-old bound for Tenerife with a giant ghetto-blaster, I bought a little Walkman with portable speakers. I'd left all tapes behind, the idea being to listen to current cultural Kenyan music and the BBC World Service, only to get here and discover that the only thing I can pick up is East Africa's *Songs of Praise*. Admittedly, if I put it on the loo and twiddle the dial for ages, I can sometimes get the odd melody from Culture Club, but this is crap because (1) having travelled several thousand miles to be in a new country, it's not really the 'culture' I was looking for, and (2) it's a lot easier and more enjoyable to nip next door to Marjorie and Quentin's and watch EastEnders on BBC Prime in a comfy leather armchair with Dolby surround-sound.

I suppose the one thing I should be missing is Alex, especially as normally when I split up with someone they metamorphose into George Clooney and I, having seen nothing but problems with the relationship when I was in it, suddenly think I want to marry them. That's it, though. I'd spent the best part of three years trying to make *myself* want to marry him – getting out and freeing myself of such mental torture is largely a relief. It's like convincing yourself that what you really want to do on a Friday night is stand in the middle of a deafeningly loud overcrowded All Bar One in Fulham, fight your way through groups of blokes in rugby shirts and baseball caps all called Rupes, fork out twenty pounds for three drinks, then spend the rest of the evening nodding, smiling and saying, 'What?', when you know that a much better time would have been had eating cheese and crackers in front of *Friends*.

Of course there are things I miss about him – for a start, he made me feel secure, loved and comfortable. But then I remind myself that it's not enough for one's boyfriend to be the equivalent of an electric blanket: there has to be the 'spark', that essence that makes you feel alive, because, let's face it, an electric blanket is a fat lot of use without electricity.

I tried presenting this reasoning to Marjorie, who has clearly, in her somewhat dubious choice of Quentin, eschewed the National Grid voltage for the rubbing-two-sticks-together variety. She says it's all to do with long-term versus short-term, and made the whole thing sound like the car park at Heathrow. According to her, the blokes with what she calls 'spunk' are the ones who set your heart racing to begin with, then break it just when you've reached top gear. They are the short-termers. The 'decent chaps', as she puts it, are the ones without 'spunk', who will keep your heart ticking over, neither fire you up nor let you down and, presumably, fork out for the pacemaker when your system dies of boredom.

It doesn't look as though either variety is out here – not, of course, that I'm interested. People do keep going on about someone called Tommy, who's clearly quite a character because practically everyone I meet asks me whether I've seen him yet. However, I'm not going to hype him up – bound to be a disappointment if I do that and, as I say, I'm not interested.

How are you and John? He's clearly a bloke parked in the long-stay and, if your recent pregnancy scare is anything to go by, doesn't seem lacking in spunk. And what's the latest from hippie self-sustaining life in sunny Spain? Our trusty ex-colleague, Lou, tells me you're up at six irrigating the fields and have to cook pulse stews in solar ovens you've built from clay – and I thought I was the one who'd gone to the primitive country! It sounds like my history project: 'Jethro Tull and the Invention of the Seed Drill'. Do you do merry jigs at barn dances and have five sovereigns a year to spend on staple crops? What are the others like? Lots of large German women with white socks, sandals and a gerbil under each arm spring to mind, but I suppose that's like assuming someone called Hugh will have floppy hair and only be familiar with the environs of Eton.

I must say, I wouldn't mind being surrounded by some hirsute Helgas and Hughs. When I was told I'd be working for a family in the middle of nowhere I hadn't counted on Nowhere having the population equivalent of the moon. Obviously, it's very stunning, with acres of red-soil grasslands dotted with those flat-topped acacia trees that look as if God got a bit over zealous with the strimmer. And the wildlife's extraordinary – it's like living with the cameraman from a David Attenborough documentary. And it's *wonderful to breathe fresh air, as opposed to the car-fume variety that passes for fresh in London. I just wish there were a few more people around. The only human contact I've had so far, apart from the family – and, to be honest, when Noah's at his Gameboy it's not immediately evident that he is a human – has been with a couple of teachers at the school. But this has just been the odd comment about homework, not really enough to base a social life on. Marjorie and Quentin are always insisting I join their dinner parties, which is very kind of them, but I can't help feeling they're doing it because they feel sorry for me, like picking the school nerd to be on your rounders team because his mum's complained everyone excludes him.*

The one occasion I believed I was forging a new and lasting friendship was when I struck up conversation with some of the African workforce. Every time I said something, they'd all smile at me wide-eyed with wonder, then, if I cracked a joke they let out loud peals of laughter, slapping their thighs heartily. This went on for a couple of days, with me convinced I was hilarious and getting more and more chuffed that, despite the supposed culture-specific nature of humour, I, with my ingenious, innovative and devilish wit, had broken through the boundaries. There is nothing more flattering than thinking people find you funny.

Then one day I decided to pluck up courage and ask Barundi, the groundsman, if there was a Kenyan version of Clapham's Jongleurs, imagining myself touring the comedy circuit of Africa, possibly as a double act with Lenny Henry. He burst out laughing, rather cruelly, I thought. Hurt, but trying to put on a brave face, I pointed out that we comedians can't always be amusing and do have our sensitive side, then asked Oginga the same question. It was only when Oginga laughed too that I realised, miserably, that they had not been laughing because I was funny but because they hadn't understood a word I'd said.

It reminds me of a wedding I went to where the bloke beside me kept cracking up, leading me to believe that I was being hilarious, until a computer drongo on my other side piped up with a banal remark about the table decoration to similar guffaws and it became bitterly apparent I'd just been entertaining someone with a nervous-laughing disorder.

I've decided I'm just going to enjoy the scenic calm of the African landscape, rather than ferret around in search of friends to get pissed with. After all, I came here to find myself, not a pub. I will commune with nature, possibly fostering a little lion cub in the manner of Born Free *and forget about . . . Oooh, goody, Quentin has just walked in, handed me a gin and tonic with fresh lime from the garden – love lovely Kenya – and told me that the school are hosting an induction dinner for all new staff of which, because I nanny for two of their pupils, I am apparently a member. Yippee!*

Mustn't get excited, though – there's nothing more guaranteed to ruin a party than building it up into a Belisha beacon of hope on one's social calendar. Still . . . I wonder what I should wear. I seemed to have been labouring under the misconception, when shopping to come out here, that somewhere between Gatwick and Nairobi I would transform from a perfectly normal jeans-and-nicetop girl into a 1970s male safari guide. Thus, while sensible people might have gone round purchasing leopard-print bikinis and little floaty see-through dresses as seen on Tampax adverts, I chose to prowl the racks of Millet's snapping up a bewildering array of khaki shorts, shapeless dark green shirts and heavy-duty masculine sandals – none of which, funnily enough, I've since felt the urge to wear.

To be honest, though, I think I was going through more than just a gender crisis before I came out – as in, came out to Africa, not *in the homosexual sense. It's a big decision ditching job, flat and boyfriend in exchange for six months in the unknown – not least when every fucker you meet rejoices in saying, 'Gosh, you're brave.' Hate the word 'brave'. Why can't people say that you're being interesting or dazzlingly unconventional or that you're an inspiration to them? But brave? They might as well have done with it and tell you you're a raving nutter.*

Admittedly, the raving-nutter option did cross my mind on

occasion – like when I arrived at the departure lounge and finally got round to reading the traveller's-health advice booklet the nurse had handed me. Contrary to finding little pictures of sandcastles and smiley suns with hats on, I was met with the script of a particularly harrowing ER episode: 'fatal . . . severe . . . no cure, ultimately death', with the insinuation being that if I managed to escape the jaws of a rabid dog I was sure to contract cholera, bilharzia and typhoid, so that were I to return at all, it would be in an oblong wooden box.

I decided I needed to set out on my travels on a more optimistic footing and went straight to the duty-free perfume shop. I wanted to find the scent advertised by the stunning girl all over London's bus shelters in the hope that I, too, by exuding it, could have my neck mauled by a shirtless Adonis with chiselled chin. But, as often seems to be the drawback of advertising, I'd remembered everything from the campaign except the product. So, after drenching all available pores on my neck and arms, and being eyed suspiciously by a sales assistant whose skin colour suggested she ate too many carrots, I decided to abandon my search and get on the plane.

Once aboard, however, all the perfumes began amalgamating to produce a vicious toxic smell of the sort found in petrol-station forecourts and the paint department of B&Q, causing the girl beside me to start doing strange sniffing noises and then inaudible whimpering to her boyfriend, who eventually leaned over and asked if I was wearing Rayon. I marvelled at his ability to identify anything from the fumes, jovially informed him that Rayon was about the only fragrance I wasn't wearing and suggested he became a sniffer dog. He told me rayon was a fabric and Ailsa was allergic to it.

So Ailsa got my window seat and failed to look either out of the window or happy. She was one of those people whose main enjoyment in life stems from looking suicidal and has the kind of peculiar relationship with her boyfriend where neither of them acknowledges the other, preferring instead to sit rigidly hand in hand and fixate on the seat in front. Naturally, this caused problems both for seatbelt fastening and more especially mealtimes, which became a remarkable feat of dexterity where spreading frozen butter one-handed with a plastic knife put the blindfolded egg-and-spoon race well in the shade. At no point in the journey did they (a) separate or (b) communicate. Perhaps this could be the key to a successful relationship.

Anyway, despite my earplugs, eye-patch and deeply unattractive nylon bedsocks, I didn't get to sleep until 4.30 a.m., by which time they'd started serving breakfast and I was awoken with a sausage being waved under my nose. Then the captain came on and started being all jokey and informal and telling us his co-pilot's wife had just given birth to a baby girl, prompting the entire plane to break into applause as if they were Americans. Can never decide whether I like such frivolity and familiarity from someone who's supposed to be in charge of my life, or whether I wouldn't prefer a more aloof, formal character with no sense of humour who would never ever do anything so silly as crash a plane.

Luckily, our own cockpit jester landed us crash-free, though not without incident. Just as we touched down he announced that we'd be stopping somewhere different to drop off a very 'important and special' person. Got slightly pissed off at this – I mean, if I'd known that airbus literally meant 'a bus in the air' then I'd have planned my route differently. It would have been very handy to get off in Paris, say, for a couple of days to visit my old schoolfriend, get back on again and maybe make a quick stop in Kuala Lumpur before – and then an altogether cheerier thought struck: maybe I was the important and special person!

Suddenly had images of lots of little black kids leaping up and down on the runway waving flags and cheering as I, standing majestically on the plane steps in the manner of Prince Philip about to descend and make a hideous racial gaffe, smiled winningly for the paparazzi. But then I looked out of the window. Instead of cute kids with flags, there were men with guns, lots of them, pointing directly at our plane. Felt my body go into premature rigor mortis as the penny dropped. He wasn't a jocular pilot at all. He was a terrorist.

I racked my brains for anything I'd read on how to deal with inadvertently finding yourself a hostage – despite its encyclopedic listing of tragedy, my traveller's-health advice booklet didn't cover it – until a brass band struck up, a red carpet rolled out and the stewardess told us that we were about to set eyes on someone famous.

Ecstatic to discover I was in the midst of a juicy Hello! *scoop rather than a hostage seize, I leaped to the window to join her, contemplating whether I could be arsed to heave down the concrete elephant that was my hand luggage in order to get my camera. Then, despite all hopes of George Clooney or, more realistically, Posh'n'Becks wheeling an animal-print-clad Brooklyn up said red carpet, three unidentifiable men in grey suits emerged, hurried into a waiting car and drove off at high speed. The important, special and extremely famous person was the President of Kenya.*

The whole thing felt like having a friend rush up to you and shriek excitedly, 'Guess who I met?' You get excited too and can't guess, and then they tell you it's some singer you've never heard of or someone from a telly programme you never watch and it's all a bitter disappointment to both of you.

Needless to say, I didn't get quite the same treatment when I disembarked: a decidedly dodgy number thirty-four bus with limbs hanging out of the window. But I'm here precisely to absorb myself in third-world customs, to become culturally enriched and . . . oh, shit, just noticed the time – EastEnders *omnibus about to start.*

Lots of love,

Jess

xxx

PS I wonder if Tommy will be at this dinner thing. No! I'm not going to obsess. I've just come out of a long-term relationship and don't need another. Especially not with someone called Tommy.

Benefit of the Doubt

'A kiss for the first person to spot Tommy,' Quentin shouted, as he manoeuvred the truck along what Kenyans called a road and everyone else took to be the aftermath of a volcano.

'Ergh, yuk!' Noah squealed, accurately summing up, Jess thought, her own feelings about the prospect. He was standing on the back seat with Bea, holding on to the frame that would normally support the roof and looking out across the arid grasslands like something from a Timberland commercial. Jess was sitting up front with Quentin on what felt like a pneumatic drill, wishing she'd thought to wear a support bra.

'What d'you mean "yuk"?' Quentin said, in mock offence. Noah giggled. 'People come from far and wide to get a kiss from me. Everyone wants me to kiss them. Isn't that right, Bea?'

Bea thought about this carefully. Jess turned round and grinned at her affectionately. She was unbearably cute. 'Jess wants you to kiss her.'

Jess froze in horror. Apart from being categorically untrue, it was, etiquette-wise, a tricky one to deny. Bea, she decided, was no longer unbearably cute – merely unbearable. 'Anyway,' she said, after a long and awkward pause, 'I thought we were supposed to be spotting Tommy,' then regretted what such a blatant subject-changer might imply.

'Exactly!' Quentin said, flashing her a complicit grin as if she were his secretary and they'd deftly managed to field office rumours about their affair. 'Right. Eyes peeled, troops.'

They obediently searched the horizon, uncomfortably silent. Jess was now even more intent on finding Tommy, flirting with him outrageously, and proving to all the world that her interests in Quentin lay strictly and solely in looking after his kids, not making some with him.

'Watch out, Daddy! Zebra crossing!' Bea shouted, jumping up and down, grinning and pointing at some bushes by the roadside. For a country still struggling with the rudiments of road-building, Jess thought, a zebra crossing seemed redundant. And then a herd of zebra approached and ambled their way out in front of them.

Jess laughed. 'That's really funny, Bea,' she said, horrified that she'd only been in Kenya a matter of weeks and had already become too blasé to notice the wildlife on her doorstep. Like a child who saw nothing special in having a swimming-pool in his own back garden. Like Noah, in fact.

'Actually,' Noah piped up, 'I made that joke. It's mine,' he stated, in a tone he would no doubt use in later life to boast about a fart.

'Codswallop!' Quentin said. 'It's *my* joke or I'm a hairy bear.'

'You're a hairy bear,' Noah and Bea shouted unanimously. Jess glanced at the Amazonian rainforest sprouting from Quentin's half-open shirt and was tempted to agree.

'Grrrr,' he roared, rather convincingly, and instructed them once again to find Tommy for Jess.

It seemed fitting, Jess thought, as the sun began to slip down the sky and tinge everything with the kind of reddish glow favoured by Thomas Cook photographers, that her first meeting with Tommy would take place against such a romantic backdrop. Despite promising herself she wouldn't, she'd set high hopes on him, undecided whether he'd be George Clooney in tight-fitting safari T-shirt, combats and rifle strung sexily over one shoulder, or a more innocent Leonardo DiCaprio astride an elephant. She hadn't asked any questions about him for fear of appearing keen, but everyone was so intent on them meeting that an almost fate-like inevitability hung about the outcome. Indeed, the only impediment she could foresee to their dating was that no one seemed able to find him.

'So, Jess, you left a man behind?' Quentin struck up, grinning.

This, Jess realised, was Catch 22: answer no, and he might assume she *was* after him, answer yes, and it might jeopardise her chances with Tommy. She thought about it and opted for 'Sort of.'

'Sort of . . . a man? Or sort of left him behind?'

'We split up shortly before I came out here,' she replied, watching his grin recede in the opposite direction to his hair. He looked solemnly ahead and muttered an awkward apology in the embarrassed manner of a lad who'd just told the group a joke about a spastic in front of someone whose brother was a spastic.

Jess waited to dismiss his loaded '*Tommy*'s single,' but when none seemed forthcoming she settled for plotting how she could engineer her future boyfriend an invite to the evening's induction dinner.

'Well, troops, think we're going to have to turn back,' Quentin announced, as if they'd run out of artillery rather than daylight. He began doing a thirteen-point turn in a ditch.

Jess felt a surge of panic. It was like going to a party because the bloke you fancied was supposed to be there, then a friend dragging you away before he'd arrived. 'That's a shame,' she said limply, hoping she'd kept the desperation out of her voice.

'Don't worry, Jess. We'll keep looking,' Bea reassured.

Evidently, she hadn't.

The drive back passed in a haze of dust and daydreams. Having concocted all sorts of scenarios with Tommy appearing on the horizon at sunset just when she'd given up all hope bearing a bunch of freshly picked African flowers and a picnic hamper, Jess reminded herself that she was in Kenya, not a commercial, and resolved to enjoy her surroundings and Bea's singing. Until she listened properly. Bea was singing 'Wannabe'. It was difficult to know what was more incongruous: that she was performing a Spice Girls hit in the middle of rural Africa, or that, aged seven, she was stipulating her requirements in a sexual partner.

'Over there, Daddy! Look – Tommy! Over there!' Noah was jiggling up and down and pointing.

Jess, overjoyed, catapulted round and followed the direction of his gaze but, frustratingly, couldn't see him.

'By Jove, son, jolly well spotted!' Quentin exclaimed, turning off the engine and grabbing for the binoculars via the unnecessary route of Jess's lower legs.

'Where? Where?' Bea yelled.

'There, by that big bush,' Noah instructed. 'You must be blind.'

Jess once again searched the horizon, to no avail.

'Oh, yeah, I see,' Bea squealed. 'Hello, Tommy.'

'Can *you*, Jess?' Quentin barked.

Jess hesitated. It was like being told an anecdote about a famous person you'd never heard of: you had a split second to decide whether to own up and claim ignorance or spend the rest of the time doing fake laughter. She opted for the latter. 'Oh, yes, gosh,' she said, squinting in the required direction and giggling. 'Nice thighs.'

Quentin looked at her oddly. 'Here, have a gander with these,' he said, handing her the binoculars. 'You can see how his backside differs from Grant's.'

Jess flinched. Why should Quentin be interested in Tommy's backside? Or Grant's, for that matter? And who the hell was Grant?

She felt a little uncomfortable as he looped the binoculars round her neck and instructed her on how best to grasp the shaft. As she brought them up to her eyes to focus, she felt even more uncomfortable. This was called voyeurism. And people got arrested for it. 'I'm not sure I—'

'That's it. Jolly good. Focus on the bush.'

She scanned down from where she'd been looking at some sky and, after scrutinising uninspiring scrub, finally located the bush. But no Tommy. Not even his backside. There did seem to be something moving about behind it, but if it was a person they were very small.

Suddenly, she began to wonder whether she would like Tommy. At the end of the day, how much would she really have in common with a nudist who hung out in bushes? It wasn't exactly a lawyer who hung out in Pizza Express who . . . She scolded herself. She'd come to Kenya to have new experiences and meet different people: a relationship with a local nudist might be culturally and spiritually fulfilling. She searched again, making a mental note to suss out Grant, just in case things with Tommy didn't work out.

'Me see, Jess, let me see,' Bea pleaded, snatching at the binoculars.

Jess looked uncertainly at Quentin, who smiled and nodded. After all, Jess conceded, as she passed them back, for someone who'd just been singing about her lover, a naked male torso was hardly likely to shock.

'I can see . . . one, two, three, four . . . five, six . . . seven horns, Daddy.'

'My word, that's clever, Bea,' Quentin congratulated.

Indeed it was, Jess thought jealously, given that she was yet to see *one*.

'Bet I can see more,' Noah said, in predictable male panic at the prospect of being outdone by a female.

'But can you tell which are the mummy ones?' Quentin said.

Jess frowned, confused as to how it had turned from checking out whether Tommy had a fit bod to a birds'n'bees lesson using deer.

'The mummy ones are the strong ones and do the work and the daddy ones look after the babies,' Bea said, matter-of-factly. Jess was pleased to see the Spice Girls influence had not been entirely corruptive.

'The daddy ones have more bigger horns,' Noah stated.

'That's right,' Quentin said, smiling. 'They also have bigger brains, better judgement and no irrational mood swings.' He looked at Jess and let out a disgusting chauvinistic cackle.

'Daddy?' Bea struck up, earnestly. 'What's Tommy's last name?'

Jess turned and smiled, feeling a wave of renewed tenderness towards her. Bea had not only displayed supportive sisterly intolerance of such sexism but had brought things round deftly to the more interesting topic of Tommy.

'It's just Tommy, noodlebrain,' Noah said, scathingly.

'Tommy's full name,' Quentin cut in authoritatively, as if he were an officer instructing the troops on defence strategies, 'is Thomson's gazelle. So you're both right.'

Jess blinked slowly as her own noodlebrain absorbed the news. 'Tommy' was not her future boyfriend. 'Tommy' was not a wacky nudist who might *become* her future boyfriend. 'Tommy' was not even a random bloke who, despite cavorting around naked and living in bushes, she could fancy as a fallback option should no one better turn up on the scene. 'Tommy', the much talked-about, hyped-up and fantasised-over, was a sodding gazelle.

'You look pretty,' Bea offered, when two hours later, after a bath that looked as though it doubled as a rhino's mud wallow, Jess was contorting herself on the edge of the loo trying to check her bottom in the mirror.

'Thanks, Bea,' she replied, wishing men could have the tact of a seven-year-old. 'D'you think this skirt makes me look fat?'

Never one to take things lightly, Bea studied it closely. 'Yes.'

Always one to take things personally, Jess exploded. 'Well, it's the only buggering one I've got, so it'll have to do.'

Bea opened her eyes very wide. 'You said a naughty word.'

'And so would you,' Jess snapped, jumping off her perch and marching through to her dressing-table, 'if you looked like a water buffalo.'

Bea looked like she was going to cry.

'Sorry, Bea. It's just' – she scrabbled around for how best to explain PMT to a child – 'I'm going out tonight and I don't look very nice.'

'Your hair looks nice.'

Jess ran her hands through the towel-dried nest on her head. It was the only part of her appearance she hadn't yet attended to. She changed her mind: seven-year-olds were clearly as useless as men.

'Are you going to meet a boy?'

'No, Bea,' she said, the perils of tempting fate all too fresh in her mind. 'I'm going to have supper with the other nannies and teachers.'

'So why do you want to look nice?'

Bea was just about the limit. 'Because, Bea, it's nice to look nice,' she said, glancing at her reflection and realising how far removed she was from this aim.

Bea seemed to be doing the same. 'I'll let you borrow my Spice Girls eye-shadow,' she said, as if it held the key. Multi-millionaires all of them, Jess considered, maybe it did.

'Thanks, Bea. D'you want to borrow one of my lipsticks?' She might not have made much headway with Bea's understanding of maths, but she was doing a wonderful job coaching her in the basics of girlie friendship.

'No, thank you,' Bea replied, looking at it solemnly and shaking her head. 'I don't suit pink.'

By the time Jess had reached the conclusion that she didn't suit anything, it was after seven and she was late.

'Bea, can you go really quickly and ask Daddy if I can use his car?' Daddy's car was a BMW convertible and about as practical in Kenya as a Range Rover in Chelsea.

Bea stood still and eyed her suspiciously. 'Why?'

'Because the one we normally go in isn't working properly,' she said, dismissively, as if she were a car mechanic and couldn't be bothered explaining brake-calliper functions to a female.

'That's what Amy always said,' Bea announced, studying a tube of foundation, 'so she could go in Daddy's posh one and make the boys like her.'

Amy was the previous nanny who hadn't lasted for reasons Jess wasn't yet secure enough to ask. 'And did the boys like her?'

'No,' Bea replied, still studying the foundation. 'That's why she went home.'

Jess tried to pretend she wasn't interested by fishing around in her bag. 'Because the boys didn't like her?'

Bea smiled condescendingly. 'Because she couldn't find any boys.'

Jess baulked. Although her reasons for coming out to Africa hadn't been man-related, it would have been nice to know, like supermarket shopping, that the Häagen-Dazs was there if she wanted it. After the day's search for a non-existent Tommy and the suspicion that not many rich and witty Adonises had a habit of becoming nannies, she began to fear she might end up leaving the country equally empty-handed.

'Daddy says don't hit any heffalumps,' Bea said, returning with a set of keys and giggling.

Tell Daddy I'll hit *him*, Jess was tempted to retort, but in the light of how it might be misinterpreted, she controlled herself. ''Anks, Bea,' she garbled, grabbed the keys, kissed the little girl's forehead and charged out. 'See you later.'

Bea shot her a sceptical look. 'I think we'll be seeing each other tomorrow,' she said, and flashed Jess a knowing smile.

After racing over enough potholes to make the journey seem akin to something on which Alton Towers would issue a health warning, Jess arrived at the school hot and flustered. Intent on making her late entrance as unobtrusive as possible, she parked round the back, checked her makeup in the mirror, slithered out and closed the door. Immediately a cacophony of ooooeee-ooooeee-ooooeee belted out, lights flashing in manic accompaniment.

'Fuck, *fuck*!' she yelled, yanking at the door handle then pointing the keys frantically at the car, as if they were a TV remote control and she needed to change the channel before her parents walked in.

'Thought the disco started later.'

She glanced up from where she was attempting a break-in from the passenger side. A tall bloke with dark floppy hair was standing confidently in the distance, legs apart, one hand in pocket, the other wrapped around a can of beer, grinning.

'Yeah, well, I'm the warm-up act,' Jess shouted back, as the alarm, in keeping with her nerves, switched to a more frenetic distress call.

He moved closer, tapping out a beat against his beer can and jerking his head forward like a turtle trying to itch the back of its neck. 'It's kinda catchy.'

Jess turned towards him intent on issuing a don't-mess-with-me look, then immediately wished to change it to a please-mess-with-me look: he was unnervingly attractive. She fumbled distractedly with the keys.

'You a burglar, then?' he continued, ambling up sexily and taking a sip of beer. 'Or just a female?'

Jess wanted to be angrier at his arrogance than she was. 'You a bastard?' she said, unable to stop smiling, 'Or just a sexist pig?'

He laughed, then took the keys from her, pressed a button and silenced the car. 'Both,' he said, giving them back and proffering his hand. 'Andy, for short.'

Jess shook it. 'A burglar who, despite your sexist stereotyping, also happens to be female,' she said. 'Jess, for short.'

They stood grinning at each other – for a little longer, Jess noted gleefully, than was strictly necessary. He had the look of someone who knew he was gorgeous. She had the look of someone who agreed.

'Nice,' he said, nodding appreciatively at the car in a way

Jess couldn't help wishing he would do to her. 'You steal her from your boyfriend?'

'Don't have a boyfriend,' she replied, immediately regretting the speed and eagerness of this response. 'Not one with a car like this, anyway.'

'Would you like one?'

A spark of lust flared up inside her and charged headlong through every nerve in her body. There was something indescribably thrilling about such a direct approach to flirting. ''Fraid I only date good-looking blokes,' she offered, smiling coquettishly up at him.

'I was meaning the car,' he said, smiling less coquettishly. 'And I'm afraid I only date my girlfriend.'

Jess tried not to look as if he hadn't just taken the wind out of her sails but sunk the boat plus crew. 'Yes, lovely . . . I would like one,' she stammered, then added, 'A car. Not a girlfriend. Obviously.' She gave an uncertain laugh.

'Oi, Brownie,' a voice bellowed up from the door. 'Get yer flirting arse back here. It's speeches.'

Andy necked his can and crumpled it – much as he had done with her ego, Jess reflected. 'You coming?' he said, head tilted invitingly. 'Or do you only *dine* with good-looking blokes too?'

'Guess I could make an exception,' she replied, wishing, as she trotted besottedly after him, that the all-attractive-blokes-are-attached rule had made a similar exception for him.

Once inside it felt less as though she'd entered a dining hall than a different century. A long thin wooden table stretched the length of the room, upon which was laid enough crested silver to fill a particularly tedious episode of the *Antiques Roadshow*. Solemn black men lined the back walls dressed in what appeared to be doctors' coats, holding more silver crested trays containing bits of dried meat. Several blokes in suits were finding phallic and technical pleasure in the mending of a broken microphone, a gaggle of girls in long floral skirts was talking earnestly about a kid called Pube, and three big-bosomed women were standing in a corner swaying, clapping and singing lots of hallelujahs for reasons Jess was unable to fathom until she spotted a table adorned with copious supplies of free alcohol.

'Wine?' Andy was hovering in front of a wine box brandishing two glasses.

'Wine-ot!' Jess said, giving a surprised laugh at her own wit.

He rolled his eyes heavenward as the box weed into the glass. 'Fools laugh at their own fun, you know,' he said, smirking.

Jess smiled. 'So . . . I take it you spend a lot of time laughing.'

He laughed. 'Especially when I meet female burglars who can't get out of their stolen property without setting off alarms.' He handed her a drink. 'Cheers.'

'Or just one female goddess who's so hilarious and stunning you simply can't control yourself,' she joked, then noticed he looked awkward and wished she hadn't. Flirting was like tennis: you got comfortable in a rally with well-placed shots that bounced off each other, then got that little bit cocky, tried to do something clever and ended up losing the point. In this particular game, she hadn't just crossed the line, she'd lobbed the ball right over the back wall.

'So, Andy!' she said, brightly, as though he were four and about to cry. 'What do you do?'

Suddenly, without any warning, he was lunging for her – as if, surroundings, convention and girlfriend were no longer strong enough to hold back his compulsion to kiss her: an urgent, passionate, uncontrolled animalistic declaration of . . . But it turned out to be his mate – slapping him over-heartily on the back.

'Matthew,' he said, extending a cuff-linked hand towards Jess's chest. 'Don't trust him.'

Andy play-punched him in the stomach.

'Jess,' she replied, reaching out to shake the hand just as Matthew removed it and returned the punch. 'Nice to meet you . . .' Her voice trailed off, along with her confidence.

'Matthew teaches maths,' Andy announced. 'It's just his personality that doesn't add up.'

Matthew guffawed. 'Andy teaches nothing,' he said, swigging at a bottle, 'and doesn't have a personality.'

Jess smiled wanly, pretending to enjoy being the audience for a game of Lads' Larks. While female friendship worked on the basis of being as nice to each other as possible, it was little wonder that the cross-gender version had so many problems when male friendship worked on the reverse.

'Anyway, Bollocks-for-brains, you're wanted,' Matthew said.

Jess watched, smitten, as Andy ran a hand sexily through his hair. Wanted was an understatement. 'OK, No-bollocks-or-brains,' he retaliated and, excusing himself with a nod in Jess's direction, followed his friend to the podium.

After a predictably dull introduction from the headmaster, who seemed intent on welcoming everyone bar masked gunmen, Andy took to the stage and delivered a hilarious account of his first impressions of the school. By the time he'd stepped down, Jess was somewhere between intrigued and in love.

'Sally,' a girl introduced herself. They'd all been invited to find their names on the table. Jess had been disappointed to find hers.

'Jess,' she said, trying to look interested.

'I take Bea for Moral Education,' Sally explained. 'She's got a good grasp of what is right.' Sally, in turquoise blouse and purple jodhpurs, evidently hadn't.

'I nanny for the Montagues,' announced a posh voice on her other side. 'Harriet. But everyone calls me Tatty.'

Jess turned round to where, contrary to visions of a dishevelled potato farmer, a tall slender girl was standing, gin and tonic in hand. She had the aristocratic look of a well-bred horse and managed to make ripped combats and an inside-out sweater seem effortlessly designer-scruffy rather than, as Jess suspected the same ensemble would look on her, scruffy. 'Jess,' she said, offering her hand as Tatty descended on a round of what appeared to be her Swiss finishing school's version of snogging.

'Why Tatty?' Sally asked, already in awe.

Tatty gave a little neigh. 'When I was born my brother, Roo, couldn't say Harriet – bless him – so he called me Tattiet, which became Tatty and soon the whole of Surrey was using it and it stuck.'

Up in the air along with your nose? Jess wondered.

'Doesn't make Harrington-Forster any easier to say, mind you,' she added, chortling.

Clearly, Jess decided, a double-barrel of laughs.

By the time the avocado and prawn cocktail arrived, the seat in front of her was still ominously empty. It was like being in a rowing boat: the conversational weight needed counter-balancing fast to prevent the whole thing sinking. She searched anxiously up and down the table for a potential oarsman.

'Hi. I'm that bastard sexist pig you met earlier.'

And found him with oar extended. 'Hi. I'm that female burglar you patronised earlier.'

Sally jerked round and stared, then surreptitiously brought up a protective hand to her pearl necklace.

'Don't worry,' Andy said, jumping into the empty seat and leaning over to Sally confidingly. 'She tends to steal cars rather than jewellery.'

Jess laughed, as Sally smiled unsteadily.

'Although,' he added, in a stage-whisper, 'I'm sure there's some fast cash to be made on this cutlery.'

It always came as a surprise to Jess how quickly, in mixed gatherings, people gravitated to their equal. It was like making a vinaigrette dressing: no matter how hard you shook the oil and vinegar it was only a matter of time before they separated again. Come the arrival of pudding, she'd not just found her matching oil but had a suspicion neither of them wanted to remain extra virgin.

'. . . so they took one look at my six-pack and promoted me to Outdoors Instructor instead.' Andy had swapped seats with Sally, swivelled it round so that he was facing Jess and was sitting, legs apart, hands behind head, grinning. If bodies could really speak a language, she decided excitedly, this one didn't require a translator.

'So. What brought you out here, then?'

Andy looked pensively into the distance. 'Umm . . . a Boeing 747, I think.'

Jess pretended to find this tedious. He fiddled with the corner of his napkin. He was gorgeous.

'Sarah, I guess.'

Jess flinched. The mention of a girlfriend in the middle of such a wonderful evening was the equivalent of eating a meal and unintentionally swallowing a chilli: nothing felt the same thereafter. 'Your girlfriend,' she confirmed, hoping it didn't sound too like she cared.

'*Ex*-girlfriend.'

She tried to look calm. 'But I thought . . . you said . . .' she began, then remembered, miserably, that an ex-girlfriend didn't necessarily preclude a present girlfriend.

'We split up. So I came out here.' He looked sad. Maybe there wasn't a present girlfriend.

'Why?'

He refilled their glasses. 'It just didn't seem enough. I mean, it was good, you know, it was fine. She's lovely. A really lovely girl.' He massaged the stem of his glass in fond recollection of just how lovely. Jess nodded encouragingly, hoping he hadn't picked up on her desperation to hear the *but*. 'But I just doubted it the whole time. Doubted what it was, doubted whether it could ever be what I wanted it to be. Doubted *why* I doubted.' He paused.

She was speechless. It was her relationship with Alex. To a T.

'I felt trapped,' he went on. 'Trapped in a vacuum of stale-ess. Every time I thought about our future together it seemed like this long flat line stretching out dismally in front of me, no ups, no downs, just flat.'

Jess felt every cell in her body light up like an inundated switchboard. There was connecting with someone, and then there was this. 'Like the line on a heart monitor of a dead person,' she said, a little too enthusiastically.

He looked searchingly at her as if they'd simultaneously dialled each other's number. 'Yes! Absolutely.'

There was a reverent silence. The flirting game had ended. It was now match point.

'D'you fancy going outside for some air?'

Jess grinned uncontrollably.

'Because we seem to be running a bit short in here,' he added, endearingly embarrassed.

Once outside it was no longer air they were short of but conversation.

'That's Orion's Belt,' he announced, stiltedly, as they walked in no particular direction.

Jess followed his gaze. 'Gosh, the stars are very bright here,' she offered, with dazzling Mills and Boon originality. Why was it that when you wanted to snog someone, you had to pretend to be interested in anything but?

'And if you look really carefully,' he continued, as she stood, head back, trying to concentrate on the celestial position she was being shown, rather than the compromising one she wished so dearly to get into, 'you can see Uranus.'

She searched the studded sky unaware of what she should be looking for.

'See?'

'Umm . . . is it, what exactly does it look like?' she said, falteringly.

'I can only see what surrounds it,' he said, a wry grin spreading across his face, 'but from where I'm standing it looks pert . . . cute . . . and very . . .' suddenly, she twigged and turned to him laughing '. . . damn sexy.'

'Cheeky!' she shrieked in delight, as, laughing too, he reached out and drew her towards him.

'Two nice ones, yes,' he whispered approvingly, squeezing her bottom with both hands before cupping her face and giving her the kind of kiss that suggested his Outdoor Instruction lessons might well be worth enrolling for.

When they pulled back and stood staring at each other soppily, Jess felt the first pangs of panic. He was wonderful. He was on her wavelength. And he was with her. Something had to be wrong. Then she remembered. 'Thought you only dated your girlfriend.'

He smiled and pecked her on the nose. 'When I can find one. Yes.'

She imploded with joy and, kissing his neck, resolved to make sure he didn't have to look very far.

Sects Education

To: *Claire.Voyant@hotmail.com*
Date: *Monday 29 May*
Subject: *Sects Education*

Wishing Andy would look further than my tits.
  Wanting to become a more stable version of
  'girlfriend'. Paranoid I've become a more literal
  version of Phil Collins' Easy Lover.

Dear Claire,
  I have a new boyfriend. Well, to be strictly honest, he's 'new'
and therefore, by male association, probably not yet a 'boyfriend'.
Even though we're in a relationship. Although maybe we're not in
a relationship per se, *but in a sort of laid-back Kenyan . . . Oh,*
God, this whole labelling thing does my head in. It's obvious he's
my boyfriend, really, I'm just scared that if I call him that he'll
get offended – like when I failed my French oral because I addressed
the male examiner as tu, *thereby insinuating that we were inti-*
mate friends and/or sleeping together. But unlike French, which at
least has rules, this boyfriend-title thing relies on intuition, in the
same way that there's an unwritten code as to when you can start
calling your friend's parents Mike and Leslie, rather than Mr and
Mrs Dalrymple.
  Anyway, boyfriend or no boyfriend, we're certainly doing lots of
shagging, which can never be a bad thing. In fact, I can't remember
having quite so much sex with anyone in my life before, but then
again, I can't remember having sex before. It seems to be an un-
explained sexual mystery that whenever you start shagging someone
new, you're automatically unable to recall shagging anyone else.
Why does this happen? Is it like Hollywood actors – that you're

only as good as your last performance? Or is it some arrogant ingredient of sperm that whitewashes our brains (and sheets, for that matter) into assuming that no one who's come before – so to speak – is comparable?

Obviously, I'm really enjoying it, it's just that . . . well, we don't seem to do anything else. Surely the more normal way to spend an evening with a new partner is at least to pretend *you're interested in getting to know each other via cinema trips and nice meals, etc. I feel as though I'm a fruit machine, but instead of him having laboriously to feed me until I come up with the goods, all he has to do is pull my handle – or, more usually, I pull his – and, hey presto, he hits the jackpot each and every time.*

The problem is, our trips to the amusement arcade are a bit erratic. He teaches at Colobus – Noah and Bea's school – in the somewhat baffling dual role of Outdoors Instructor-cum-Choir Master, and lives on campus. It's officially the local school – 'local' in the way Chiswick isn't a million miles away from Clapham, just seems like it because the District Line's so crap – and is a forty-five-minute drive over roads with enough potholes to make you feel as if God's playing snooker with you. As a result, we tend just to see each other at the weekends, unless I can find some crucial missing chord in Noah's music that requires immediate and thorough investigation beneath Andy's duvet.

I'm in his apartment now because he only has to teach in the mornings on a Monday, meaning we can do something nice together this afternoon like . . . well, like . . . like possibly have sex. Again. For the third time today. In fact, I'm currently sitting at his desk on his minuscule laptop computer (laptops and mobile phones – the only things blokes will compete over for whose is smallest*) trying to convince his housegirl – the poor Kenyan woman who gets paid 3p a week to do the jobs for which Hotpoint invented eight different machines – that I'm not the prostitute I appear to be. She's a lovely lady but doesn't speak a word of English, meaning a simple request to wash a window has me performing the camp moves of a Gary Barlow backing singer.*

This morning's charades were particularly creatively challenging: the water has been cut off. This in itself isn't anything special: if the electricity, phone and water are working at the same time here you get suspicious, in much the same way that if you board a train in Britain that is on time, has no broken air-conditioning, doesn't stop outside Doncaster for no apparent reason, has a buffet service with food you might want to eat and toilets with no puddles of urine on the floor, you can't help but feel something nasty is waiting to meet you at the other end – or possibly that you are about to meet your end.

Anyway, the trouble with the water is that where normally it just cuts off because an animal's got stuck in the tank, this time they're saying there's something wrong with the pipes and we have to conserve every drop because we might be without it for three whole days. Trying to explain this to someone who only understands Swahili is not easy: every time she reaches for a tap I have to mime throat-slitting gestures to the extent that I think she suspects I want to kill myself.

It's at times like these that I wish I was back in England where you can at least be guaranteed that the water will run and the plumbing will work. But I suppose, like ex-boyfriends, there's no good appreciating what you've left behind, so I'll just have to fill the kettle and wash myself in a puddle in the bath, which is stained a dubious orange colour – hopefully not because the previous owner used it as a second loo.

Mind you, I suppose I should count myself lucky: a urine marked bathtub must seem like a luxury en suite at the Ritz in comparison with your bamboo shower hoses and recycling-compost toilets. Am particularly concerned about the latter. Are you saying the turds get dried out and used to fertilise the same fields in which you grow your dinner? Please tell me I've missed a vital link in this disturbingly worthy eco-chain. While I'm in favour of doing one's bit for the environment, I'd sooner repair the hole in the ozone layer single-handedly than eat something grown in my own excrement.

Ergh! Just had a horror thought that the previous owner pooed in the bath too. Might get the housegirl to give it a good scrubbing, although I can't help wishing she'd just go. One of the best things about being left in a house after a bloke's gone to work is the snooping opportunity, and I can't take full advantage of this with her around. So far I've only done some photo albums, which are much better to look at on your own because you can just whiz through the boring ones without appearing rude and uninterested – the 'boring' ones, in this case, being bits of nondescript buildings and eighteen identical shots of a valley that must have seemed awe-inspiring and fascinating when Andy was taking them. I've decided that anything without people in it makes for tedious viewing – like books with long waffly descriptive passages and no dialogue.

I've moved on to having a little peek through his computer files, which I know is not terribly morally justifiable but neither is having a brand new Sony laptop when thousands in Kenya are starving. Typically the ones I can open are boring school reports while the password-protected ones give rise to two possible paths of paranoia: (1) Is the password the name of another woman? (2) Is the need for a password another woman? I mustn't venture down either route. I did that once with a boyfriend whose password I worked out by watching and remembering key sequences in the manner of James Bond about to open a safe with his watch. Ended up getting myself into the most horrendous state when I realised it spelt 'Amber Lotus', convinced myself he was having an affair with her and ended the relationship. It wasn't until months later that I discovered Amber Lotus was the make and colour of a car.

Ergh – have a horrible headache suddenly. Suspect it's because I've been staring at this tiny computer, which is only tiny because it uses font snitched from the bottom line of an optician's eye chart. Or maybe it's a symptom of sex-overload syndrome? The trouble is, I can't help thinking it's malaria. But that's the problem with living somewhere like Africa: you think the slightest ache or discomfort is not just tiredness or a cold, but the onslaught of some fatal tropical disease. It's like when you think you might be pregnant and immediately diagnose nausea as morning sickness rather than a hangover or, as it usually is, PMT.

To be honest, it's probably not malaria, just another vile side-effect of the pills I'm taking to prevent malaria. So far they've given me insomnia, stomach cramps, diarrhoea, dizzy spells and cold sweats, making the prospect of malaria seem positively appealing. It reminds me of being a child and feeling sick and my parents spooning something that tasted suspiciously like melted chalk down my gullet. Contrary to their promises that it was a 'magic cure', it had me barfing up my innards within seconds.

Anyway, I shouldn't worry because apparently if you've got malaria you become like those smug people who've already met their life partner and 'just know'. The problem is, be it malaria or marriage, I permanently feel I just don't know. I spend so much time comparing what I should feel with what I do feel that I end up in a negative peat bog assuming headache = malaria, or because Alex did not make my heart miss a beat every time I saw him = end relationship. At least with malaria you can get your symptoms checked by a doctor. If I'd had someone to check whether my doubts about Alex were Incompatible Couple Syndrome or just hypochondria, I might right now be going for dress fittings and boring on about tiaras. But that's the trouble with relationships: you're constantly striving towards a destination you've never reached with only failed attempts behind you to guide your way.

In fact, my whole relationship with Alex felt like one long trip on the M4 when you've come out of a service station and followed the wrong sign. The further we went, the fewer exits there seemed to be and the more panicked I became that I'd never be able to turn back. But maybe if I'd just kept going we'd have found ourselves in somewhere unexpected but equally good – like when you go into a changing room to try on a pair of trousers and the assistant hands you two tops from the reject rail because they can only count in multiples of three, and you end up buying one of the tops rather than the trousers you originally went in for.

It's not that I'm having regrets about splitting up with Alex, more that I regret taking so much of him for granted. I just assumed it was normal boyfriend etiquette to phone and check you got home all right, or cook you dinner when you've had a shit day at work, in the same way as you move out from your parents' house and discover that balsamic vinegar isn't 'just there' or that the phone bill isn't 'just paid'.

It's weird how it's only since I've been going out with – or whatever you call non-stop shagging – Andy that I've started to think more about Alex. I guess it's a comparison thing, like when your computer at work gets upgraded to a snazzy new version and suddenly all the icons aren't where they used to be, or the mouse is so sensitive it disappears whenever you touch it, and before you know it you're praising all the little foibles and eccentricities of your last computer, which previously you spent most of your time swearing at. Not that any of Andy's icons aren't where they should be, nor his mouse likely to disappear when I touch it – quite the opposite, to be perfectly honest about it – just that there was a familiarity and reliability about Alex that where before seemed annoying now seems comforting.

I think the whole thing has a lot to do with Marjorie's theory. She claims you are one of two types when it comes to relationships: a tap or a plug-hole. The tap is the giver (unless you live in Kenya where, like now, it seems to be more the giver-upper) and the plug-hole the taker. For a partnership to work best you need one of each. Obviously Alex is the tap and, although in many ways Andy is like the tap too – i.e. only functions when turned on – I suspect that when it comes to the more crucial aspects of a relationship he is the plug-hole. Which leaves me – a plug-hole complete with waste-disposal unit, if what Andy has been doing to me lately has any relevance.

And therein lies the problem: we want and need the same things from a tap! When I first met him I was so amazed to have found a bloke intent on holding out for 'the one' – rather than giving in and being 'won over' – that I assumed we were destined for each other. But – as my interrailing days taught me all too well – just *because you've found a friend who wants to go to Portugal doesn't mean you'll make ideal travelling companions. Andy and I have already hit rocky seas and we're barely off the coast of Britain. Storms so far include:*

Beaufort number	Atmosphere	Description of Argument	
2	Uneasy	Andy:	Going to bed wearing Mr Happy boxer shorts given to him by ex-girlfriend Sarah.
		Me:	Mrs Unhappy: loud huffing, followed by age-old wall-facing tactic.
5	Tense	Andy:	Dashing off to play football, announcing after one-sided sex that 'I'll make it up to you later.'
		Me:	Furiously pointing out that orgasms do not work on deferred payment in manner of cream sofa from Land of Leather, but in manner of Mastermind questions: 'I've started so I'll finish . . .'
7	Near gale	Andy:	Happily talking all night about his career while watching me struggle to make dinner in blatant assumption that that was mine.
		Me:	Exploding along with non-microwavable bowl at his self-obsessed, sexist arrogance

			and for the first time admit- *ting to myself that I might* *have made a mistake leaving* *Alex.*
12	*Hurricane*	*Andy:*	*Admitting for the first time* *that he might have made a* *mistake leaving Sarah.*
		Me:	*You fucking WHAT?!?!*

I think the bigger problem is less that we're plug-holes trying to turn each other into taps – or, more specifically, Alex and Sarah – but two people with rather too much baggage trying to share one seat. It's as though we've sneaked through Check-in by hiding our overweight hand luggage, enjoyed a celebratory drink in the departure lounge, then spent the rest of the journey lugging it around with sore shoulders and an increasing regret that we didn't just face facts, pay the excess at the time and enjoy an unencumbered and stress-free trip.

Anyway, I'm not going to get stressed but just enjoy it and accept that . . . Urgh, head is still thumping, not helped by the fact that Andy's flat is next to the music room where some kind of perpetual keep-fit class is going on – at least, I hope that's what it is. Britney Spears seems to be making the same mistake over and over and telling everyone with trademark fake naïvety that 'Oops, she did it again,' and a rather excited female voice is shouting, 'Up . . . and down . . . That's it, with your partner . . . Up . . . and down, then innnnnnn and out and in, out, in, out, well done, Jenny, that's it, Simon . . .' Maybe it's beginners' Kama Sutra and any minute now — oh, God, must stop being such a bloke and reducing everything to sex. Don't know what's got into me – apart, obviously, from Andy three times a day – but I seem to have contracted an alarming ability to see the sexual in anything.

The other day Andy had to take the First Eleven cricket team to an away match and asked if I could stand in and take forms

Three and Four for football. Although I can't play or understand the game and don't particularly like it, I agreed, since showing a lack of interest in sport in front of someone whose life is sport is like trying to apply for a job in television without having done five years' unpaid work as a photocopier. I don't quite know what makes sport-enthusiasts like this, since I'm sure if I was equally passionate about, say, metallurgy, I wouldn't insist on a rundown of the chemical properties of iron sulphate before deciding whether or not to bother with someone. Anyway, he rushed off, left twenty-nine little faces staring up at me as if I was Mary Poppins about to tap my umbrella on the ground and produce sweeties from my carpet-bag, and a note that instructed me to: 'Divide into sects. Rotate – dribbling, positions, marking each other, ball work, shooting.'

Not entirely clear what this had to do with football, I sent them running round the pitch and then, assuming he'd misspelt 'sex' (he is an Outdoors Instructor, after all, not an English teacher) split them up boys versus girls, which everyone seemed very happy about. However, just as I'd solved the problem of not knowing the rules by enrolling a nine-year-old who did as referee, the headmaster turned up, informed me that Cherry Orchard School had arrived for the tournament and told me to get the team to the pavilion ASAP.

The minute he'd disappeared I turned pleadingly to the kids as if I were their mother and had just received a text message on a phone I was still struggling to turn on. They were all doing something with their hands that we used to recognise as a little bunny finger-shadow-puppet, but I suspect, much like Dick from the Famous Five, it has a different meaning now. Only when I overheard a bunch of boys saying Cherry Orchard were a 'bunch of girls' did I suss out what was going on and promptly dismissed the girls' team to the pavilion.

Everything went smoothly after that. The boys played football, I walked around saying, 'Good kick,' and by the time the bell went for the next lesson, they were all reluctant to go – which I think is perhaps less to do with my skills as coach and more because they had double maths.

Exhausted by my non-participation in the game, I retired to Andy's flat with a beer and plans of a little nap until, just as I'd got settled, a fuming Andy stormed in. The First Eleven had lost – an event seemingly on a par with the Battle of Hastings – and Cherry Orchard's 'bunch of girls' had been a 'bunch of big-balled boys' who did not take kindly to Colobus's dig at their football skills by sending a team of girls. Play had ended before half-time with two broken ankles, several bruised egos, and an irate Cherry Orchard headmaster demanding a written apology.

I explained calmly to a not-very-calm Andy that I had just followed his instructions and shouldn't be to blame, especially as he was the one who, despite prolific practice in the act, had still to learn to spell it. He looked at me with the blank expression of a foreigner who hasn't realised you've asked them a question, then closed his eyes and hung his head as if saying a little prayer. Then, Hell.

S-E-C-T-S, he shouted, much like the YMCA song, only with less friendly hand movements, was an abbreviation of the word 'sections' and was an instruction to divide the pitch up so that different football skills could be practised by different groups in rotation. It had nothing to do with sex and even less to do with sending 'a bunch of pissing girls' to lose a crucial qualifying match. I felt like that bloke Southgate who missed the penalty and had to spend the rest of the year being verbally abused because everyone – while claiming that the beauty of football lay in supporting the team – blamed him alone for England getting kicked out of the World Cup.

So what was supposed to be a forty-five-minute favour for Andy ended up with me making a formal apology to both headmasters, offering everything short of a blow-job to get Cherry Orchard's sports master to agree to a rematch, and resolving never to offer Andy my services again – sectual, sexual or otherwise. Which reminds me, I'd better just check I've put the photo albums back in the right order before he appears – one sec . . .

Jesus wank! Fucking fuck. I've just read a postcard on his mantelpiece that's signed off: 'PS Have you shagged Pippa yet?' Who the fuck is Pippa? He's having an affair. Worse than an affair because he's told someone how desperate he is to shag her and . . . I must calm down and study it properly. After all, it could be Jess, just written funny. Although it definitely starts with P. Or is it a D? Could it in any way be a J? Maybe it's 'have you shagged PEOPLE *yet?' Oh, God, who the fuck is Pippa? I keep trying to find other Ps and Is to compare them, like a graphologist about to conclude someone has a mother fixation because they do curly Ys and – maybe Pippa's his mother? But then that would mean – yuk, do not even want to let brain imagine what that would mean . . .*

Oh, Christ, this is hell – like playing hangman, but instead of watching a little stick man being hanged because you haven't guessed the right letters, I'm on the verge of hanging myself *because I have. Although just thought – could Pippa be his nickname for me, one he's still too shy to use in front of me? Maybe. Probably not, to be honest. Sod it – I give up. Off to find a noose.*

Jess

xxx

PS Might just let Andy know why, though. Don't want a Romeo-and-Juliet-style botch-up, after all.

Brief Encounters

'Why?' Andy said sleepily, first-thing-in-the-morning-sex being his routine equivalent to everyone else's trip to the loo. 'What's wrong?'

Jess grunted huffily, swivelled round so that she had her back to him, then announced – should he still be in any doubt that something was very wrong indeed, 'Nothing.'

Andy laughed. 'Ah, the good old nothing problem,' he said, nuzzling into the nape of her neck. 'Nothing a bit of coital action won't cure, I'm sure.'

Jess manoeuvred as close to the edge of the bed as she could. There was only one thing worse than 'nothing' being taken literally and that was 'nothing' being taken light-heartedly. 'Why don't you try elsewhere?' she mumbled, sulkily. 'After all, we all know you want to.'

Far from denying this, he seemed, if anything, more excited. 'Does this count as elsewhere?' he whispered, sliding his hand down her back and playfully patting her bottom. 'If so, I'd very much like to try.'

'Nothing' ventured, absolutely nothing gained, Jess, furious, resorted to silence.

He drummed his fingers on her right buttock as if waiting to be served at the bar. 'Methinks the lady doth protest too much,' he murmured in her ear.

'You don't think. Period,' she snapped, when it was clear neither version of saying nothing was going to work.

'True. But I think this little strop might be something to do with *your* period,' he said, chortling.

Jess flipped round. Then just flipped. 'One, it's not a "little strop". Two, I haven't got my period. And three . . .' she paused – the idea had been to suggest *calmly* that she knew about his infidelity '. . . just piss off back to Pippa and leave me alone.'

Andy fell back against his pillow offering up both palms in surrender as if she'd just brandished a sawn-off shotgun. 'Explanation, please.'

Jess stared at him hard. 'I don't think *I*'m the one who should be doing the explaining,' she said, wishing she sounded more cheated-lover than no-nonsense teacher.

'Then at least tell me what you'd like explained,' he replied, all wide-eyed innocence, 'bearing in mind I'm still a bit unclear on the finer points of reproduction.' He smiled.

'OK, then. What about reproduction with, say, Pippa? How are you on that?'

He looked at her, scratching his head with the exaggerated confusion of a cartoon character. 'Who's Pippa?'

'Thought *you* might be able to tell *me*.'

He shook his head. ''Fraid not. Don't know a Pippa.' Then he leaped on top of her and buried his head in her chest. 'Only know a sexy Jess.'

'Andy!' she exploded, pushing him off her as if he were a dog that had just stuck its nose up her skirt. If men had a one-track mind, Andy's was a monorail driven by Hugh Hefner. 'Can't you see I'm upset? Has it completely escaped your notice that something – Pippa, to be exact – is bothering me? Don't you understand that having sex with you is the last thing short of giving myself a lobotomy with a knitting needle that I actually want right now? Have you not—'

'Got the slightest clue what you're waffling on about, never known anyone called Pippa and want to know what I'm being accused of.' He looked angry.

Suddenly it struck Jess that if she was going to accuse him of infidelity, she'd have to own up to how she came to *know* about his infidelity, which meant stepping down from her high horse and on to a more deferential donkey. Instead, she chose to concoct a complicated lie about the housegirl developing a pressing desire to learn English, not from the easy-to-understand Swahili/English phrasebook but from an illegible, handwritten postcard. Just as she was working out how best to launch into this lie, Andy leaped up and shot out of bed.

'I don't do paranoid,' he said, as if it were a sexual position and Jess a porn director. 'Nor do I do random accusations about girls I've never heard of.' He was picking up T-shirts from the floor, sniffing them, then chucking them back again, in much the same manner, Jess suspected, he did with women. 'The whole point of a relationship,' he continued – she was intrigued to hear how he'd couch 'is to shag as many people as possible without getting caught' – 'is trust.' She flinched. 'Without it, it doesn't work.' Then he stormed into the bathroom and slammed the door.

Jess lay staring at an ant as it struggled with the back-breaking load of a crumb. When it came to relationships, she reflected, everyone had their crumb to bear – an unresolved problem to which the carrier was sensitive, their new partner oblivious. Andy's crumb was obviously that of trust and she had just unwittingly displayed the very girlfriend-behaviour he'd run away from. Moving from a failed relationship to a fresh one was like recovering from malaria: everything would look rosy and dandy to begin with but there was no certainty that the same symptoms wouldn't recur at some point in the future. Like now.

'Andy, I—' she began, when he emerged from the bathroom as if it were a morgue.

'I've got choir,' he said, pushed past her and disappeared angrily through the front door.

It wasn't until several hours later that, caught half-way between feeling awful about Andy and paranoid about Pippa, Jess hit on the perfect solution to unearth the truth.

'So, Bea, how was school today?'

Bea was sitting at the kitchen table struggling with the complexities of three times four. 'We're only allowed to talk when we've finished our homework, Jess,' she replied, with the unnatural goody-goodyness of an Enid Blyton creation.

Why was it, Jess wondered, that the only time kids could be guaranteed to do what they were told was when you didn't want them to? 'Well, look, we *have* finished,' she said, hurriedly writing '7' and closing her jotter. 'So. How was school?'

'Boring.'

'Even sport with Mr Brown?'

Bea nodded.

'But I thought you liked Mr Brown.'

'Sometimes,' she said, comparing the lengths of her pencils in a way that would make her, one day, a rather intimidating girlfriend. 'Which one d'you like best?'

Jess smiled. 'I think I like Mr Brown best.'

Bea cast her a disparaging look. 'I meant the pencils.'

'Oh . . . right . . . um, the blue one. So. Who does Mr Brown like best?'

Bea furrowed her brow in concentration. Jess composed her expression for the name 'Pippa'.

'I like . . . the red one best, the yellow one next best, the . . . green, no, the blue one . . . the green, yes, the green—'

'That's lovely, Bea,' Jess said, trying not to look, sound or feel irritated. 'Now, if they were teachers, which one d'you think Mr Brown would like best?'

'But they're pencils, silly,' Bea said, laughing.

'But let's *pretend*,' Jess whined, in adult-child role-reversal.

Bea looked deeply unimpressed. 'I think that's a bit stupid, Jess,' she said, picking them up and packing them into her pencil case.

Just like getting information from a bloke, Jess decided, subtlety got you nowhere. 'Who's Pippa?'

'Depends. Do you mean Pippa Illingworth or Pippa Cassidy?'

Jess froze. Of all the Pippas Andy could be shagging, she hadn't counted on them being seven years old.

'This doesn't look like homework.' With excruciatingly bad timing, Marjorie had just entered, cradling what appeared to be a live rabbit.

'Peepo!' Bea shouted, leaping down from her chair and charging towards her mother's groin.

'Not so fast, young lady,' Marjorie said, lifting the rabbit above her head as if about to lob it into a netball goal. 'Peepo only gets a cuddle from girls who've done their homework.' Peepo did a dropping.

'But I *have*,' Bea whined. 'Jess says I have.'

Marjorie placed the rabbit on the draining-board, where it promptly did several more droppings. She marched over to the table and picked up the jotter. 'OK, what's three times four?'

Bea searched the ceiling. 'Twelve.'

'Right. So why have you written seven?'

Bea looked at her indignantly. 'I haven't written seven.'

Marjorie showed her the jotter. 'That looks like a seven to me.'

Bea looked even more indignant. 'Jess wrote it.'

Still reeling from visions of Andy and under-age Pippas, Jess regained consciousness. 'Wrote what?'

'The wrong answer,' Bea said, irritated.

Marjorie ruffled Bea's hair and beamed conspiratorially at Jess. 'I've heard a lot of excuses for shoddy homework, Bea,' Marjorie said, looking from her daughter to the jotter with the disbelief of a customs official trying to match the face with the passport photo, 'but blaming it on your nanny is—'

'But she *did*,' Bea pleaded, snatching the jotter and, much to Jess's horror, pointing at her hastily scribbled seven. 'Look.'

Terrified of what Bea might be capable of, especially when cuddling a rabbit was at stake, Jess realised she had to own up. 'Oh . . . gosh, yes . . . um, I think I did write that,' she stuttered, smiling nervously. 'Silly me, eh?'

Marjorie looked at her as if she'd just discovered ten kilos of cocaine in Jess's suitcase lining. '*You* wrote it?'

'Told you, told you, told you, told you!' Bea sirened, jumping up and down and squealing. 'Can I hug Peepo now?'

'Sorry, Marjorie,' Jess said, meekly. 'I don't know what I was thinking of.'

'You were thinking of Mr Brown,' Bea announced, in full devil's-spawn mode.

Jess grimaced. Wanting to kill someone else's kid was all very well when alone with them. Wanting to do it when surrounded by their parents was the equivalent of being forced to listen to fingernails scraping down a blackboard while chained to a seat with spikes on. 'No, I wasn't, Bea,' she said, as sweetly as she could muster. 'I was helping you.'

'Helping her,' Marjorie boomed, 'would have been waiting for her to write in her own answer, which in this particular case' – she peered at Jess suspiciously – 'would also have been the *correct* one.'

Jess hung her head in shame, ready at any moment to be moved to the Naughty Table. Bea was let out to play.

'I'm more than happy for you to date Andy,' Marjorie continued, 'but I don't want it to come between your role as nanny.'

Jess nodded obediently, head swimming with what had really come between . . . well, Andy's legs, for starters. 'I'm sorry, Marjorie,' she said, close to tears. 'It won't happen again.'

'Forgetting your three times table, or dating Andy?'

Jess forced a smile. 'Both,' she said, wishing one didn't seem likelier than the other.

When it became clear that she'd been let off the hook as if she was a fish deemed too puny to be worth killing, Jess gathered her belongings and scuttled for the door. Unfortunately, though, Marjorie reeled her in again before she got there.

'You couldn't possibly run Bea to Swahili, could you?'

Jess turned round. As a punishment to fit the crime, this

was excessive. 'No problem,' she lied and waited, miserably, while Bea plus rabbit were bundled into the car.

'Guess who used to be Peepo's daddy?'

Jess stared thunderously ahead. 'Dunno.'

'Guess, Jess,' Bea pleaded, trying to plait the rabbit's ears.

'I'm *driving*, Bea.' She swerved round a pothole.

'But still guess.'

'Oh, for Christ's sake, I dunno. Peter Rabbit?'

'Guess again.'

'Bea, listen. I'm very tired. It's been a long day and I'd just like to . . .' Bea looked as though she was going to cry. 'Big Ears?'

'Nope.'

'Buzz Lightyear?'

Bea laughed. 'Nope. D'you give up?'

Jess nodded, tempted to include the rest of her life in this response.

'Mr Brown!' Bea squealed.

'Where?' Jess shrieked, losing grip of the steering-wheel in the excitement, as the car skidded and the rabbit catapulted to the floor.

'Peepo's daddy, silly,' Bea said, heaving the near-dead bundle up from where it was cowering under a crisp packet. 'Mr Brown is Peepo's daddy.'

Jess regained control of both wheel and composure. After her recent experiences with Andy, his having fathered a rabbit did not greatly surprise her.

Bea, however, seemed to think it required explanation. 'He found Peepo in his garden and started being her daddy but then Peepo got ill because he didn't feed her enough carrots so Mummy said she'd take her to the bunny doctor and get her fixed' – Bea gulped for air – 'and the bunny doctor said Peepo needed to be loved properly not just on Wednesdays so Mr Brown said we could be her mummy and daddy instead.'

Jess smiled, wondering whether she'd now be nannying a needy rabbit on top of two spoilt children.

'That's why Mr Brown is sometimes sad,' she continued – and has to shag around, Jess concluded, bitterly. 'Because he loved her and called her . . .' Bea paused, giggling '. . . called her, called her—'

'Called her what, Bea?'

'Called her his' – Bea bit her lower lip and smiled coyly – 'girlfriend.'

Suddenly, Jess sat bolt upright like a . . . rabbit. Pippa was not sexy, shagging Andy or seven years old. Pippa was Peepo, the pet rabbit.

'In the name of all flying arses!' she exploded, caught between feelings of jubilant relief and humiliation that yet another person she'd obsessed about and fixated on had turned out to be an animal.

'Don't worry,' Bea piped up, reassuringly, 'I'm sure you can be his girlfriend too.'

Jess smiled patronisingly and refrained from telling her that that had been precisely what she'd been worried about.

By the time they got to Bea's Swahili lesson, the class was in full swing – or, rather, the teacher was. He seemed to be doing some sort of Kenyan jig to emphasise a point about verb conjugation. Too preoccupied with thoughts of her own conjugation with Andy, Jess left them to it and was just on her way to grovel for forgiveness when she spotted a tantalising white box protruding from her pigeonhole.

All her mail came to the school on the understanding it would then be hand-delivered by a local Kenyan boy. Whether the local Kenyan boy shared this understanding or it was just that everyone except the accounts department at Visa had misplaced her address, nothing interesting ever arrived. Hence, this – a gift-wrapped box – was a big event.

She charged towards it, yanked it out and tore off the ribbon. Then she removed the lid and yelped in delight. Laid lavishly on swathes of soft tissue was a set of sexy red lace underwear. Without an accompanying envelope, address or postmark, it could be from only one person. Exploding with joy, she skipped off to find him.

'If you're going to have another go, I'm not in the mood.' Andy was straddling a stool at the kitchen table bent over his computer.

'And why would I want to do that?' Jess squealed, rushing up behind him, hooking her arms around his neck and pecking him as though she were a hen.

'If I knew that, Jess,' he said, pretending to be busy with an Excel chart, 'I would be a rich and much-envied guru.'

Jess made as if to strangle him. 'Watch it, sexy chops!'

'Given, however, that I'm merely a poor naïve man,' he continued, swinging round to face her, 'perhaps you could enlighten me as to what has caused this particular, dare I say it, "good" mood?'

Jess beamed at him gooeyly. 'I wonder . . .' she said, mounting him in a way that would have been seductive had the stool not made an ominous cracking sound beneath them. 'I think it might just possibly, maybe, have something to do with some rather nice . . .' she hung her head then looked up at him through her eyelashes in a style she'd watched Bea perfect '. . . underwear.'

He smiled endearingly. 'Thought it might.'

As they sat entwined in renewed affection, Jess couldn't help feeling guilty. Surely if anyone should be giving reconciliatory gifts it was her. 'You're the bestest boyfriend in the whole wide world,' she said, in a rush of joyous love.

Suddenly, she felt him tense. An almost imperceptible stiffening – though not in the desired location. She knew, immediately and miserably, what it was. She'd used the boyfriend word.

'I'm afraid I'm not,' he said, pulling away.

Jess concentrated on forcing the corners of her mouth

upwards, resulting in a manic, insincere, Tony Blair-type smirk.

'Must be from another bestest boyfriend.'

She stared at him, confused.

'It arrived this morning from the UK addressed to the "Sexy Brit".' He smiled. 'Obviously I assumed that was me, opened it up and . . . well, realised it wasn't. So that left Tatty, Matthew or you. Tatty says her mail gets flown here by the Queen's corgis and, anyway,' he adopted Tatty's high-pitched bleat, ' "Charlie knows red doesn't suit me." Matthew doesn't suit anything and would never be described as sexy. Nor, I suspect, is he a 34C. Which leaves you.' He studied her chest, pursing his lips and tilting his head from side to side like a plumber working out how best to remove the washing machine. 'Maybe not a 34C either, but a damn sight sexier than any of the other contenders.'

Jess blinked slowly, taking in the news. While pleased that he'd reached the stage of describing himself as her boyfriend, she was somewhat disappointed to learn he was yet to reach the stage of cementing his commitment with gifts. 'And there's no letter attached? Nothing to signify who it's from?'

'No, Sherlock,' Andy said, grinning. 'Hence the guessing game.'

She got up and fetched the box, emptied it on to the table and fished around in the tissue paper. 'Well, blow me,' she said, slumping down on the sofa.

'I was rather hoping,' Andy said, sidling up beside her, 'that you might want to blow' – he raised one eyebrow suggestively – 'me.'

She punched him playfully, he grabbed her hands, and before long they were using the sofa for something other than sitting on.

'Put on the underwear,' he whispered, with an urgency he usually reserved for encouraging the opposite.

Jess scampered over to the table and hastily donned the

red lace, suspecting that whatever had been the sender's motive, this wouldn't have been their chosen outcome.

'*That* is very sexy,' he purred, as she rejoined him on the sofa feeling like something found pouting from the walls of telephone boxes. He admired the ensemble momentarily, then seemed more concerned with a detailed examination of what lay underneath.

Suddenly, Jess remembered: 'Fuck!'

'That would appear to be the way we're heading,' he said, panting towards his destination.

'Bea! I've forgotten to pick up Bea!' she shrieked, springing up as rapidly as the underwear had caused him to.

He pinned her back down. 'Tell her we're just coming,' he murmured, grinning.

'I'll get the sack,' she protested, freeing herself of his grip as if he were several armed riot police wrestling her to the ground.

'For *being* in the sack,' he added, still grinning.

''S not funny, Andy,' she said, leaping around the room as she tried to find her clothes.

'You're telling me.' He sighed, then groaned with frustration

'I'll make it up to you later,' she yelled, in roguish echo of his own past promises, then fled.

She found Bea sitting on the steps with her rabbit on her lap like something Steven Spielberg would film to a melancholy orchestral movement.

'Sorry, sorry, sorry, sorry,' Jess parroted, engulfing her in a large overcompensatory hug.

'It's OK,' Bea said, in uncharacteristic forgiveness. 'It was just Peepo that was worried.'

'And me,' a voice bellowed above them. Jess peered up to see the Swahili tutor bearing down on them, not looking in quite the exuberant form of earlier. 'The lesson ended twenty minutes ago.'

'Yes, I'm sorry,' Jess said, standing up and smoothing her hair. 'I was . . .' she noticed he was staring directly at her chest '. . . um . . . busy.'

'So I see,' he said, still staring. 'Well, anyway, she was safe with me.'

As they made their way back to the car, Jess glanced down to check whether he'd been staring because her top was inside out or because he was a pervert. She stopped in her tracks. A white card was protruding like a prostitute's payment out of her bra.

'You've got something on your boobie,' Bea pointed out, giggling.

Jess pulled it out. It was blank except for a typed message that read: 'I'm coming over to try to win you back.' She closed her eyes as everything finally made sense.

The Sarah Doorstep Challenge

To: *Claire.Voyant@hotmail.com*
Date: *Sunday 18 June*
Subject: *The Sarah Doorstep Challenge*

Totally confused and befuddled. Feel as if brain
    has been Magimixed so that all thoughts are
    just brown sludge. In awe of how Posh Spice
    makes this look painless.

Dear Claire,
    *Whoever lauded email as a saving grace in the manner of Jesus
was obviously not stuck in Kenya in a bizarre cyber-lovetrap. Wish
to be back in Jane Austen time where handsome messengers came
galloping up to deliver wax-sealed love letters tied with little bows
from dark, smouldering Colin Firths standing pensively by fire-
places. Do not wish to be sitting in front of an IBM computer with
unhelpful 'server not responding' message.*
    *One of the problems with moving out to Kenya, other than the
fear of getting snappled by a lion and, obviously, guilt for leading
decadent lifestyle next to the natives – and possibly the threat of
skin cancer if you spend too long drinking cocktails by the pool –
is that email takes on an importance of gargantuan dimensions.
Where normally an empty incoming mail folder is mildly disap-
pointing, here it becomes the equivalent of every single one of your
friends telling you simultaneously that they never really liked you.
When you're waiting for a response from a bloke, however, it is
the stuff of an Amnesty International appeal.*
    *In this particular torture, the bloke I'm waiting to hear from is
Alex. He sent me some uncharacteristically racy underwear and a
note that said he was coming to try to win me back. As endearing*

and flattering as the proposal was, I couldn't help panicking that we might have a rather messy version of Fatal Attraction *on our hands – especially as Bea already owns the requisite boilable bunny. So I emailed back to find out when he was planning to arrive, not least so I could remove all large saucepans. Ten days on, I haven't heard a peep.*

Surely it cannot be that no-messing, straightforward Alex is playing the treat-'em-mean-keep-'em-keen game? He isn't normally a game player. Obviously he's a great Scrabble enthusiast and likes the odd go at backgammon – but manipulative tactics to keep women gagging? But, then, if he's not playing games, he must just have not got round to replying or, worse, forgotten *to reply, meaning I'm no longer special, fluffy-place-in-heart ex-girlfriend but normal bog-standard mate. Ergh, I really cannot cope with such a demotion – after all, the whole point of ex-boyfriends is that they're there as a constantly keen safety-net should you not find anything better. Instead, I'm going to focus on all other possibilities for his lack of contact:*

(1) He hasn't replied because he hasn't received it.

(2) He has *received it but, for various complicated computery reasons, can't open it.*

(3) He has *received it and* can *open it and is just taking his time to compile a really witty and loving reply, possibly to arrive in conjunction with large floral bouquet.*

(4) He's ill.

(5) It's two in the morning there – all the time.

(6) He's been away on a really long business trip in a country that doesn't have phone sockets.

(7) His computer doesn't work.

(8) Even his one at home.

(9) And all the ones in London.

You see, this is entirely the problem with email, it's so – oh, Christ, just thought, maybe he has *replied only I haven't got it! I hate blind-man's-buff style torture of communicating abroad, like being stuck in one long traffic jam and not knowing if it's due to roadworks, a multi-car pile up or, as is usually the case, no reason whatsoever.*

I suppose I could try phoning him. The trouble is, the lines here are so abysmal that you hear everything repeated as if you're standing in a large cave. Also, because every minute is costing you a fiver, you panic and end up having a conversation of How-are-yous and Fines because anything else seems too expensive to say.

Of course, the logical answer is good old pen and paper which, albeit more time-consuming, can at least be relied upon to work. I now understand why old people go round praising things like mangles over Hotpoint spin-dryers, though I suspect that if I owned a mangle I'd be mangling my own head by now.

I really didn't envisage being like this in Kenya. The whole point of coming to a new country is to experience a different culture, become rejuvenated and inspired, and for trivial things like worries over looking ugly and blokes to be put into stark relief by the bigger picture – third-world famine, enormity of world outside M25, poor people with no shoes still being happy, etc. – not to obsess and moan and behave as though you've never left England.

It's hardly surprising, mind you: every time I try to do the African thing, e.g. walk barefoot on the red-soil arid plains, heart beating to the rhythms of the earth, rejoice in the simplistic beauty of a sunset, commune with hippos, I'm immediately invited to forget all reminders of where I am, in favour of re-creating where I've come from, by attending some hideous cucumber-sandwich event of the sort I'd move heaven and earth to avoid if I was in England.

Last weekend took the biscuit – or, rather, lightly buttered crumpet. Andy took me to the 'Fun For All the Family Sports Day', which was never going to be a winner: since when do fun and family go together or, for that matter, fun and sports? Contrary to images of playing African hockey with bamboo canes and mangoes on a little red-dust pitch with baby baboons obliging as goalposts, we were greeted at the electronic gate by an umpire from Wimbledon who handed us a fixture list and a glass of Pimm's and instructed us to sign in at the clubhouse. The clubhouse was filled with the kind of people who do that aggressive sexual grunting when they play tennis, and give you death stares whenever your ball trickles on to their court. They were all bedecked in regulation white shorts and dresses and stared at my orange Topshop hotpants as if I'd turned up at Royal Ascot in a bikini.

There then followed a day of humiliation and boredom as, thanks to me, we encountered defeat on bowling green, football pitch, manicured golf course, croquet lawn, netball court, at swimming-pool water-polo (I mean – what is going on?), and, obviously, on the tennis court. The only advantage to being such a sporting retard was that – in good old British spirit – there was a gin and tonic after each game for the losing team. Thus, by the time it came to sit down (thank the Lord!) for the roast beef and Yorkshire pudding banquet, I was plastered enough not to find team-mate Henry's dissection of the eighteenth bunker the tedious-beyond-all-good-English-manners conversational diarrhoea it clearly was. I'm beginning to think I'm not in Kenya at all, but a perpetual rerun of Open Day at Eton.

Luckily, however, today is Sunday, the good Lord's day of rest – i.e. no bloody sport – although it's proving anything but restful. I seem to be living in a region that is both devoutly religious and tone deaf, a head-achingly bad combination: 'worship' takes the form of relentless drum beating interspersed with painful wailing – as if everyone on Oxford Street has been told simultaneously that they've missed the Next sale.

I think I need a stint in that meditation garden of yours. It has to be calmer than this – even with naked dreadlock man quoting explicit poetry. Is he still insisting on eating naked as well? I guess you could say it puts the organ into 'organic', although I suspect you've got enough to put you off your human-poo-cultivated food without a side order of dangly genitals.

Talking of which, I'm supposed to be going round to Andy's

for dinner tonight but if they keep up this racket for much longer I might have to go earlier. I'm under strict instructions to wear the red-lace ensemble (presumably under some clothes), which he's become quite attached to. I know it's a little insensitive to be wearing Alex's underwear while shagging someone else but, then, what is not returning an email for ten whole days if not bloody insensitive?

Oh, Lordy, can stand this cacophony no longer! I sincerely hope that whatever God they're worshipping, He is wearing a set of ear-plugs. Will send this when the God of Cyberspace stops arsing around . . .

Fucking, fucking. FUCKING. To say tonight was an unparalleled cataclysmic disaster would be like saying Titanic *had a bit of an altercation with a lump of ice. I'm so distraught it defies description.*

Naturally, the evening began well. I'd donned the underwear under something I'd bought in Topshop's 'smart evening wear' section, i.e. a nightie, and, unusually for me, was both looking and feeling good – always, always a bad sign. Having wangled use of the family's second car by telling Quentin I thought he'd lost weight, I flounced off in the manner of Nicole about to turn on all males by saying, 'Papa?' in provocative, come-to-bed-with-me French accent.

The minute I started driving, there was this sort of popping noise then a weird sinking sensation, almost as if the car was a boat. I decided the best thing was to ignore it and hope it went away, which turned out not to be the best thing at all.

Driving at night in Africa is the equivalent of walking round Brixton asking if anyone wants your handbag. Aside from the normal things – drunk drivers, zebras with no road sense, invisible potholes you only find after scraping the undercarriage off the car – you are also likely to get mugged, raped and killed if you stop.

I stopped. Or, rather, the car did. It turned out that the popping and sinking was a slow puncture that decided to be a quick puncture when I rounded a corner, hit a rock, lost control and careered across the road. Ended up, half in a ditch, huddled behind the wheel in a terrified bundle.

Tried to remain calm and wait for common sense to kick in, while hoping a little roadside phone would pop up from nowhere and a cute, smiley man in fluorescent cagoule would appear with a toolbox, fiddle under the bonnet, while I sat hunched beneath a large tarpaulin looking vulnerable yet sexy sipping a steaming cup of tea, then wave me off in a way to suggest a forthcoming dinner invite might not be out of the question. Then I remembered I was in Africa where the only things at roadsides, other than large ditches, are little stalls selling oranges and/or – for some inexplicable reason – hub-caps. Sometimes the Africans seem so clever and enterprising with their ingenious means of, say, making baskets from plants, but I really feel that selling stolen hub-caps by the side of the road is not one of their better ideas.

I sat there and contemplated death. There's something strangely appealing about doing this, particularly once you start working out how many people would miss you and be sad. When you think about it, including primary-school teachers and friends' parents, it amounts to quite a lot. In fact, I'd just got to the stage of imagining all the lovely things they'd say at my funeral (because, like Hello!, no one makes anything but saccharine, white-lily-type comments) and was rather looking forward to the event, when a BMW pulled up and a man not dissimilar to William Hague offered his assistance.

There's a kind of unspoken agreement among the white community in Kenya that you stop and help one another on the road, in the same way, I suppose, that all girls know tacitly to rally round and call all blokes bastards when someone is dumped. Conveniently, William seemed to have been born with both a silver spoon and a spanner in his mouth, and the tyre-change was over in a shot. I did lots of gushy over-the-top thank-yous, he swatted the air, we made implausible arrangements to go for a coffee, and an hour and a half later than planned I got to Andy's.

Andy was very sweet and concerned, but I was torn between wanting to appear the brave and independent cope-with-anything type of woman and, well, wanting to cry. Little did I know, however, that what I'd just been through was but a mere saunter in the park beside what was to follow.

Despite my late arrival, he was still in the midst of 'cooking' – this being a euphemism for dirtying every saucepan in the kitchen, slavishly adhering to a recipe book such that would never exist if recipe book was female, and meticulously, laboriously and painstakingly chopping up a pepper as if engaged in brain surgery. Whenever I asked if he needed help, he assured me he was fine, which was bollocks because every time I tried to make conversation he looked at me distractedly then put his head in the oven.

When we finally sat down to eat I'd passed the stage of hunger but chose not to make this obvious to Andy, who looked on the verge of passing out. He claimed it was not the exertion of 'cooking' but that the heat had got to him, which, given that I've seen him still going strong sixty minutes into a game of ferocious rugby in forty-degree blistering sunshine, held about as much water as a sieve. So, I put on relaxing music, lit some candles and poured him some wine in my new role as ineffectual man.

Everything had become much more chilled and we were having a nice evening, when there was a scuffling outside the door. We didn't give it much attention at first, assuming it to be a grazing lion or askari, i.e. African security guard dressed like an escapee exhibit from the Jorvik Viking Centre in duffel coat and helmet, whose duty it is to protect schools, houses, etc., by walking around with a bow and arrow. But then the scuffle became a knock and we shot each other quizzical, suspicious looks as if we were Mulder and Scully just about to work out where the green slime was coming from.

Andy got it. I don't know what it was – perhaps psychic powers heightened by being so near the equator – but I just knew something wasn't right. The fact that Andy was saying repeatedly, 'Jesus, I'm in shock,' was a clue, but not enough to prepare me for the unwelcome sight of him rounding the corner carrying a large suit-case, arm in arm with a girl.

There was a split second when she and I looked at each other like two dogs undecided whether to go all out for the snarling attack or just amicably sniff each other's bottoms. Then Andy stepped in and dropped the next grenade: the girl was Sarah, his long-term ex.

She's nothing like I imagined. When you hear a lot about someone you've never met it's quite frightening what the brain can create. It's like when one of your friends goes on and on about a bloke they fancy, encouraging images of a larger-than-life demigod, and then he turns up and he's just this normal bloke with bad taste in trainers, and you realise how blind love can be.

For a start, she's blonde, or at least mousy blonde, which is unsettling given that I am not. Ex-girlfriends are supposed to be helpful signposts towards your boyfriend's choices and tastes: a blonde accountant in M&S T-shirt, pearl necklace and knicker-bockers is totally disorientating – like the horror mouse with the human ear on its back.

She looked thrown to see me – not, however, as thrown as I was when Andy introduced me as 'one of the nannies'. Something about the way he was acting told me he hadn't so much as mentioned me to her. Anyway, we all behaved as if everything was normal, with Andy going on about what a lovely surprise it was, while scanning the room guiltily – for what, I hate to imagine.

We talked – in that wary way you do when trying to make light conversation and simultaneously process everything the others say in order to work out whether or not you like them. Overall results suggested I did, but for reasons that weren't very positive: she seemed bland and non-challenging.

Quite remarkably, it turns out she's a close family friend of Sophie (my boring married friend). Chances are we've probably met before but, a bit like everything Sophie-related, I suspect she blended rather too well into the wallpaper.

Anyway, it was just when she was boring on about an in-flight sausage and I was doing parrot-nodding trying to imagine her and Andy shagging (Sarah seems an unlikely choice for such a sexual man – like Ricky Martin going out with Anne Widdecombe) when – hideous. Truly, truly hideous. I got up to fetch more wine and when I sat down again she was staring at my chest – not lustful-lesbian staring but the furious axe-murderer variety. Then she kicked the chair leg, thumped her glass on the table and shouted, 'Why the fuck is she wearing my bra?'

The whole thing was like watching a car accident unfold really slowly on a Christmas drink-driving campaign, only instead of the mannequin flying through the air and slumping into a dead heap, it was me.

Sarah assumed that Andy had received the underwear but requested I wear it for some kind of warped sexual fetish of his such that would seem but bread and butter for a Jerry Springer guest, then started calling him things that would merely be a string of beeps had she chosen to appear on the programme. Andy kept saying he could explain, he could explain, but, a bit like my Higher Grade history paper, didn't seem able to explain at all. And I, after telling everyone to calm down as if I were a 999 operator, was left to flee home by myself, feeling like a call-girl who'd just discovered her client was a transsexual.

But now all excitement and drama is over and I'm stuck, alone and miserable, as they, no doubt, have a nice shaggy reunion. Why does my entire romantic life make me feel like I'm struggling to get uphill using an escalator going downhill? I keep hoping Andy will come screeching to a halt outside on a motorbike or a very fast giraffe and whisk me off to look at the moon. Maybe I should just go out and get eaten by a lion – although crying in bed is probably easier and I won't have to put on shoes. Right. Well, I hope at least Cyberspace God is going to take pity on me and let me send this.

Lots of love,

Jess

xxx

PS *Jesus wept. I've just remembered. Alex! No wonder he hasn't replied. He thinks I'm some sad gagging act sending loaded emails asking him when he's coming over. But I don't want him to come over. Oh, God, God. I'm going to have to find a really subtle way of ensuring he doesn't come, like asking guests when they're leaving without making it sound as if you're looking forward to it. Cannot believe that after all the anguish of earlier, Alex is now the last person I want to hear from.*

The Star-cross-wired Lovers

Sorry for delay in replying. Just finalising flight details. Will arrive Nairobi, Sat. 24th, 08.30, and will expect nothing less than full VIP treatment. Can't wait!
  Love'n'stuff,
  Alex

PS Don't doubt red lace suits you, but can't claim any glory for it. Ciao.

Jess stared at the computer screen as the initial excitement of receiving an email nosedived into disappointment when she discovered who it was from. As much as she still cared for Alex, she couldn't help feeling that as he was one of her reasons for coming to Africa it was pointless for him to join her. Like signing yourself into the Priory with a suitcase full of narcotics.

She clicked on to a game of Solitaire, all too aware of the poignancy in doing so. It had been a full twenty-four hours since the underwear fiasco and still no word from Andy. Whoever had coined the saying 'No news is good news' was evidently not talking about men. In her experience, no news was a head crammed full of suspicions why – none of them good.

'Where's your bloke, then?' Quentin had just strolled in, hiking up his trousers as if about to stick his thumbs behind his braces and leap into a chorus dance from *Oliver.* 'Thought today's his half-day.'

'It is,' Jess replied, despondently, clicking repeatedly to deal a new and better hand in a way she wished she could do with her life.

'Hrrmph. Well. Can't have you playing with yourself,' he said, as Jess smiled politely and hoped this wasn't an invitation to have sex. 'Fancy a stiff one? A drink,' he added, chortling repulsively.

'Thank you, yes,' she said, shelving the game when the ace of hearts – predictably – failed to show.

'Thought you'd be with Andy today.' Marjorie waltzed into the room and out on to the veranda. Rubbing salt into the wound wasn't in it, Jess thought, bitterly: they were craning in the rock variety from Siberia.

'So did I,' she said, joining Quentin and his stiff one on the wicker sofa. Marjorie raised her eyebrows expectantly. 'His ex-girlfriend's turned up,' she spat, as if Sarah were dry rot.

'Ex-girlfriend, shmirlfriend.' Quentin said, swiping the air dismissively, jowls wobbling, belly ballooning over belt, every bit, Jess decided, the look of someone who'd never had one.

'I wouldn't be so sure,' Marjorie crowbarred in. 'Exes can hold a surprisingly strong sway,' she said – on her day off from Tact School.

'Peter's a buffoon!' Quentin erupted from nowhere. 'Can't even hold a cider.'

Marjorie shot him an indignant look. 'Well, he can hold a conversation, which is more than some people I can think of,' she snapped – a little too defensively, Jess decided.

'Peter proposed to Marj in the . . .' Quentin turned to Jess, beckoning her closer and lowering his voice to a confiding whisper, '. . . in the, in the . . . the . . .' he let out a loud guffaw '. . . the cinema queue, wa-ha-ha-haaaarrr!'

Jess smiled uncertainly, torn between trying to laugh *with* Quentin and not *at* Marjorie. What was it about couples that made them want to use single people like divorce lawyers? It was the equivalent of bad Christmas pantomimes: men in drag trying to get you to shout, 'Oh, no, you didn't!' and someone from *EastEnders* wearing lots of petticoats insisting you bellow, 'Oh, yes, you did!'

'It was very romantic,' Marjorie said, 'and I cried all the way through the film.'

'At the prospect of saying yes,' Quentin roared, with another guffaw.

Marjorie flashed Jess a look that suggested it had more to do with twenty years' regret at having said no.

As they continued in their picking at and protecting of Peter, Jess sank further into both sofa and despair. Was this what she was destined for: a husband she made do with, an ex she wasn't through with? Then, suddenly, she sat bolt upright. If exes really held such sway, then surely Alex's imminent arrival was the trump card she needed.

'Sarah?' Andy sounded desperate.

'No. It's me. Jess,' she said, feeling disappointment daggers dart down the line towards her.

'Christ. I mean, hi. Yes. Shit.'

Jess paused. Shit wasn't even the half of it. 'Is that me you're referring to, or shall I call you back when you're finished?' she said, acerbically.

'No, look – oh, Christ . . . I didn't mean, look, I'm sorry, I . . . Look, Jess, I'm having problems—'

'Forming sentences? Forming relationships? *Sustaining* relationships by using that thing with numbers on that you dial and hear—'

'With Sarah,' he barked.

Jess flinched. Problems with ex-girlfriends were always a bad sign – namely that someone had a problem with the ex bit. She decided that this was her moment to attack. She positioned her missile and fired: 'Know what you mean.'

There was an expectant pause. He'd soon learn about besotted exes, she thought gleefully.

'Christ!' he said, alarmed. 'Has she been to see you?'

'Who?'

'Sarah.'

'No, *Sarah* hasn't but . . .' she waited, drawing out his pain '. . . someone—'

'Shit. I was really hoping . . .' He gave a long sigh. 'She probably just needs time.'

Jess battled on, determined: 'I don't really think it's Sarah we need to be—'

'I'd just feel so much happier if she'd stayed.'

Jess brightened. 'Has she gone?'

'God knows. I think she's in some hotel or other. Listen, you don't fancy meeting for a drink in town, do you? I'm feeling really rotten and trapped here.'

'Umm, well . . .' Jess stammered, weakening. She thought about it. At the end of the day it wasn't exactly his fault that Sarah had turned up and, well, she could keep Alex's love crusade as reserve ammunition. 'OK,' she said, pleasantly, and went to put on the rest of her armour.

By the time she made it to the local village it was dusk, and the place had turned from a few men dozing quietly under trees into Africa's equivalent of Piccadilly Circus. Barefoot cyclists were weaving all over the road swinging indeterminate animals in cages and narrowly avoiding large women strolling slowly with babies strapped to their bosoms. Stallowners selling little pyramids of overripe fruit were shouting things she didn't understand and inviting her to look at their bananas, children were chasing chickens, trucks were reversing into boys pushing samosa carts, and lots of farmyard animals were snuffling about idly getting beeped at.

Suddenly Jess felt a stab of guilt. While she'd been obsessing about Alex being too keen and Andy not keen enough, a whole community was struggling to eke out an existence selling whatever they could and eating the family goat. She resolved to leave a large tip after her gin and tonic.

'Sorry I'm late,' Andy said, dragging a stool over to join her at the bar, then, as an afterthought, planting a perfunctory kiss on her lips. 'What you having?'

Frenzied attacks that you're going off me, mixed with para-noia about Sarah and a dash of angst over Alex, she contem-plated saying, then opted for, 'Um, I'm fine, thanks,' and gestured to the only part of her that was.

Andy leaned over and did not so much get the attention of the barmaid as her cleavage, a flirtatious smile and the heavy insinuation that she wasn't doing anything particular after her shift. Jess tried to sip her drink calmly and wished that watching Andy with other women didn't feel quite so like watching a toddler totter close to the edge of a swim-ming-pool.

'I just feel terrible, Jess, terrible,' he suddenly announced, hurling his head into his hands and fixating on an ashtray.

Jess couldn't help warming to this admission of bastardom, but vowed not to give in until a full apology was forthcoming. 'Well . . . no good crying over spilt milk,' she began, then decided that this transition into her mother might suggest she'd already forgiven him. 'I mean, it was selfish and unthink—'

'Selfish?' he cried, jerking his head round and staring at her incredulously. 'Jess, it was downright unacceptable.'

She flinched. She had no idea he'd be taking it *this* badly. It did feel a bit peculiar, a bloke getting emotional over an argument about a phone-call, or lack of phone-call – like a female not being able to form sentences when there was foot-ball on the telly. 'Don't be too hard on yourself,' she offered, softly. 'An apology should probably be enough.' She smiled.

'I tried,' he said, pleadingly, 'but the phone kept buggering up.'

A functioning phone in Kenya was, indeed, a novelty. However, Jess recalled, his seemed to have worked perfectly when *she*'d called *him*. 'Well, we're here now,' she said, not sure that he was mentally strong enough to cope with any more confrontations.

'*Why?*' He thumped the bar. 'Oh, God, Jess, look, I'm

sorry, I . . . just, I can't . . . can't stand the thought of hurting someone who is so . . . so—'

Jess glanced coyly at the floor in anticipation of her compliment.

'So sweet,' he said, looking at her so beseechingly, so endearingly that it was all she could do not to leap on top of him, protesting, 'No, no, you are the sweet one, you are the lovely one, you are the one I want to be with for ever and ever, amen!'

For the moment, however, she decided to opt for the winsome smile. 'I'm not hurt,' she said, reaching over and massaging his neck affectionately. 'At least, not any more.' She moved towards him in preparation for the reconciliatory kiss, but he remained motionless, focused on something dangerously close to the barmaid's bottom.

'I just keep thinking – what must it look like?'

Jess bristled, following his gaze. 'What? Naked?' She didn't like where this was headed.

'In her underwear,' he said, hypnotically, as the barmaid turned round and flashed him a knowing smirk. 'And me just . . . just . . . there beside her . . . feeling—'

'Hello?' Jess shouted, reaching over and waving a hand in front of his eyes like a doctor with a coma patient. 'Reality check. Girlfriend sitting beside you. Not greatly tactful to lust after other women with her there,' she singsonged, trying to remain calm.

He jerked backwards, then blinked very fast. 'Sorry. Shit, I'm not much company, am I? It's just that I . . . well, I can't stop thinking how she must *feel*.' He turned and forced a smile. 'Drink?'

'Why don't you go fuck her and find out?' Jess spat, folding her arms across her chest and staring lividly at the barmaid, who was massaging a wine bottle as if it were something entirely different.

'I thought you of all people would understand,' Andy said,

sulkily, draining his beer and slamming the bottle down on the bar.

'Understand what exactly, Andy? That you're an insensitive, self-indulgent, arrogant pig? Yes, I understand that more and more with every miserable second I have to spend listening—'

'That I've upset someone very close to me!' he shouted, exasperated.

Jess spun round, mouth agape. She might be sitting next to him, but right now she felt emotionally closer to her tax return. 'Well, you've got a very unfunny way of showing it.'

'I just find love so confusing,' he said, anguished, then beckoned to the barmaid in a way that suggested he didn't have the same problems with lust.

Jess felt her entire body explode with excitement. He'd used the L-word. Not directly. Not sandwiched between 'I' and 'you', but better than that – in passing. Like it didn't need to be said, just assumed, a tacit understanding. 'Well, I just find *you* confusing,' she said, boxing him playfully in the arm.

The barmaid arrived with two drinks and a gushing grin for Andy.

'Cheers, Jess,' he said, bringing his glass to hers. Then he smiled, holding her gaze – lovingly. And there was something about the way he was looking at her, something about a vibe she felt, something about the moment, sitting there, just the two of them: he was going to tell her he . . .

'I love her.'

She froze. 'Who?'

'Sarah.'

Her jaw dropped along with the penny. She closed her eyes, mind darting backwards over their conversation, forwards to its implications, sideways to its repercussions and upside down, inside out, and round and round, until it eventually crashed to a standstill in a resolute determination not to cry.

'As a friend, Jess,' he said, looking at her as if she hadn't just jumped to conclusions but threatened to hurl herself off Mount Kenya. 'Which is why I feel so terrible about the whole thing.'

Jess sat, stunned and miserable, prodding a slice of lemon in an attempt to drown it along with her sorrows. He hadn't so much as given her a thought, let alone a second one. She stared self-pityingly out into the street, trying to put things into perspective by imagining she was a goat-herder. But it didn't work and before long she was enviously eyeing up a young couple canoodling on their way out of a shop called, intriguingly, Men Who Care. She made a mental note to check out whether they sold boyfriends and turned back to her man, who didn't seem to care at all.

'So. How are you?' he said, caringly.

She raised her eyebrows at this *volte-face* and gave a wan smile. The true answer would have him running not just a mile but a marathon. 'Yeah, fine.'

'I was thinking, maybe we should take off on a safari trip when term ends. You know, just to get away?'

Jess let out an unnatural noise. As much as the suggestion appealed to her, she couldn't help feeling it was the equivalent of a murderer slicing off her nose, then asking whether he could take her and it out for dinner. She paused, carefully contemplating what card to play, then, suddenly, joyously, remembered the ace up her sleeve. 'That could be a little tricky,' she said, enigmatically.

'Going on safari? Or going with me?'

She let him have his little chortle. After all, she thought eagerly, he would not be anywhere near chortling when she delivered her news. She waited patiently, then released the bomb: 'Alex will be here.'

'Oh, right,' he said, sipping his drink in what was clearly, she realised, a way of appearing casually non-jealous. 'Didn't know he was coming out.'

She crumpled her face into a wincing expression as if she'd

accidentally dropped her glass and was waiting for it to smash all over the floor. 'Neither did I.'

'It's not going to be *that* bad, surely,' he said, continuing his excellent performance of indifference.

'Well . . .' Jess said, forebodingly, then decided to release the next one: 'It appears he, too, is on a mission to win me back.'

Andy burst out laughing. 'I hate to break it to you, but I don't think Sarah's mission was to win *you* back.'

Jess faltered. He'd either been born with a superb talent for acting or just no emotions. 'And I'm scared that . . . well . . . that he might succeed.' She looked at him – lovingly.

'Oh, God,' he suddenly erupted, running a hand through his hair. 'Christ!'

Jess assumed a concerned expression, triumphant at having broken down the walls of his resistance and given him a dose not just of his own medicine but his entire first-aid kit. 'I know,' she said, sombrely.

'I've come to say goodbye,' a voice announced dramatically from behind her.

She catapulted round. Sarah was holding her large suitcase, staring straight ahead.

'Oh, God, look . . .' Andy stuttered, jumping up and flapping around like a baby bird. 'You can't go! We – at least, I what I mean is, have a drink. At least stay for a drink.' He looked searchingly at her as if she were an electronic kitchen gadget he'd never used before and couldn't work out whether it would heat up gently or start a mad frenzy of whirring blades.

'You already appear to have a drinking partner,' she said, coldly, looking pointedly at Jess, who looked pointedly at Andy.

'Look. Let's just all calm down and deal with this in a mature, adult—'

'Goodbye, Andy,' Sarah said, in the pleasant tones of

Hannibal Lecter about to eat someone's tongue. And, with the briefest nod in Jess's direction, she turned and headed for the door.

'Sarah, wait!' Andy implored, charging after her. 'At least let me take you to the airport.'

But she ignored him, walked out on to the street and sped off in a waiting car. Andy staggered back to the bar looking like a paparazzo who'd just missed Jordan.

'Shit, *you*'re not going, are you?' he said, alarmed.

'Off you? Yes,' Jess said, gathering her bag and downing her drink.

'But . . . what? What's wrong? I didn't know she was going to show up,' he said, petulantly.

'You've made it perfectly clear who you'd rather be with, Andy, and I'm nobody's second prize.'

He looked at her, confused. 'I want to be with you,' he said, pleadingly, 'and I thought you wanted to be with . . .' he paused, as if in the finale of a Mariah Carey song '. . . me.'

'So did I,' Jess said, then made for the exit, hoping that Alex's visit might restore her faith in love.

Has Alex Got News For You

To: Claire.Voyant@hotmail.com
Date: Saturday 24 June
Subject: Has Alex Got News For You

Losing belief in all blokes, particularly Alex.
  Losing sleep over the fact that my life is one
  long losing battle with all blokes, particularly
  Alex. Losing – let's be honest – it.

Dear Claire,

  I knew I would come out to Kenya and be struck by the humble lives of its people, suspected I might be inspired to re-evaluate whether I really need twenty-three pairs of shoes, wondered whether I'd find myself on a Comic Relief insert raising awareness of their plight (the Africans, not the twenty-three pairs of shoes), but never in a million years did I think I'd be sitting surrounded by every material possession they don't have, wishing to swap my life for theirs. Alex has got a girlfriend. If I was African I'd probably be belly-dancing in a straw skirt round a campfire with her. Unfortunately, I'm British and just want to kill her.

  Why is it that whenever you imagine what something is going to be like, it always turns out to be the one scenario you hadn't considered? When Alex told me he was coming over I really thought I had run through every eventuality: him bursting out of the arrivals lounge with a bouquet the size of a buffalo, him smiling nervously at me over a candlelit dinner clutching a little ring-type box, him sobbing pitifully when I tell him I have a boyfriend, him taking one look at my toothbrush and claiming he can't live without me, him throwing himself at a lion. Sadly, him mentioning chirpily that he has a girlfriend was the one option I'd overlooked. It was

219

not so much pride before a fall as pride before a catastrophic plummet off the top of Mount Kilimanjaro.

Of course, I was initially cautious: seeing a boyfriend for the first time in the capacity of ex-boyfriend is always a bit weird, like driving a car on the Continent – you have to go against what has become naturally ingrained, remembering to go round roundabouts backwards and not try to change gears with the handle to the window. But apart from a slight slip-up when I automatically went to take his arm then had to feign a sudden interest in palmistry, everything was fine.

I picked him up from the airport and, although not bearing the buffalo bouquet, he seemed genuinely pleased to see me (not, obviously, in a bulgy-trouser way). We spent the day driving around with him whooping delightedly at all the things I no longer notice, and me conforming to the jaded long-term visitor rule of moaning about the natives.

In fact, it was all going so well I'd got myself into a tormenting internal quandary unable to figure out whether the fact we got on as 'friends' was because that was all we should have been in the first place, or because it was indicative of just how special and compatible we really were. By the time it came to dinner, I was trying desperately to remember why I'd ended it at all, and was seriously considering taking him up on his offer of getting back together – when, that is, he offered it.

Then, suddenly, through a mouthful of ciabatta, he said it: 'When me and my girlfriend were . . .' Ergh, very nasty diarrhoea-type feeling. Hate the fact that one minute you're having a lovely time and being all laughy and happy, then someone mentions the word 'girlfriend' or 'cancer' and everything goes very black indeed. The problem was I was torn between wanting to know all the gory details about her and wanting to pretend none of it was happening – like driving past the scene of a car crash and not wishing to look yet at the same time being morbidly intrigued by what might be lying underneath the plastic sheeting.

Obviously my face mirrored my mangled emotions because Alex

explained in a calm lawyery voice who she was and how they'd
met, in the quiet understated way that suggested they were about
to get married. She is French, which – aside from all the normal
phobias this throws up, i.e. sexy, sophisticated, exotically aloof,
Juliette Binoche – immediately sets her apart as an unknown
quantity.

Apparently she's come to London to do a fashion course, which
seems odd – like going to France to study the British transport
system – and has already got an American interested in some of
her hat designs. Hate her, hate her. Alex says she is 'creatively
gifted' but emotionally insecure due to a turbulent family life. So,
in a nutshell, she is your average nightmare: sexy yet vulnerable,
talented yet modest.

It's difficult to gauge how keen he is, but he's hugely impressed
by the whole French angle and has taken to doing that annoying
thing bilingual people do of using the foreign word for something
they claim doesn't translate into English. Particularly annoying in
Alex's case – he has only ever been on a two-week exchange trip
to Lyon.

I keep imagining the two of them in little cobblestone Parisian
cafés, Alex in a beret, her in something Jean-Paul Gaultier has
lent her, both of them laughing gaily in French. Or walking hand
in hand along the banks of the Seine, occasionally dancing with
lamp-posts while Frank Sinatra sings 'I Love Paris' and little rose
petals float – oh, oh, must stop it. It's bad enough feeling jealous
and unhinged about it all without torturing myself with the full
X-rated version.

Anyway, how are things with you? Has John recovered? Was
he properly ill or just needing an excuse to get out of singing
medieval Spanish songs with the 'Solar Sisters'? I must say, I too
would be tempted to eat poisonous berries when the alternative is
six a.m. choir practice on a yoga mat. And I'm currently tempted
to feed them to evil ex-boyfriends as well.

Urgh. Hate the murky world of exes – like being in the army
and having to pretend you have no emotions and that inching

through snake-infested pits full of landmines doesn't faze you. But what are my emotions? Is it jealousy because she has something I now want, in the same way as you um and ah about buying, say, an expensive coat, faff around unsure whether you like it enough, then come back to find someone else has bought it and suddenly realise it was the ideal coat for you? Or am I just pissed off because he is an ex and therefore not supposed to find someone until I am happy and married and completely over him?

Of course, if I had my own love life sorted none of this would be an issue – like little old ladies who take an inordinate interest in a wonkily parked car and can hold an entire morning's conversation on wheelie-bins because nothing nearly so exciting is happening in their own lives.

Ever since the Sarah débâcle, things with Andy have not been right. Our sex life has cooled to three or four times a week which, given that this used to be our daily quota, feels like being back in wartime Britain and having to ration the sugar. According to Cosmo, sex is the barometer of how your relationship is faring, but since it also advises you to 'discuss sexual problems openly with your partner', I'm not going to take it too seriously: every simpleton knows that nothing is guaranteed to kill passion quicker than talking about why you think it is dying.

As a remedy – advocated also, as it happens, by that same erudite publication – we went off on a short break to the Maasai Mara. Their SOS (Save Our Sex) guide gave short breaks a nine out of ten shag rating, promising erections galore and orgasms to blow your socks off (unsettling non-sexual image of wearing socks while shagging). Unfortunately, the only erections turned out to be canvas ones with guy-ropes and any besocked orgasms were being enjoyed by the hyenas – or someone sounding embarrassingly like a hyena. The idea that you can pack a problem into a suitcase then get to your destination to find it has become a white dove is the stuff of garishly face-painted children's entertainers. The reality is ten times the crumpled mess you began with.

I didn't realise this at the time, though, and thought everything was going to be fine, especially when I met Andy on the school's airstrip to discover we were not only going in a little plane, but Andy was to fly it – deeply, deeply sexy notion, like dating a surgeon, or being in bed with an army officer who suddenly has to rush out and drive a tank.

Four-seater planes are Kenya's equivalent of the tube – only, at a cruising altitude of twelve thousand feet, you have slightly more reason to 'Mind the Gap'. A lot of white Kenyans own one and think nothing of hopping on and off them, as demonstrated by my last trip with the family, where the kids looked slightly bored then fell asleep and I bounced up and down hyperactively, oohing, ahhing, pointing and behaving like, well, a kid.

I can't help feeling, however, there is something not quite right that while private jets in the western world are the preserve of the élite, i.e. film stars and Richard Branson, here in the third world, where starvation is rife and many are without homes, they are the main mode of transport. Next thing, they'll be having baths in Moët & Chandon and using caviar to fertilise the fields.

Anyway, Andy was being very laid-back – chewing gum, wiping the windscreen with his sleeve and laughing at my anxious expression when he told me one of the wings was . . . LEAKING PETROL! Crikey mikey! But that's the trouble with flying: the concept itself is so against what is normal and right that you just have to accept leaking wings and suspicious clanking noises as being normal and right too. Admittedly, however, it's easier to accept when not above cloud level in something that is losing fuel and tilts when you sneeze.

Miraculously, we made it alive and arrived at something that called itself a 'camp', in order, I can only assume, to let American tourists believe they are 'roughing it'. I now realise we were swizzed at Girl Guides:

	Camping Girl Guide style vs	*'Camping' African style*
Bed	Sleeping-bag smelling of dirty hair and bonfires, on top of a thin layer of green polystyrene, on a slope with a large boulder digging into hip and scrunched-up damp towel masquerading as pillow.	Majestic four-poster bed lavishly draped with muslin and elevated on a throne in the manner of Posh 'n' Becks' wedding.
Bathroom	Juggling act with torch and packet of tissues, trying to drop neither down the fly-frenzied long drop, while pinching nose, squatting in thigh-aching manner and fighting back a (surely unnatural?) desire to have a look at all the turds.	*Marble* en suite *with soap in shape of flamingos, loo paper folded into little pointy end, and diamonds cascading out of shower (at least, felt like).*
Food	String floating in grey water and quivering chunks of burnt flesh eaten with someone else's fork off the lid of the billycan.	Sumptuous Bacchanalian banquet with so much food it could feed . . . well, embarrassingly enough, Africa.

Leisure facilities	Rope hanging from tree.	Heated swimming-pool, cocktail bar, balloon rides, walking safaris, horseback safaris, night-time game drives, visits to local Maasai villages and – very, very nice but felt I should really be six-foot Russian goddess with Roger Moore and glass of champagne – jacuzzi on veranda.
Evening activities	Crouched on a wet log drying socks by the fire while comparing blisters, eating charcoal-encrusted goo formerly known as a marshmallow and singing 'There Were Ten In The Bed' with little concern for how much this would fail to be a singing matter when still awake at three a.m. squashed up against someone's hiking boot with damp tent plastered to cheek.	Shag, shag, shaggety-shag . . .

Or, at least, it should *have been shaggety-shag, which is why it was all such a disaster. There's nothing worse than going on holiday with your boyfriend where everything is all sultry and seductive and naked-fleshy and geared for you to have lots of sex – and then NOT HAVING IT! Aside from the sheer physical frustration, you get all neurotic and panicky because you're not doing the done thing – like going to Paris for the first time and not climbing the Eiffel Tower.*

The trouble was, there was no *Eiffel Tower. In fact, we seemed to be dealing more with a Leaning Tower of Pisa situation, or rather* not *dealing with it, hence the neurosis. I kept trying to coax him into shaggy-type situations, as if he were an escaped wild animal that the wardens were luring into a cage, but gave up when even the jacuzzi on the veranda at sunset didn't do the trick. I mean – not shagging in a jacuzzi on a veranda at sunset is the equiv- alent of having a jackpot-winning lottery ticket and not collecting the money.*

If I could have relaxed about it all maybe everything would have been fine. But that's the problem with holidays: there's so much pressure to be having a really fun time all *the time that the minute you're not you get all worked up and stressed about why you're not, and the whole thing becomes one enormous headache.*

The ostensible point of the trip, i.e. to see the animals, went very well. We went out every day in an army-style truck with a guide, several Americans and Dixons' entire audio-visual department. Great fun – rather like a more expensive way of playing I-Spy. Spotted heaps of things. Well, to be honest, we didn't*, the guide did. He'd suddenly focus for no apparent reason on a piece of scrub miles in the distance then tell us it was a cheetah. I would strongly suspect he was the cheater, the Americans would claim it was awesome, Dixons' gadgetry would whir into action, and ten minutes later – hey presto! – there was the cheetah. Most impressive. In fact, I'm tempted to take him home with me and harness his talent for knowing exactly where to look into, say, finding my house keys when I'm running late and can't for the life of me remember where*

I last put them or, more importantly, finding me a boyfriend. The trouble is, I don't suspect Maasai warriors work particularly well in London.

This animal-spotting business is somewhat absurd, though. It's truly wonderful to see giraffes and hippos in the flesh – sometimes, in the case of a poor impaled impala, rather too much flesh – it's just that everyone seems to treat the experience as some sort of frantic dash round Sainsbury's, passing truckloads of tourists and barking things like, 'Have you seen the rhinos?' and 'Where are the elephants?' as if there's been a massive stock reshuffle and nothing's on the right shelf. No one just sits quietly observing and absorbing, so consumed are they with ticking shopping lists and getting to the checkout. Suspect they might also be victims of the syndrome that causes people to say they've 'done' rather than 'been to' Kenya.

Anyway, by the end of the 'holiday' we'd come away with a rather impressive array of ticks, more literally for Andy who had, if not ticks, then something equally unpleasant to have to lie next to. He'd refused to wear insect repellent, as strongly advised by an abhorrent-looking American, who insisted on smearing it lavishly over his blubbery body – somewhat pointlessly, I suspect, given that any insect would've been repelled merely by looking at him.

Alex, of course, has come out equipped to star in Arachnophobia if required. He's one of these people who follow instructions to the T and always buys the suede-protector cream needlessly foisted upon you by shoe-shop staff. His 'toiletries' bag (unsettlingly camp notion in itself) was bursting at the seams with anti-bite lotions, bite-treatment potions, aloe vera cooling gel, Vitamin E – ergh, yuk, YUK, just had a vile image of him massaging aloe vera cooling gel into Aurélie's inner thigh, then no doubt giving Aurélie orally sex. Gruesome. And she'll have lovely long lean thighs like a giraffe's and . . . oh, God. She flew out here two days after Alex did, or probably just galloped on her giraffe legs, and now they're on safari together, no doubt shagging in the jacuzzi on the veranda at sunset, shaggety-shaggety-shag.

It's probably all for the best anyway. It's a well-known fact that it takes something like death, a car crash, discovering ex-boyfriend has new girlfriend to throw life into perspective and really learn what is important. I now realise that I'd been hoarding Alex in the back of my mind much like one hoards leftover casserole. Too precious to throw away. I'd wrapped him in clingfilm and kept him in the fridge, ready to reheat when nothing tastier was available. But Alex/leftovers can't hang around for ever, they go off: some with giraffe-legged goddesses, some just with vile green fuzz. I must therefore chuck him out – out of sight, out of mind – and start again with some fresh ingredients and a . . . Oh, just had another nauseous vision of them feeding each other pawpaw and passion fruit and Alex telling her how beautiful she is, in stiltedly-endearing French.

Well, I'm going on a romantic walk with Andy, so there! And we'll have no language barriers because we'll just be communing in the language of love. So. Great. In fact, I'll just get the picnic hamper ready and find a suitable rug to make love on. As Baden-Powell would say, 'Be Prepared', though I have a suspicion he didn't mean for sex. Which reminds me – condoms!

Lots of love,
Jess
xxx

PS On second thoughts, might leave the condoms. Suggests I do not see the walk as entirely walk-related and, anyway, must remember wise logic gleaned from university days: if prepare for sex, i.e. shaved legs and sexy underwear, sex will not happen. And what is taking condoms if not preparing for sex!
PPS No. Will take them. It is only sensible and we can always use them to carry water.

High Infidelity

'Carry water, Jess?' Andy said, a wry smile creeping across his face as he peered into something that had become less a picnic hamper than a hamper to the picnic.

'Or as a glove when tending stabbed HIV patients,' Jess offered, aware that making excuses to one's boyfriend for carrying condoms wasn't normal.

'I was rather hoping we'd be going for a walk,' he said, rifling through the blankets and pulling out a first-aid kit, 'not joining Médecins Sans Frontières.'

'Always best to insure against the unlikely,' she said, looking mournfully at the condoms.

'And what about back pain?' he suggested, heaving the wicker basket over his shoulder and pretending to buckle under its weight. 'And loss of earnings due to no longer being able to use my right arm?'

'I just trade you in for a better model,' she said, laughing, then followed him out to the gate.

Walking in Kenya, Jess decided, as they set off down a track stared at by a baboon picking its nose, was like having Sky Television: you could always guarantee there'd be something good to watch. The trouble came when there were two of you and it happened to be on different channels.

'Wow, look at that funny blue bird thing,' she enthused, pointing at the living version of something John Lewis would bedeck with gold-sprayed holly and sell as a Christmas table decoration.

'Yeah,' Andy replied, with no attempt to feign interest, then nodded to the distance. 'See that hill to the left? Snowboarders' heaven, that. Just need to put in a few lifts. And get some bloody snow!'

'It's like life, though, isn't it?' Jess continued. 'There are these beautiful shiny colourful birds that everyone likes looking at, and then there are these poor mangy pigeons that are all dirty and scraggy and everyone thinks are vermin. It's not *their* fault they're not pretty.'

'You boarded before?'

'Nope. Anyway, I bet they've got much nicer personalities.'

'Snowboarders?'

'Pigeons.'

Andy burst out laughing. 'Nicer than who?'

'Than all those pretty birds who flutter around showing off.'

'Jess, birds don't have personalities,' he said, smiling as if talking to a small child. 'And neither do the feathered variety.' He let out a self-congratulatory chuckle. 'So. Fancy some boarding lessons?'

Jess looked at him with raised eyebrows. 'In return for lessons on how not to be a chauvinist wanker?'

'I'd as happily settle for you chained to sink and bed, if that would suit.' He grinned. 'Though I suspect this might pose a few problems for the snowboarding.'

'Not to mention your life-expectancy,' she said, thwacking him on the backside.

As they continued the journey in their own private thought-worlds – his, half-way up a hillside reliving a snowboarding jump; hers, reliving the past half-hour of their relationship – an unwelcome realisation dawned. Andy wasn't the person she'd thought he was. Or, more accurately, not the person she'd hoped he was.

Dating in your late twenties, she decided, was like launching a murder investigation: you assumed everything was solved when you found someone matching your description and in possession of the weapon you were searching for. Initially, Andy had fitted the bill perfectly: description, gorgeous; weapon, large. But as time wore on little clues had begun to pop up, suggesting he might not be the correct suspect after all. Things that didn't match up. Things that didn't work. He lived in a world of sport, didn't understand her, didn't think like she did, didn't really think at all. And yet, rather than face up to them, she'd convinced herself they were unimportant, airbrushed them out – always manipulating the evidence so that it pointed to the conclusion she wanted. After all, accepting the truth meant starting the whole investigation again, with no certainty you'd ever get the right person.

'I think we're lost,' her murder suspect announced, as the track symbolically petered out in front of them. 'Get us the map, will you?'

'What map?'

Andy stopped and looked at her. 'You mean to say that in this gargantuan goods vehicle that is currently parked on my upper spine we have everything from a cheeseboard to the kitchen-sink taps, but no map?'

Jess nodded.

'And you're in charge of children?'

'Anyway, we don't need a map,' she said, as Andy dropped the hamper and collapsed on to the ground as if it were the finishing line of a gruelling Territorial Army obstacle course. 'We can just wander down there beside those pretty flower things.'

A bemused smile crept across his face. 'Wander beside some pretty flower things.' He adopted a newsreader's voice: 'Two British tourists were found savaged to death in Kenya's Rift Valley after embarking on what the locals overheard them describe as "a wander beside some pretty flower things".'

Jess jumped on top of him, laughing despite herself. 'One British tourist was found stabbed with a cheese-knife after repeatedly taking the piss out of his girlfriend. The girlfriend, a normally mild-mannered character, is reported to have said, "I have no regrets. He was being rude and condescending and there seemed no other option."'

They dissolved into a tickling heap.

'Right. I'm having a beer,' Andy said, delving into the hamper.

Jess lay on her stomach, head propped up on her elbows, feeling uncharacteristically free and happy in the manner of a Calvin Klein model. This, surely, was what being in Africa was all about: picnic hampers, tickling fights with your boyfriend and lots of wonderful wildlife roaming at will. 'Look at that cute little cow,' she exclaimed, delightedly.

'Lovely,' Andy said, not looking up. 'Even lovelier if I could find a beer.'

'It's so cute, Andy. Look – its horns look like a head-dress.'

'Jess, please tell me that this yawning chasm contains a beer.' He was ransacking the hamper like a burglar running short of time.

'I don't think I packed any beer,' she said, unconcerned, fishing among the discarded contents and picking up a stick of pepperoni. 'D'you think cows like pepperoni?' She peeled back the unsettlingly condom-like wrapper to reveal something no man would boast about. 'Or is that a bit insensitive – like making us eat human—'

'No. Beer,' Andy announced, in a stunned 'Me, Tarzan, you, Jane' monotone, before keeling backwards with his hands over his face as if he'd just been refused asylum.

'There's some herbal wine stuff,' Jess offered, throwing bits of pepperoni at the cow.

'Wonderful,' Andy exclaimed, staring up at the sky. 'Glad I've been breaking my back carrying herbal wine rather than cold beer. That's marvellous news.'

'How cute,' Jess squealed, 'all his friends are coming to join him. Look. I bet they're thinking, What are those funny humans doing lying down and moaning about having no beer?' She prodded Andy. 'Look, they're moving closer. Hello, little cows.'

Andy lifted his head reluctantly and glanced round, then let out a strange noise. 'Ohmyfuck!' he shouted, bolting up.

'Jess, they're not little cows. They're fucking buffalo.'

If one's life was supposed to flash past when drowning, it seemed suddenly to stop ominously dead when flanked by a herd of highly dangerous animals, Jess decided, leaping to her feet in terror. The pepperoni, it would appear, had merely been their starter.

'Oh, oh,' she yelped, trying to use Andy as a shield. Andy was putting things back into the hamper in slow, deliberate movements, keeping his eyes fixed on the buffalo as if they'd just picked up a megaphone and instructed him to lay down his weapons.

'Do not move. Any sudden activity could cause a stampede,' he stated in the dramatic hushed tones of a commentator from a wildlife documentary that always seemed so exciting, Jess reflected, when watched from the comfort of the sofa.

She concentrated hard, wishing it didn't feel like a game of musical statues with the death penalty.

'I want you to turn round very slowly,' Andy instructed, confidently, 'and walk with me to that boulder.'

Jess stared in horror at the boulder. 'Andy. It's a buffalo.'

'Okaaay,' he said, less confidently, 'in that case we back away gradually, then run when I say. OK?'

Of all the situations she could be in, Jess thought, this one was not OK. Not OK in the slightest.

'Nice and gently,' he whispered, as they started stepping back. The buffalo watched intently in the manner of the Gestapo in *The Sound of Music* when the von Trapp family perform 'So Long, Farewell' before running off to hide in the graveyard. Despite plans of a similar escape, Jess feared they would end up not so much in a graveyard as in a grave.

Suddenly, the buffalo were shuffling forward.

'Don't panic,' Andy advised, as Jess felt her heart rattle at her ribcage like a prisoner frantic to get out. 'They'll sense your panic and might charge.'

'Oh . . . fuck,' Jess stammered. It was just the dating game, she told herself, trying to remember how to breathe. You had to be calm and indifferent, not show any signs of neurotic behaviour or desperation and, once safely ensconced on the other side, you could relax and be yourself.

'OK. After three we're going to turn and bolt,' Andy said, in a masterful manner that would have seemed sexy, Jess decided, had she been able to feel anything but blind fear. 'Ready? After three. One, two—'

'Bolt where?' she said, alarmed. They were stranded in the flat, open-spaced savannah of a Land Rover commercial.

Andy looked slowly behind him. 'The foot of that rockface to our left. We'll climb it if need be.'

Jess glanced backwards. The rockface was so far in the distance it was the size of a pebble. 'Um . . . I'm not very . . . I don't – I won't be able to run that far.'

'Believe me, you will,' he said, with the unquestioning conviction of someone who could. 'After three. One, two . . .'

Suddenly, adrenaline sweeping over her like a tidal wave, Jess turned and fled – charging headlong across the scrubland, limbs flying, feet stumbling, knees buckling, terror turning her body to jelly. On and on, feeling sicker by the second, she forced herself forward, blood pumping, heart thumping, head a mass of throbbing veins. Too frightened to look behind, too deafened by the drumbeat of panic, she could only imagine the thundering hoofs of the herd on her tail, kicking up seas of dust as they pounded on to pulverise their prey: her.

Then the real horror hit: she glanced to her side. Andy was no longer there. This was turning into something Hitchcock would direct. How long had he been gone? *Where* had he gone? To get help? Up the rockface? Under a buffalo? *Inside* a buff—

'Jess! Stop! Stop!'

He was shouting. He was still alive. And he needed her. If she was going to die, she would do so heroically. With a bravery she didn't know she possessed, she ground to a halt and turned on her heels, ready to face whatever fate awaited her, ready to rush to his side, ready to meet their bloodied slaughter . . . together.

But something wasn't quite right. Andy was standing several metres back waving. And the stampeding, flesh-hungry buffalo were nowhere to be seen.

'It's OK, it's OK,' he shouted, beckoning her over.

She approached him warily, eyes darting suspiciously around in their sockets like someone in the midst of an unfortunate experience with an Ecstasy tablet. 'Where are they?'

'It's OK. Calm down. It's OK.' He reached out and pulled her to him. 'Look.' He swivelled her round. There in the distance, miles in the distance, were the buffalo, standing exactly where they'd left them with what she could swear was the hint of a sadistic smirk curling about their chops.

'I really thought I was going to die,' Jess reflected, later that evening when they emerged from under Andy's duvet having celebrated the beauty of being very much alive. *Cosmo* was wrong, she decided. It wasn't a holiday that rekindled your sex life, it was a near-death encounter with buffalo.

'So did I,' Andy said, squeezing her affectionately. 'Your little legs were working so fast I thought they would just, like, come off at the hips.'

Jess laughed. This was the third time they'd relived the experience. Like repeatedly reminiscing about how they first got together, it never seemed to lose its appeal.

'Brits Bored to Death by Buffalo,' Andy joke-headlined. 'Not bad, eh? Or . . . Tourists Tell Their Tortured Tale of . . . of Trampled Terror.'

Jess joined in. 'How about . . . We Won't Charge You, says Bank of Buffalo.' They both chuckled. 'You were so funny when they started coming closer,' she said, then dropped her voice to imitate his doom-laden warning, 'Don't. Panic.'

Andy pinned her to the bed, grinning. 'Look at the cute little cows,' he retaliated, in high-pitched jest. 'D'you think they'd like to share our picnic? Hello, little cows, my name is Jess and I live on a fun fluffy planet called Stupider.'

Jess tried to wriggle free. 'Hello, big-bollocked buffalo,' she bellowed. 'My name's Andy and I've got such gigantic balls I'm going to run backwards up a rockface.'

He relinquished his grip and, still laughing, collapsed into her neck.

When Jess woke in the morning, Andy had gone. Trying not to jump to the more lurid conclusions of the last time he'd disappeared from her side, she glanced calmly round the room and was overjoyed to find a note on his pillow. Notes on pillows, she decided, as she grabbed it eagerly, happened in films or fantasies, never real life.

> *To my cute little cow,*
> *Gone to run backwards up a rockface. See you soon,*
> *Your Big-Bollocked Buffalo.*
> *xox*

She let out a squeal of delight and read it eight more times. It would seem that they were not just back on track but heading for a trip up the aisle. Dreamily, she picked up an outdoor-pursuits magazine by his bed and flicked through it, imagining the two of them in a spectrum of romantic poses on clifftops and river rapids. A couple of catalogue order forms cascaded out, full of photos of grinning men with side-partings, standing stiffly in fleeces and hiking boots, looking keener to pursue each other than the outdoors.

Then, suddenly, as if by a miracle, another note appeared on the pillow. It had obviously fluttered out with the forms – unless Andy was gorgeous, thoughtful, totally in love with her and a magician. Excitedly, she picked it up, thrilled to discover it wasn't so much a note as a letter. She opened it out, then stopped short. It was addressed to Andy.

The trouble with stumbling across something private, she realised, as her eyes involuntarily scanned the page, was that it took unimaginable restraint not to . . .

> *Dear Andy,*
> *William, as you know, will no longer be staying on at Colobus.*
> *My husband has been posted to Dar-es-Salaam where we*
> *will be joining him at the end of this week. We have enrolled*
> *William at . . . teaching standards are   which I'm sure*
> *William . . . obviously this will mean . . .*

Jess skim-read on, discovering that the other trouble with stumbling across something private was that it rarely turned out to be interesting. And then her eye picked out the word 'sex' and it suddenly became very interesting . . .

> *. . . a trait of our sex. At another time, in another place,*
> *things might have been – but I mustn't torture myself with*
> *what-ifs. Life is as it is for a reason. Regretting the path*
> *we've chosen, wanting the path we haven't, is a futile way*
> *to exist. I do not know if what I feel for Michael is right –*
> *is there a right way to feel? – but I know in my heart that*
> *I shall never forget my . . .*

Blimey, Jess thought, turning the page. She'd never seen Andy as an agony uncle before.

> *. . . weekend in Nairobi with you.*

She froze. A piercing pain punctured her senses. Everything started to go blurry.

> *You made me feel a woman. Not a housewife! Not a wife!*
> *An irrepressibly sexual, voluptuous, desirable woman! And*
> *for that, my delicious toyboy, I owe you the world. Good luck*

in everything you do. When you meet that special lady, she will be luckier than all the stars. With love, lust and fond memories . . .

Jess felt sick as, like a jigsaw puzzle of the devil, she slotted in the final piece.

Pippa.

'How's my little cow, then?' Andy had just come clattering into the hall with skittles, ropes and pieces of laminated map. 'Guess which wanker's just tried to set up an orienteering course with a broken compass?'

Jess lay stunned on the bed, staring at the ceiling, the letter crumpled in her fist. 'Wanker,' she spat.

'Yup, that'll be me,' he chirped, ambling into the bedroom, planting a kiss on her forehead, then wandering through to the loo and releasing a long stream of urine.

'Wanker. Wanker. Wanker,' she repeated, in a drugged monotone, still too numb to vary the insult.

'I think we've established that,' Andy said, poking his head round the bathroom door, smiling, then clocking her zombied expression. 'You OK?'

Jess continued to stare rigidly ahead of her, in the corpse-like manner of a royal guard.

'Hello-ho? Anyone there?' he singsonged, zipping up his fly and joining her on the bed. 'Little cow? Moo? Is little cow not going to—'

'Fuck off, Andy!' she snapped, lashing at him with her legs.

Andy sprang back as if he'd just tried to pet a crocodile. 'What, in the name of arse, is wrong with you?'

Jess threw him a disgusted look. 'You tell me.'

He started glancing anxiously around the room like a cornered thief checking his best escape route. 'I haven't tidied my sock drawer?'

'Glad you find it amusing.'

'No, good heavens, not at all,' he protested, shaking his head in concern. 'Quite the contrary. A messy sock drawer is not something to be taken in the slightest bit lightly. In fact, socks must be—'

'I know,' Jess cut in.

He looked at her warily. 'Kept in pairs at all times,' he trailed off, uncertainly.

'I know,' Jess repeated, wishing to mutate into a viper and hiss him down with venom.

'Know . . . what exactly?' he ventured, with a nervous swallow.

'About Pippa.'

She waited for his begging pleas for forgiveness, fixing him with a stare from *The Shining*.

'Oh, God, we're not redoing the old Pippa performance, are we?' he said, relaxing back against the wall as if he'd just been told his test results were negative. 'I thought that was last month's affair.'

'Evidently so. And a great affair too, by all accounts. Well, her account, anyway.'

Andy laughed. 'Oh dear, Jess,' he said, grinning condescendingly, 'I don't know where you get your information from but I'm afraid—'

'Oh dear, Andy,' she mimicked, seething. 'I get my information from the horse's mouth,' she hurled the crumpled letter-ball at his head, 'or, should I say, the ass's mouth? Poor deluded woman.'

Andy tried to appear calm while he picked it up and opened it out. She watched, with bitter-sweet pleasure, as the realisation did not so much come crashing down around him as left him looking like someone who'd chosen to visit Etna on the wrong day.

'I – look – listen . . .' he stuttered, as if launching into a road-safety appeal.

'I'd rather do neither, thanks,' Jess said, getting up and pulling on her clothes.

'Don't go, please don't go, Jess. I can explain. See, look, Sarah turning up like that made me and . . . well, things with you and I were . . .'

Jess stopped and looked at him distatefully. 'Were what, Andy?'

'Were . . . Look, it's complicated when—'

'You're trying to juggle three women at once? Yes, I can imagine it's very complicated indeed. So I'm going to do you a little favour, Andy. I'm going to walk out of that door and – if it's not too complicated for your minuscule malfunctioning brain to comprehend – never walk back in again.' With that, she picked up her bag and headed for the hall.

'I was confused,' he wailed, tripping after her with the tortured expression of a child denied the pick'n'mix at Woolworths.

'No wonder,' she said, turning back and staring at him coldly. 'I should imagine having to choose which woman to shag gets very confusing. Goodbye, Andy.' She then walked with dignity to the car, got in, drove out of the gate and cried all the way home.

As soon as she got in, she went straight to the computer in an attempt to make electronic contact compensate for the real thing. If it was true that life flowed in peaks and troughs, she was currently in line for a Mount Everest of good fortune. She clicked on the inbox file and discovered, joyously, yet freakishly, that the theory was right. There, like a guardian angel, was an email from her dear friend, Jo, thrillingly titled, 'Fab News'.

Immediately, her mind tumbled through the possibilities. She was dispatching a heavy mob to murder Andy? A mysteriously sexy man was on his way out to woo her? Antonio Banderas wanted her phone number? George Clooney wanted her kids? Excitedly, she clicked it open.

Mark's just asked me to marry him. And guess what?

Jess scrolled down.

I'm so happy I'm fit to burst!

In the Doghouse

To: *Claire.Voyant@hotmail.com*
Date: *Wednesday 19 July*
Subject: *In the Doghouse*

So depressed I'm fit to appear in EastEnders.
*Desiring for the first time just to fuck it all and
go home. Confused by the realisation that when
I was at home I wanted to fuck it all and go to
Kenya. Am I just an emotional ping-pong ball?*

Dear Claire,
*I feel as though I'm a nomad who, instead of roaming from
place to place in search of fresh pasture, is lurching from one continent to another convinced the pasture is fresher and greener wherever I am not. Right now, however, I'd settle for slopping around
in mangled entrails if I could guarantee they were Andy's.*
*The bastard's had an affair with a married mother, which is
hideous for a number of reasons:*

(1)   The married mother is Pippa.
(2)   The Pippa he said didn't exist.
(3)   It is the stage version of The Graduate *with a naked
       Jerry Hall.*
(4)   Ergh – but they will like . . . really have had sex.
(5)   Which is more than we've been bloody doing.
(6)   Oh, God.

*And what's worse is that I've been gagged from telling anyone
because until today our pissing email's been buggered. Feel like I
did when I was unemployed and bombarded my flatmates the*

second they came through the door with tedious, long-winded tales of Hoover bags because I hadn't spoken to anyone all day and everything had welled up inside my head getting inflated and out of proportion. But none of this is inflated – except Andy's bloody ego. Oh, God.

He claims it was a friendship that 'got out of control', making it sound like some innocent playground antic that wasn't his fault, rather than the wild, abandoned, unbridled-lust lunge that the expression suggests to me. Apparently they met on a school sailing trip on Lake Baringo – immediately bringing to mind all sorts of sunset shots of them standing on the ship's bow, arms outstretched Jesus-style, liberated spirits laughing captivatingly into the wind, later to retire below deck for naked sketching sessions and steamy sex.

Nothing happened, according to Andy, until they bumped into each other in Nairobi when he was drunk and she was going through a bad patch with her husband. He's like a lion-in-waiting, targeting the poor vulnerable gazelle with the broken leg – not that I have an ounce of sympathy for the over-greedy witch.

I feel certain he spoon-fed her the same sentimental I'm-searching-for-my-soulmate bollocks that he did me. And even more certain that she secretly believed the fraudulently untrue subtext that she was it. The trouble is, it's mightily hard not to believe it could be you, a national weakness that the big smiley lottery finger has been exploiting for years. Especially when he's got the persuasive talent of a salesgirl who wanders Oxford Street clutching a clipboard, appealing directly to your vanity by convincing you to part with fifty pounds for a makeover and model shoot, the results of which, you will only discover once you've signed something waved fleetingly under your nose, legally bind you to paying five hundred pounds per photo.

He told me, in what I can only assume was a misguided attempt at dumbing it down, that it was 'just sex'. Very wrong thing to say – like being dumped, and dumper saying it's 'just me', rather than *explaining it's because they find you repugnant/have fallen in love with someone else/want to shag around. Now I can only see them in terms of rampant shagging, which is vile in all respects, particularly the one concerning our own non-rampant shagging.*

Anyway, I've banished him from my mind as one would nasty thoughts about murderers when alone in the house at night with unexplained noises downstairs. Or, at least, I'm trying to. The trouble is, like the ominous noises, it doesn't take much to trigger a whole series of unpleasant associations that have you desperately wishing you weren't on your own. Not that I want him back. Not at all. It's just that he was kind of my only friend out here, and did make me laugh, and was fun to spend time with at weekends and really was very sexy and strong so could fight lions if – No, God, what on earth am I thinking? He is a vile, adulterous, deceitful, cheating, wanking wanker.

I just wish that . . . well, that I could always remember this, particularly when I see him. But it's like revising for an exam – you sit on your bed and can quite easily recite all eight points to the radiator, then get into the exam hall and can only remember one. He's come round a couple of times to 'explain', in much the same way that quietly spoken men turn up on your doorstep claiming to be on the run from the harsh political regime of their country while guiding you through a photo album of their eighteen children all of whom are going to be beheaded next Wednesday if you don't sign a petition and, presumably from the way he's pointing at the other suspiciously generous donations, a large cheque. So far I've been very strong, listening stoically then saying something like 'The damage is done,' or 'If we could change the past' before, equally stoically, showing him the door.

The problem comes, however, when I see him in public – an attractive man roaming at large in the manner of a peacock attracting many peahens with his beautiful erect tail – not, of course, that Andy walks round with an erection. At least, not at school. At least, I hope. Almost immediately I find myself wanting to rush up to him and resume being his girlfriend, and can't work out whether this is because of some animalistic, peafowl-type attraction, or because single men, like most good things in Kenya, are in short supply. Or maybe it's simply that being a single woman here is a fate worse than going out with Andy.

I really had no idea it would be so hideous. All attached white women in Kenya, rather than being smug or condescending as they might be in our own country, seem to be gripped in a perpetual state of paranoia that their partner is going to bugger off with someone else – not unreasonable in the light of what's just happened to me. They're so fiercely territorial you'd think their spouses were top-secret MI6 files capable of causing widespread warfare if peeked at for a second. As a result, all women are seen as a threat, single women as scavenging jackals ready to steal mercilessly what rightfully belongs to others.

This became terrifyingly apparent at last week's end-of-term play. I really didn't want to go for the obvious Andy reason, but Bea was being both a toadstool and Baby Spice – which seemed to require no costume change – and Marjorie and Quentin insisted it would be 'fabbo'. Knew immediately I'd made a cataclysmic error when I entered what appeared to be a refugee camp. Exhausted women were slouched on the floor trying to distract bored babies, who were wailing at top volume, while their menfolk huddled in corners swigging beer, and kids in ragged tunics charged around with cardboard axes, screeching. At the far end of this bedlam, the headmaster was shouting the running order with the success of a reporter doing a piece to camera from the Gaza Strip.

To begin with, everything was fine – apart from the war-zone – but then I spotted Andy and felt as if I'd just been machine-gunned in the stomach. He was standing by the stage with lots of little children clambering all over him like monkeys. So completely sexy. What is it that makes men with small infants seem divine sex-Adonises, when women with same just look like harassed dishrags? He nodded at me and attempted to wade over but a kid was holding on to his ankle with the tenacity of a rabid dog.

I hovered uncertainly in the programme queue wondering

whether I, too, was a clinging weight he couldn't shake off, when I began to notice lots of women checking me out in the suspicious manner that suggested they'd just smelt gas. Despite being two and a half times the size of Britain, Kenya is a small parish in Surrey when it comes to gossip. Thought they might just be feeling sorry for me, which would have been enough of a humiliation to bear, then noticed, mortified, that they'd started taking hold of their partner's hand as if I were the scary candy man in Chitty Chitty Bang Bang *trying to lure him into my van. Surely if I'm going to seduce someone else's husband I'd have the nous to do it somewhere more private than the school play?*

Anyway, I took small consolation from the fact that there seemed to be a hearty all-single-girls-together ethos – not in a lesbian way, or so I understood it – and had just got chatting to a very nice divorcee called Ruth when the looks started up again. Almost at boiling point with being treated like a contagious virus, I was ready to shout, 'What you starin' at?' in the manner of a skinhead outside McDonald's, when a little boy in a tutu tapped me on the bottom with his wand, brought his finger to his mouth in a ssh and pointed to the stage where, to my embarrassment, the play was under way.

In fairness to me, though, this wasn't immediately obvious. Two tiny girls were speaking not so much in stage-whispers as whispers, a boy with a crown was sitting on a throne picking his nose, someone wearing a sheet was guiding a pooing sheep into the wings and an inexplicable pen of barnyard animals had been erected in the far corner: a donkey trying to bolt, a piglet chomping through a cable, various flapping poultry and a perpetually bleating goat.

Tried to work out what was going on, but it was a bit like listening to a badly tuned radio that keeps switching into Russian. Just when I'd finally managed to establish that the person in the sheet was significant, everyone was bowing and clapping and the stage was being set for Act Two, entitled 'Teachers'. I had visions of staff members making fools of themselves wearing face-paint, but it turned out that the sixth-formers would be doing it for them – remarkably accurate impersonations of each one. It was all highly amusing until they got to Andy. A kid dressed only in very short shorts strutted on to the stage flexing, in his case, invisible muscles and flirted demonstratively with a selection of gushing girls, all of whom broke into a high-kicking dance formation, chanting, 'Mr Brown, the ladies' man, kisses any girl that he can, can, can' – astutely summing up what has taken me several months and a broken heart to work out for myself.

Oh, Jesus. It seems that I'm never destined to get what I want. With Alex I had the security but wanted the spark. With Andy I had the spark but blew my fuse when I discovered there was no bloody security because the bastard had selfishly overloaded his socket.

Surely it can't be that the two are mutually exclusive – security and the spark, not Alex and Andy – in the same way that if you're in Kenya you can't also be in London unless, of course, you're in Marjorie and Quentin's front room, which confusingly seems to be the second floor of Harrods. But, then, if I have to choose, what do I go for? The safe trundling dodgem cars or the roller-coaster? Maybe the solution is simply to be a man about it, marry the replica of one's mother, then have it off with the secretary for kicks. Oh, God, why did I think such anti-feminist thoughts? I'm supposed to be hating men, not turning into a Conservative MP.

I'm trying not to wallow, especially since I'm sure I'll look back on the whole sorry discovery of his infidelity as a blessing in disguise even if at the moment it feels not just in disguise but under a cloak wearing a mask running around invisibly. After all, it's much better I find out now that he's a no-good philanderer, rather than ten years down the line when I'm a single mother of three.

Talking of sprogs, well done on becoming an aunt. Will you insist little Ralph eats puréed lentils and recycles his sick? Might be a problem identifying which is which, mind you. I couldn't open the photo attachment, but I'll take your word for it that he's very cute, rather than John's description of an albino frog.

Very jealous to hear you're sweltering in ninety-degree sunshine – however unpleasant the effect on the compost toilets. We're in the height of winter, for which read summer in the west of Scotland, i.e. rain. Marjorie and Quentin have escaped to warmer climes on the coast, leaving me in charge of the kids and a fluctuating supply of wildlife. You'd be greatly impressed by the living food chain going on in the dining room, with the dog chasing a cat trying to eat Peepo, the pet rabbit, behind the telly.

They're now on school holiday – the kids, that is – a prospect that loomed up in front of me like a smear-test appointment. But rather than being strangled by PlayStation leads and force-fed Twix bars while playing never-ending Monopoly in my pyjamas, it has been painless so far. They disappear outside for large chunks of the day, only returning briefly for food, like boisterous kids from a Sunny Delight advert. In fact, they've been so angelic it's almost spooky – like something Henry James might have created. Maybe I'll start seeing terrifying apparitions of the last governess hovering silently near creepy lakes, or haunting figures peering in through . . . No, but see, this is exactly what's happened: Andy has corrupted my mind like a nasty computer virus that sweeps through the system, damaging and infecting everything in its path.

The only thing that seems to have escaped my tainted outlook is Alex. I see him now as my saviour, a god whose worth I hadn't appreciated until coming into contact with the devil – Andy. All his faults seem like nothing in comparison – like when you're faffing around worrying about which weekend you should visit your friends in Oxford, and then you go into work and get told your job's on the line, or get a call saying your granny's died, and suddenly your goalposts move and what before was this colossal concern now seems a trivial detail.

Alex was my reserve oxygen tank, the one I thought I didn't need. But now I'm eighteen metres under, the tank I assumed was fine is faulty, there are no other fish in the sea (or, at least, none that I can bloody find!) and I can't survive without him. There is obviously one rather major airlock in the system, his girlfriend, but I feel a three-year relationship holds more sway than a three-month one, even if the three-month one is with a French giraffe.

I know I will have to tread carefully. Storming in and reclaiming what I see as mine is not always successful – look at Saddam and Kuwait – so I've decided to write him a letter expressing my feelings, as seems only fitting given the British tradition of great lovers, e.g. Plath and Hughes. It's been very hard and I still don't think it's right. Can certainly see why Plath was such a screw-up, though. I've copied it below with my thoughts and would really appreciate your advice, though not sure Sylvia would have emailed her friend before sending poem to Ted.

> *Dear Alex,*
> *It was lovely to see you here in Kenya. I hope you enjoyed the rest of your stay[1] and saw lots of wonderful wildlife on safari – other than Aurélie!!![2]*
>   *You will no doubt agree that being in Africa makes you reflect on life's deeper meaning. It pits you against a world of extremes, where life is at once beautiful, vivid and throbbing,[3] yet unyielding, sinister and cruel. By this very contradiction, it holds all to command, laying bare the fragility of humankind,[4] like the carcass of an animal on the dusty savannah.[5]*
>   *When I split up with you I was searching, but I didn't know what for. Now I have found it. It is not in looking at a mountain range or wading through a stream. It is not in soaking up a sunset or running in the wind. It is all of these*

---

1 Tone not quite right. Sounds like welcoming leaflet in rural B-and-B, as if I should be enclosing map of local walks and small sachet of Nescafé.
2 Tone definitely not right. Suggests Aurélie could be water buffalo or hippo (if only). Good to have humour, but not sure it's ethical to make joke of ex-boyfriend's girlfriend – like being rude about someone's parents.
3 Throbbing?
4 Danger of sounding like Sunday-night BBC documentary.
5 Danger of sounding a prat.

things, yet none. All of these things because they are beautiful. None of these things because they are only beautiful with you.[6]

I know you have a girlfriend,[7] *but love should not be confined to the here and now.*[8] *My heart will always be beating to the rhythm of our love. But two hearts are better than one.*

I love you.

Jess

xxx

PS If replying, remember to enclose PO box number otherwise postboy fucks up and delivers it to runner-bean farm.[9]

Obviously, I don't envisage us going out properly until I get back, and even then it should not be something that's undertaken lightly. Returning to a long-time ex is the equivalent of getting a tattoo: reversing the decision is a damaging process so you must be very sure you're still going to want it – Alex/snake on shoulder-blade – in ten years' time. I'd imagine we'd get married pretty sharpish once we were back together, though. After all, the whole point of our previous three-year relationship was that it was a testing ground – much like university is preparation time for a degree (plus for reaching optimal alcohol tolerance). If you've already passed the exams, what is to be gained from resitting them?

I wish I hadn't wasted so much time on Andy now. But I guess it's like shoe-shopping: only by trying on other sizes and styles do you realise the first pair you had were the right ones all along. Not that Andy's size wasn't right, exactly. In fact, it was very right, to be strictly honest about it. I just had a problem with the fact that

---

6 Very much like poeticism – am I maybe hybrid of Plath/Shakespeare?

7 Beautiful poeticism ruined by reality?

8 Might suggest I'm interested in a threesome.

9 Not sure desperate need to ensure I get his reply doesn't slightly ruin poignant moment?

he was being worn by several others at the same time. Sharing shoes, like sharing toothbrushes, is not something I'm a great fan of.

Oh, God, though, however much I try I can't shake off recurring reminders of him and Pippa. It's like constantly having a hangover and knowing you did or said something very bad, but being unable to remember quite what. And to think it all started so well, too – but nights that end up in a hangover usually do. Here was this ideal I'd been searching for, seemingly searching for me! And then . . . misery. The whole thing's like one big package-holiday phone-booking fuck-up. You scavenge around trying to find a good deal, stumble across something that looks and seems fantastic – almost, one might say, too good to be true – give Tracey your address and credit-card details while imagining sipping piña coladas on white sand under clear blue skies, then get told, only once the transaction has been processed and your bank account emptied, that there is 'structural work in progress on the adjacent complex', i.e. you are going on holiday to a building site.

If only Andy were a building site. I could dump heavy skiploads on his head, or bulldoze him with JCBs before— NO! Just because he has wronged me does not mean I need to turn into Gazza. The most effective way to deal with criminals like him is to show them that you are strong and will not be beaten and – although I think I might just go and do some comfort eating to build up this strength. Kala, the housegirl, is making very nice smells in the kitchen. Cooking smells, obviously. And even though it's wrong to keep servants, it's more wrong to offend them by not eating yummy almond cake they've spent all afternoon baking. Oh, dear, I hope this isn't insensitive in view of your gruel and yam broth diet.

Looking forward to receiving your editorial advice and — Ooh, someone's just knocked at the door! See! Even in adversity, fortune knocks. Perhaps in the shape of a floral delivery from Alex?

Off to find out . . .

Jess

xxx

Indecent Proposal

'Miss Jess, Miss Jess, he insist and I saying no but he say I wrong and you—' The *askari* gasped for air, panting and sweating at the door. He was clutching his bow and arrow, looking at her as if she were William Wallace and the English army had just appeared over the brow of the hill.

'It's OK, Yusef, calm down.' Jess said glancing nervously around for men with Kalashnikovs. But Yusef looked closer to breaking down, so she began rubbing his upper arm in the reassuring way she couldn't help feeling that, as their security guard, he should be doing to her. 'What's happened? Who's—'

'Arrest me.' A figure in combats ambled up, hands behind head in surrender. Andy. She'd given Yusef strict instructions not to let him through the gate.

'I saying no, no, but, Miss Jess—'

'It's OK, Yusef,' Jess said, staring at her ex-boyfriend, whose choice of muscle-defining tight T-shirt and mischievous grin made her wish involuntarily to prefix the *ex* with an *s*. 'I'll deal with this.'

Yusef looked suspiciously from one to the other as if they'd both opted to eat a bomb.

'Told you, Yusef, mate,' Andy said, slapping him heartily on the back. 'Women say one thing but mean another.' He tapped his nose in an all-lads-together way, and Yusef backed off uncertainly down the track.

'True,' Jess said, leaning against the doorframe with folded arms and feigned composure. 'Women say fuck off and mean don't ever come near me again!' She went to slam the door.

Andy threw his hands back behind his head. 'Don't shoot!'

'Give me one good reason.'

'I deserve a prolonged and painful death. Shooting's too quick.'

'True again,' she said, trying not to smile. 'I gather Milosevic does a good line in torture. Why don't you go and see him?' She started to close the door.

'Wait. Listen, Jess, I've got a proposal.'

'The answer's no.'

'Give me a chance,' he implored. 'You don't know what it is yet.'

'I've given you far too many chances, Andy,' she said, feeling dangerously close to giving him another.

'A hot-air balloon trip over the Mara,' he announced, like the compère of a raffle. 'You, me, the kids, a sunrise. Camping overnight, and, oh, a champagne breakfast. How does that grab you?'

The truth was that it grabbed her in a way that made her want to grab *him* – against the door, passionately, breathless and sweaty. He was like a drug. However much she knew he was bad for her, however much she told herself she'd regret it, however much she'd promised that the last time was *it*, *finito*, over, never ever . . .

'I'd love to,' she squealed, then remembered what had happened to Adam and Eve when they'd found themselves similarly tempted by a serpent. 'But as the children's responsible guardian I can't accept.'

Andy seemed to find something amusing with the responsible bit. 'What about as their fun and irresponsible one?'

'They aren't old enough to drink champagne,' she replied, for Mrs Killjoy.

'More for us. Next excuse?'

'Why are you doing this?'

'Invalid question. Next?'

'Why would I want to do this with you, then?'

'Good question. Umm . . .' He looked sheepishly at his

feet. 'As a means of making me feel less of a bastard for the way I've treated you?'

She paused. The forbidden apple looked very tasty. 'I'm not going to sleep with you, though.'

Andy laughed. 'No, I shouldn't imagine sex in a hot-air balloon is a terribly safe idea. Condom melts. Apparently.' He grinned. 'So is that a yes, then?'

'Yes, please!'

Jess looked startled, almost as if someone else had answered for her. And then a creature appeared from out of her bottom and she realised someone had. Bea. 'What's a comdom?'

'Hello, Bea,' Andy said, bending down to her level. 'Would you like to go up in the sky in a big balloon?'

'Is that what a comdom is?'

Andy looked beseechingly at Jess. She raised her eyebrows to indicate this one was his. After all, she conceded, a condom was the tool of his trade – it would be like a joiner explaining the function of a hammer.

'Um, sort of, yes . . . in a way,' he stuttered. 'Why don't you go and see if Noah wants to join us, too?'

'In the comdom?'

'In the *balloon*, Bea. It's just called a balloon. A big balloon that floats in the sky with a basket attached that we stand in.'

'Does the comdom make it keep up?'

He stifled a laugh. 'To be honest, it tends to do the opposite,' he said, smirking up at Jess. 'No, Bea. The *balloon* stays up because of hot air.'

'What's hot air?'

'Most of the stuff that comes out of Mr Brown's mouth,' Jess said, smirking back.

Andy did a dragon roar. Bea giggled.

'Now, why don't you go and find Noah before I melt you into a puddle?' he said.

Bea looked suspicious for a moment, then scurried off in search of her brother.

Like cinemas that got you spending money you never planned to part with courtesy of strategically timed popcorn adverts, Andy's successful targeting of the kids soon had Jess packing her overnight bag. Or trying to. Wherever she went she found it necessary to guard against all possibilities: a ball-dress for a black-tie event that might loom up in the middle of a family walking holiday in Skye; a pair of sandals lest the glacial slopes of Verbier gave way to a freak Bahamian heat-wave; her entire lingerie drawer for a one-night ~~stand~~ stay in a campsite.

'The idea, apparently, is to lift off the ground,' Andy said, with a wry grin, as Jess piled more of her wardrobe into something that looked incapable of being lifted at all.

'Just in case,' she said, gesturing to a second pair of jeans.

'Or *not* in the case,' he replied, nodding to the over-flowing luggage.

A good hour later, like Railtrack passengers, they were still waiting.

'Ready?' Andy said, when Jess appeared in the doorway looking like a Peruvian packhorse.

'Think so,' she said tentatively. She had one air-hostess suitcase, one canvas bag, one large toiletries bag, one other little bag and one overwhelming feeling that she'd almost certainly forgotten something. Bea had a minuscule Spice Girls satchel. Noah had a camera.

'Then let's get off!' Andy said, enthusiastically, hoisting the kids into the Land Rover with considerably more ease than he did the bags.

Road journeys in Kenya were unpredictable, Jess decided, a bit like Andy. One minute you were coasting along surrounded by breathtaking panoramic scenery, feeling wild and liberated, exotic animals popping up on demand like waiters, and next, you were stuck behind a huge lorry spewing out thick black diesel smoke, plastic bags littering bleak waste-lands full of rotting carcasses. Very occasionally, usually when there didn't seem to be anyone around to save you, you found yourself in the middle of armed warfare.

'Wow! Look at his big spear!' Noah exclaimed, as barely fifty yards in front of them a tall Kikuyu tribesman was standing in the road facing a large group of Maasai, holding the weapon at his side as if he were a lollipop man. Something about the way he was looking, however, suggested to Jess that he wasn't interested in their safe passage to the other side.

'Ssh, please, Noah,' Andy warned, in a manner that sounded ominously as though he might be scared.

'I like his necklace,' Bea whispered, always ready to appreciate the aesthetic in a situation. Jess surveyed his bizarre adornment. He'd obviously had a somewhat unconventional time at the jeweller's that had left him wearing bangles round his neck and having his ears pierced with a pastry cutter.

'Is everything all right?' she ventured, as the rest of his tribe began to move in, banging their spears on the ground in a way that implied everything was not nearly all right.

'Cattle dispute, I suspect,' Andy said, glancing in the wing mirror.

'Is there going to be a war, sir?' Noah asked, wide-eyed.

'Not as long as you keep quiet,' Andy said, then, realising his mistake from the look on Noah's face, added, 'Maybe. But only if you stay really silent.'

The Maasai had started muttering among themselves like old ladies in the post-office queue. It wasn't clear what they were planning but, given that they had a couple of bows and arrows and a stick, Jess hoped for their sakes it wasn't an attack. The increasingly impatient Kikuyus watched them, hawk-like. It was the House of Commons road show. 'Perhaps we should, like, reverse, or something?' she stammered, when getting caught in the crossfire looked more and more likely, less and less appealing.

Andy nodded to the overhead mirror. 'Could be tricky.'

Jess glanced behind. Herds of skeletal cattle had encircled the vehicle. 'Shit.'

'Look, sir! They've started fighting.' Noah was pointing excitedly to a group of Maasai who seemed to have misunderstood the orders and had begun attacking each other.

'Don't worry,' Andy said. 'It's a tribal thing. They're not interested in us.' He then undermined his reassuring words by activating the central locking.

Gradually, a loud whooping sound started up, almost like cheering. Jess instantly felt relieved: they were calling a truce. 'Chuh! Typical blokes, eh? A lot of fuss over nothing.'

Andy looked at her in alarm. 'Jess,' he shouted, 'that's their war cry!'

Before she had time to utter her own terror cry, the two tribes were charging at each other, spears jabbing, arrows flying, sticks clashing. They were dressed in tartan and shouting incomprehensible things that presumably weren't very flattering. The upsurge had all the hallmarks of the aftermath of a Rangers–Celtic match.

'I'm scared,' Bea wailed, climbing through to the front and clutching Jess as if she were a koala bear.

You're scared, Jess narrowly refrained from screeching. 'Don't be silly, Bea. It's just a little tiff,' she said, as a Kikuyu jumped on to the bonnet of the Land Rover, shaking his spear and roaring.

'Like Missiles Attack!' Noah added, for whom life did not imitate art but one of five computer games. 'Neeeeeeaaawwww – SPLAT!'

'We can do without the sound effects, thanks, Noah,' Andy said, inviting the demonic Kikuyu to step down from the bonnet as if he were a celebrity attending a première.

'Can he break through the windscreen?' Bea squeaked.

'No, Bea,' Andy said, smiling comfortingly. 'We're perfectly safe, nothing can – arghhh!'

Suddenly, there was a violent, blinding flash. They all

screamed in horror. Jess buried her head in Bea's neck. The windscreen had fallen in. She'd been impaled, her and Bea, like a shish-kebab. This was her dying moment. The one where her whole life sped past in a white flash, then drifted off into a calm, silent, empty . . .

'You idiot!'

Was God scolding her, or had she bypassed heaven for the eternal flames of—

'Blazing idiot!'

She opened one eye. If He was shouting at her, He looked uncannily like Andy. She opened the other. 'I'm alive!' she cried, rapturously.

'Not for much longer, thanks to paparazzo here.' Andy yanked something out of Noah's hand. Jess was relieved and perturbed to discover it was the camera. 'You do not. Take photos. Of the natives. Fighting,' he articulated – pointlessly, as they were just about to find out.

'Open now!' The Kikuyu from the bonnet was standing with his spear over his shoulder, pointing it at the car, reminding Jess, amusingly, of a Highland Games Toss-the-Caber event, until she and the others noticed that everyone else's spears were pointing in the same direction.

'Oh, God,' Andy announced.

'Perhaps we should give them the camera,' Jess suggested, as if it were Hallowe'en and they'd run out of apples.

'No way!' Noah protested.

'It's that or your head,' Andy said, in a way Jess prayed was a joke.

'I think they're getting angry,' Bea understated.

Intertribal warfare had seemingly been forgotten. Instead, Maasais and Kikuyus were swarming round the vehicle, rapping at the windows and shouting with the fervour of besotted Hear'Say fans. It was when they started to rock the car, however, that Jess suspected they were after more than just an autograph.

'Right!' Andy shouted, trying and failing to restart the engine. 'Shit.'

Bea burst into tears. 'We're going to die,' she wailed.

'Are we going to die, sir?'

'Would everyone please shut up and calm down!' Andy exploded, wrenching at the ignition and beeping the horn in a not very calm way at all.

Suddenly, a much louder horn was hooting, crescendoing into a frenzied screech. If whooping was a war cry, Jess didn't even want to contemplate what this heralded.

'Thank the Lord,' Andy exulted, in what she took to be a Kenyan last rite.

But then a strange thing was happening. The tribesmen were scattering away from the vehicle and the road. Once they'd fled, Jess could see why: a large *matatu*, Kenya's version of Stagecoach, was hurtling towards them, weaving across the potholed highway like a drunk.

'God help anyone in *his* way,' Andy said, managing to start the Land Rover and swing into the ditch just in time to ensure they wouldn't be His first candidates.

Jess watched as the bus lurched onwards, ignoring speed restrictions, safety rules and, given how many passengers were hanging off it, the death penalty. It had a placard on its back windscreen that said, 'Shag.' From the quantity crammed inside, Jess imagined it was more of an orgy.

The remainder of their trip was a subdued affair, peppered only with a bout of swearing from Andy when they were forced to inch along a muddy track whose signpost read, seemingly intentionally unpunctuated, 'Slow roadworks ahead.' By the time they had made it to the campsite, put up the tent, cooked something that tasted of Tupperware boxes, and tucked Noah and Bea into their sleeping-bags, the idea of drowning themselves in gin seemed not only desirable but medicinally sensible.

'Is that too bland?' Andy asked, as Jess sipped from a plastic mug of gin, lemonade and black bits she was glad the camp-fire light was too weak to illuminate.

'No, not at all,' she replied, smiling. The truth of it was that nothing with Andy was bland. It was both his charm and his downfall. Things just seemed to happen with him – exciting things, terrifying things, hideous Pippa-type things. Life was never boring. And yet, she mused, crunching charcoal, she felt exhausted by it all, like a mother whose desire to have a baby is overwhelmed by the screeching, bawling, puking, pooing reality.

'I've been thinking,' he announced, as if it were a disgusting personal habit to which one shouldn't confess in public. 'I'm going to cut short my stay here and fly home next month with you.'

Jess flinched. Why was it that the minute you believed you were over someone, they expressed a desire to sleep with you? Not that he'd said as much, she acknowledged, but it was like an invitation to come in for coffee – perfectly clear what he meant. 'And you really think that would work?' she said, both repulsed and impressed by his unflagging arrogance.

'I haven't told Sarah yet. She might be a bit . . .' he looked pensively into the smouldering embers in a way that was presumably meant to be symbolic '. . . but yes. At least, I hope.'

'And when were you planning on telling *me*?' Jess enquired, marvelling at how he'd blithely plotted their future together, like a charity's assumption that a single contribution obligated you to be a donor for life.

'Well, I'm telling you now, aren't I?' he said, crossly.

'And do you normally "tell" people to go out with you?'

'To be honest,' he said, smirking, 'it was more her telling me.'

Jess felt her brain fog up like a car whose demister wasn't working. Her? Her who? Her, Sarah? He'd always said she was kind and well-meaning, but *telling* him to go out with the person who'd been wearing her underwear after she'd come all the way out to Africa to woo him back? That wasn't just kind, it was kind of weird. And then it hit her. 'Pippa.'

Andy cocked his head in confusion. 'I'm sorry?'

'Pippa. I assume it was Pippa who told you to go out with me. Like a kind of guilt atonement. You know – I feel bad so I'm going to tell you to go back to that poor pathetic woman I seduced you away from. Well, I'm not a charity case, Andy. Not a ping-pong ball that you can just bat to and fro to alleviate whatever marital disharmony you've—'

'Whoa-wo-wo!' he shouted, as if she were a neurotically rearing horse. 'Planet. Different one. Confused,' he one-word sentenced, like a kid whose language has been reduced to text-message speak. 'Do you mean . . . did you say – go out with *you*?'

Jess moved her eyes from side to side to emphasise the lunacy in the suggestion that he could have meant someone else. 'I did. Ye-es,' she said, encouragingly.

'It's just that . . . heavens, I don't really know how to say this, Jess.' He glugged back the remains of his mug to help him. 'I'm going out with Sarah.'

Mortification (*noun.*): shame or humiliation (deriv. *mortis* death). Jess sat with the fixed expression of a puppet as Andy described how he and Sarah had been reunited, courtesy not so much of her 'telling' him as issuing the kind of ultimatum even Saddam might have felt obliged to adhere to. His shortened stay in Kenya was so that he could start serving his sentence sooner.

'I do feel scared it mightn't work,' he mused, as if the relationship were an electric gadget, 'yet being with her makes me feel secure and *un*scared. Weird, eh?'

Not really, Jess thought. Sarah appeared to possess the equivalent might of the UN. 'And you don't think you're going to get itchy feet again two months in?'

'Nope,' he said, assertively. 'Got some athlete's foot powder for that. Zaps the fungus, apparently.' He smiled, then turned serious. 'Who knows? I hope not. I mean, that was sort of what Kenya was all about. A testing ground.'

Jess thought about suggesting that Kenya's thirty million inhabitants might not see their country in such terms, but stopped when she remembered that she, shamefully, had. 'It's certainly made me see sense with Alex,' she said, then realised from the lack of jealousy-inducing motive behind her comment that it wasn't just Alex on which Kenya had given her a perspective. 'And appreciate what's really important in a relationship.'

Andy nodded with the earnestness of an *Oprah* guest. 'To enjoy what you have rather than fantasise about what you don't.'

Jess didn't think it the moment to point out that he had done more than just fantasise about what he didn't have. 'But what about all your doubts?' she asked, as much of herself as him. 'Have they just, like . . . gone?'

'Not exactly,' he said, refilling their mugs with neat gin to ensure that the two of them certainly would be. 'More . . . exorcised out of my system.'

'By shagging me three times a day?' She laughed. 'Or playing lots of football?'

'Ex*or*cised, Jess,' he corrected, solemnly, as if she'd just made light of his dead grandpa. 'Freed myself of them by not being afraid of them. By confronting them. By seeing whether they were endemic to my relationship with Sarah or to all my relationships.'

By shagging me three times a day, Jess concluded.

'With Sarah, I had all the basic ingredients to make the cake,' he announced, inexplicably. 'The staple things, you know, flour, eggs, and it was a nice, wholesome cake.'

Jess blinked back visions of Sarah as a Victoria sponge.

'And yet I wasn't satisfied. It felt drab. I wanted the icing on that cake, too. So I came out here. And met you.'

Jess bowed her head coyly, waiting for Radio One's Our Tune to strike up from the long drop.

'And you were that icing.' He paused dramatically.

She held back to hear whether he was going to elaborate on this compliment – assuming that being a sugary paste was a positive thing – then smiled her acceptance. 'That is so sweet, Andy!'

'Yes. Icing tends to be,' he retorted, grinning. 'But that's not the point, is it?'

She shook her head and waited eagerly to hear more of her favourable points.

'Without the cake, icing is useless.'

She baulked. The analogy might have been cute, but the insinuation was clear: he wanted to go out with Sarah, and go to bed with Jess. He wanted, quite simply, to have his cake and eat the icing too. 'It's one or the other,' she snapped.

'Exactly!' Andy exclaimed. 'That is exactly my point! It is either the cake or the icing. And I know now that it's the cake. The cake with its basic, staple ingredients. I need and want the cake.' He looked at her with the expression of an anguished philosophy student. 'I just had to live off a diet of icing to know that.'

Jess felt her jaw drop open in disgust, head swimming with images of her as a sticky goo into which he dipped his wick regularly to reassure himself he wasn't missing out. But then she thought about it from a different perspective. If their relationship could be reduced to a cookery lesson, surely she had sampled her way to the same conclusion. 'You were tasty icing, too, while you lasted,' she said, smirking, 'but I've got a very nice Alex cake waiting for me in a tin at home.'

'So you two are getting back together as well?' Andy said.

Jess nodded, then smiled. What had connected them in the first place was dissatisfaction with their exes. It seemed somewhat of an irony that a mutual desire to return to those exes was connecting them once more. 'Just don't get any ideas about a foursome,' she said, realising from the look on his face that they were no longer just connecting, they were mind-reading.

'Night,' he called, as they stumbled their way to bed. Separately.

Like a party where the best bit is getting ready, the balloon ride the following morning was a bit of an anticlimax. Hampered by Bea's vertigo, Noah's kamikaze camera stunts and wet mist, it wasn't quite the uplifting experience Jess had envisaged. The champagne breakfast, on the other hand, was.

'Jess is *still* drunk,' Bea squealed, when they returned home and tried to heave their bacon-larded stomachs out of the car.

'Jeshish snot.' She'd just awoken with a trail of dribble down her front.

'Jeshish got a phone call,' Andy said, gesturing to the house-girl.

'Miss Jess, it is good time, Miss Jess. There is man on phone.' Kala was beckoning her inside in a way that suggested the man wasn't just on the phone but in the bed, naked, with some massage oil.

Jess lurched after her and burped into the receiver. 'Hello, man on phone.'

'Jess, hi. It's Alex.'

'Alex!' she shrieked.

'I've got some news,' he announced, excitedly.

'Yippee,' she rejoiced, giggling. 'You love me!'

'Love me,' the echo pleaded, rather desperately.

'Well . . . I . . .'

'You're pregnant!'

A pregnant pause.

'I'm engaged.'

Otherwise Engaged

To:	*Claire.Voyant@hotmail.com*
Date:	*Thursday 24 August*
Subject:	*Otherwise Engaged*

Engorged. Slumped at a computer terminal
  discovering the pitfalls of consuming the entire
  population of the Indian Ocean for lunch. In
  particular – ergh – fishy farts.

Dear Claire,
   When Marjorie and Quentin said they were taking me on
holiday to the coast as a thank-you for being their nanny, I under-
stood that we would be splashing through waves in the manner of
boisterous Labradors, not having to invest in a winch/helicopter/
whole cast of Baywatch *to rescue me from drowning in my own*
whale blubber. Next thing I know Warner Brothers will be
approaching me to feature in Free Willy 4.
   Admittedly, I can't hold my generous hosts entirely to blame for
this recent metamorphosis into cumbersome marine mammal.
Finding out Alex is getting married was definitely an incentive to
stuff larder and fridge down gullet, not to mention slit wrists and
eat twenty-four paracetamol. It seems tragically unfair that when
you're falling in love you get the added bonus of appetite loss,
meaning you're not only happy but skinny too, whereas when you
discover that the person you have fallen in love with has fallen in
love with someone else, you get the misery compounded by the
uncontrollable need to eat yourself into a hog.
   I'm trying not to dwell on it, which, of course, has had exactly
the same effect of trying not to eat – i.e., I do it all the more. I
just can't help feeling I've been the victim of mercilessly bad timing

265

– as though I've got to the shop at five thirty-one and the security guard is shaking his head and lowering the heavy steel grating in my face. But at least with the shop you can go back tomorrow and get what you want. By tomorrow what I want will already have been sold to someone else.

Ergh. The whole torture is vile. I was so sorted about where Alex and I were headed – as in, up the aisle. It was like sailing on a beautiful crystal clear ocean where everything was ripply sand and cute little blue fish. Now my emotions are all churned up like murky seaweedy sea where moving forward in any direction seems an unpleasant and potentially jellyfish-filled experience.

I think the worst thing – other than the pulsating Portuguese man-of-war currently stinging the shit out of my heart – is the shock. I'd only ever seen Alex in relation to the bearing he has on my life. Naturally, I realised he was a person with his own life too, but I only knew about the bits connected to me and didn't consider the existence of the rest – like that philosophy theory: does a falling tree make a noise if no one is around to witness it falling? Yes, apparently. And not just a noise, a full 'Will you marry me?' explosion.

And now it seems that everyone's at it. Just days after this suicide-enticer, a smug little envelope from Spotty Simon plopped through my door. Only I didn't realise it was from him at first and did that pointless thing when faced with a strange letter of trying to work out from the postcode and handwriting who it might be from, rather than just opening it and finding out. I recognised the writing but couldn't quite place it. Associated it with someone nice and quite attractive, then got this feeling it was someone I fancied and – YUK – it was Spotty Simon. There is nothing more alarming than having your subconscious thoughts thrown into such stark relief in this way. (I'm now worried this means I fancy Spotty Simon. Could I fancy Spotty Simon? What if I've fancied him all along but refused to admit it to myself? Ergh, the thought is too repellent. And redundant, given he's now married.)

Anyway, I don't know why I thought he was nice. He isn't. All the envelope contained was a showy-offy new-address card for 'Simon, Marie and baby Ellie' with, 'Got married yet?' written on the back. I can but hope this was a grossly misjudged attempt at humour and not his idea of tact.

The only thorn to be extracted from my sorry situation is that I didn't get round to sending Alex the letter I planned, despite your editorial expertise turning it into a piece of literary brilliance. Instead, I was the bigger person (literally, I now miserably suspect) and sent him the following:

> To Dearest A,
> Congratulations, or, as they say here, vizuri sana! She is very lucky.
>> Wishing you a long and happy life together,
>> J
>> xxx

. . . which is obviously a load of bollocks, but I fear the truth would not so much have hurt as had me locked up with a restraining order.

I thought going on holiday might make things better, help get it all into perspective, but, of course, it's done the reverse, allowing me endless hours of staring at blue skies imagining them in a selection of loving embraces. The problem with going on holiday, I'm rapidly discovering, is that you have to take yourself with you.

In the rare and wonderful moments I've managed to lose myself, it's been very nice indeed. Going from rural Kenya to the coast is like switching from broadsheet to Hello!: everything is glossy, colourful and happy – though obviously Lady Victoria Hervey doesn't keep popping up at every turn. We're staying in a rented cottage south of Mombasa, where I share a room with Bea and a cornucopia of wildlife. Guests so far include: one pair of copulating cockroaches, an army of safari ants, enough mosquitoes to open up a blood bank, and a spider you could ride on.

I've yet to work out what's worse – Bea screaming at eardrum-damaging volume at a weird flappy thing, or the athletic work-out required to ensure weird flappy thing doesn't get into the room in the first place. It is not by accident that the insect repellent they use here is called Doom. The trouble with not being native to Africa, though, is that you don't know whether the fluorescent-winged beetle climbing into your bed is a friendly inquisitive little fellow or about to have you for breakfast. Nor do you have the innate ability to ignore what in Britain would quite reasonably warrant a call to the Noise Pollution Police. In fact, sleeping has become a skill I no longer possess as night-time takes on the soundtrack of a horror movie – distant shrieking, nightjars sirening like car alarms and bushbabies cackling with witch-style malice.

Daytime easily makes up for this, however, with nice hot sunshine and sea the temperature of a recently vacated loo seat. The beaches are everything Bounty adverts promised, except for the wet, sun-kissed Adonis, who in this case has, unfortunately, been replaced by a skinny, ginger-haired satellite-dish installer from Dundee. Sample chat-up lines include: 'My job is to give you good reception,' and 'I'm able with my cable.' So, in answer to your query as to whether I've met any dishy blokes: yes, but I don't suspect this is quite the 'dish' you had in mind.

We haven't really done much except eat. It's so hot that even picking your nose requires Herculean effort. We went on a boat trip yesterday and did some snorkelling, which was great fun. Feels like you've inadvertently fallen into a tropical fish tank, although given my current whale status that would clearly not be possible. I can't get over how many vibrantly coloured and patterned creatures there are just inches below a seemingly unprepossessing surface. Marjorie says I should remember this when it comes to blokes.

How are you and John? Will you be coming back for Jo's wedding? Ergh, God – just had a diarrhoea thought. Do you think Alex will invite me to his wedding? What is the etiquette with exes? Surely inviting them is an insensitive, showy-offy act – like asking your infertile friend round to watch you give birth to triplets. Yet not inviting them suggests there are still feelings that shouldn't be there.

I must say, returning to Britain to a newly engaged Alex wasn't the plan. But, then, nothing in my life ever seems to go to plan. I'm not sure what I envisaged would happen to me in Kenya, but unless my last two weeks have me undergoing a seismic change of the sort regularly experienced by Oprah Winfrey's poor body then I'll be going back much the same person as I came out, in a depressing reversal-of-Big-Brother type way.

I did a questionnaire in one of Marjorie's magazines about the 'you' you'd like to be versus the 'you' you are. I fear a similar set of miserably opposed answers would result if applied to my Kenyan experience:

	Hoped-for Kenyan Me	Real Me
Q1. What do you look like?		
(a) Bronzed in a well-travelled manner rather than Michelle-Collins orange, with svelte toned body effortlessly achieved via jaunts up Mount Kenya.	✓	
(b) As ugly as ever, only with added whale fritter.		✓
Q2. What do you like chatting about?		
(a) The juxtaposition of neo-colonial Africa with disintegration of grass roots infrastructure, incorporating sub-argument pertaining to humanitarian aid and how best to administer it.	✓	
(b) Big Brother.		✓

		Hoped-for Kenyan Me	Real Me
Q3.	**What is your best physical attribute?**		
	(a) N/A: there is no place in this world for vanity when millions have no legs.	✓	
	(b) ~~My legs~~ My hair? Without the dandruff? Probably my ears – after all, not much can go wrong with ears. Although mine could possibly be a bit too loby. Maybe my knees minus the hairy bits. Oh, sod it – have no good attributes.		✓
Q4.	**What are your career aspirations?**		
	(a) Touring the globe with Bob Geldof campaigning for the cancellation of Third World debt.	✓	
	(b) To be rich enough not to need a career.		✓
Q5.	**What would your friends say about you?**		
	(a) 'Oh, Jess, she's so wonderfully generous and compassionate with a staggering intelligence, which is so modestly expressed through her bellyaching sense of humour.'	✓	
	(b) 'Who's Jess?'		✓

I hope not all of my friends will have forgotten me. According to Jo's mate, Pooch, coming home from a stint abroad is like going back to school after being off sick. You expect the trumpeting fanfare of a returning war hero but get the distinct impression no one noticed you were gone. Apparently the thing to do is not witter on about your travels to anyone who will listen, but wait patiently until someone asks, then give a condensed summary of your experiences in no more than one minute, otherwise their eyes will glaze over. She made it sound like a demeaning radio panel game of the sort Chris Tarrant might be involved in.

I'm sure my friends won't be so egomaniacal. At least, they'd better bloody not be, seeing as the last few weeks have been ruined by nagging dilemmas about what on earth I can bring back for them. Hate this about holidays. I mean, surely the point of them is escapism and relaxation, not rushing around with Christmas-Eve-on-Oxford-Street stress, buying up pointless African artefacts that will look absurdly out of place next to the Bang and Olufsen stereo, but which everyone will feel obliged to display, while politely disguising the clear insinuation that what they would really have liked is two hundred fags from Duty Free. What's more, it's been made doubly torturous by Mum, who keeps digging out ever more distant aunts and uncles with the skill of a palaeontologist. It's bad enough trying to find presents for people I know. It's Pin-the-Tail-on-the-Donkey finding something for an amorphous abstract unit who only comes into existence to send you Paisley-patterned address books and matching pen sets at Christmas.

And then there's the related going-home stress of making sure you've taken enough photos, not just of tiny blobs that were enormous buffalo through the lens but of more normal things, like where you stayed and who you spent time with. I tend to suffer from the syndrome that makes you overlook the sightseeing potential on your doorstep – like people living in London who've never been to the Albert Hall. Like me. Mind you, I don't know why I'm worrying. I will only get home, look at them a couple of times, plan to put them into a photo album with accompanying witty comments, then dump them in a large cardboard box along with eleven years of other Kodak packs I've planned to put into a photo album with accompanying witty comments.

Maybe the solution is not to go home at all. After all, what am I going back to? Unemployment, homelessness and an ex-boyfriend's wedding. Hardly the most grabby of selling points. The only positive is that Andy's coming too, so we'll both be in the same position – alas, not a sexual one, because he's got back together with Sarah.

Ergh. Suddenly had horrible panicky feeling that everyone has a partner except me. Reminds me of Brownies and game where scary lesbian Brown Owl laid down hula-hoop rings and when the music stopped you had to jump into one with your partner. Only I wasn't quick enough off the mark and kept trying to become an appendage to another couple, until I was shouted at and made to stand in the naughty corner.

Perhaps, though, this was a wise lesson I didn't heed, and now I must stand for ever in the naughty singles' corner as punishment for not grabbing a partner sooner. There certainly seems to be some degree of Sod's Law in the irony that I came to Africa because I was running away from a relationship I didn't want, and am now returning from Africa running after the relationship I cannot have.

Am I just doomed never to be in the right place at the right time, like London's buses? I realise I'm a child of the Alex Garland generation, permanently on a quest for something better. I just wish he'd warned me that this turned you schizophrenic. For example, one minute I'm seeing myself through the eyes of my friends back home as a daring, strong and brave person where a, 'when-I-go-to-live-in-Kenya' anecdote immediately earmarks me as 'interesting'. Naturally, this is ego-comforting and makes me feel rather pleased with myself. The next minute I am actually in Kenya and seeing myself through African eyes. Here, I am not some fascinating Bohemian type challenging convention, but a bog-standard Brit among a whole host of other bog-standard Brits, living in Africa not because we are daring or strong or brave but quite the *opposite: because we are running away from something at home i.e. we are weak.*

Wish to develop a third personality where life is just led, rather than picked over as if it were a plate of congealing turnips. It's very depressing travelling several thousand miles to 'find yourself' only to discover that what you've found are the things you'd gone all the way there to lose – e.g., entire personality. Maybe, though, it's like dieting and weight loss. You can't expect miracles simply by starving yourself for a day, but must instead accept that it's a cumulative process and be patient. Maybe I will arrive home a thin goddess purged of neurosis. Oh, but, no, I won't – I'll have a sedative harpooned into my backside and be craned in on a gigantic hammock.

Oh, God, a spooky man is staring at me over his computer screen. I gave him a friendly smile, which he has mistaken for the beginnings of a relationship. I must say, I'm very disappointed by these Internet cafés. Cosmo rated them number three on their list of places to meet men, immediately installing images in my mind of Indiana Jones and cheeky email banter.

Initially, mind you, their theory did seem to bear out. Soon after I arrived I went into one in Nairobi and was innocently tapping away when a dazzling sex-god appeared on the opposite terminal. He was wearing a sexy Nike T-shirt and kept looking across at me and grinning in a way that suggested an invitation to a secluded safari lodge would shortly be forthcoming. Then he got up and disappeared out of the door hand in hand with another bloke, revealing the sexy Nike T-shirt to have arrogant parting 'Just Do Me' shot emblazoned across the back.

Ever since then I've been leered at by creeps (see above), ignored by Japanese tourists, or chatted up by a fungi specialist who, in the same way pet owners look like their pet, bore a disturbing resemblance to a mouldy growth.

Talking of which, I seem to have something alarmingly unappealing mushrooming out of my inner thigh. I'm hoping it's a bite from one of our many room guests, or an adverse reaction to

273

bikini line cream, rather than full-blown gangrene. There also seems to be a whiff of baked beans coming from my underarms. Christ's sake! No wonder I'm having the pulling success of a dead mule when I both look and smell like one.

Right, I'd better cycle back and join my hosts. We're going snorkelling again, then probably out for a gargantuan meal to devour all the creatures we were snorkelling with. I swear if I eat one more thing I'll explode in the repugnant manner of Monty Python's Mr Creosote. Dinner is no longer a pleasurable activity but synonymous with Dark Age torture.

Lots of love and blubber,

Jess

xxx

Who Wants To Be a Married?

'Dinner!' Marjorie called, appearing out of the kitchen with a bowl of floating candles.

Quentin, Jess and Andy were lined up on the sofa like expectant baby birds – or, in Quentin's case, an overstuffed vulture.

'My, my,' he roared, heaving himself up and waddling over to peer into the bowl, 'that does look tasty. Do we eat the wick too?'

'The wick's for pudding,' Marjorie replied, placing the bowl on the table with no indication that this was a joke.

Jess got up and followed her into the kitchen, hitting the sort of warm humid air normally associated with arriving in a foreign country. It was her last night in Kenya and this was supposed to be her farewell dinner: if the food so far was anything to go by, she suspected she might be saying farewell a great deal sooner. 'Can I help?'

Marjorie was whisking frantically at a sauce that couldn't decide whether to be runny or solid so was opting for a bit of both. 'No, no, everything under control,' she replied. She was someone who treated domestic duties as army assignments. Cooking was target practice, Hoovering minesweeping and supermarket shopping a military exercise where the aisles were trenches, the trolley a tank and the enemy everyone else in the shop. 'Go and beat up Quentin,' she advised, handing Jess some knives.

The meal, much to everyone's relief, turned out to be both digestible and enjoyable. The conversation, however, was proving neither.

'. . . so I shot the brute – pow – right between the eyes. Bloody good shot, to tell the truth. Killed him. Dead.' Quentin popped open another bottle of champagne in celebration of the murder.

'The man?' Jess said, terrified.

'Pfwah-har-har-har. The man. Pfwah-har-HARRR!'

She looked uncertainly to Andy and Marjorie for clarification. But they, too, were cackling in the manner of demons. 'But . . . isn't that against the law?'

'The dog, Jess,' Andy spluttered. 'He shot the dog with rabies. Not the man.'

'Here's to Jess,' Quentin announced suddenly, picking up his champagne. 'For being top value and a jolly good nanny to the sprogs.'

They all clinked glasses and brayed like politicians, as Jess smiled coyly and chose not to dwell on the ease of association from rabid dog to her.

'Right, troops, I think a game's in order.' Quentin strode over to a drawer and returned with the kind of hinged box that organised people kept drugs in. He then removed some Rizla papers and a lump of something that suggested he was one of those organised people. 'I have never had sex with a wildebeest.'

Sometimes Quentin seemed a genial, harmless soul. At others he seemed mildly offensive. Now he seemed to have lost the plot.

'You drink if this is true, i.e. you *haven't* had sex with a wildebeest, and don't if it isn't,' he explained, lighting the roll-up, as everyone was quick to glug back their champagne. 'Then the question stick,' he continued, waving the joint in the air as if it were incense, 'is passed to the next person who makes another "I have never" statement, and so on.'

Marjorie looked like Barney Rubble trying to make sense of Fred Flintstone. 'Why?'

Quentin guffawed.

'It's a drinking game, Marjorie,' Andy said, patronisingly, filling up the glasses. 'An excuse to get lashed.'

'In that case, can we do it without resorting to bestiality?'

Andy flashed her his most seductive smile. 'Are you propositioning me, Mrs Robinson?' She gave a little giggle.

He was like a girl with a new top, Jess thought: he'd try it on with everything.

'Jess'll show you how it's done,' Quentin bulldozed in, placing the joint at her lips in a way she didn't wish to over-interpret. 'Won't you, girl?'

Jess inhaled obediently, as her mind fuzzed up with unlikely enough scenarios to get everyone drinking. With Andy as a participant, this wasn't easy. 'I have never shagged . . .' She paused. Where had Andy *not* shagged?

'I suspect *that*'s not true,' Quentin interjected, raising his eyebrows.

'. . . in a hot-air balloon,' she completed. She grinned knowingly at Andy as they both picked up their glasses. Quentin and Marjorie grinned too – but didn't pick up their glasses. The thought was too repugnant to bear.

'I've got one!' Marjorie announced, excitedly, reaching for the joint. Everyone looked on in anticipation. 'I have never been to Tajikistan.'

A hushed silence descended on the room as if the school nerd had been bold enough to make a suggestion, and the head bully was deciding whether it was cool in its off the wall-ness, or deserving of being beaten to a pulp.

'Fair enough,' Quentin grunted, clearly disappointed.

The point of the game, Jess was learning, as they all drank obligingly, was not just to get sloshed but to get so sloshed you divulged intimate sexual secrets in the process. She might not have been to Tajikistan yet, but if she played for much longer she would be packing her bags and emigrating there.

'Andy's turn,' Quentin boomed, keen to return things to the gutter.

Andy leaned over, took the joint from Marjorie, then sucked at it provocatively. 'I have never been attracted to . . .'

Jess waited eagerly to hear the rare creature that had escaped Andy's roving libido.

'To someone who's . . .' he grinned, mischievously '. . . married.'

Marjorie sipped her champagne, grinning back at him winningly, as he folded his arms and looked coyly at the table. Jess was about to break up the happy couple with the news that he had another married woman in mind, when it became uncomfortably evident that he wasn't the only one.

'Quent! Why aren't you drinking?' Marjorie snapped, in contradiction of her usual nag for him to stop.

'Well, I mean, obviously it depends on how you interpret "attracted to",' he muttered, squirming.

'And? How *do* you interpret it?'

Quentin stared at a pot plant. 'Appreciating the beauty of another, without wishing to act on this appreciation,' he articulated, in the over-calm manner of someone who knows they're in a lot of shit.

'And which *other*'s beauty have you been appreciating?' she barked, as Andy pretended to be busy with a cork and Jess feared the recital of a list the length of a blockbuster's credits. 'No! Don't tell me. Let me guess.'

Quentin looked alarmed at this suggestion – understandably, Jess decided: female guesses were rarely wrong.

'Pippa.'

An indeterminate noise escaped Jess's mouth, as Quentin sealed his fate by not saying anything at all.

'Bastard,' Marjorie squeaked, then yanked the joint from Andy and slammed her way out to the veranda.

Quentin pulled an expression that said, 'Women, huh?' and grovelled his way after her. As an advert for marriage, it was as compelling as that for B&Q.

'I take it we're talking about the same Pippa,' Jess said, when sounds of cats being massacred abated, 'that you had a stint with.'

Andy nodded and shoved a newly rolled joint into her mouth as if it were a dummy. 'I should imagine so. She's a bit of a fox.'

'Sly with a bushy tail?' Jess suggested, sucking eagerly on her dummy.

'Certainly a bushy . . .' He smirked, then took his turn with the joint. 'An attractive woman, shall we say?'

Jess smiled benevolently, suddenly feeling a huge rush of love towards both Andy and Pippa and everyone, including beautiful Quentin. Happiness was growing inside her like a little baby rose bud blossoming into . . .

'You're deeply majestic, Andy.'

A divine spirit seemed to think so too, because lots of little Andys were hatching in front of her. Ploppety-plop!

'Majestic both in a skin meaning but only also in a core of a golden nugget.'

'Jess, perhaps you—'

'Golden rays tinkling down and touching nuggets that is a force of goodness and happiness in all bright colours of traffic lights that can change red, stop, allowing flowing of other rays around in the circle . . .'

A band of bright light was zapping Jess's forehead like something out of *Star Wars*. She raised herself up on the bed and squinted into the room as a kettledrum beat itself repeatedly inside her remaining brain cells. Something wasn't quite right. A tree had sprouted outside her window, for starters. And her bedside lamp had shrunk. And someone, it would appear, had stolen her dressing-table. Then it hit her. It was Marjorie and Quentin's room.

She stared at the carpet in alarm. What in Christ's name was she doing in here? *When* had she got in here? How? Why? And – with *whom*?

She peeled back the covers, and began to stalk the room like an ostrich, desperate for any morsel of a clue that might fill in the gap between the happy, free sensations she'd remembered enjoying and the current hideous ones fogging up her head. She lifted up the duvet, peered under the bed, checked the bin for used condoms. Nothing. Then she stopped short. Very short. Where the hell were her trousers?

'Morning, handsome. Sleep well?' Quentin had just entered.

'Umm . . . I,' she stuttered, looking at him searchingly, trying to figure out whether . . . perhaps . . . in some disturbing drug-induced frenzy they could have . . .

'You OK? Looking a bit green behind the gills.'

He didn't seem fazed to find her trouserless. Oh, God. Maybe they had.

'Your trousers are next door. Marjorie's de-vomiting them as we speak. Bless the woman.'

He was being normal. Maybe they hadn't.

'Oh, gosh, yes,' she faltered, with no recollection of having thrown up. 'Quentin? Were you . . . when, what I mean is . . . well, last night did I—'

'Sleep with me?'

Jess looked at him in horror.

'Yes, ma'am. You sure did.'

There was waking up after a nasty nightmare and there was waking *into* a nasty nightmare. And then there was discovering you'd had sex with your boss. As a note on which to end a job, it was a sick one.

'You've been great,' Marjorie praised, as Jess stood at the door with all her bags, feeling the furthest she'd ever been from great. Despite having the entire day to prepare for her departure, she'd ended up fleeing around at the last minute resorting to the kind of panic packing that entailed sitting on suitcases and forgetting everything in the bathroom. 'Thank you so much for all you've done.'

Jess hugged her, wondering whether this thanks extended

to shagging her husband. 'It's been a pleasure,' she managed, and hoped this didn't cause Quentin's head to swell – either of them.

'I don't want her to go,' Bea whined, charging up and clamping herself to Jess's leg with the tenacity of a suffragette to railings.

Jess prised her off and scooped her into her arms. 'I'll be back,' she said, a less intimidating Arnold Schwarzenegger.

'With more presents?' Noah asked, excitedly.

'Noah!' Quentin scolded, then readjusted his trousers and gave her the kind of hug that made it perfectly clear what present *he* wanted.

'Oh, fuck,' Jess said, when she and Andy were safely out of earshot in his car, travelling to the airport to board symbolically – separate planes. 'Life is a shite pile of piss.'

'Interesting analogy,' Andy mused, overtaking four people on a bicycle. 'You mean, like a mountain made of shit with rivers of piss running down it?'

'It's not funny, Andy,' Jess protested, lashing out at the dashboard. 'I mean . . . I slept with Quentin, for fuck's sake.'

Andy chuckled. 'I know.'

'You *know*?' she screeched, undesirable things exploding in her stomach. 'How do you know?'

'Mmm, let me see now . . .' He grinned. 'I put you there, you fool.'

Jess felt her brain freeze over, like a crashed computer with scrambled screen. 'Why? When?'

'Hmm, couldn't tell you *exactly*. Somewhere between you chucking up in my hand and falling asleep in the bath. Wine gum?'

'But . . . in your hand?' The thought was inspiring a repeat performance.

'I don't think we can really say it was limited to my hand. No. Especially when you see my shoes. Covered in . . . Anyway, don't want to put you off sweetcorn for life. But, yes, my hand seemed to be the desired direction of the projectile. Sure you don't want one?'

'And then I had sex with Quentin.'

Andy burst out laughing. 'I hardly think so!'

It was like having a conversation with the taxman: nothing made sense. 'But you just said I slept with him.'

'In the same *bed* as him, yes. But, Jess, if there was any action at all, it was happening with the mosquitoes. Mmm, these black ones are nice.'

'So I didn't shag him?' Jess squealed, as if she'd just discovered she could get her money back.

'Put it this way. Quentin was snoring like a walrus and you . . .' Andy seemed to be enjoying a hilarious private moment '. . . you were . . . well, comatose would be a euphemism.'

Jess mulled over the good news with a wine gum. 'So why did you put me into bed with Quentin, then?' It wasn't so much frying-pan into fire, as frying-pan into Dante's blazing inferno.

'Well, I didn't think you wanted to sleep in your own sick on the sofa. Would that be correct?' He looked at her with raised eyebrows. She nodded with lowered head. 'And Marjorie had stormed off and passed out in the spare room. So, unless the bath would have been comfier, it seemed like the only option.' He smiled. 'Request to step down from the witness box, your honour.'

Jess smiled back. He may have been a lousy boyfriend, but as an ex he was exemplary. She turned to him with renewed affection. 'So, where on earth did *you* sleep?'

He glanced sheepishly down at the steering-wheel, then looked up at her with a cheeky grin. 'With Marjorie.'

Touching down at Gatwick airport was not just an anticlimax but a reason to reach for the antidepressants. It was grey, drizzling, and five a.m.

'Have a nice stay,' a bored stewardess parroted, as Jess

descended into the igloo and followed the streams of people as they trudged through empty carpeted corridors, finally popping out into the bright lights of Baggage Reclaim.

Fighting with a trolley, she joined the congregation of mourners huddled round the carousel. An obligatory lone bag was chugging along obediently, disappearing and reappearing with the depressing regularity of Anthea Turner.

'Poor woman,' a man in front mumbled, to what appeared to be his wife. Then he retreated out of the mêlée leaving Jess a ringside view.

She stared morosely as the rotating conveyor belt continued to convey the message that all their baggage appeared to be lost. Then the lone bag trundled past again, this time close enough for her to notice that lots of Tampax were oozing out from a broken zip. She glanced about at her fellow mourners, feeling a genuine sense of embarrassment for the poor owner of the bag. Then she looked again: the poor owner was *her*.

Not being one for public displays of attention, she tried to grab-and-run, but failed on the grab and was forced to watch it complete another circuit, before lunging at it in a way that prompted every head to jerk round simultaneously, like a badly animated cartoon crowd scene. Pretending to be calm, she stuffed the remaining escapee tampons back in, then waited, mortified, for her five other bags to arrive. When eventually she made it to Customs, bright red and on the verge of screaming, it felt an irony indeed to be walking under the sign 'Nothing to Declare'.

'*Jambo! Karibu!*' a familiar voice shouted as something whacked her on the shoulders.

Jess spun round in delight. It was Lou. 'What are you doing here?' she screeched, as if there might be another reason she was loitering around at Gatwick at an unsociable hour of the morning. Lou was an old work colleague and a good friend, soon to be upgraded to best friend, Jess decided, for this unexpected yet greatly appreciated appearance.

'Thought you might be missing your servants,' she said, smiling, then gestured to the pile of bulging bags, 'although it looks as if you've had the foresight to pack most of them.'

Jess laughed. 'God, it's so good to see you.' They performed a stop-start hugging routine. 'I want to hear everything! All the news I've missed.'

'I take it we're talking gossip, rather than Blair's latest position on the single currency?'

'I think it's important to be well informed on all matters,' Jess said, earnestly. 'Gossip.'

'In that case, d'you want the good first or the bad?'

'Bad.'

'Jo wants us to be flower-girls at her wedding. And wear puffed cerise.'

'The good better be fantastic.'

'Depending on how you look at it. Alex's fiancée has called off the engagement.'

Jess froze. She didn't know how to look at it, but right now she didn't know how to breathe. 'Crikey,' was all she could mumble, then, head swimming, she gathered her baggage, both literally and metaphorically, and made for the door.

What would have happened if Jess had given in?

To find out turn to page 17 . . .

Otherwise turn to page 285 . . .

EPILOGUE

The Beginning of the End

To: *Claire.Voyant@hotmail.com*
Date: *Thursday 5 October*
Subject: *The Beginning of the End*

Entering a phase in my life that I can only hope
*   will be like crap sex: painful and frustrating*
*   but over very quickly. Wishing I could adapt to*
*   change in the manner of a crafty chameleon,*
*   not a hibernating tortoise. Blaming my mother*
*   as it's easier than accepting fault lies within.*

Dear Claire,

*   I feel as though I've not so much made a fresh beginning as squelched my way to the starting line in a three-day-old nappy. I'm trying to remain buoyant – obviously difficult with nappy – and accept that life cannot be expected to fall into place like a Jennifer Aniston haircut, but must be worked at and tended. To this end, I'm repeating a mantra Mrs Beagle, my home-economics teacher, used to say after I'd produced a burnt soufflé: 'Things turn out best for the people who make the best out of the way things turn out.' The trouble, I suspect, is that even Mrs Beagle, Carol Smillie and the* Changing Rooms *team would be stumped to find anything good to say about the way my life has turned out. To pick a few random areas:*

Home Life
Since I no longer have a home Lou said I could stay in the spare room in her new flat until I got myself sorted. This is a very kind offer and greatly appreciated, given the alternative – i.e. no alternative. It's just that I didn't realise the spare room meant the airing cupboard. As a result, I'm sleeping naked with an ironing-board on a single bed.

287

It's the single-bed thing that's the worst, especially since I am single. Obviously I'm not expecting to turn the cupboard into a knocking-shop, but it would be nice to know I had the option. A single bed suggests I've already given up, like having a hysterectomy, or leaving body hair to sprout at will.

The only other drawback, excluding the fact that my wardrobe is a Gordon's Gin box and I can't have the lamp and radio plugged in at the same time, is that I'm next door to the bathroom. Initially, I thought this would be quite nice, imagining watery sounds permeating the walls in the relaxing manner of whale music. Unfortunately, however, it is less watery sounds than urinary odours – vile, pungent and not the least bit relaxing. Plus the walls seem to be made of loo paper so I hear pretty much everything that happens on the other side of them – can almost make myself believe weeing is a cascading waterfall but poo . . . Anyway, not very pleasant.

The rest of the flat is lovely – very tidy in the style of an Ikea showroom with Oriental stick things and wooden bowls full of conkers. Somewhat alarmingly, I keep finding myself looking round with genuine interest at linen baskets and kitchen-unit tiling with plans of how I would kit out my own flat (should the requisite quarter-million happen to plop into my bank account). Where does this come from, though? One minute I'm being young and carefree and seeing home merely as a place to dump belongings and sleep, then suddenly, without any warning, I find a discussion on the merits of roller blinds versus Venetian endlessly fascinating. It's like when you're little and will go to the ends of the earth to avoid bedtime, then something invisible happens as you grow up and the next thing you know the one moment of the day you're really looking forward to is bedtime. Not that there's much to look forward to with regards to my particular slimline version.

Anyway, I'm scarcely in the flat because I have a crap . . .

Work Life

Strictly speaking, it's not the work that's crap, more that I am crap at doing it. It's a researcher job in a production company that does a weekly women's-issues programme called Girls on Top *which, despite sounding like something on the front of* Loaded, *is actually very cerebral. Well, for daytime telly anyway. The only reason they've employed me is because Lou knows one of the producers and the interview was disguised as a 'chat': a beneficial strategy for everyone – i.e., make you think you're just having a friendly informal coffee, when really you're being screened in the manner of 007 shagging Pussy Galore for vital information on Fort Knox.*

I feel a fraud being there at all – like an illegal immigrant who's constantly in fear of someone tapping them on the shoulder and asking to see their papers. Which would be very terrifying in my case given that my CV is a greater work of fiction than War and Peace.

So far – that's a week – I've been shadowing another researcher, which has been fine. Her contact book seems to be the 192 database so that finding a woman who's written a thesis on 'PMT in the Middle Ages', is the equivalent of phoning up for the number to Pizza Express. The problem will come, I suspect, when I'm left to do it on my own and will have to resort to copying her work when she isn't looking in the way copiously dull and baffling physics lessons have fortunately equipped me to do.

It's the hours that are going to be the killer. If you leave before seven thirty you're seen as some kind of slack-arse dosser of the sort found scowling out of grainy crime-prevention posters. Hate this about London – as if you're not really a whole person unless you're overworked, underslept, stressed, starving and struggling with the imminent onslaught of a nervous breakdown. People seem to have forgotten that the point of a job is to earn a living, not ruin any chance of living beyond forty. Hmm, might suggest as a possible item 'Working Women: Womb to Tombstone', though given how little work I've done myself it might be a bit like John Prescott driving to a rally to promote the ecological and practical benefits of taking the bus.

Anyway, it's certainly promising to be more mentally stimulating than my last job, not that this would be hard, and it would probably do me good to focus on something meaningful and substan-

tial for a change, rather than my non-meaningful, non-substantial and crap . . .

Social Life

Ergh. I swear if you don't haemorrhage away your existence at work, you'll explode like an overheated pressure-cooker trying to establish a decent existence outside it. I realise I've been off the scene for a while but I had no idea organising a social life was the equivalent to being a theatre box-office manager: the strain of ensuring every night is booked up is unbearable. If you don't have a fully packed weekend and something planned for at least three out of the remaining four nights, you're deemed a social leper of the scabbiest order. So, you scurry around filling up your diary in the manner of a GP's appointment book, rejoice at the sight of lots of ink-filled pages, live in fear of a friend phoning you up and being free *on the night they suggest meeting, and generally behave not so much as a social butterfly but a flea-ridden kangaroo.*

But what for exactly? No one gives a shit. No one says, 'What did you do a week ago last Tuesday?' or 'Did you stay in and feel lonely on Thursday?' because they're all too busy making sure they *didn't stay in feeling lonely on Thursday. I find the whole thing utterly pointless, as if we're slogging away to pass some sort of exam that will never be marked because there are no examiners. Which is probably just as well in my case: from what I can remember from uni, resits are a pain.*

Anyway, I usually enjoy the social events I manage to ensnare, especially going to the cinema (though dubious as to whether this counts as social given that you sit in darkness not talking). I'd forgotten how much fun it is going to watch a film – like taking a mini-holiday from yourself, with the added bonus of being allowed to stuff overflowing pails of popcorn into your mouth, because, as everyone knows, consuming lots of E-numbers is a mandatory condition of cinema-going. Went to see Miss Congeniality *the other day. Love coming out after watching something like this because it makes you think life is just a happy, fun thing where it's perfectly* normal for an attractive man to approach you in the street and invite you round for a bagel. Rather than no man, no bagel and no bloody . . .

Sex Life
N/A: Not Applicable/Not Available/Not Again ever by look of things.

I sincerely hope life is more upbeat with you. How was the end of summer fiesta? Did large Bob get stoned and insist on everyone blowing his horn – his bamboo one, I mean – or was it a more subdued and tranquil meditate-with-tinkly-goat-bell-music occasion? Either way it's got to be better than a night in a smoky Slug and Lettuce, feeling like the slug.

Oh, God, really must try to grasp a more positive perspective. I think the reason everything seems particularly bleak at the moment is because I'm still confused about Alex. One minute I just want to forget all the crap, rush back and start all over again with him, and the next I'm thinking, Don't be so ridiculous, he's not in a fit state to start anything other than a fresh pack of tissues.

My friends' advice has been to steer clear of him for the time being and go out on the pull instead. While I appreciate their input, this is the biggest load of bollocks I've heard in a long while – like telling a bereaved person to get over the loss of their loved one by buying a teddy bear. Nevertheless, I obliged them and spent last Saturday night at a place called The Swan. I don't quite know what I was expecting – lakes full of graceful people in tutus, Tchaikovsky playing in the background perhaps? – but it was the nearest place to hell I've ever been in. Three floors of sweating, pulsating hormones drenched in alcohol and pelvic thrusting to Stereo MC. Lou says I've got to stop seeing everything through the eyes of my mother and accept that I don't go to such places to meet my future husband but simply to have a laugh. I know she's right, it's just that I can't help feeling I'd have much more of a laugh with a bottle of wine and a nice meal with friends. Oh, God. I am my mother.

I must say, though, I'd rather strut around a place that makes no attempt to disguise that it is just a seedy jungle full of hungry sexual predators than drag myself to a dull party in a bar and pretend to be enjoying tedious conversations on venture capitalism with drips called Lloyd. What's going on with parties these days? Since when did they change from being wild fun things in people's kitchens, where everyone gets sloshed on tequila and jumps into bed with a stranger, into sedate art-gallery-opening style affairs in posh wine bars where everyone has two glasses of claret then disappears home with their partner at half past ten? Feel as though I've horribly mistimed things – coming out to play just as everyone's been called in for tea, except for a couple of fat unkempt things with dirty T-shirts and dried snot on their upper lip.

Ergh. Mustn't get into negative all-fanciable-men-have-gone mode, even if the whole situation seems to be heading that way. As Jo points out, I've just entered the market and should be fresh and positive like a gay-looking boy band, not jaded and cynical. Oh, God, though, 'market' – hate the implication of being up for sale, as if we're all paintings at a private view where the ones with red dots are the couples who've already been bought and the ones without are the crap ones that everyone will look at politely, but no one will buy – except possibly some bearded forty-year-old.

I think what I object to most is the assumption that you're single because there's something intrinsically wrong with you. The idea that you might be single because there's something intrinsically wrong with most of the male population is deemed to be as absurd as suggesting Posh Spice is talented. The trouble is, I keep finding myself feeding this misconception, crowbarring in non sequiturs about my 'ex' and when I 'dumped' my 'ex', with such force and insistence as to suggest my 'ex' might turn out to be extraterrestrial.

Anyway, I've decided the trick is simply to carry on as usual, much as you would when lost on a motorway – if your desired destination happens to pop up on the way, all the better. The thing is, this is fine as long as you don't hit a crossroads and have to make a decision, as happened last Friday: either out with friends from work, not very exciting but good for career, or party with Jo, not very good for career but very exciting. *Or is it?* This is another drawback of being single – you have to be psychic to know in advance which option is going to offer the most potential. There's nothing worse than making the wrong choice and spending the whole evening imagining all the George Clooneys you might be meeting if you'd just made the right one.

In this particular instance, however, Lou gave us no *choice* – it was to be her screenwriting party. She's been going to screenwriting nightclasses, which I didn't know and was slightly jealous about, until she admitted that part of the reason was to meet someone. Urgh. I thought the whole point of romance was that it was to do with fate and chance encounters, not something you engineered and managed in the manner of a prudently invested unittrust portfolio. Next thing I know she'll have a box number in Time Out's *lonely-hearts column and be describing herself as funloving and attractive with a GSOH. Actually, she won't because, ironically, by* not *going to the screenwriting party she's now got a boyfriend, Mike. She met him by accident in a record shop and they both seem keen – although, according to her, they're still in the intensive-care stage where it could go either way.*

So Jo and I went on her ticket and had a somewhat bizarre time. I sincerely hope Lou gets something usefully script-related out of the classes because as a mating ground it would appear to be about as promising as the waiting room of a venereal-diseases clinic. Scriptwriters do not appear to be the most attractive species, taking the notion of suffering for their art as far as fashion boycotting and – rather unpleasantly – deodorant abstinence. They seem to live in a sort of underworld of smoky surrealism where reality is Hollywood and fantasy something they write about to get there. And some of it is very fantastical indeed. One man cornered me with a scene-by-scene account of his latest work, summing it up as Nightmare on Elm Street *meets* Pretty Woman. *I suspect from the way he was addressing my chest, this particular nightmare doesn't meet any women.*

I do have a great deal of admiration for them, though. Their *unflagging optimism in the face of not very optimistic odds, is an example to us all – although I fear that jacking in a job to concentrate on writing yet more scripts is taking this optimism into the realms of lunacy, like jacking it in to concentrate on choosing lottery numbers.*

Initially, I thought there might be good reason for such positivity as everyone I talked to seemed to be excitingly on the brink of hitting the big time. One bloke was sure his latest work was set to become the next Working Title blockbuster and called it his Orgasm – likening his previous experiences of submitting scripts to the frustration of having sex and almost, but not quite, having an orgasm. I had to stop him, however, when he looked a little too enthusiastic to expand on this analogy.

But he wasn't the only one. I listened eagerly to tales of how Justin was 'waiting to hear from Working Title' and Sandy was 'waiting to hear from Working Title'. It was when Chris, Steve, Alan and Ted also told me they were 'waiting to hear from Working Title' that I suspected Working Title might need to rephrase their rejection letter.

It certainly made me realise I didn't want to become a scriptwriter – not that I've ever thought about it. It's bad enough waiting to hear from someone you fancy and suffering from all sorts of delusions as to whether they like you back; the idea of doing this for a living makes me want to stop *living.*

Becoming an agent, on the other hand, appears to be an entirely different kettle of fish (surely this should be tank or bowl – kettle suggests lots of boiled goldfish with popped-out eyes). In contrast to being a scriptwriter – a sort of desperate Blind Date *style contestant where one's success is dependent on being original with words – agents get to swan around being picky and arbitrary while still being revered and adored in the manner of a celebrity.*

The one agent at the party – female and not what you would call conventionally attractive, or, come to think of it, unconventionally attractive – was being chatted up and lusted over by hordes of blokes as if she were Anna Kournakova with balls in her knickers

– their *balls, or so they appeared to hope. Apparently she's done a book on how to write for television and runs expensive courses on the subject, proving that those who can, teach; those who can't, join screenwriting classes. Very much envy her job. I mean, you'd certainly never be miserable if you were an agent, secure in the knowledge that at the tiniest onset of insecurity you could just pop down to the local writers' group and have an ego massage. Mind you, I guess it'd be difficult to know if someone was shagging you because they liked you or because they wanted you to invite them round to dinner with the Spielbergs.*

Anyway, Jo and I made do with our lesser-citizen status and joined a selection of self-conscious scriptwriters doing jigging-type dancing on an empty dance floor. It felt like a party in Neighbours *when they haven't forked out for enough extras so three of the core cast are pretending to be having a wild time in Madge's lounge popping party poppers and doing fake whoopy laughing. Luckily the raffle was called before I had to accept an invitation to dance with a man who was doing something extraordinary with his arms – like a bald baby sparrow learning to fly. Not attractive.*

Well, I say luckily, but it was actually extremely embarrassing. We'd blagged our way in on Lou's ticket, which had been fine because Lou hasn't been to the classes enough for many people to know who she is. What was not fine, however, was her name being called out as a prizewinner several times as everyone looked round in hushed anticipation like eager kids in assembly when the head-master is about to give someone a bollocking. Felt a complete tit going up and accepting the prize with the whole audience laughing – presumably because I'd forgotten my name. Wouldn't have minded if the prize had been worth it, but a Boots cleanser and moisturiser gift set is not enough to make up for such humiliation.

Indeed, the only real highlight of the evening was making excitingly frequent eye-contact with a very cute guy sitting by the bar. He was one of those people whose eyes smiled irrespective of what his mouth did. Unfortunately, he was also one of those people who never left the bar. Despite finding endless excuses to return for

extra ice, a bendier straw and another slice of lemon for my wine,
I was unable to find the courage to say hello, and ended up having
to make a rapid exit post-raffle in fear of anyone discovering my
true identity, like a Labour MP scarpering from Clapham Common.

And now it's Thursday night and I should be out laughing at
a dinner party or watching King Lear at the Globe with eight
friends. Instead, I'm hunched over Lou's laptop in a jumper with
hummus on it. Ergh. I suppose I could tidy my airing cupboard,
except that the floor is like earthquake rubble with bits of dead
limbs and jaggy metal. I keep making little stabs at clearing a
space on it, like a caterpillar munching a leaf, then get distracted
by something more interesting – e.g., putting a letter in the old-
letters box leads to three and a half hours reading old letters.

Yesterday it was my university alumnus magazine. Trauma-
tically bad idea. I've never read it before and can now see why.
I'd always assumed the point of it was tedious articles on the restora-
tion of a wall, interspersed with black-and-white photos of strange
looking fifties men in mortarboards. I'd no idea it was a slight
against single people. Whole pages are devoted to showy-offy smug-
ness: 'Penelope Gertrude married William Cuthbert after a romantic
nine-year courtship and is delighted to report they're (still!) insanely
happy living in Hull'; 'Joy Anastasia has spent a fascinating year
researching Tibetan communities in Kathmandu with her partner
and is now running her own successful salmon hatchery'; 'Having
spent seven wonderful years jointly heading up the most prestigious
investment bank in the world, Rebecca and Andrew have left their
successful careers to concentrate on making a further success of
their successful marriage by having lots of successful children and
rearing Zion, their successful pit bull terrier.' Found myself un-
accountably seeking solace in the obituaries.

Am I the only one not successful?
Lots of love,
Jess
xxx

Blind Date

'Yes!' Claire squealed down a crackly phone line. 'I said yes, yes, yes.'

Jess tried hard to drum up similar enthusiasm. 'That's great. When's the wedding?'

'Crikey. Dunno. To be honest, I'm still reeling from the proposal. I mean, it was like – arghhhhh!' Claire dissolved into giggles.

Why, Jess wondered, when something was so clearly a foregone conclusion did people feel the need to pretend it wasn't? It was like driving a car with the petrol warning light on then being surprised when it splutters to a standstill in the middle of the dual carriageway. Maybe it was a grown-up version of Santa Claus and the Tooth Fairy: you knew the truth, really, it was just more exciting not to confront it.

'Don't worry, darling. Won't dress you in –' the phone crackled in and out of reception '– carpet and . . . up the aisle . . . won't happen, apparently . . . I'm having twins.'

Jess froze. So that was why she was getting married. 'Twins?'

'Harry and Caroline.'

'You've already named them?'

There was a fuzzy pause, then Claire burst out laughing. 'No, you ninny. Not *my* twins. My godson and . . . get me sprogged up for years . . . got to . . . running out of cash but . . .'

'Well. Congratulations again,' Jess said, limply.

Claire's response became a series of bleeps as if she'd said the F-word before the watershed.

'Isn't it fantastic!' Lou exclaimed, nodding at the phone as she dashed past in her underwear. 'Never doubted that they'd marry, mind you.'

Jess smiled weakly and hoped Lou held similar convictions about her.

'Number two, mate, number two!'

Following what sounded like military potty training, she wandered into the front room where Lou's new boyfriend, Mike was slouched next to Jo's fiancé, Mark, yelling at Cilla Black and a bloke with a tragically short fringe. The shot then switched to three girls in various states of undress, number two seemingly naked.

'Number two?' she cried, incredulously. 'She looks like a mushroom – look at her neck.'

But Mike and Mark were looking at something a little lower down, which also seemed to have caught the attention of the cameraman. 'It's a C. Bet ya,' Mark said, smirking.

'Nah. It's gotta be a D minimum,' Mike confirmed.

Jess was undecided whether they were talking about her chest size or her A-level results. 'Number one's heaps prettier.'

'Nah. Moose,' Mike said, dismissively, slurping from a can of Foster's in a deeply unattractive manner. 'Looks like that bird from last night, though, eh?'

'What bird?' Lou had just entered with wet hair.

'Oh, *mate*,' Mark shouted, 'very bad choice.' Number one was shrieking in delight – rather prematurely, Jess thought, given what lay in store for her behind the screen.

'Mike? What bird?' Lou persisted, towel-drying her hair a little over-zealously.

'Oh, just some girl in the pub. Beer?'

Lou shook her head, pretending to be fine with this response. Being single may suck, Jess decided, but being in a relationship and feeling paranoid sucked you dry.

'You OK?' she said, following Lou through to the kitchen where the table was mysteriously laid for eight. 'I thought there were only seven of us.'

'D'you think he snogged her?'

'Nah, course he didn't,' Jess said, swatting the air. 'Now, who's this mystery guest?'

Lou bent down and started clattering around in a cupboard. Something about the frenetic cacophony she was creating suggested the mystery guest might turn out to be a bottle of vodka. 'If you ever get into a relationship,' she struck up from inside, as Jess tried not to dwell on 'if', 'don't believe anyone who tells you the beginning's the best bit. It's not. You spend all the time you're with them wondering what they're thinking, and all the time you're not, wondering what they're doing.' She popped her head out and banged it intentionally and repeatedly against the cupboard door. 'And, yes, I have fallen in love with Mike.'

'Ah . . . I, um . . . at least, I . . . the beers are in here I take it.' Mike.

Lou swung round, bright red.

'Um. Girlie bonding session,' Jess said, jumping to the rescue, as Lou picked herself up from her confessional head-banging position.

'It looks painful.' He smiled, nervously. 'Blokey bonding session,' he said, gesturing to the beers. 'Torturous.'

Torturous wasn't the word for it, Jess thought, as they all stood awkwardly waiting for someone to break the ice, wind or anything to alleviate the tension. Luckily, they were saved by the bell.

'Mike, this is Jo,' Lou said, as a figure dressed in what appeared to be a slinky wetsuit leaped Catwoman-style into the room. 'She's a recruitment consultant, very quiet and shy.'

'All right, babes,' Jo said, engulfing him in a flurry of kisses that were neither quiet nor shy, while adeptly checking him out for a later post-mortem. 'I'll look at your CV and get back to you,' she said, which he naïvely took to be a joke. 'And who are you?' she added, sarcastically, turning to Mark.

'I'm not sure,' Mark said, grabbing her round the waist.

'But you definitely look familiar.' They started smooching uninhibitedly as Mike tentatively reached for Lou's hand.

Trying not to feel like a spare tyre, Jess set about helping everyone to gin and tonic – herself more to gin than tonic. When she returned, Jo was giving Mike the third degree, cunningly disguised as first aid.

'So, how often do you play rugby, then?' she said, prodding his foot as he attempted to turn a wince into a winsome smile.

'Not for much longer with you as nurse,' he replied.

Lou beamed down on them proudly as if he were her son at a school prize-giving. She'd been single and selective for so long that if a bloke made it as far as base camp, i.e., got introduced to her friends, it was tantamount to declaring marriage. Men might speak in a macho way of career targets and sporting ambitions, but little did they know that their greatest challenge was the scrutiny of their girlfriend's mates. She watched Mike chat animatedly to Jo, blissfully unaware of the multiple-choice exam he was sitting.

'D'you think he heard?' Lou whispered, keeping a watchful invigilator's eye on the proceedings. 'The L-word, I mean.'

'So what if he did?' Jess whispered back, then acknowledged exactly what, as images of Mike scrambling for the door reared up in her mind.

'He'll think I'm a psycho,' Lou confirmed.

Jess patted her arm in sympathy. She was right. The beginning of a relationship wasn't fun at all, it was a game of precision timing without a clock: the right time to phone, the right time to start having sex, the right time to say the L-word. Like deer-hunting, a mistimed shot scared them off for good.

'Mike, this is Sophie and her husband, Richard,' Lou announced, breezily, guiding the newly arrived couple into the room as if she were a waitress in a posh restaurant and they were the dessert trolley. 'Sophie used to live with Jess and Jo,' and comes with cold custard, Jess thought of adding as Lou gestured to Richard, 'and Richard's an accountant.'

Mike looked as if he wanted to skip to coffee. 'Nice to meet you.'

By the time they'd all obediently shuffled to the table it became obvious that the mystery guest was a mystery ghost.

'Hi. My name's Jo. Like your tie.' Jo was handshaking the empty seat.

'Pete's running late,' Lou said, filling the ghost's glass. 'Red or white?'

Jo looked intrigued. 'Who's Pete? Jess, have you got a new bloke? You crafty slapper!'

There was a hushed silence.

'Maybe.'

Jess stared at Lou, baffled. 'Maybe?'

Lou grinned.

'Lou. What's going on?' she said, threateningly, sniffing the traces of a set-up. It was usually about now that Jeremy Beadle appeared disguised as a lollipop lady.

'He's a really nice guy,' Lou began, in a way that Jess could already hear herself repeating with the addition of a 'but'. 'A friend of Mike's.'

Jess rolled her eyes. Why was it that couples, not content with wafting their smugness under your nose, felt the need to matchmake each other's single friends like a chef using up leftovers in a pie? Was it because they wanted to spawn clones of themselves in a heady, self-aggrandising scientific experiment, or did they simply see it as a charitable gesture on a par with adopting a mange-ridden donkey from a donkey sanctuary?

'Just give him a chance,' Lou pleaded.

Jess nodded nonchalantly. This was the kind of thing her gym teacher said when no one picked fat Kelly.

'Top nosh, Lou,' Mark said, as they all tucked into something that had clearly taken fifteen times longer to prepare than it would to eat. 'Can you teach Jo how to do it?'

'And Sophie,' Richard joined in – pointlessly, given that teaching Sophie how to cook was the equivalent of teaching Mozart how to play the piano.

Jo and Sophie didn't feel the need to fight their corner of feminism. They were too busy speaking some kind of foreign language that at first glance appeared to be Hungarian. '. . . organza at Dickinzinjones . . .' Then seemed to switch into Russian: '. . . damask satin, shantung . . . Swarovski crystals . . .' Enjoyed a passing flirtation with French: '. . . Liberty's silk dupion, tulle or chiffon, vis-à-vis diamanté brocade?' Touched briefly on Hindi: '. . . veil . . . veil . . .' And finally crashed to an intelligible standstill in the international language of money: 'Two grand and that's only the dress.'

It was a truth universally acknowledged that a woman in possession of a wedding date must also be possessed. Something seemed to happen to them, Jess decided, between the moment of proposal and the declaration of 'I will' that turned them from human being to harassed Topshop sales assistant. For a day that was supposed to be the happiest of your life it seemed to cause several hundred previous ones of misery. Like the cooking–eating ratio, it didn't make sense.

'Ooh, that'll be Pete,' Lou said, as the bell prompted Jo to confer on wedding hymns.

'Did you have "Be Thou My Vision"?' she chorused, already looking as though the wine had blurred her own.

' "O Lor-hor-hord of my heart," ' Sophie serenaded back.

'Get. Me. Out of here,' Jess only part-joked.

'Why don't you let Pete in?' Lou suggested. 'While I warm up his starter,' she added, as if they were a call-girl duo.

Jess picked up her glass and slobbed her way to the door feeling like Annie when Daddy Warbucks wants her to be nice to potential parents. The trouble was, she couldn't help a tiny part of her wondering if this might be . . .

'Hi. You must be Jess.' A hairy hand extended towards her

chest. She was curious to know what Lou had told him that had encouraged him to jump to such a sure conclusion. 'A keen wine drinker, I believe. Pete.'

Jess pretended to hide her glass behind her back as they shook hands and gave each other the once-over. He was small and stocky and clearly of the belief that the best way to combat receding hair was not to have any at all. Much in the way that the quality of a film could be predicted from the trailers it follows, Jess wasn't optimistic.

'Got bored of the other party, then?' Mike joked, visibly cheered by Pete's arrival.

'Yeah. Not enough totty,' Pete replied, scoring his first foul of the evening.

As the two blokes became entranced in animated banter, Jo and Sophie talked more Hungarian, and it came as no surprise to Jess that John Gray had made himself a millionaire out of *Men Are From Mars, Women Are From Venus*.

'So? What d'you think?' Lou whispered excitedly, as Jess went to fetch the solution to the evening from inside a glass bottle.

'That I'd rather eat my own head.'

Lou looked as though she'd insulted her mother. 'I think he's lovely,' she said, from the safety raft of a relationship. 'What's the problem?'

'Everything,' Jess replied, sulkily, feeling as if she was sixteen and being coerced into a pair of brown brogues.

'He's fun. Nice eyes. Sparky. Full of life.'

He sounded like the Australian Chardonnay. 'Your taste isn't my taste,' Jess snapped. And then a horrible realisation came over her. Maybe Lou had picked him not because she thought he was Jess's taste but because she thought he *should* be Jess's taste. They had long acknowledged the theory that people went for their looks equal. What, then, did a bald dwarf say about her?

'. . . very dull and unattractive,' Pete snuffled at his food, pig-like, as Sophie nodded in agreement and Jess and Lou returned to their seats, 'but beggars can't be choosers.'

If *she* was a beggar, Jess thought, gulping furiously at her wine, *he* beggared belief.

'So. What do *you* do, Jess?'

'Oh, you know, scavenge for food in dustbins, play the penny whistle on the Underground, eat old socks. The usual beggarly pursuits.'

Pete looked baffled. He was clearly one of those people for whom the question wasn't merely a formality but a necessity: something that must first be established in order to form an opinion of someone. Like the use of fingerprints in criminal investigations, a one-word answer 'lawyer' immediately provided a character profile replete with information ranging from 'bars likely to frequent' to 'loo paper likely to purchase'. It defined a person better, Jess decided, than had they been stuffing candles up their nose or munching the tablecloth.

'I work in television,' she said, watching him mentally label a computer file 'Creative' and drop her into it. 'And you?'

'Oh, I'm very boring,' he said, needlessly she suspected. 'IT consultant. Computers. Conversation stopper.'

The conversation stopped.

'Who's for more wine?' Lou announced, when things had dried up at her end too.

'Not for Soph and me,' Richard said, putting a protective hand over their glasses as if she were trying to force them to eat liver. 'We're going to have to shoot off in a bit.'

Lou checked her watch in disbelief. 'But it's only ten thirty.'

'We're driving down to Dorset tomorrow,' Sophie explained, 'to babysit my sister's baby, and . . .' she looked coyly at Richard '. . . and . . .' To receive our welcome pack for middle-age? Renew the bridge-club membership? Look into retirement homes? Jess's mind raced through myriad exciting possibilities.

'And our therapist's suggested hot baths and a few early

nights to see if we can produce one of our own,' Richard concluded, turning the whole idea of making love into a chemistry experiment.

With the departure of the party-animals-cum-laboratory-rats, the dinner dissolved into something Bacchus would have approved. Jo and Mark seemed to be in the process of prematurely consummating their marriage, Lou and Mike were discovering they didn't have compatible music tastes but liked the taste of each other's ear, and Jess and Pete were proving that a guide dog was an indispensable attendant on a blind date.

'I didn't . . . I wasn't meaning to offend you,' he slurred, slopping wine liberally over his trousers.

'No 'fence taken,' Jess said, suggesting the opposite by heaving herself unsteadily out of the sofa and making for the bathroom.

'Is looking really good,' Lou said, bursting in to join her, sporting the kind of melted makeup effect that made it hard to believe she could be talking about her appearance.

'Whatiz?' Jess said, slumped on the loo.

'YouanPete.'

Jess looked at her incredulously. 'Good?'

'Yes. Like a film.'

'A horror one,' Jess replied, burping.

'Name a film that doesn't start with the girl thinking the bloke's a wanker from Tossoffland. Really hates him then slowly realises he's ashilly wonderful and by the end they're in love.'

Jess flushed the loo. 'Name a film where that bloke looks like Pete.'

'Anyway,' Lou breezed, after a pause that said she couldn't, 'he really likes you.'

Jess felt herself warming to this news. However little she thought of him, it was difficult not to have a soft spot for someone who had, well, a hard one for her. 'No, he doesn't,' she fished, grinning.

'Yeah, he does. Watch,' and with that she vanished fairy-godmother style leaving Jess to check her reflection in the mirror and conclude that she was by no means the fairest of them all.

'All right, mate?' Pete was slouched exactly where she'd left him but everyone else had vanished. It wasn't very subtle, but she was flattered that he was so intent on getting her alone.

'Where they all gone?' she said, collapsing next to him and trying to find something stationary in the room to focus on.

He shrugged, then turned and looked at her. He had two heads. 'Bed?'

Blimey, she thought, he didn't beat about the bush – he was heading straight on in there. ''Fraid I've only got a single.'

'No,' he said emphatically, thumping the armrest out of – presumably – frustration. She smiled at the thought of being so desired. 'The others've gone to bed.' She stopped smiling. 'And I'm going . . .' he leaned forward, put down his glass, took both her hands in his hairy ones and looked alarmingly as though his next words might be 'to be sick' '. . . to go there too.'

Then, suddenly, it was happening. The twin-headed bald dwarf was moving in, looming closer in the manner of an ominously encroaching underwater shadow from *Jaws*. She closed her eyes to ease the seasickness and waited with gold-fish lips, too drunk to fend off the beast.

'You're a really nice girl, but . . .'

She opened her eyes. He'd all but pecked her.

'I should be going.' Then he staggered to his feet and left.

'Maybe he didn't want to rush things,' Lou suggested, the following morning over a breakfast that, at ten past one in the afternoon, had certainly not been rushed. 'Or was about to vomit.'

'Thanks, Lou,' Jess muttered, feeling not so far off doing the same. 'I don't care, really. I didn't even like him, it's just the humiliation. I mean, blokes are supposed to want it twenty-four seven, come volcano or . . . England–Germany game.'

Lou raised her eyebrows.

'OK, well, straight after an England–Germany game. I offered it to him on a plate,' she whined, chasing a rubber mushroom around her own, 'and he walked away.'

Lou nodded as if she were a doctor listening to the symptoms of gonorrhoea. 'I think he's gay,' she diagnosed, piercing her fried egg so that the yolk ejaculated over the sausage. 'Mike? What do you think?'

Mike didn't look like he did think. He was too busy doing the male equivalent: eating. 'Uh?'

'About Pete being gay.'

'Dunno. Never snogged him myself.'

'But surely you—' She was called away by the doorbell. 'You must get vibes, though,' she shouted from the hall.

Jess watched, frustrated, as Mike chomped. Getting blokes to analyse other blokes was like trying to break into a password-protected computer file. You knew that the information was in there but getting hold of it required lots of ingenious guesswork.

'Has he ever displayed gay signs?' Jess took over, keen to cling to the idea that she'd been rejected because of her sex, not because she'd appeared too up for some.

'You mean, in his car window? With one of those nodding dogs – "Bark if you're gay – woof, poof."' He chuckled.

'No, Mike. I mean, as a person, like . . . say . . . wearing cardigans, or being oversensitive . . . or—' She stopped.

Mike was wearing a cardigan. 'What are you saying?' And was being oversensitive.

'Just that if he's gay he might like to—'

Lou reappeared in the doorway, barely visible behind a bouquet of lilies.

'Pick you pretty flowers?' Mike completed.

Jess felt her expression melt into something from a Ferrero

Rocher advert. Gay or not, sending flowers was like check-mate: a very good move. 'They're gorgeous,' she gushed, getting up gracefully to accept her gift.

'I never get flowers,' Lou said, bringing them to the table.

'Nor do I,' Jess squealed. 'Until now!'

Lou stared at her oddly. 'They're for me.'

A cavernous silence descended the room.

'That's great,' Jess managed through clenched teeth.

'No, it's not.' Her mind spoke *Exorcist*-style through Mike's mouth. 'Who the hell are they from?'

Lou looked up in confusion. 'You, I thought.'

Mike shook his head. 'Wrong.'

Delving into the foliage, Lou removed the little envelope and opened it as if she should be standing in a low-cut designer dress at the Oscars announcing, 'And the winner is' while all the nominees pretend not to care. 'From a secret Hollywood agent.' She smiled as Mike sulked, and Jess searched the congealing bacon fat on her plate. Lou got boyfriends and bouquets; *she* got blown out by a bald dwarf. Something had to change before she gave up and went to live in the Gobi desert.

Con Artist

To: *Claire.Voyant@hotmail.com*
Date: *Wednesday 15 November*
Subject: *Con Artist*

Living in the Gobi desert. Feeling like a camel
with dried-up humps plodding towards an oasis
that will inevitably turn out to be a mirage.
Contemplating burying my head in the sand
and leaving it there.

Dear Claire,

Is it me, or is life one big disappointment pitted with just enough tantalising pinpricks of hope to fend off suicide? I don't know whether it's perfectly reasonable to expect more in the manner of Oliver Twist and a bowl of gruel, or whether it's all the telly's fault for making instant success and money appear as easy to get as a Big Mac and fries, even for normal people like hairdressers. Especially for normal people. Either way, I can't help feeling as though I'm constantly waiting for my life to happen – like a plane lining up on the runway: everyone else is taking off and I'm stuck somewhere in a queue I can't see. Occasionally, there are noises that sound temptingly like action but turn out to be false alarms, or I get a sense that I'm moving forward and get really excited, then discover it's just a reversing luggage truck giving me the impression I'm moving forward. I'm beginning to suspect I've got a faulty engine.

Lou says it's wrong to think your life is directed by some divine being or air-traffic-control tower because, ultimately, 'you make your own luck'. I find this a deeply unappealing thought – like having to sit down and cook a crème brûlée from scratch rather than waltzing into M&S and getting a ready-made one with a spoon. Still, I can see her point. Expecting things to plop on to your lap is the equivalent of hoping to win the lottery without buying a ticket, so I've decided to tackle my life face on, starting with learning how to draw it.

Or, at least, this is what I understood was meant when I enrolled myself for life-drawing classes. Lou, who sees night classes as the pulling ground everyone else commonly associates with nightclubs, had left the course booklet lying around on the kitchen table with the subtlety of my mother and the ironing. Bored one evening, I started flicking through it, oscillating between images of myself becoming a Russian-speaking, ping-pong playing, computer-literate potter and feeling exhausted by the mere effort of filling in a registration form. But then I caught sight of something that sold itself on 'learning about perspective' and thought that might be the one to attend first.

Wrong. Contrary to visions of slouching around sketching the meaning of life and sharing a joint with someone sexy called Johann, I walked late and panting into a room with a naked man perched half-way up a ladder staring fixedly into the distance, presumably concentrating on not having an erection. He was surrounded by lots of people in painting smocks with palettes under their arms, straddling easels and doing flouncy, sweeping brushstrokes as if conducting an orchestra. I had an HB pencil and a pad from the newsagent.

Hoping quickly to retreat and join the local playgroup for a round of join-the-dots, I got collared by the 'teacher' – a bloke in pantaloons called Jed – and told to assemble an easel quietly. The problem was, I'd never used an easel before, so of course the thing immediately collapsed and knocked a jam jar of green water over someone else's painting, thus ensuring that the only drawing I was doing was attention to myself. I ended up crouched on a windowsill trying to sketch a foot.

I simply can't fathom what possesses someone to be an artist's model. Jed stopped the class for a good ten minutes to demonstrate how to draw the bloke's fat rolls. How horrific. The idea of standing naked in front of myself is something I try to avoid. The idea of standing motionless for two hours is close to torture. The idea of standing naked and motionless while my fat rolls are scrutinised by twenty art students, all of whom have already had a good gawp at my genitals, makes sitting in an electric chair seem a really fun pastime.

No sooner had I got to grips with his big toe than Jed told us to stop working and turn our easels for the class to see what we'd achieved. Absolute mortification. The place was transformed into the Louvre and I discovered I'd been painting with Picasso's grand children. Everyone smiled sympathetically. They thought my dismembered toe was a penis.

It's no good. Doing an activity just so you can meet people is like having a baby because you want to buy cute little Baby Gap trainers. I've decided the trick instead is to do something you enjoy and if you happen to bump into some cool people in the process, why, that's a nice little extra. But what do I enjoy? Hmm . . . watching telly's quite good, although not exactly the most people-meety activity. I suppose I like eating, but am I brave enough to sit at an empty table in a restaurant pretending to read a book?

Oh, sod it. What I really enjoy is cuddling up with a boyfriend and having lots of sex. Which, I suspect, is the nub of it. No matter how much I convince myself that being single is liberating and fun, the stark, bitter reality is that there's always a sense that something is missing – like forgetting to put on knickers or drinking tonic without any gin. You snuffle around trying to find ways to fill this void in a vain attempt to make your life feel fuller, all the time denying it – like Liz Hurley and collagen lip implants.

In fact, I suspect no man will ever pop up and fill the hole – so to speak – and wonder whether the trick doesn't lie in proactively pursuing them. For example, I wouldn't mind initiating contact with cute smiley-eye bloke from that screenwriting party, assuming he isn't gay and/or girlfriended. Except that I don't know his name, never spoke to him, and have no way of tracking him down. So he's probably not a very good example.

Anyway, I'm not going to obsess over guys but instead become preoccupied with sorting out my body, working on the logic that there's little point in throwing myself into a new social arena while I look like a wildebeest. I'm clinging to the notion promoted by all beauty magazines that only by transforming one's figure into Geri Halliwell's will one get a man – while overlooking the minor inconsistency in this theory that Geri Halliwell is single. So far I've done three jogs round the park, gone swimming once and contemplated joining a gym (which counts as an exercise in itself given the mental energy required to sustain it for longer than three and a half seconds).

I do find it somewhat nonsensical, though, that when I had a boyfriend and someone to appreciate my body (or, at least, to see it), I did fuck all about keeping it in shape, and now, as I mutate into a lithe swimwear model, I remain an undiscovered ruby. Still, as Geri says, you must do it for your inner sanctum – and, perhaps, as an enormous boost to your singing career.

In conjunction with this new-me regime, I'm also eating healthily. Or trying to. The problem is that every time I go to the supermarket, eagerly snatching at organic broccoli and pints of goat's milk, I end up getting home and discovering I've bought nothing I fancy eating, then dashing out to raid the chocolate counter of the local newsagent's.

Ergh. I wish life didn't seem like such a battle. I feel as though I'm constantly fighting it with a blunt sword and a shield made of soggy bog paper while everyone else glides effortlessly to victory with the aid of B52 bombers and cruise missiles. Lou, for example, who already has a boyfriend and therefore shouldn't even be on the battlefield, is being pursued by some bloke from her screen-writing class. This is simply not fair – the equivalent of dropping off a sack of grain at Posh 'n' Becks' rather than a Sudanese village – although it does suggest that love works on a Sainsbury's buy-one-get-one-free offer, which is a cheering thought. He's already sent her a bouquet of lilies – my favourite (Cupid has clearly joined forces with the goddess of tactlessness), and a really cute note inviting her out for a drink – with a friend if she wants, in case she thinks he's a weirdo.

She thinks he's a weirdo. He calls himself a 'secret Hollywood agent', which she's decoding into flobbery gross man who made a pass at her in a dialogue class. She's refusing even to reply, terrified of jeopardising things with Mike.

The thing is, I think he sounds really nice. His note was witty and complimentary in a laid-back charismatic way and he's got gorgeous handwriting. I keep trying to persuade her to check him out, if only to make sure he's not some dynamic love-god. And, anyway, she doesn't need to worry when he isn't because he's going off travelling soon, thus giving her the perfect get-out clause. Although – oh, God – maybe the reason I think he sounds nice is not because he is nice but because, without knowing it, I've lowered my standards, in much the same way that, desperate to find an outfit for a wedding, you end up returning to the vile purple number you did bulgy-cheeked vomit signs at seven hours previously.

However warped my perspectives might be, I think I was wrong to be so critical of Alex when I was going out with him. All the time I'd been working on the oxymoron that there was such a thing as the 'perfect' man – which, of course, I now realise is the equivalent of a scientist basing his life's work on the assumption that the moon is made of cheese. Alex, therefore, was constantly being compared and found wanting, as one does with various parts of one's anatomy and pictures of Kate Moss. But just as you discover from an ITV docusoap that half her bum had been airbrushed out, so too do you discover from endless crap parties that the perfect man doesn't exist. I have a strong and unpleasant suspicion that I have given up Alex for a ghost – which, quite frankly, is enough to send me searching for a noose and give up the ghost too.

Jo says I've got to be patient, that the right person will come along when I'm least expecting it and not looking. I find this an unbelievably shite theory – like telling someone who's lost their house keys that the only way they'll find them is not to search for them. It's all very well for her, nicely ensconced in pre-marital bliss, to put a happy, shiny, romantic sheen on what is really a bog-awful game of hide and seek with an egg-timer, but as any single female will tell you, there's never a bloody moment when you're not expecting it.

I'm sure there must be a medical explanation for what happens to people when they get engaged that makes them forget they were ever 'I' rather than 'we', like a celebrity who lunches in the Ivy as if they'd never spent their pre-famous years as a toilet cleaner for Burger King. They certainly seem to undergo surgical removal of the sensitivity cells, finding nothing wrong with subjecting their single friends to Saturdays of nine a.m. wedding-dress fittings, standing in front of mirrors looking beautiful and happy, expecting whoops of appreciation from those with toxic hangovers for whom the prospect of ever doing the same is one of extreme uncertainty.

I think I could cope if the whole wedding thing was happening underground – like an illegal gambling den – and we only had to turn up on the day. It's the expectation that everyone will want to share and delight in every little hand-tied bouquet dilemma that makes me want to fry my head. It presumably comes from the same Blissful Oblivion Family as the one that causes the parents of new-born baby Lily to believe the rest of the world is equally captivated by her beauty, charm and vomited milk.

At the moment, I'm trapped in hen-party-organisation hell. I hate the whole notion of hen nights – lots of pissed females wearing fake veils and carrying giant blow-up penises, screeching at high volume in tacky clubs at orange strippers in thongs. But what option is there? Tradition decrees that the bride marks her exit from the single life and Jo, who's been in a relationship for four years, sees no paradox in complying. She also sees nothing wrong in the presumption that what her single friends really want to do at a weekend is not go out and potentially meet a husband of their own but celebrate her success at having done so.

However, if you would like a hen party I, of course, would be *more than happy to organise it – after all, I will have become a pro by then . . . a professional, not a prostitute – fingers crossed. Have you decided where you're having it yet? What about an organic wedding on a Spanish hilltop where everything is recycled at the end? Mmm, very much like the idea of recycling the men. Particularly Alfonso, the goat-herder.*

Without being rude or tactless I'm trying to block out wedding thoughts and concentrate instead on being a lonely, successful career woman. The lonely bit is going supremely well and I'm sure the successful part will come too – probably when I'm least expecting it! I've got to the stage with my job where I can no longer claim to be learning the ropes – the stage where they take the stabilisers off your bike and you wobble your way to a sobbing, elbow-grazed, blood-spattered destination, usually in the gutter.

It's the pre-production meetings that are the worst. Like university tutorials where, if you haven't done the reading – which happens to be all the newspapers cover to cover by ten a.m. – you spend the whole time staring at the dried froth on your cappuccino lid, concentrating on appearing invisible and praying that no one asks you a question. Unlike university, however, it's seen as cool if the producer likes your idea, thus spawning a meeting room full of eager Jeremy Paxman protégés vying for attention and approval in the manner of eight-year-old stage-school auditionees. On the one occasion I did have an idea it took me so long to rehearse it in my head that by the time I'd plucked up courage to suggest it without using a strangled sheep-voice they'd moved on.

I could just about survive if we were then given the rest of the day off to have coffee and read Heat, *as would be the natural course of events at uni. Instead, we're expected to scurry back to our desks and spend the next seven hours with a phone stuck to our ear. Hate the phone. Well, I mean, obviously I don't hate the phone when the person on the other end of it is a friend or an attractive bloke. When they're a scary government minister you've never heard of and you're supposed to be asking them their views on a subject you don't understand, it's a tool of torture on a par* with a branding-iron. I keep finding myself in vile Catch 22 situations, putting off calling such people, hoping when I eventually do I'll get a secretary or answer-machine, while at the same time acknowledging that a secretary or answer-machine isn't going to be any bloody use at all. The whole thing reminds me of feeling ill and knowing the only way you're going to feel better is by chucking up your intestines into the toilet bowl.

I think they're beginning to suss me out in the manner of finally locating the source of a bad smell. They've taken to giving me what they call 'soft slots', which are basically the equivalent of the 'and finally' items on ITN news. I'm torn between feeling miffed and undervalued by this demotion, and enormously relieved not to have to be Brain of Britain when brain is the size of a raisin.

So far there's only been one major cock-up – or, more accurately, not a cock-up. Some Oriental sex therapist for domestic animals had written an article on how lack of human shagging in the home affects the sex drive of pets, and the producer wanted me to find some guests to support this. Not the easiest of conversation-openers, I must say, but it really is quite incredible what people will do to get on telly.

By four o'clock I had a woman called Helen with two non-shagging dogs willing to tell the nation she hadn't had sex for five and a half years (?! – terror prospect of neon-lit proportions). Plus, if we could guarantee a plug for her book, The Interrelationship of the Sexual Dynamic between Humans and Animals: Morecombe's Theory Investigated – nice grabby title – the Oriental woman would do a therapy stint on the show. Spent the rest of the day swanning round the office, rejoicing at my new position as talented guest-booker for juicy X-rated Pet Rescue.

Unfortunately, the non-shagging dogs turned out to be non-socially adjusted, and within five minutes of being in the studio had bitten one of the sound engineers. Helen seemed to have mistaken the occasion as her last chance to pull and arrived in something Jordan might wear to the beach. And Onki, the Oriental therapist, insisted on doing everything sitting cross-legged on a small stool.

These proved merely to be the raw ingredients for what was clearly not just a recipe for disaster, but nationwide catastrophe. The minute we were on air, the dogs started doing savage barking while Helen, with the dexterity of a politician from the Today programme, twisted all the presenter's questions into a platform from which to air her anxieties about impending childlessness, clearly hoping to invoke the sympathy of a kind and potent man in the manner of an earthquake relief fund appeal.

Onki, sensing a straying from the subject, came crashing in with all sorts of bollocks about symbiosis and animals picking up on desperation and how getting them to mate was the key to sexual harmony in the house – which was fine as our viewers like bollocks – then suggested various methods of achieving her aim. Solutions ranged from experimenting with warm soya milk to doing strange things with pot plants, before climaxing with the horrifyingly inappropriate recommendation that will no doubt prove the death-knell of my television career, and possibly my life: 'manually arousing' one's dog. I could actually feel the fury vibes zapping down at me from the viewing gallery like Darth Vadar's light sabre. Talented guest-booker? My 'guest' was sitting on live daytime television wanking off a toy bone.

I'm beginning to suspect I've made the wrong career choice, which is as nightmarish a prospect as burning the dinner-party food half an hour before the guests are due: starting all over again seems too much effort and a hopeless gamble, yet continuing as if everything's fine is lazy and unappealing. In fact, the reality is that I can't be arsed working at all. When I first came out of uni, I saw a career as this breathtakingly beautiful mountain, which I would relish climbing. Four years on, I'm still at the toilets in the visitor's-centre car park with a stone in my shoe.

Jo says it's not that I'm work-shy or bone idle, it's the alarm going off on my biological clock. It's telling me to stop getting up and going to work because it's time to lie in bed and make babies.

By ignoring this and trying to pursue a career, I'm just repeatedly hitting the snooze button, which, as everyone in denial knows, is merely a torturous means of prolonging the inevitable.

Obviously I like this theory, and hope that my particular clock is set to Californian time, thus giving me an extra eight hours to find a fellow baby-maker. Oh, God. I detest the way that everything comes back to not having a boyfriend. If I'd known it was so bleak and barren out here in single life, I'd never have left the centrally heated cocoon of coupledom. Mind you, I still foresee a happy ending for me and Alex. I've watched too many Meg Ryan films not to suspect, after much misunderstanding and lots of tears, that we'll get together in the final scene, possibly under twinkly stars watched by a cute kid. In the meantime, I'm going to concentrate on not expecting the unexpected.

Lots of love,

Jess

xxx

Great Expectations

'Guess who!' a thrillingly unexpected male voice boomed down the line.

Jess felt her heart attempt a Russian-gymnast number with her ribcage. Could this be the one she hadn't been looking for? The one that happened when she least expected it? She swallowed, nervously. It was possibly safer to start with a smaller question. 'Is it Finn?'

'It's quite fat now I'm ashamed to admit,' he chortled heartily, 'but still ticking over. How the hell are you?'

'Oh, you know . . . good,' she offered, mind whizzing backwards and forwards in search of a reason for his call. Finn was a friend of Jo's whom she hadn't seen for over a year. They'd always got on well . . . very well, now she thought about it – and although nothing concrete had ever happened between them, the chemistry was there. He was quite attractive . . . very attractive, now she thought about it. And they had similar interests . . . very similar interests, now she thought about it. She beamed happily down the phone: suddenly it all made sense, now she thought about it.

'Still heading up BBC Factual without breaking a fingernail, then?'

'Naturally,' she purred, grinning. 'Still single-handedly underpinning the entire financial world without breaking sweat?'

'Not a drop!'

And then they were off, enthusiastically filling in the past year's blanks as if completing a Dateline questionnaire.

'So,' he said, coming up for air, 'I assume you're going to Jo's wedding.'

'As her chief flower-girl it's a humiliation I can't refuse.'

He laughed. 'In that case, since I've left it too late to book a room, might I be able to bunk down with the flower-girl?'

Jess let out a strange noise. They'd be planning their own wedding in a minute.

'If I promise not to deflower her,' he added, a promise she sincerely hoped he would break.

The remainder of the conversation seemed to pass through the warm soft-focus lens of a Westlife video as Jess planned their life together. A Scottish-themed wedding would be nice – would Finn look good in a kilt, though? – and it'd have to be in spring before the midges came out. They could go travelling for a couple of years, perhaps sail round the world, then come back and . . . would they bring up their two children (three? What if Finn wanted, like, six?) in Britain or would Finn's job take them somewhere more exotic? Did they need bankers in the Caribbean? And if they quarantined the dog . . .

'Well? What d'you think?'

Jess jolted back to the more immediate future. Something about the fact that he was a bloke told her that perhaps he wasn't ready to hear exactly what she thought. 'About what?'

'Me in a morning suit. For the wedding.'

Was he suggesting . . . 'The wedding?' she choked. But she hadn't said yes yet.

'Go on. Say yes. I'm dying to.'

Jess grinned smugly. He was clearly checking out his chances for the real proposal. 'Since you ask so nicely, yes, I will.'

There was a hesitant pause. 'Will what?'

'Marry you!'

He laughed. A warm, loving, husband-to-be laugh. She could already hear them reminiscing about this moment, lying in bed giggling over what might have happened had they really got engaged over the phone, rather than on a gondola in Venice sipping champagne at sunset. 'I'm afraid that's out of the question,' he said, cheekily.

'And why's that?' She grinned, excitedly. 'Because I'm just too damn beautiful?'

'Because I'm already married.'

Jess recoiled from the handset as if she'd just got too close to someone with halitosis. 'Married?'

He laughed again. 'No need to make it sound quite such torture. Yes. Last year. To the lovely Emma.'

Jo was right: it did happen when you least expected it – to someone else.

'But, unfortunately, she can't make it to the wedding,' he bludgeoned on, 'and doesn't want me wearing my morning suit because she thinks . . .' short pause, followed by giggle '. . . she's such a sweetie, she thinks I'll be molested by females. Imagine!'

Blind ones, perhaps, Jess thought bitterly, forcing out a hyena laugh.

'So, if you promise not to molest me, I'll wear it.' He then left a loaded pause for her to fill with objections to such a promise, before saying goodbye in Italian.

'When's the stripper coming?' Lou shouted, several hours later when they were standing at the bar of a tacky club watching Jo dance with a blow-up penis.

'Now,' Jess mouthed, gesturing to a fireman strutting his way through the dry ice in a way that wouldn't have inspired a great deal of confidence had there been a fire. 'Although I suspect Jo might come first.' Jo was screeching in delight as he placed his helmet on her head and pulled a hose from somewhere that left little doubt what it was supposed to represent.

'Mine's bigger,' a voice boasted from beside them.

Jess looked round to find an attractive bloke waving a twenty-pound note in the air. 'Perhaps you'd like to do a follow-on act, then,' she suggested, grinning. 'My friend's got an insatiable appetite.' She nodded to where Jo was licking cream off the end of the hose.

'And what about you?'

She looked him up and down with all the subtlety of a Channel 5 porn film. 'I, too, enjoy a good meal but . . .' she paused, eyeing his crotch '. . . I try to avoid light snacks. Sorry.'

He laughed. 'In that case, can I buy you a light drink?'

And suddenly it was happening all over again: the expected unexpected. Meeting someone new like this, she decided, as Lou developed a nervous twitch, then an urgent need to go to the loo, was like buying a scratchcard: there was always that wonderful moment of hope. The moment when you had in front of you the possibility of untold happiness. The moment usually followed by confirmation that you hadn't.

'So,' he said, when their James Bond style *double-entendres* hadn't given way to the requisite bedroom scene, 'you organise all this?'

Jess nodded proudly, as if Jo were her daughter. Jo was taking off the fireman's thong.

'Done a great job, by the look of things.'

The look of things suggested the job was yet to begin.

'Thanks,' she said, grinning. 'It was tough, you know. You've got to choose your stripper carefully.'

'You clearly have good taste,' he replied, in a way that made it hard to tell whether he was a latent homosexual or just arrogant. 'Another drink?'

By the time they'd got down to introductions and conversation deeper than a puddle, Jo had almost got down to her undies.

'I think your friend's forgotten which one's the stripper,' he said, as Jo was escorted off the dance floor dragging the symbolically deflated penis.

'I think she'll be wanting to forget most of the night,' Jess said, then gave him a winsome smile to suggest the same wasn't true for her.

'Anyway, as I was saying, they were foolish enough to promote me to senior level, meaning that . . .'

Jess nodded distractedly as her mind busied itself with filing him into positives and negatives as if he were hospital-test results. It was like her English tutorials: a perfectly good story couldn't just be enjoyed, it had to be sabotaged to death by analysis.

'. . . said, "Mate, we think you've got potential but the climate's tough and there's no telling . . ."'

He had nice eyes, she mused, and in profile a nice nose, except face-on he looked a bit . . .

'. . . so I said, "Fine, I understand, I'm willing to give this a go if you think . . ."'

. . . like a turtle. But he seemed quite dynamic and travelled a lot, which was promising. Although could she go out with someone who wore grey shoes? And kept saying 'like'?

'. . . like I'd even thought about it. But, like, at the end of the day . . .'

He was good-looking and moderately interesting and clearly keen on her.

'. . . which of course didn't go down particularly well with the girlfriend.'

Jess froze. The filing system had just crashed.

'You want another?'

She tried to force her face not to reflect what was going on behind it, but her smile seemed constipated. 'No, thanks. I've had quite enough for one evening,' she said, proving her point by stumbling off her bar stool, stomping to the loo and bursting into tears.

'Babes, babes!' Jo cried, finding her, moments later, crouched by the bin. 'What's wrong?'

'Every-ry-thing,' she sobbed, as blackened tears left her looking like a Hallowe'en mask.

'No, is not,' Jo slurred, removing the helmet and sliding down the wall to join her. 'You've got me. Look.'

'But you've got M-Mark, and I've got nuh, nuh, nuh—'

'Nice friends who lurrrrrrve you,' Jo completed, as if it were the third prize in a raffle.

Jess snorted into her sleeve. 'Everyone's together,' she whinged, 'in a happy love nest. Everyone's got a . . . a girl-friend or's married.' She kicked one of the cubicle doors. 'Even the bloody toilet's engaged!'

Jo burst out laughing. 'To someone who's doing a dump on its head, probably. I'd rather be single.'

Just then one of the latches switched to vacant and a girl matching that description walked out. 'I was actually doing a piss,' she announced, 'but whoever he is I'll dump on his head for ya.'

Jess smiled in appreciation of her sisterly support, then watched her strut out and throw her arms round the very bloke she would have targeted for the dumping.

''Snot fair,' she exploded, hitting her head against the bin. 'I'm doomed. Doomed to be alone and mi-mi—'

'Don't be ridiculous,' Jo soothed. 'Mr Rightzout there, I know he is,' she said, as if reading from the opening line of a self-help book. 'And he'll come along – whee! – just when you're least—'

'DON'T!' Jess screeched. 'In the name of Christ, Cupid, Venus, and Aphrofuckingdite, please do not tell me that he'll come along when I'm least fucking well expecting it!'

Jo didn't so much bite her tongue as look as though the whole thing had been lopped off.

'You waiting?' a girl interjected, rather tactlessly.

Jess threw her head back against the wall. 'For ever, probably.'

'Go ahead,' Jo said, heaving herself off the floor and attempting to do the same with Jess. 'Come on, babes,' it was the blind drunk leading the paralytic, 'let's have a cheer-up boogie.'

Jess staggered to the sink and struggled with the complexities of washing under a tap that would only produce water if pressed down upon by both hands. It had clearly been designed by the same bathroom engineer who'd introduced the hand-blower as a hygienic means of hand-drying, unaware that it would force everyone to resort to the unhygienic means of drying their hands on their trousers. Then she walked back into the club and felt as if she'd just been resuscitated with electric-shock treatment.

'I don't believe it!' he said, his face breaking into a seductive smile as he insisted on exchanging the sort of kissing routine Jess suspected he didn't do with his granny. 'Me. Sexy Jess. Seedy joint. Who'd ever have expected it?'

'Not me,' Jess singsonged, then stopped in her tracks. For once, to her bewildering joy, this was true. 'It must be fate, Andy.'

He grinned. 'Or just mutually bad taste in night spots. How are you?'

'Oh, you know,' she said, shrugging. 'Pissed. And you?'

'Aside from being ecstatic to see you, *obviously*,' he charmed, 'thirsty.'

After inviting her to sit down and taking her drink order as if they were in a very posh hotel, he ambled up to the bar looking so sexy and hot that, were he to get lost on a mountain, there'd be no need for thermal imaging. Or, indeed, thermals. She stared lustfully after him: absence might make the heart grow fonder, but it played havoc with one's libido.

'Psst,' Jo hissed, concisely summing up her state. 'You know he's got back together with Sarah.'

'And?'

'And heez bad news.'

'So are daily reports of stabbings,' Jess retorted, 'but you still watch them.' She wasn't quite sure what *that* proved.

'I jush don't want you getting stabbed, babes,' Jo slurred,

smirking at someone over Jess's shoulder. '*My* helmet!' she shouted, giggling. 'No, mine. *Mine!*' Then she stumbled up, helmet obscuring what was left of her vision, and went charging hell-for-his-leather-thong towards the fireman.

'Come here often?' Andy said, returning with two vodkas. 'Or just when God gives His angels the day off?'

Jess laughed, then looked at her watch. 'I didn't know Slime School had finished. Need help with your homework?'

Andy raised a suggestive eyebrow. 'So, come on then, why *are* you here?'

'Hen night,' she said, as if it were synonymous with a public hanging.

'Not yours.' He didn't look quite as perturbed by the possibility as she would have liked.

'No. That will be taking place in the year two thousand and sixty-four involving a Zimmer frame race, false-teeth snogathon, and a brandy with departed friends at the graveyard. Husband to be picked from the mortuary.'

'I'm sure it's not that bad,' he said, after a telling hesitation. 'So, who's the hen that's beating you to it?'

'Jo,' she replied, glugging her vodka at the reminder that marriage was a race. 'Which you should know, because Sarah's supposed to be here.'

Andy suddenly looked at the floor with a pained expression, as if he might be having trouble moving his bowels. 'Sarah and I have split up.'

Jess stared. For a fleeting moment this news hit her like stepping off a plane into the warm air of the Caribbean. It held a hint of promise. But that was exactly what Andy was: he was a holiday. All things good and fun and sexy. And when you were stuck in the daily grind of normality, he was the escape you needed. But holidays ended and, as a long-term option, something more than just a treat, he wouldn't be viable. The prospect of him would always seem alluring, but he was respite not reality.

'For good? Or just while you get over your latest bout of doubts?'

'Sarah did it,' he said, as if Jess were the teacher.

This struck her as odd – like the crash victim offering to go to prison for the drunk driver. 'Why?'

'Because she wants to get married.'

The crash victim had clearly been injured in the head. 'Well, that makes sense.'

'She's a woman, Jess,' he said, sitting back and sucking on his cigarette. 'They don't make sense.'

'Could it, perchance, be a comment such as that that made her want to leave, I wonder?'

'I doubt it,' he replied, grinning. 'I think she's always known she's a woman. At least, that's the impression I got. Can't see how my pointing it out should cause anything untoward.'

Jess rolled her eyes. Fighting chauvinism with feminism was a losing battle on a par with the American War of Independence. 'So, who does she want to get married to?'

'Believe it or not,' he said, closing his eyes and exhaling in a long, satisfied breath as if it wasn't just a cigarette he'd finished, 'me.'

'Which is why she's split up with you,' Jess confirmed, confused.

He nodded. 'And is refusing to have me back without a marriage proposal.'

Jess flinched. No wonder she was having such difficulty finding her soulmate. 'Since when did love become a military order punishable by court martialling?'

He stubbed out his cigarette. 'Since Sarah decided that if it *was* love, we'd have been married by now.'

'She's got a point,' Jess said, wondering whether that was also the sad reality of her and Alex.

'Two, actually,' he replied, grinning.

'Hilarious, Andy. So. D'you think she's right?'

He looked pained again, then sighed. 'Maybe.'

Jess waited, feeling as though she was extracting a splinter from his foot.

'She's been part of my life for so long, giving her up for ever would be like . . .' he searched his empty glass for inspiration '. . . like putting my dog down.'

'I see,' Jess said, knowing from her own experience that comparisons with domestic pets were never a good thing. 'So it's a kind of habit thing.'

'In a way,' he said, nodding into the distance. 'But there are lots of things I love about her, which makes her such a hard habit to give up.' He lit another cigarette, suggesting his problem was less of love than of limited will-power.

'Like what?'

'Lots of things.'

'Like?'

He stared at the ashtray, pausing for what was too long, Jess decided, to be a nostalgic relapse, then announced, with no hint of irony, 'She's good at cooking.'

And suddenly, in that one comment, sitting in a sleazy night-club, drunk, everything became clear to Jess: she and Andy were idealists, constantly trying to reconcile their expectations with reality. What they thought they wanted was to be swept off their feet. What they needed was to be brought down to earth.

As if ordered to implement this, a bouncer the size of Brazil began ushering them out into the cold, where she queued for a taxi, resolving no longer to wait for the sunsets, love letters and bouquets of lilies.

'You got the lilies, then?'

Jess frowned into the phone, too early into her hangover for anything to be working yet. Like the office after a party, the cleaners were still clanking around her head mopping up the mess. 'Ergh?'

'Oh, God. This isn't Lou I'm speaking to, is it?'

There weren't many things she could be sure of, but her name was one of them. 'No.'

'It's someone with a really big hangover.'

Jess lurched. How did he know?

'Who's thinking, How does he know I've got a hangover?' This was getting creepy. Maybe it was Uri Geller. 'Who is this?'

'I can't believe you don't know.' He sounded hurt. 'I'm gutted. I really thought last night meant something.'

Jess froze. What had . . . when . . . but . . . ?

He chuckled. 'I'm just joking. We've never met before. My name's Dan and I'm after your flatmate. Oh, God, that sounds really bad. I *am* after her obviously but, um, I also do want, but . . . what I mean is not. Is she around?'

Jess smiled. There was something quite endearing about a bloke who got tongue-tied over a girl. Even more so, she mused, had the girl been her. 'No, I'm afraid she's not,' she said, wondering why Lou had never mentioned him. 'Do you want to leave a message?' Then, in light of his last attempt at forming a sentence, added, 'I can edit out the buts and ums, if that would help.'

'But, um, but, oh, um, I don't know,' he replied, laughing.

'How about "Dan rang. No buts. Call him"?'

He laughed again. 'Excellent. Except that she doesn't know me as Dan.'

Jess paused. 'Does that mean you're a kind of Superman figure, then? Clark Kent by day, caped crusader by night?' she suggested, warming to the image.

'Damn!' he shouted, grinning audibly. 'My cover's blown. What gave it away?'

'You forgot to take off your glasses last time you flew by. I just kind of put two and two together.'

'Wow. You're smart,' he praised, and they both laughed. 'You'd better promise not to tell Lou, though. She knows me as her secret Hollywood agent.'

Jess reeled. Surely this couldn't be flobbery gross man from the screenwriting classes? He didn't sound flobbery or gross, but just, well, nice. No wonder *Blind Date* spawned so few successes: she'd have gone for him right away. 'What's the message, then?'

'Just that I don't normally do this, that despite appearances I'm not a perverted stalker and that if she'd like to go out for a drink I'll be at this number until next Saturday, at which point I will leave her well alone, shed Clark Kent for the very becoming tight Lycra of Superman and fly around the world.'

'Short and concise, then,' she said, pretending to take down his number, knowing Lou would only throw it away. 'Will that be everything, Mr Kent?'

'Oh, and, er . . . good luck with the hangover.'

'Thanks,' she replied, smiling, replacing the handset and feeling an inexplicable desire to call him straight back.

I Will

To: *Claire.Voyant@hotmail.com*
Date: *Saturday 9 December*
Subject: *I Will*

Have met someone. Not in the way one's mother
  might coincidentally bump into Jean
  Barrington in the post office then bore on
  about what all her children are doing, but in a
  fate-like meant-to-be type husband way.
  Though, obviously, very much wish to bore on
  about him. And possibly our children!

Dear Claire,

I now realise weddings are not a torture device by which the smug and insensitive foist showy-offy displays of coupledom on depressed single friends forced to disguise tears of loneliness under hats with bits of dead pigeon on. No! They are but a grand and generous gesture of love, where those already in it selflessly take it upon themselves to encourage others to be in it too by organising a large fun party and seating people like me next to people like Will!

I didn't immediately like him. In fact, if truth be told I thought he was a bit of a wanker. But this is usually a good sign – look at **When Harry Met Sally** – and I certainly don't think he's a wanker now. It was a work friend's wedding and we were both the only colleague they'd each invited, such as will no doubt make a cute and romantic story for our grandchildren. His name is Will, as in 'I Will' – which, come to think of it, could prove to be a confusion at the ceremony, unless of course it's short for William in which case . . . anyway, might hold off addressing such practicalities for the

331

moment. He's a management consultant, twenty-seven, and looks a bit like Brad Pitt. Sometimes. Well, in certain lights. Possibly not very bright ones.

Anyway, after guzzling champagne as if it were, well, champagne, we were soon hitting it off at the table and, come dancing time, it was clear we were on the way to having it off in the bedroom. Or so I thought. The problem was I was staying in one of those B-and-Bs where it is all very sweet when the muffin-baking Mrs Tiggywinkle landlady lends you her iron, and all hideously embarrassing when you lurch up at two in the morning with a bloke hovering sheepishly by your side, both of you too pissed to work out how to open the door. She took one look at us and told us not to be sick on the duvet.

Fortunately, we didn't make it as far as the duvet, Will deciding my clothes needed urgent and speedy removal from the vantage-point of the wardrobe mirror. It was all very sexy and heated, and welcome in view of the Gobi desert that has been my sex life, except that half-way through I remembered the embarrassment that was lurking under my dress. I'm not talking about my body (that is just a normal everyday embarrassment), but my bra.

I was wearing something that went by the name of 'Pump and Go' (perhaps inspired by the sexual habits of the male drunk?) and is an unsightly padded monstrosity with twin airbags – much like those seen on adverts for the Volvo estate, only in this case you're provided with a little pump to inflate them, rather than having to crash into a wall. Quite a rigmarole, I must say, but apart from feeling as though you've attached a rubber dinghy to each nipple, the overall effect is very beneficial which is, ironically, the problem. So crazed with lust was he for my Jordan-inspired assets that he punctured the thing with his cufflinks in a frenzied attempt to get at them, then stopped, horrified, as I emitted a hissing noise, almost as if my breasts were farting. It wasn't very erotic. The result was the equivalent of taking Yorkshire puddings out of the oven and watching them collapse into little blistered pancakes. And, unfortunately, I'm not just referring to my chest.

Nevertheless, the following morning he stoically took my phone number and said he'd call – which, miraculously, he did, but not before I'd chewed off half my fist. It's all very well and exciting meeting someone new but I'd forgotten that the minute their back is turned you reduce them to the telephone: staring at it longingly and charging at it whenever it rings. I'd even got to the stage of playing games with it, teasingly delaying responding, which is great fun until you discover it's Callminder with a message and you realise you've just been flirting with an automated woman from the Home Counties.

We arranged to go out for a drink, which was lovely. Well, quite lovely. Oh, sod it, it wasn't lovely at all. Some unpleasant and very unwelcome alien bug has seemingly been mutating inside me, eroding all sane cells (admittedly not many left now) and replacing them with wedding panic-buttons. As a result, a 'date' is now something frighteningly unrecognisable – I just don't know at what point it changed from going casually to the Fine Line with someone you fancy, to interviewing them for marriage. At any given moment this was the flow chart surging through my system:

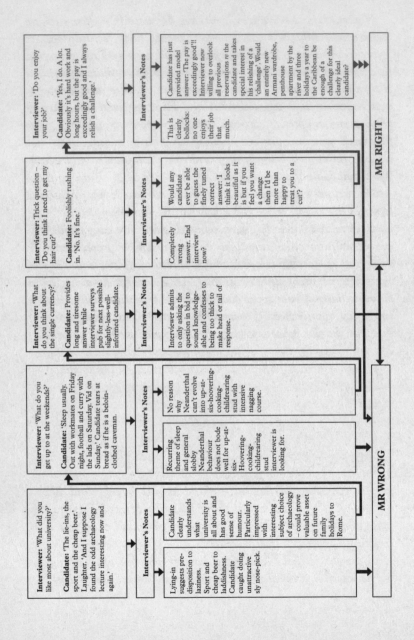

Interviewer: 'What did you like most about university?'

Candidate: 'The lie-ins, the sport and the cheap beer.' Laughter. 'And I suppose I found the odd archaeology lecture interesting now and again.'

Interviewer's Notes

Candidate clearly understands what university is all about and has good sense of humour. Particularly impressed with interesting subject choice of archaeology – could prove valuable asset on future family holidays to Rome.

Lying-in suggests pre-disposition to laziness. Sport and cheap beer to laddishness. Candidate caught doing unattractive sly nose-pick.

Interviewer: 'What do you get up to at the weekends?'

Candidate: 'Sleep usually. Out with workmates on Friday night, football and curry with the lads on Saturday. Vid on Sunday.' Candidate tears at bread as if he is a beloin-clothed caveman.

Interviewer's Notes

No reason why Neanderthal can't evolve into up-at-six-hoovering-cooking-childrearing stud with intensive nagging course.

Recurring theme of sleep and general slobby Neanderthal behaviour does not bode well for up-at-six-hoovering-cooking-childrearing stud interviewer is looking for.

Interviewer: 'What do you think about the single currency?'

Candidate: Provides long and tiresome answer while interviewer surveys pub for next possible slightly-less-well-informed candidate.

Interviewer's Notes

Interviewer admits to only asking the question in bid to sound knowledge-able and confesses to being too thick to make head or tail of response.

Interviewer: 'Trick question – 'Do you think I need to get my hair cut?'

Candidate: Foolishly rushing in. 'No. It's fine.'

Interviewer's Notes

Completely wrong answer. End interview now?

Would any candidate ever be able to guess the finely tuned correct answer: 'I think it looks beautiful as it is but if you feel you want a change then I'd be more than happy to treat you to a cut?'

Interviewer: 'Do you enjoy your job?'

Candidate: 'Yes, I do. A lot. Obviously it's hard work and long hours, but the pay is exceedingly good and I always relish a challenge.'

Interviewer's Notes

Candidate has just provided model answer: 'The pay is exceedingly good'!! Interviewer now willing to overlook all previous reservations re the candidate and takes special interest in his relishing of a 'challenge'. Would an entirely new Armani wardrobe, penthouse apartment by the river and three holidays a year to the Caribbean be enough of a challenge for this clearly ideal candidate?

This is clearly bollocks; no one enjoys their job that much.

MR WRONG

MR RIGHT

The end of the night was a bit odd. Granted that after such an intense and exhausting interview it would have felt improper to tear at each other's clothes in carnal frenzy – especially given the farting-breasts experience. Indeed, nothing more than a perfunctory handshake and a remark about the weather seemed appropriate. Yet surely it's not normal to part in separate taxis having pecked one another on the lips like sparrows.

I keep replaying the evening as if I've just sat an exam – one minute thinking it went well, I got most things right and everything will be fine, a split second later thinking what a fucking fuckup, everything went disastrously and I'm doomed to a life of eternal resits.

And now I'm in the agonising position of waiting for him to phone to tell me whether I've passed, which is deeply unjust – everyone knows the candidate is supposed to be the one cacking his pants, not his interviewer. Then again, maybe he too is interviewing me and I will be invited to attend a practical next Tuesday as the second, and not unappealing part of the process.

Ergh. Really must stop this. It is no good to man or beast. I have to remember that the relationship is still embryonic – not literally – and there is nothing to be gained from letting it gallop off into Ga-ga Land. I'm determined to stop taking such a long-term view to every encounter with a bloke. As Jo astutely advises, I must treat each date as the equivalent of buying a single to Earl's Court rather than an entire year's travelcard.

Anyway, I'm going to a party tonight where all kinds of things might happen. It's so much more wonderful being single when you've got someone floating around in the background like a lifeboat. It's when the whole thing feels like a fated Titanic trip with nowhere near enough lifeboats to go round that you start thinking how best to kill yourself.

Hope you're well. Would send this off now but am keeping the phone line free for Will to call. Any minute now, I can feel it! See ya . . .

*

Ergh. The above was written when there was such a thing as hope, and happiness wasn't just something belonging to Zoë Ball. It is now nine miserable sodding days later. I am at work. I am also, it would appear, still single.

Will hasn't called. I must accept, like relatives of missing mountaineers, that he is not coming back. There have been the odd promising glimmers – unrecognisable 1471 numbers, moments when the phone's been engaged for more than three minutes – but with each day that passes, hope dwindles, and there comes a time when you can no longer convince yourself he's just got lost in some bushes.

It reminds me of my linguistics course where lectures were dedicated to the theory of silence as an effective means of communication. At the time I thought it meaningless waffle. I had no idea it would prove so devastatingly right. The worst of it is the guessing – wondering what he is communicating to me by not communicating with me. Found myself desperately scouting for possibilities, phoning up friends and either feeling huge pangs of love and harmony towards them when they gave me the answer I wanted to hear, i.e. he likes me and will phone, or wishing to strike them dead with an axe if they told me the truth.

Anyway, I don't know why I'm getting into such a state. If he doesn't have the balls to call me, he's hardly going to be much cop at negotiating our mortgage, or assisting at our baby's birth, or, for that matter, at school parents' evenings. I'm just fed up with constantly thinking I might have met Mr Right, then discovering he's Mr Write-off. Maybe it'll be like the fire alarm at school. I'll get so blasé with all the test runs that when the real thing happens I'll be like poor Sally Smithers and almost get burned alive in the music room.

Thanks for your email. I'm touched to hear you're treating my manhunt in the manner of an international murder inquiry with Wanted posters, and intrigued to know what it is about this newly arrived Adonis that leads you to think you've found my ideal man. Who is he? Where did he spring from? And how ideal exactly? Naturally I'm quite happy for you to matchmake us at your wedding, but my experience of both matchmaking and weddings is that they're miserable fucked-up disasters. (*Your* wedding, obviously, to change this.)

I think I should just enjoy being single and try not to give off any vibes that might suggest otherwise. Men, while thick and unperceptive, seem to possess an almost uncanny sniffer-dog ability to detect the slightest whiff of desperation, and, like fish, will dart for cover the second they sense you're out to catch them. It's becoming increasingly clear to me that getting a boyfriend is not just a case of picking him off a shelf (even if you're on that shelf too – particularly if you're on that shelf), but something that must be researched, worked at and prepared for in the conscientious way one approached one's finals – or would have approached them, had there not been the minor distraction of a fantastic social life.

It's hard work, I tell you: self-help books to be studied, horoscopes to be cross-referenced, agony-aunt columns to be related to, Ally McBeal to be watched. And that's before you take into account the weekly seminars in the pub to try to get to grips with all the contradictory theories and information you've amassed. For example, according to How To Make A Man Fall In Love With You, you must let them make seven moves before you let them know you're interested. Yet my horoscope says that the time is ripe for Pisceans to seize control. And when Ally did neither with Billy, she still cocked up, went bright red and fell off her chair.

I'm sure I wouldn't be panicking so much if the whole world hadn't suddenly mutated into couples, as if it was boarding Noah's Ark. I feel as though I'm going to be the only one left drowning in the flood. In an attempt to keep buoyant, I suggested Jo and I spent Saturday shopping – an offer on a par with suggesting no-strings-attached sex to a bloke. She said she couldn't because she was going on a 'Walk of England'. I'm no longer just losing friends to coupledom; they're deserting me for anoraks and compasses.

Ergh. And it's Christmas soon, which is bad enough in itself without feeling that everyone is strolling arm in arm through crisp winter air before snuggling up in front of a roaring fire and feeding *each other roasted chestnuts. Even the pigeons seem to be pairing up in festive cheer.*

The worst of it all is that Mike's moved in. Like nuclear warfare, it was bound to happen. He's a nice enough bloke and I'm glad Lou's with him, it's just that being single, miserable and living with a couple who are happy is the equivalent of festering in a Bangkok jail where even the lesbians don't want you. It's not that they make me feel uncomfortable but there are times – after a Sunday-morning giggling session and before Lou's third orgasm – when I'd give anything not to be lying alone in the adjacent room.

And, just in case I wasn't feeling enough of a love leper, it was Jo's wedding on Saturday: I was a flower-girl in a see-through nightie with bits of twig in my hair. The whole thing felt like a performance of A Midsummer Night's Dream *except that it was midwinter and a nightmare. Celebrating other people's happiness is hard enough at the best of times, but when the cause of that happiness is the one thing you think you'll never have, it's like being a starving Somalian watching* Gary Rhodes. *As much as I try to convince myself that one day I, too, will be beaming euphorically from underneath curtain netting, I've a sinking feeling that if I ever did make it as far as the altar it would be like* Four Weddings and a Funeral: *I'd be Hugh Grant marrying the Duck Face character I didn't love, or Duck Face getting jilted. Or, and this is fast becoming an attractive third option, I'd just plop down dead.*

Jo had tactfully themed the event 'duality', meaning that everything from the candles to the bog paper was in a couple. She'd even arranged it so that we all got two chicken legs. Presumably not to disrupt this consistency, I'd been paired up with another stray – Mark's brother, Jake, a twenty-two-year-old music student and borderline homosexual. While I'm grateful for all donations to my cause, even Oxfam occasionally has to turn away substandard goods. I'm beginning to feel like a spare sock who's lost its partner in the washing machine and gets perpetually mismatched with other randoms.

But, then again, maybe I haven't lost my partner. Alex was there too, also single, and also being mismatched, unless he's into six-foot engineers with moustaches. Although a wedding wasn't the perfect venue at which to meet, it was lovely nevertheless. But that's always been the problem with Alex: it's lovely. Yet, when I listen to couples exchanging marriage vows, 'lovely' feels the equivalent of 'fine'.

In an effort to make sense of this, I found myself turning into Ruby Wax, uninhibitedly accosting anyone who looked happy and asking them why they got married – not as daunting a task as you might imagine: if there's one thing people enjoy more than talking about themselves, it's romanticising their relationship. The standard reply seems to be, 'Because I couldn't imagine life without them.' Either they didn't play enough let's-pretend games at nursery school, or I've just unearthed the hallmark for love. In which case . . . the sheer thought of my life is so unappealing that I can't imagine me choosing to be in it, let alone . . . but, then, maybe if Alex . . . oh, bollocks! Kate, the producer, is staring at me evilly, as if she knows I'm not really typing 'notes'. She's given me an item for January about successful career women being unable to find a bloke to match their standards (I'm enjoying the thought that I inspired this), but the truth is that every successful woman I phone is too busy being successful to talk to me. Just going to pretend to be working for a moment . . .

A spectacular thing has just happened. I was in the middle of doodling on Mo Mowlam's head when my mobile bleeped and there was a text message from Alex: 'Lovely 2 C so much of U on Sat. When can I C the rest? A.' Love the cheeky innuendo and feeling of intimacy and appreciation the see-through nightie has clearly brought about, although slightly alarmed by the prospect of it being similarly appreciated by all one hundred and twenty guests. And can't help finding the tone of the message uncharacteristically flirty. Still, it's obviously a sign from the heavens! A helping hand from Fate, via Vodafone. Why else, just when I was thinking about him, would he contact me?

Suddenly everything seems to make sense. The reason I'm single is not that I'm unlovable or the world is made up of wankers, but because I'm meant to be with Alex. God threw Will, the tosser, at me because, like a crafty car salesman, He knows that by test-driving a clapped-out banger I'll appreciate the worth of the considerably more expensive Alfa Romeo. And what is Alex if not my Romeo?

I'm not going to rush into anything, though – after all, look what happened to Juliet when she got all impetuous. Alex and I have too much of a past together to go gaily leaping into the future. We need to wipe the slate clean, like naughty drivers with points on our licences who must wait patiently until such time as they are removed before getting back into the driving seat and heading off into the sunset. Still, though, a bit boring waiting. Might just send a little reply for the road.

Hope you have a lovely Christmas in snowy Spain (are you sure there's snow? It sounds a bit weird, like 'sunny Scotland' or 'icy India'), and good luck with the New Year resolution. I've decided there's no point in taking the usual eyes-are-bigger-than-belly approach, making endless lists of promises that I'll only break on 2 January, then feel crap and useless. Instead, I'm going to pick something significant yet manageable, like not chewing my nails. And, for once, STICK TO IT!

Lots of love and unused mistletoe,
Jess
xxx

Oxford Blues

Jess was sitting at her desk chewing her nails.

'. . . has had to cover another story and since you've been working so closely on this item we thought you could have a bash at it.' Kate launched herself from the desk, whizzed backwards across the floor in her chair, grabbed a pile of papers from her own desk, then came hurtling back like a dud firework.

'What? Interview them?' Jess squeaked, taking her fist out of her mouth.

'Don't look like that,' Kate said, laughing. 'They might be successful career women but they're not going to eat your head.'

Jess fought back images of her face staring up from a corporate platter.

'These are the proposed questions,' Kate continued, handing her an all but blank sheet of paper, 'but they're only guidelines. Remember, you're not interrogating them. If they give you a lead, go with it. Just make sure we get loads of bollocks about no man being good enough, refusal to drop standards, fear of dying alone, blah, blah.'

It was all very well for Kate, Jess thought, with her designer merchant-banker husband, but it was not blah, blah if the likelihood of procuring the same was as slim as Kate Moss.

'And look sympathetic, for heaven's sake! Don't want our viewers thinking we're hard-nosed Hitlers.'

Jess grimaced: *that* was who Kate reminded her of.

'And interested. But don't speak over their answers – makes it easier for the editing chaps. Okey-dokey?'

No. It was not okey-dokey at all. Jess nodded.

'Mike's on camera, meeting the sound guys there at eleven. You've lined up the women for twelve. Plenty of time.'

Jess nodded again.

'And we've got a stylist on stand-by. Anne. Very talented. Might even be able to do something with your hair.' She laughed. 'Any questions?'

Only about securing a gun licence, Jess decided.

'Here's the production vehicle,' Kate barked, throwing her some keys. 'Shouldn't take you longer than a couple of hours to get there. 'Member to take the bags. Know where you're heading? Map's in there if you need it. Okey-dokey. Good luck and, hey, *have fun!*' she concluded cheerily, as if it were not the most daunting challenge of Jess's television career to date, but a make-your-own *Blue Peter* board game. She sprang to her feet and left.

Jess shoved her fist back into her mouth. She didn't just feel under-qualified, it was the equivalent of being asked to help in a road accident on the strength of a first-aid course at Brownies.

'By the way,' Kate added, her head reappearing round the door, 'it's a Previa.'

Jess gave a friendly wave. 'Okey-dokey,' she said, smiling. What was a Previa?

By the time she'd carted down a number of indeterminate sports bags, she'd ascertained that a Previa was a car. The problem came when she had to decide which one.

'Can I help?' a voice struck up.

She was bent down studying the bumper of a Ford Escort. 'Just looking, thanks,' she murmured, righting herself and discovering that she'd been looking in entirely the wrong place: the voice had a very handsome owner.

'For anything in particular?'

'My car, actually,' she said, wondering, as she studied him, whether he might turn out to be . . .

'And you think this might be it?'

She smiled coquettishly. 'Perhaps.'

''Fraid not,' he said, grinning. 'But good luck.' Then he unlocked the door and drove off.

It was no good: men and cars were as indecipherable as each other. She wandered vacantly up and down, reflecting on how much easier the task would have proved had she been told to look for something purple with a sunroof. Eventually she resorted to zapping the key unlock button at every parked vehicle on the road, watched by two builders, who were clearly convinced she was trying to steal one.

'All right, love?'

'Fine, thanks,' she mumbled, then stopped short. The magic key had opened the treasure chest, but the treasure chest was a brand new people-carrier the size of a small cottage.

She clambered up and stared in horror at the dashboard, feeling more as though she were in a cockpit than a car. Beside her were the directions, photocopied from the spine of the map so that all the important bits were missing. It seemed to be suggesting she went to Rye, which was peculiar, she mused, because she could have sworn the filming was taking place in Oxford. And then she discovered she wouldn't be going anywhere, because the key wouldn't work.

'Oi, 'scuse me, love.' One of the builders had approached the car and was doing something effeminate with his hand, which she took, after much puzzlement, to be a request for her to wind down the window.

'Can't,' she mouthed, after searching the door panel for the handle. 'It. Does. Unt. Open.'

The other had now turned up and was peering in at her as if she were a turtle that retracted its head if he tapped on the glass.

'This your motor, missus?' He'd now opened the door.

'No, it isn't,' Jess snapped.

The men exchanged significant looks.

'Then youse going to tell us why youse driving it?'

'I should think it's perfectly obvious,' she said, twisting angrily at the ignition, 'that I'm not.'

It took several minutes to prove that she was an

incompetent not a thief, but it was well worth the effort. They showed her how to disengage the steering lock, electronically open a window and find reverse. Soon she had enough confidence to lurch off alone, thanking them with what would have been a friendly toot, if she hadn't mistaken the windscreen squirter for the horn.

'How we getting on?' Kate crackled into her mobile half an hour later.

'Oh. Yes. Fine,' Jess replied, dislocating her neck as she swung on to the motorway, drenched in the kind of sweat reserved for sportsmen and McDonald's staff.

'Okey-dokey. Won't disturb you. Let us know of any problems.'

'Will do,' she chirped, dropping the phone and almost crashing into an overtaking lorry.

She'd decided to plump for the Rye option, which was fine, except that every time a junction appeared all signs to Rye disappeared. It wasn't until a clearly inaccurate map had sent her in the wrong direction twice that she located the correct road, relaxed and realised, delightedly, that people were staring at her. She smiled, wondering whether this was because she looked important and in control, or just because she looked rich. And then a man signalled to her: black smoke was billowing out of her exhaust pipe.

'The thing is, it's very black,' she gabbled, after spluttering in terror to a service station.

The assistant behind the counter looked blank. 'Very black, you say,' he repeated, nodding.

'Yes. Very black and I think—'

'Excuse me.' A woman resembling Princess Anne pushed forward. 'Packet of Marlboro Lights, thanks.'

'D'you know what it might be?' Jess begged, as he handed over a packet of Silk Cut. Today was supposed to be her big break – not breakdown.

'I am thinking it is your engine, no?'

344

'I said Marlboro Lights,' Princess Anne snapped.

'Oh, *fucking* fuck! I'm supposed to be – this is – I really need—'

'Madam. We do not like this words in our hearing.'

'I'm going to get fired. You do realise that? This was my – Look, is there someone here who knows what to do?'

He looked out thoughtfully into the forecourt. Something about his expression led her to suspect that that someone wasn't him.

'A mechanic?' she prompted. 'Someone who fixes cars? A black smoke specialist? Anyone who can fucking – sorry, sorry,' she threw up her arms in defence, 'who can help?'

He swallowed, then blinked in the long, slow way of the uncomprehending.

'You checked the petrol gauge?' Princess Anne suggested, marching towards the exit. 'Probably just run out of fuel.'

Jess stormed back to the car, both relieved and humiliated to discover the woman had been right: relieved because it was so simple, humiliated because she couldn't open the tank. It was little wonder that workmen whistled at women, she decided, as she was forced to crowbar the cap off, when people like her were perpetuating the dizzy-bimbo myth to such marvellous effect.

By the time she made it to Rye, it was well after eleven. It was also deserted. The directions said everyone would be at the mini roundabout, but when she got there it was a primary school. After driving around in circles, she pulled in at a beach car park and stared out of the window. It was then that the thought struck her: maybe she was supposed to be in Oxford, after all.

Trying not to panic, she shuffled through the papers on the seat next to her. They all said Rye very clearly. So why did she have this fixation with Oxford? It was like waking up in the middle of the night and being frightened by an ominous shape in the corner. She'd know rationally it was just a mound of dirty washing but that didn't stop a tiny part of her suspecting it was a rapist, murderer or 'Aghh!'

A man was rapping at the window. 'No sign of the birds.'

Relieved to discover this was the cameraman, not the prelude to a Hitchcock film, Jess turned off the engine and got out. 'They're probably running late,' she offered, then added, as he looked ostentatiously at his watch, 'even later than I am!'

'Or just too busy with their heads up their holes,' he said, lighting a fag.

Jess smiled. This was a good point. She might not know much about cars or directions or, indeed, anything, but at least she wasn't preoccupied with being a career woman to the detriment of everything else. And then a pleasing realisation dawned on her: very shortly she *would* be preoccupied with being a career woman. She looked out over the ocean, the symbolism of the moment swelling up in her like the tide: it was a stunning location in which to make her début as a reporter.

'You Jess?' a bearded bloke in jeans enquired. Jess assumed, because he was carrying a microphone on a stick, that he was a sound guy – and, from the way he was leering at her chest, in the technical sense only. 'Got Kate on the blower. Says she needs to speak to you urgently.'

Jess took the phone, rolling her eyes as if to say, 'It's murder being this much in demand,' then reached into the car to get her busy-person's notes and pick her own phone off the floor. There were seven missed calls. 'Hi, Kate,' she said, pleasantly.

'Where are you?'

'Beside the seaside,' she chirped, smiling at all her men-in-waiting, then bursting into 'Oh, I Do Like To Be Beside The—'

'So why do I have eight angry women waiting for you in Oxford?'

Jess froze.

'And half my production crew sitting around doing squat all?'

A very dark cloud seemed to be descending. 'Um . . .'

' "Um" isn't good enough, Jess. These women were told by you to be in Oxford. Oxford is the location for the university rowing item. Rye is the location for the career women item. *Your* item. Or was. These people have better things to do than waste their precious time hanging around for idiots. As do I!'

'But,' Jess attempted by way of an apology. The line went dead.

'Didn't like your singing, then?' the sound guy acknowledged perceptively.

Jess stared ahead, stunned.

'Don't worry, love. We think you've got a great voice, don't we, lads? See us a fag, Jeff.'

'I've fucked up,' she managed, when the news sank in.

'What? The birds somewhere else, are they?'

'Oxford.'

There was an awed silence.

'Jeez. That is a fuck-up,' the cameraman agreed. 'Which twit told them to go there?'

Jess nodded. 'Me.'

'That mean we can go, then?' Jeff asked eagerly, then started miming something dangerously close to wanking. 'Any of youse up for a swift half?'

Jess felt her eyes fill with tears. The only thing she was up for was the sack.

' 'Scuse me, dear. Are you from the BBC?' A frail old lady had just tottered up, clinging to something that looked as though it might once have had a heartbeat. 'This is my husband,' she said, referring to the corpse. 'He used to work for the BBC.'

'I did, that,' the corpse – alarmingly – confirmed. 'Fifty-seven years, and don't regret a day of it.'

Jess forced out a polite smile. 'Well, I'm afraid I *don't* work for the BBC, or for any other organisation after this morning's terrible . . . anyway,' she trailed off, sensing the return of tears. 'Nice winter day.'

'You filming the sea?' the old lady persisted.

'Not exactly. No.'

'The car park?'

'We was supposed to be interviewing successful career women,' Jeff explained. ''Cept Jess, here, bless you darlin', ballsed it up.'

The old lady was amused. 'So *you*'re not a career woman,' she said, chuckling.

'Or successful,' Jeff felt it necessary to add.

'A total failure, one might say,' Jess concluded, bitterly.

'Never mind, dear,' the corpse said soothingly, with considerably more sensitivity than his living companions. 'What were you to be asking them?'

Jess sighed. 'All about their successful careers, the high standards they set themselves, and how they can't find a bloke to live up to them.'

The corpse smiled. 'Well, let me tell you something, m'dear. The only thing we can be certain of in this life is death.'

Oh, joy. Her day was going from bad to diabolical.

'Which means life must be lived. Not by having successful careers. Not by setting standards. Not by searching for a better this, a greater that. But by good old-fashioned love.' He turned to his wife with the schmaltzy timing of a Spielberg creation.

'That's right, dear,' the old lady said, flashing the corpse a toothless grin. 'Success is all well and good, but loneliness . . . loneliness is very sad.' As if on cue, she looked searchingly at the sand-duned wasteland. 'Give me the love of a good man any day.' And then they kissed.

Suddenly, Jess was gripped by a volt of vision.

'Do you think you could repeat all that,' she said, smiling encouragingly and signalling frantically at the blokes, 'into this camera here?'

An hour later, Jess was leaving Rye with footage that spoke

right to the heart of the issue. She could already hear the dramatic voiceover: 'All too often we overlook the wisdom of our elders: in this groundbreaking account, our very own reporter, Jessica, discovers the truth about success and love.' She grinned proudly. It had not only salvaged her career, it had shown her the importance of holding on to what really mattered.

'Alex? It's Jess.'

There was a loaded pause – the sort of pause she hoped was loaded with excited anticipation, not with the words 'piss' and 'off'.

'Jess. Hi.'

'Have I . . . am I calling at a bad time?'

'No, no, I'm just – thanks, Graham – no, not at all. How are you?'

The wonderful thing about Alex, she recollected, as she regaled him with her morning's catastrophes and narrowly missed another one with a motorcyclist, was that whatever he was doing he could always be relied upon to put her first.

'Sounds mad,' he concluded, laughing.

'No more mad than usual.' She swallowed nervously. Asking an ex-boyfriend on a date was like returning to the battlefield unarmed. 'Alex, I think we should meet up.'

There was another pause, only this time it wasn't just loaded it was firing. 'Jess, you're cracking up.'

'No, no, I'm not, Alex,' she said, laughing. It was ironic, but she'd never felt saner. 'I promise you. I've seen sense. Please, can I take you out for dinner and explain?' She smiled expectantly into the phone, wondering whether he'd insist that *he* take *her*.

'I can't,' he said, anguished. 'You're crack—' and then he was gone.

Jess reeled. She'd always suspected she might have to fight for him, she'd just never envisaged being knocked out in the first round.

'He's – he's hung up,' she wailed, moments later.

'Who is?' Lou replied, concerned.

'Alex. I asked him out for dinner and he said – he said—'

'He said what, sweetheart? I can barely hear you. You're cracking up.'

'That's what *he* said,' Jess cried, 'but I'm not, I'm—'

Lou burst out laughing. 'Your phone, you daft nut,' she squealed. 'It's the one cracking up. You're already mad, remember?'

Jess felt a huge wave of relief wash over her. 'Oh, thank the Lord.'

'Call him right back this instant,' Lou ordered, ''Bye.'

Just as she went to obey the command, a text message bleeped through: 'Luv 2 meet 4 dinner. Oxford Circus, 7.30? U choose restaurant. A.'

Jess grinned and put her foot to the floor.

By nine o'clock, Alex was regretting his suggestion. 'What's wrong now?' he said, smiling bemusedly.

They were standing outside a bistro that called itself 'Authentic Thai', its menu board headed up with steak and kidney pie.

'It's empty,' Jess complained.

'Which means we'll get better service.'

'Exactly. Look at the waiters,' she said, as three moustached men on stools waved like *Blind Date* hopefuls. 'They're all eager. They'll make me feel self-conscious and then I won't be able to eat anything.'

Alex looked at her the way he always did when he didn't understand her – like a child in awe. 'That'd make it cheap, at least,' he said, giving her an affectionate squeeze.

'I just want it to feel right,' Jess said, gazing up at him in a manner that suggested she wasn't only referring to the restaurant. 'Anyway, I told you, I'm paying for it.'

'That may be, but I seem to be the one paying for it at

the moment,' he said, feigning hunger pains. 'What about this one, then?' He'd stopped at a brightly lit place with plastic tablecloths. 'Looks nice.'

'Too light,' Jess confirmed. 'It needs to be much cosier, with candles and little alcoves. The problem is, it's stark. They need to break it up with potted shrubbery and those hanging—'

'Jess!' he implored, grabbing her by the shoulders and looking her intently in the eye. 'We're eating in the place, not taking out a mortgage on it.'

Once they'd compromised on somewhere that was miraculously still serving food, Jess had almost forgotten what the evening was all about.

'Today made me realise something,' she launched off, as Alex swooped like a vulture on his bloody steak.

'Oxford isn't the same place as Rye?'

She laughed. 'That as well,' she conceded, then turned serious. 'But more, well . . . something about me . . .' she looked coyly at the plastic flower arrangement '. . . and you.'

Alex paused mid-munch, eyes darting from side to side as if he'd been told there was a monster behind him. 'Right.'

'Right, well . . . and . . .' She pulled at a nylon petal. This had been a lot easier to do at rehearsal, whizzing along the motorway with Magic FM providing the requisite sentimental songs in the background. She took a deep breath. 'And I realise . . . I've made a big mistake.'

She watched his face as if she'd just let off a firework and was waiting for it to light up. But nothing happened. No elation. No disappointment. No surprise. Nothing. It was like sitting an exam paper with a four-word sentence followed with 'Discuss': you could just about rise to a four-word sentence in reply, but it was clear from the two hours and blank-paged booklet in front of you that they were expecting a little more.

'I love you, Alex. I know . . . well, that I haven't always shown it.' She glanced up to check. He wasn't showing anything. 'And that I've treated you badly in the past. And

351

I'm sorry. I . . . the thing is. Well, the thing is, what's important now is the—'

'Dessert menu?' A man in an apron was thrusting a laminated photo of ice-cream in their face.

They shook their heads, as if getting shot of a fly.

'What's important now is that I recognise how I feel for you and no longer want to run from it. No longer want to deny it.' She bowed her head, pulling off the nylon petals one by one, hoping the daisy game would conclude that he loved her. 'I guess what I'm trying to say is . . . well, what I'm . . . Could we start again? Me and you. Us.'

She looked up at him and smiled. This was the moment. The moment their fingers would touch, their eyes would meet, their lips would . . .

'No.'

She reeled. This wasn't the moment she was meaning.

'You don't love me, Jess. You love the *idea* of loving me.' He untucked his napkin from where it had been acting as a bib and started dabbing the corners of his mouth. The gesture had a finality about it she didn't like. 'I wish you did love me. Trust me, there's no one in this world who wants to believe it more.'

She felt her foundations rock. 'But . . . couldn't—'

'We don't work, Jess,' he said, staring down at his glass and wrapping a protective hand around its stem, 'we don't work because' – he brought his head up, locking his gaze with hers – 'because you will never feel for me the way I will always feel for you.' And then he tried to smile.

She broke, the painful way glass shatters. 'Alex, I . . .'

A tear carved itself a channel down his face. It seemed a piercing irony that he should finally understand her at the very moment he was turning her away.

'I'm . . . sorry,' she managed, before her eyes brimmed over and her world flooded.

Plumbing New Depths

To: *Claire.Voyant@hotmail.com*
Date: *Friday 16 February*
Subject: *Plumbing New Depths*

Where the fuck is the fucking plumber? Beginning
   to suspect twenty-four-hour emergency promise
   includes the sub-clause 'unless it's Friday'.
   Beginning to suspect he's in the pub or
   enjoying a romantic post-Valentine dinner.
   ~~*Beginning to suspect*~~ *I've gone mad.*

Dear Claire,
   A very bad disaster has struck. I'd just shoved all my white
underwear into the washing-machine and was staring inside a
cupboard wondering what to shove into my mouth when, out of
the corner of my eye, I spotted it: a rogue rugby sock tumbling
happily around in the drum turning everything bright green.
Panicked, I started prodding buttons and twisting dials while the
machine sloshed this way and that. Then I decided to turn it off,
but I could actually see the dye draining from the sock and attaching
itself to my lovely lace bra and, in the end, could stand it no longer.
I kicked it. I don't recall it being a particularly hard kick, except
it seemed to be hard enough to break the safety lock because the
next thing I know the door is flying open, water is everywhere, and
. . . oh, Jesus. It is Friday night. Kitchen is the Lake District, wet
green washing is slopping everywhere like slime, I was supposed to
be meeting Lou an hour ago, and the fucking, fucking plumber is
Christ alone knows where. The only thing that could possibly restore
my will to live is a gin and tonic.
   Mmm, love the way alcohol washes through one's system

smoothing over all the sore spots in a warm Mummy hug. Can quite see the appeal of being an alcoholic where happiness is found inside a bottle of vodka, rather than in relation to whether someone loves you. I think it might be something to do with the passing of Valentine's Day – unmarked, very dark day – but I feel as though I've sunk to a depth untraceable even with the most sophisticated sonar equipment.

My plans for a sentimental reunion with Alex mirrored those for a suicide attempt. He pointed out the truth, never pleasant, and I've barely stopped crying since. I now realise that all the time I'd been moaning about being single, I had secretly squirrelled him away for a rainy day, much as you complain about being poor, safe in the knowledge you've got two grand in a trusty savings account. Only now it's pouring and I can't bank on either.

Consequently, life seems horribly black – as if I've been plunged into a power-cut, fumbling around, bumping into things and cursing myself for not having the foresight to organise backup. It would be nice to think Andy was there, carrying that torch for me, but although there have been little glimmers – turns out the sexy text message of my last email was from him, not Alex – I've learned my lesson re playing with fire.

Still, I can't help wondering whether my life will take the course of a thriller – signs are already in place for lots of terror and mess, cf washing-machine – where the murderer/my husband will end up being Andy, the last person I suspected. We've arranged to meet for a drink twice now, both times he's cancelled, and are supposed to be going for third time lucky next week but, a bit like watching the second half of a two-part drama, returning a video before it's due back, or flossing, I don't imagine it will happen.

Thus your wedding or, more accurately, that ideal man you're going to be setting me up with at your wedding, has become a jewel of hope, a lighthouse towards whose welcoming glow I chug rudderless and half sinking. I know it's dangerous to be holding out for something as yet unseen, but when you're lost and miserable any semblance of promise is welcome, however much of a white elephant it may turn out to be. Yuck – suddenly had an unappealing image of this bloke as a monstrous grey thing snuffling food off the table with a long swaying trunk, although obviously the long trunk wouldn't be so much of a problem.

Lou says I've got to check that you *don't* fancy him. She says that when someone talks about setting their friend up with a bloke, it is usually because they fancy him themselves, just haven't quite admitted it. I think she might have missed the point that I'm meeting him at your wedding, but still, if the theory is to be believed, it doesn't say much for Lou's taste. So far she's sent me a stunted bald computer boffin, a rap artist who goes by the name of Boz, and is currently trying to foist on me some Spanish waiter with whom she had a fling eleven years ago and whom she suspects is the sender of a mysterious Valentine card from – and this, I hazard, is where the mystery ends – Spain.

The whole undignified business smacks of a baby-sitting group clothes exchange, where I'm supposed to be eternally grateful for her out-of-date, out-of-shape and out-and-out disgusting cast-offs. In fact, my boyfriend quest in general resembles the end of a jumble sale when you're half-heartedly fishing among the dregs, still hopeful of stumbling on that perfect dress.

Maybe, though, there's no such thing as perfection and I'm hunting for something that doesn't exist, in the manner of Loch Ness monster enthusiasts. After all, blokes do seem to conform to my experience of scratchcards, often turning out to possess two of the winning requirements but never all three. Perhaps the trick, then, is not to scratch beneath the surface but live instead in a world of blissful ignorance and, oh, thank heavens, that's the door. He'd better have a bloody good excuse . . .

It wasn't the plumber. It was the downstairs neighbour informing me that water is dripping into her bedroom. Oh, Christ. No longer do accidents happen in threes; they crash into each other in a relentless and ever more horrifying M25-style pile-up. I insisted on saying sorry over and over, making hopelessly unrealistic promises of paying for the damage (How? Bank is empty and have to buy

*entirely new ceiling! From where? Habitat?) before inviting her in
for a placatory drink. It was quite nice, the sort of thing cool people
might do with their neighbours in Manhattan lofts – although,
obviously, without flooding both flats first.*

*She's much less of a weirdo than Lou and I had assumed, and
does not cut up dead bodies and store eyeballs in jars as per our
previous belief. She has a perfectly sensible job working for National
Heritage and goes ballroom dancing on Mondays. But – and this
is the scary bit – she is forty-two and lives alone. The reason for
this is not because she is mad, widowed, farts in her sleep or has
long-distance buffalo-ranch gigolo in Texas, but because, as she so
tear-jerkingly and resignedly puts it, she 'has never met that special
someone'. Holy Moses. I'd always presumed people like her were
alone because they wanted to be; it gave me an unpleasant sick
feeling to learn that it's because they have no other choice.*

*I'm going to cling to the belief, advocated by Lou, that she's
actually a lesbian – not because I want to be her girlfriend but so
that I can pretend she was hampered by having just a small minnow
pond from which to find her soulmate, rather than the whole plenty-
fished ocean I'm told is out there for me. She might be: after all,
at no point did she imply her special someone had to be male, and
she referred in passing to an ex-partner, which either means she's
being anally PC or it is a euphemism for her gay lover.*

*Anyway, lonely lesbian or not, she seems very nice. The only
black spot of the evening, excluding the swamp, was when she
suggested I come to her ballroom-dancing classes. She said, 'You
could bring your boyfriend,' then took one look at my face, and
added, 'Or your girlfriend.' It didn't take much analysis to see
what was being insinuated here: I can't help suspecting gay people
of possessing a sixth sense when it comes to sussing out potential
homosexuality in others. It's a bit like when you're talking to a
palm-reader or psychic and there is this rather unsettling sensation that they know a lot more about you than you do. I don't
think I'm a lesbian, but then again those plane-crash survivors
in the Andes probably didn't think they were human-flesh eaters.*

356

The good thing is that it looks as though I might have made a new single friend – and useful, given my eviction likelihood. Such creatures are a dying breed nowadays and, in my social group, all but extinct. Occasionally, those who have mutated into twin sets will call me up wanting to meet, I will get excited that they'd rather spend the evening with me than their twin, consequently feel warm, snuggly, very loved and popular, then discover, as it slips out that their twin is away on business, that I've merely been drafted in to alleviate an otherwise dull, lonely evening. Being single may be shit, but at least it provides you with the survival skills to cope in the wild: this lot would be eaten alive in seconds.

In an effort to ensure I can attract friends for less negative reasons, I decided to organise a trip to the theatre. Ergh – never again. The theatre bit was fine, apart from booking it. I don't know what comes over me when I'm trying to buy tickets, holidays, etc., but I always start with a figure that I'm adamant I'm not going to exceed, e.g. thirty pounds for the stalls, then get enticed by thirty-five for the front stalls, then, for just a tenner more, the upper circle at forty-five and before I know it I'm forking out seventy quid for the front row of the dress circle.

We went to see Art, *which was very good and thought-provoking, in stark contrast to the after-show drinks. I'd made the huge mistake of inviting friends from different 'friend spheres'. I simply don't understand it. Logic surely dictates that if I like X and X likes me, and I like Y and Y likes me, then X will like Y, and Y will like X. Apparently it doesn't. As I should have learned from my algebra days, anything with Xs and Ys never bloody works out. The evening ended with Cat telling me she thought Julia was up her own arse, Julia making snide remarks about Sophie, and me very nearly telling the lot of them to go fuck themselves. Felt as though, in some horrible oversight, I'd mixed orange juice with milk and was being forced to drink the resulting curdled mess.*

The only positive to be extracted from the pain was Camilla getting me to sign up for her women's football team. Contrary to visions of being pulverised by the cast of Prisoner: Cell Block H, *everyone has long blonde hair and is called Camilla. I've only been to two sessions so far, the rest being cancelled due to bad weather, which I was secretly pleased about. It's not the football I object to, but all the faffing around jogging and dribbling beforehand. I've promised myself I'm going to stick at it, though, and not do a repeat of Freshers' Week where, in frenzied excitement, I joined six different clubs, went to each for the introductory speech and free glass of wine, unenthusiastically slopped along to a random Saturday of Trampolining Club and never did anything else for the next four years. After all, I enjoy football and think I have a natural talent for it – look at Beckham-style washing-machine kick!*

Mike's being very disparaging, claiming a girl playing football is the equivalent of a bloke on the piss: no co-ordination and unlikely to score. I tried to point out that what we lacked in technical talent we more than made up for in manners, explaining that were we to bump into each other on the pitch we wouldn't automatically see it as a malicious ploy by the opposition to sabotage our chances, lashing out and spitting like barbarians, but instead offer polite apologies and great concern for their knee. Equally, rather than barging aggressively for the ball, we stand back selflessly and let the other person have a go, saying things like, 'No, after you', 'Don't be silly, you got here first', 'But I insist', 'Well, as long as you don't mind', which is surely a much nicer way of playing something that, after all, is supposed to be a team game. He remains unconvinced and can't see why I don't just spend my Wednesday nights in the pub.

This is the one area where he might have a point. If taking up football has taught me anything, it is that all the time I've been moping around saying I wanted to 'meet new people', I was actually talking bollocks: it was just a less desperate way of saying 'find a boyfriend'. Joining an all-female football team is as close to achieving this aim as sitting in an empty flat-cum-boggy-marshland.

Oh, where in arse's name is the plumber? If he doesn't come in the next half-hour I'm going to demand a free service as would be my entitlement had he been a Pizza Hut delivery boy arriving with cold pizza. Can't bring myself to tell Lou so I've said I can't come out because I'm doing my tax return – which I would if I could understand the bastard thing.

Every night this week I've revved myself up for it, sitting down with the enticingly titled 'How To Fill in Your Tax Return', which happens to be sixteen times thicker than the form. The trouble is, I'm still haunted by last year's effort – a Herculean two-day advanced mathematics Ph.D. involving writing lots of numbers in tiny boxes, following instructions to allocate chargeable event gains with notional tax to tax bands, toying with the idea of sodding it, ticking 'Death Benefit' and jumping out of the window, then turning, cross-eyed and weak with exhaustion, to the final page to discover the whole wretched process could have been averted by signing exemption box 23.2: 'Persons who are mentally incapable of understanding the Tax Return'. It reminds me of filling in the insurance claim for my car crash. Gobbledegook lawyer language all the way through, until I got to question 42: 'Draw a picture of the accident'.

If I had a proper job, I wouldn't have to go through this torture. Then again, I'd rather be sending myself insane with a tax return than the Jobseeker's Allowance application form that I fear might be next month's little treat. Every time I think I've turned a corner with work, something happens to prove I haven't.

Last week I was working on a tedious item about women being under-represented in the transport sector. It was all going fine, i.e. clearly no chance of item being used, so I'd decided to design my birthday invite.

Jo and I are planning to have a joint thing (my idea) to share the stress of no one coming, not just your fault if it's crap, etc., and are making it a 'Leathers 'n' Feathers' theme (her idea). I was just putting the finishing touches to a computer-drawn matching thong and whip set when Kate charged up, demanding to know where I'd got to with the transport item. Hate the way she possesses a spooky psychic knowledge whenever I'm not doing what I should be – the same way parents know to come into the room during the one sex scene of the film. I flicked back deftly to the tedious letter I was writing to the heads of various transport organisations inviting them to take part in a studio discussion, asked her if she'd like to check it, and flamboyantly pressed send. She looked impressed then walked off, giving me the peace and quiet to return to my invite, liaise with Jo over the guest list and email it all off. Very productive morning. And then I got back from lunch.

Sophie, Karen, Mike and Anna emailed saying they'd love to come and talk about women bus drivers and – yes – I think you can see the way this one is headed, the boss of London Underground, the vice president of the Women's Rights Movement, and the shadow transport minister wouldn't make it to the Leathers 'n' Feathers party, nor, it would seem, have anything more to do with our production company. It was when an RMT executive phoned up and told Kate he was looking out his feathered thong that I discovered I wasn't just up shit creek without a paddle: I'd capsized the boat.

It's all a punishment, I know, for thinking I can get away with doing as little and as slapdash work as possible, like driving up to a junction and being faced with a choice of two lanes – one stretching miles ahead full of stationary cars, the other completely empty. You feel sure the ones in the long queue are being naïvely conscientious so you whiz off happily down the clear lane – until you discover it's right-turn-only and have to rejoin the back of the long queue, getting beeped and rudely gesticulated at. Except, in this case, I fear the long queue I'll be joining is the dole one.

Oh, misery – and that's not including washing-machine, new ceiling, furious Lou, fucking non-existent plumber. I've called the bastard seven times now and he still hasn't turned up. Maybe he's being a bloke and I must follow the dating etiquette – not phone him relentlessly being moany and demanding, but sit back and wait for him to contact me. Which, in my experience, has the same results anyway, i.e. none.

I hope your life is better. And the wedding plans are coming *together. If there's anything I can do at this end – flood the church, perhaps? – just say so. Organising other people's weddings is becoming one of my greatest talents, a talent that remains spectacularly underused with regard to my own. Which is something I'm dearly hoping your Mr Ideal might change. I don't feel so much as though I've put all my eggs in one basket as into a large test tube eagerly awaiting his sperm. Suspect I might not tell him this yet. Always good to maintain a little mystery about – shit, Lou's back. What on earth am I thinking? I won't be meeting any Mr Ideal. I'll be meeting my death.*

Lots of love – possibly for the last time,
Jess
xxx

Holding Out or Giving In

'It's not going to hurt,' Lou said, stabbing the corkscrew into the bottle. 'And who knows? You might even enjoy it.'

Jess sat slumped on the sofa, picking her toenail. 'I just don't want to,' she protested, as her second executioner marched into the room.

'Right. What's your poison?' Mike placed three glasses on the table.

'Jess is wimping out,' Lou said.

Mike looked confused. 'Why?'

'Because it's Claire's wedding tomorrow,' Jess explained, flicking a toenail clipping at the fireplace, then cleaning her ear with a pen lid. She could tell from the expression on his face what he was thinking: No wonder Jess never goes out – she's really a cavewoman.

'And?'

'And I want to spend tonight getting ready for it, not lugging myself to another crap party.'

Mike glanced at the discarded toenail as if to suggest that it would take longer than an evening to transform her from a slob on the fringes of society into a creature people could look at without feeling nauseous. 'Maybe I'm missing something but I understood Claire was the one getting married. Not you.'

'Not necessarily,' Lou said, with a knowing grin. 'If Mr Ideal lives up to his name we could be looking at a double wedding. Couldn't we, Jess?'

Jess felt herself turn red. It was all well and good sharing the hopes of her soulmate search with her closest friends, but when they were thrown out into the rational world, i.e. relayed to a bloke, they seemed very sad indeed.

'Call me stupid,' Mike said, the smug way people did when

they clearly thought they were anything but, 'but are you saying you're giving up a Friday night to beautify yourself for a bloke you haven't met yet?'

Jess shifted uncomfortably. That was exactly it. 'No.'

Mike looked unconvinced.

'I just . . . Anyway, the party'll be shit.'

'Nice positive thinking, that's what I like,' he said, pouring out the wine. 'And have you perhaps considered the possibility that this "Mr Ideal",' he suggested, as if he were a *Mr Men* character, 'might be equally as shit as the shit party?'

Jess shook her head grudgingly. That was the problem with being romantic: blokes weren't.

'He comes highly recommended,' Lou supported.

'So did *Titanic*,' he said, chortling.

'Look,' Jess said, exasperated, 'why can't I just stay in on my own and wallow in self-pity?'

'Because last time you did that I seem to remember you took it out on the washing-machine.' Lou was grinning in a way that made it difficult to tell whether she was reminiscing amusedly, or about to seek revenge with the coal shovel.

Jess decided it wasn't worth the risk. 'Who's going, then?'

'Everybody,' Lou enthused. 'Jo and Mark, Soph and Rich, Karen and Tom obviously, Becks and Adam, and I think Chris and Carla are going to look in and Mike and—'

'What about non-ands?'

Mike picked up the TV control and started flicking through the channels. 'Who's Nonands?' he said, plumping for Ceefax. 'You after him, Jess?'

'A rapidly dwindling species who exist in the singular,' Jess said, curtly. 'Like me.'

'I think Karen's brother's single,' Lou offered, as if he were the last sausage in a motorway services' café.

'Great,' she replied, glugging consolingly at her wine. 'The question is, can I really be arsed trooping all the way over to West Brompton to discover why?'

*

'Hi, I'm Tim. Karen's brother.'

Jess smiled weakly at the spotty object in front of her. Having dragged her greasy hair and negative attitude to a house of couples holding hands and sipping wine, it seemed perfectly fitting that Tim should be both dull and five feet tall. 'Jess. Karen's friend.'

'So. Did you find this place all right?'

Oh, God. Jess nodded. The only thing more tedious than detailing how you got lost was having to listen to someone detailing how they did.

'. . . said right at the second roundabout, but that was only if you'd approached it from the other set of traffic lights . . . and at one point I thought we were going to run out of . . .'

Tights! She mustn't forget to buy tights. And confetti. The little heart-shaped stuff. Although were hold-ups sexier? Tights or hold-ups? Did hold-ups hold up, though? Tights or hold-ups? Tights or . . .

'. . . hold-ups all along the South Circular . . . which, of course, I'd tried to tell him, but he was adamant his girlfriend had said . . .'

If she could get home early enough, she could wash her hair and get Lou to put those curler things in overnight to give it a bit of a . . .

'. . . lift, never again I said, and guess what he said?'

Would red nail varnish clash with pink sandals?

'Do you give up?'

Jess nodded. After all, she wouldn't be able to tell until she was wearing the sandals.

'He said, "Well, why do you think the train only stops at West Brompton during the week?" Bah-ha-ha-ha!'

'Save me from carving out my own womb and eating it,' Jess implored, in the sanctity of the loo queue.

'Give him a chance, babes,' Jo advised, hugging her

husband – the uninspired result of what had happened when she'd done that. 'He's probably just shy.'

'-Ite at making conversation, you mean. Oh, God. I want to go home.'

Jo laughed. 'But you've only just got here.'

'Quite.'

Mark looked stealthily from side to side as if checking the corridor for MI5 spies, then leaned conspiratorially towards her. 'Would food make things better?' he whispered, in an uncharacteristic moment of male-female understanding.

Jess nodded like a four-year-old and followed him back into the throng to comfort-eat herself into oblivion. Just as she'd set to work demolishing a pizza slice, there was a foreboding tap on her shoulder.

'Loo?'

She swung round. An attractive, familiar-looking bloke was grinning at her expectantly. Unfortunately, there was also an elasticated string of mozzarella connecting her to her pizza in the manner of a leash.

'I—' she began, as the mozzarella snapped and pinged against her cheek like something out of *Alien*. It was typical that the sexiest man at the party had only wanted her for directions to the bog. And then she realised he didn't want her at all. 'Over there,' she muttered, pointing to where Lou was already lapping up the attention of another admirer.

He glanced over, puzzled, as she studied his face, which, in contrast to her own, seemed to get better the more she looked at it. She had definitely seen him somewhere before, but she decided not to challenge him on it.

'You don't know who I am, do you?' he said, a seductively cheeky glint in his eye. 'Dan.' He held out his hand. Jess shook it. 'But I think you know me as your secret Hollywood agent.'

She couldn't think and didn't know. 'But . . . I . . . the person you want is—'

'Lou,' he confirmed. 'At least,' he smiled mischievously, 'that was your name last time we didn't meet.'

Jess blinked. It was like waking up with a hangover: impossible to get a grasp on anything.

'Not that you seemed particularly certain of it even then,' he added, laughing.

Suddenly, the most incredible possibility struck her. 'Then when?' she gabbled.

'Screenwriters' party. Months ago. I'd been plucking up courage to come and talk to you all night, watched you collect your raffle prize – a rather flashy Boots cleanser and moisturiser set, if I remember rightly – and was all set to make my move. The next thing I knew you'd bloody well buggered off. I was gutted.'

Jess stared in speechless ecstasy. So *that* was why he looked familiar: he was the cute smiley-eye bloke she'd fancied. The same cute smiley-eye bloke who'd fancied her. It was Hollywood happening right there in West Brompton. 'Oh, my God.'

'Quite. I was bedridden for days, unable to stop howling even to eat.' He grinned. He was gorgeous. 'Eventually I braved it to the phone, weeping obviously, got the mate I'd gone to the party with to get your address from the class register, and sent you the lilies.'

Jess squeaked.

'Which you ignored. Then the note asking you out for a drink. Which you also ignored—'

'But I—'

'No, no,' he continued, still grinning. 'Please don't worry. By now, I'd developed this,' he lifted up his shirt and grabbed a chunk of flesh from his side, 'a pretty impressive thick skin, I think you'll agree.'

Jess laughed. 'I know, but—'

'Which proved very necessary for when I phoned and left a message with your flatmate – who, incidentally, sounds a much nicer person than—'

'Thanks, but—'

'Which – yes – you ignored. And so, heart shattered into a thousand pieces, I was left with no other option but to flee the country.' He adopted a melancholy gaze into the distance. 'And confine my unrequited love to an anonymous Valentine card.'

'But you don't understand,' Jess implored. 'I—'

'Please,' he interrupted, holding his arm out to silence her. 'I understand completely. I'm a broken man. There is nothing you could possibly say to heal me.' He smiled.

'I'm not Lou.'

He stopped smiling.

'My name's Jess – the much nicer flatmate.' She grinned. 'I went to that party on Lou's ticket, picked up the prize under Lou's name, then scurried off as quickly as I could before anyone realised I wasn't Lou.'

He looked as though he'd eaten a porcupine. 'You mean to say that—'

'You've been wooing the wrong person.'

He threw his hands over his face. 'And have just made a pillock of myself in front of the right one. Fabulous.'

Jess fought back the urge to sweep him into a huge hug. 'Perhaps we could forgive and forget,' she suggested, beaming up at him as he peeped gingerly over his fingertips, 'and start again?'

He smiled. And two hours later they'd barely stopped.

'. . . with ice-cream trickling down my chin, cycling one-handed as this enormous dog – I mean, we're talking the size of a pony – charged after us snarling teeth and—'

'But, what . . . how,' Jess spluttered, laughing. 'Where was Simon?'

'Still half-way up the bloody tree! John was all for leaving him there but the poor bloke was . . . actually, you don't want to know what he was doing.' He walked across to the food table and returned with a bowl. 'Put it this way, you'll never catch me eating this again.'

Jess looked at him quizzically, then peered inside the bowl. It was the remains of chocolate mousse. She burst out laughing. 'That's dis—'

'Exactly! Ended up with John and me trapping the dog-cum-pony in this sort of . . .'

Suddenly, his phone started ringing. It felt like an intruder – a barman shouting, 'Drink up,' and switching on the lights, just at the best part of the evening. She watched him frisk himself to find it, their private world of two dissolving as they became mere bodies again in a roomful of other bodies. He smiled apologetically – both a stranger and someone with whom she could talk so easily that a lifetime didn't seem long enough to fit in everything they had to say.

Like a camera panning out from the action, she took in the surroundings he'd rendered her oblivious to. And then it hit her. She hadn't analysed him. She hadn't interviewed him. She hadn't subjected him to any checklist. She'd just enjoyed herself. And that, she decided, could only be good.

'Hi, Iz.'

She froze. Of course. It made perfect sense. Her perfect man had a perfect girlfriend.

'Yup, OK, yup, yup.' He rolled his eyes, grinning.

Jess looked away. If only Fate had got his arse in gear earlier, maybe she'd be on the other end of his phone checking when he was coming back to make love to her.

'OK, but don't wait up. You too. 'Bye.' He snapped his phone shut and pulled a sad face. 'I'm afraid I've got to go.'

Jess forced a weak smile. It was funny how words could punch you in places you didn't know could hurt. 'Well . . . it's been . . . um . . . it's been nice,' she said, conscious of how inadequately this reflected her evening.

'Yuck,' he exclaimed. 'Horrible word, nice.'

She laughed. He wasn't allowed to be fantastic *and* read her thoughts: it was the cute kid saying, 'I luv ya, Daddy,' before Daddy goes and gets his head blown off.

'What about fun?' she offered, smiling. 'Interesting? Un-usual? Slightly odd but still—'

'Jess, I really want to see you again.'

She paused. There was something about witty people that made their serious statements all the more powerful. They caught each other's eye and held it. It felt like for ever, the way fractions of a second could.

He smiled. She'd found her scratchcard, the unique one with all the matching signs. The winning one. And he bloody well belonged to someone else.

'I don't think that'd be a good idea,' she said, breaking the spell.

His face fell. 'What about if I promise never to get your name wrong again?'

She shook her head.

'And never send lilies or hassle your flatmate?'

She grinned. 'No, Dan.'

'OK!' he said, throwing his hands up in defeat. 'Just off to collect my OBE for Outstanding Contribution to the Cause of Persistence.' He bent forward and pecked her cheek.

'Nice, I mean, really horrible to meet you,' she said, still grinning.

'Hated it too,' he replied, 'every minute of it,' then looked at her wrist in alarm. 'Shit, I'm late. Promised Aunt Iz I wouldn't be a minute past midnight.'

Jess let out a strange noise.

'Yeah, I know, a sort of camp Cinderella thing. Too tricky to explain,' and then, before she could insist he left a glass slipper or, more conveniently, a phone number, he was gone.

'So she wasn't his girlfriend?' Jo whispered, the following after-noon when they were sitting in a cold church trying not to hat-butt each other. Having left the party early, she wasn't going to miss the first opportunity to catch up on gossip, even if it meant talking through one of her good friends' weddings.

'No! His fucking aunt!' Jess hissed back, attracting an evil glower from a befloralled object fitting that description – or just someone who liked to wear curtains.

'So why didn't you go after him? Drag him to the bed and' – she glanced at the ceiling – 'sorry, God, give him one.'

'. . . and come together in the presence of God to witness . . .'

The aunt was now transfixing them both with a look that suggested she used to be a headmistress. Who still practised caning. Jess decided to feign innocence by staring at a fruit collection on someone's head and thinking, because she'd done little else since they'd met, of Dan. It had only been a matter of hours, yet she'd already replayed their evening together so many times that, were it a CD, the repeat button would be jammed. Like checking herself in the mirror, though, it never seemed to get boring.

'. . . but when that which is perfect is come, then that which is in part shall be done away . . .'

That which is perfect *had* come – Jess reflected, bitterly – and gone. And the terrible thing about it was that she saw no way of getting it back.

'Psst,' Jo struck up again, when the aunt became lost in a hanky. 'Why didn't you go after him?'

'Because he bolted out and jumped into a taxi,' Jess whispered, 'before I could even ask him—'

'. . . to be my husband, to have and to hold from this day forward . . .'

'Phone number?'

'. . . for better, for worse . . .'

Jess shook her head.

'. . . till death us do part.'

By the time they'd made it to the reception, this news had made it round most of the guests.

'What about one of his friends?' suggested Susan, a girl with a strategically missing bit of dress.

''Fraid I don't fancy any of them,' Jess replied.

Susan frowned. Material didn't appear to be the only thing she was missing. 'No, I meant—'

'We don't know any of his friends,' Jo interjected, as self-appointed spokeswoman. 'Karen didn't see who he came with, so we're guessing he's a random – a friend of a friend, perhaps.'

It was turning into a briefing session from a Bond film. Any minute now Jo would produce a car that doubled as a parachute.

'But if he knows your home number, won't he call you there?' Emma offered.

Jo winced. 'Unlikely,' she said, sucking in through her teeth. 'She made it pretty clear she didn't want to take things further.'

Sophie smiled sympathetically and stroked Jess's arm as if it were a small animal. 'Never mind, Jess. Remember, nothing can be predicted, and love is . . .' She looked dreamily up at her balding husband. Blind? Jess considered suggesting. '. . . conquering.' And then she smirked so smugly that it was only a timely summons to dinner that saved the wedding from becoming a funeral.

'So? Is he shit?'

Jess was downing wine to drown her disappointment: she'd been placed between Jo's husband, Mark, and Lou's boyfriend, Mike.

'Who?' she said, shoving a slab of salmon into her mouth.

'Who d'you think?' Mike said, looking at her in disbelief. 'Mr Ideal. Mr Perfect Pants.'

Jess felt her jaw fall open and a bit of fish drop out. With all the distraction of Dan she'd forgotten about her soulmate.

'Crikey. That bad, eh?' Mike said, helping himself to her tomato, then pointing hopefully at the scrap on her lap. 'You want that?'

'He . . . I haven't met him,' Jess stammered, as the room suddenly blossomed with possibility.

'She keeping you hanging, then?'

Jess looked over to where Claire was sitting, head thrown back in laughter like something from a promotional leaflet for a bank loan. She'd forgotten to point him out. It was perfectly understandable, Jess conceded, only now that *she*'d remembered about him, it was like being handed a parcel: far too tempting not to find out what was in it.

'. . . a large bull, liberally endowed in areas I can but dream of . . .' John was announcing.

Everyone laughed and someone shouted, 'Didn't know bulls had big brains!'

Jess scanned the room once more. After several circuitous trips to the loo and a lot of neck-straining, she'd come to accept that, unless he was disguised as a bearded biochemist, Mr Ideal wasn't there.

'. . . that Fate himself – or herself – had put that bull there because it was at that moment, standing in a field covered in mud, that I knew I wanted to spend the rest of my life with this person.' Beaming, John lifted his glass and turned to Claire. Their love was so clear, their happiness so contagious, Jess felt it swell up inside her and spill down her cheek. 'To my beautiful wife.'

As the place descended into a clinking, braying, clapping stadium, it struck Jess that maybe Fate was controlling her life too. Despite seeming as though it was constantly conspiring against her, maybe, without her realising, it had been working *with* her, deliberately sabotaging Dan's efforts to prove to her that he wasn't meant to be. That what she hoped for didn't exist. That what she dismissed as compromise was reality. That what was right for her was what she'd always suspected was wrong. That she should never have let go of Alex.

She watched the room transform into a night-club. The more she thought about it, the more it made sense, the way safe things did. Someone had once said you knew it was love when it felt easy. Right enough, things had always been comfortable with Alex. And yet, she couldn't shake off the suspicion that what they had really meant by easy was exactly how it had felt with Dan.

'Glad to see you're getting stuck into the celebrations, babes,' Jo said, bounding up and jigging energetically on the spot as Jess stared into the distance like a recently awoken coma patient.

'I give in,' she said, throwing her arms in the air. 'What's the point of me holding out if I can't hold on to it when it comes?'

Jo looked intrigued. 'Are we talking hand-job or blow?'

Jess looked confused. 'Neither.'

'Oh,' she replied, visibly disappointed. 'What, then?'

'Never mind,' Jess said, suspecting that the side of a thumping dance floor wasn't the best place for a deep-and-meaningful. 'I'm going to get drinks. What d'you want?'

Jo's interest was suddenly reignited. 'Double vodka, please. Though you'd better get in there quick, babes. The evening posse's arriving.'

Jess did as she was ordered and slobbed through to the bar where Claire was greeting her B-list guests as if they were the Royal Family.

'Double vodka, triple gin, please.'

The barman grinned. 'Not having a bad night, by any chance?'

'I've had—'

Suddenly, someone had grabbed her round the waist. 'He's here!' Claire squealed, excitedly. 'In the bog!'

The romance of the moment was overwhelming. 'Is he laying me a special turd?'

'Eight, thank you,' the barman confirmed. Jess fumbled in her wallet. 'It'll get better, you know,' he said, smiling.

'Thanks,' she replied, returning his smile as she picked up the drinks.

'This is Jess,' Claire announced. 'And Jess?'

Jess spun round. The barman had been right.

'This is Dan.'

To be read 10 years from now . . .

About to go on my first date. Wishing my bedroom
   didn't resemble the end of a Top Shop sale.
   Wishing the date to end up in my bedroom,
   though.

Dear Jess,

   *Happy 37th birthday. I don't know where you'll be, what you'll
be doing or who you'll be with when you read this, but if I've come
away with anything this past year (excluding a cold and even
more body hair), it is the realisation that nothing works if you
force it.*

   *I'd always assumed that life was about swimming upstream.
That by battling against the natural flow, I could somehow reach
a better destination. So I went to Africa. That by treading water,
I could compensate for the natural flow. So I moved in with Alex.
I'd never considered just letting go and seeing where the current
took me.*

   *Which is a pity, because at the moment it seems to be carrying
me to a lovely posh restaurant in Notting Hill with a particularly
attractive bloke called Dan. And, after that, possibly washing the
two of us up on an island called Barbados. Who knows?*

   *What I can be certain of, however, is this: when I was taught
to drive, one of the first things I had to find was the biting point
between clutch and accelerator. My instructor would explain it and
I'd understand what he was trying to get me to do, but I knew it
only when I could feel it. With Dan, I've found that biting point.
And it feels right. End of story.*

   Jess
   xxx